# The Constant Heart

Dilly Court grew up in North East London and began her career in television, writing scripts for commercials. She is married with two grown-up children and three grandchildren, and now lives in Dorset on the beautiful Jurassic Coast with her husband and a large, yellow Labrador called Archie. She is also the author of *Mermaids Singing*, *The Dollmaker's Daughters*, *Tilly True*, *The Best of Sisters*, *The Cockney Sparrow* and *A Mother's Courage*.

# Dilly Court

## The Constant Heart

arrow books

Published by Arrow Books 2008

4 6 8 10 9 7 5 3

First published in Great Britain in 2008 by
Arrow Books
Random House, 20 Vauxhall Bridge Road,
London SW1V 2SA

www.randomhouse.co.uk

Addresses for companies within The Random House Group Limited
can be found at: www.randomhouse.co.uk/offices.htm

The Random House Group Limited Reg. No. 954009

A CIP catalogue record for this book
is available from the British Library

Penguin Random House is committed to a sustainable future for
our business, our readers and our planet. This book is made from
Forest Stewardship Council® certified paper.

Typeset by SX Composing DTP Rayleigh Essex

Printed and bound in Great Britain by Clays Ltd, Elcograf S.p.A.

*For Clive in memory of Peggy, a wonderful mother
and much-loved aunt*

# The Constant Heart

# Chapter One

London, May, 1874

The small patch of sky just visible between the sooty clouds was the same shade of blue as the forget-me-nots and ribbons on her new bonnet: a birthday present from her father. Smiling happily, Rosina stepped onto the pavement outside the milliner's shop. She was eighteen today and life was wonderful. In her world the sun was always shining. She did not see the squalor, vice and poverty lurking in every dark corner of the Ratcliff Highway – the East End's most notorious street, where even the police were afraid to go after dark. She barely noticed the crush of horse-drawn vehicles with the drivers bellowing insults at each other. To her ears, the raucous cries of the costermongers, bootblacks, match sellers and hot chestnut vendors, all vying for trade, were as musical as the wheezing notes played by the hurdy-gurdy men.

She picked up her long skirts to prevent them from trailing on the filthy cobblestones, carpeted with horse dung, dog excrement, rotten fruit and mouldy straw. She was oblivious to the stench of steaming sewers and the sulphurous fumes from the river. She was so accustomed to seeing the slatterns hanging round in shop doorways touting for trade, and the ragged, pock-marked faces of the street urchins begging for money, that she barely noticed them. She stopped to look in a shop window where exotic seashells, shimmering and iridescent, lay on a bed of white sand. Her reflection smiled back at her, and she paused for a moment, primping and admiring her beautiful bonnet. A voice from within called her name, and Rosina poked her head round the open door. 'Good morning, Mrs Sanchez. Isn't it a lovely day?'

'Happy birthday, Rosie.' Mrs Sanchez heaved her large body from the stool behind the counter and waddled to the door. 'Hold your hand out, ducks.' She took a necklace of pink-lipped shells from the window display and hooked it over Rosina's outstretched fingers.

'Thank you. It's really, really lovely.' Rosina kissed her on the cheek.

Mrs Sanchez wheezed a gale of garlic into Rosina's face. 'It's not nearly as lovely as you, my pet. You're just like your dear mother, God rest her soul.'

Rosina knew that this was a compliment. It seemed that everyone had adored her mother. 'I wish I'd known her.'

'She was a real lady. A beautiful woman, Rosie. Too good for this earth.' Mrs Sanchez rubbed her hand across her eyes and her full lips wobbled.

'Look at me, silly old fool. Making you sad on your birthday.'

Rosina grasped her work-worn hand and gave it a squeeze. 'Nothing can make me sad today, Mrs Sanchez. Papa should be home on the tide and we're having a special supper. I'll wear my lovely present tonight.' She slipped the shell necklace into her reticule.

'Goodbye, dearie. Give my best regards to your daddy.' Mrs Sanchez disappeared into the dark interior of the shop with her stays creaking like the timbers of an old sailing barge.

Rosina blew her a kiss and walked on. A small child, covered in bleeding sores, sidled up to her holding out its hand. It was impossible to tell whether it was a boy or a girl, but the eyes were those of an old person, huge and beseeching in the pinched face. Rosina pulled out her purse and placed two pennies in the outstretched hand. Claw-like fingers closed over the coins and the child was gone, disappearing into the gaping mouth of a dark alley. Rosina sighed and a shiver ran down her spine. She had chosen to put it out of her mind, but she knew only too well that poverty marched alongside wealth in the great city of London. Misfortune, disease and death could strike anyone at any time. She walked on; she would not think about that now, and she would not be unhappy today. The month was May: her favourite time of the year, when the late

3

spring sunshine warmed the cold pavements of East London and banished the pea-souper fogs into a dim memory. She had been born in May and her family name was May – the month truly did belong to her. She paused to stare at the brightly coloured parrots, waxbills, canaries and bishop birds in old Jamjar's shop window. They strutted up and down on their perches or fluttered about in cages, singing, cackling and squawking. She loved to look at them with their shiny boot-button eyes and bright plumage, but it made her sad to see birds trapped in cages when they ought to be free to spread their wings and fly away, far above the soot-blackened chimney tops. She tapped the glass and a green parrot cocked its head on one side; it seemed to wink its large eye at her and she laughed out loud.

'He likes the look of you, young Rosie.' Old Jamjar, the owner of the shop, whose foreign name had been too much of a tongue-twister for the East Enders and had been commuted to Jamjar, came out rubbing his bony fingers together. He grinned at her, exposing bare gums. His teeth had been knocked out in the days when he had been a prize fighter, or so the legend had it. Rosina had never had the heart to enquire if it were true. She laughed at the antics of the parrot: it seemed to enjoy entertaining her by standing on one leg and opening its beak to utter a string of swear words.

'I don't think I could take this one home, Mr Jamjar. Bertha wouldn't have him in the house using language like that.'

'That bird sailed with Admiral Nelson on the *Victory*, so it's said.'

Rosina frowned. 'That would make him older than my papa, older than . . .' She hesitated.

Old Jamjar chuckled. 'Older than me? He would be if it was true. But it's a good story. Maybe one day you'll buy all me birds and set them free, like you always said you would when you was a little girl.'

'When I'm rich, Mr Jamjar, that's just what I'll do. Now, I'd best be on my way.'

'Just wait a moment.' He disappeared into the shop, and came back moments later holding a scarlet, green and blue feather in his hand. He gave it to her. 'I hadn't forgotten. Happy birthday, Rosie.'

She studied the gaudy feather and smiled. 'It will make a lovely quill pen. Thank you.'

With a gummy grin and a wink of his one good eye, old Jamjar retreated into his shop and was greeted by a chorus of raucous bird calls. Rosina had always imagined that the jungles of Africa would sound just like that. She would not have been surprised if a monkey had leapt out to swing on the shop sign and tossed a few coconuts into the street. She was tempted to linger, but Bertha would be expecting her home soon.

Even though she knew most of the shopkeepers and street sellers by name, Ratcliff Highway was not the sort of place where it was safe to linger. She stepped out briskly, stopping to accept an apple from a costermonger who had apparently dandled her on his knee when she was a baby, and a second-hand silk scarf from fat Freda who owned the dolly shop on the corner. By the time she reached Black Eagle Wharf, her arms were filled with small gifts from old friends along the way. She could tell by the stench from the manu-factories in Silvertown and the iron works in Bow Creek that the tide had almost reached the high water mark, and the arrival of her father's Thames sailing barge was imminent.

She scanned the horizon for a sign of the reddish-brown sails of the *Ellie May*, named after her mother who had died when Rosina was just a few days old. There was already a tier of barges moored alongside the wharf, together with lighters, small coasters, watermen's skiffs and wherries. A gentle breeze rattled the stays against the bare masts, and the tea-coloured waters of the Thames sucked and slapped at the flat hulls of the vessels. She stopped briefly at the tobac-conist's shop to spend a few pence on an ounce of pipe tobacco as a welcome home present for her father, exchanging pleasantries with Sam Smilie, the proprietor. He gave her a quarter of her favourite confectionery, sugared almonds, and wished her a happy birthday. She thanked him, and demonstrated her delight by popping one of the sweets in her mouth. She walked along the quay wall, sucking the crisp sugar coating slowly, savouring the rose-scented flavour and anticipating the crunch of the sweet almond inside. She was passing the row of narrow four-storey houses with oriel windows overlooking the river when Caddie, the heavily pregnant wife of Arthur Trigg, the mate on the *Ellie May*, leaned out of her window on the first floor.

'Happy birthday, Rosie. Looks like you done well for yourself.'

She glanced up at her and smiled. 'Thanks, Caddie. I can't believe how many people have remembered it's my birthday today.'

'I'd have got you something meself, but I'm a bit short of the ready until my Artie gets home.'

'Don't even think about it, Caddie. You need all your money with two little ones to feed.'

'And another one soon to be born. My Artie weren't too pleased about number three, not at first anyway.'

Rosina pulled a face. 'Well, it's not as if he had no part in the matter, is it? Don't look so worried – I'm sure he'll be delighted when the babe arrives.'

Caddie gave her a weary smile. 'I'm sure he will. My Artie's the best dad in the world to little Ronnie and Alfie. I do so hope he gets back soon. I'll be in a real fix if they miss the tide.'

'If you're short of money I'm sure Walter could let you have some on account. Come to the counting house in a bit and I'll see what I can do.'

'I will, and God bless you, Rosie.'

With a cheery wave, Rosina hurried along the cobbled pathway, past the single-storey wharfinger's office, to the house that had been her home since she was four years old. The front room was used as the counting house and was run by Walter Brown, her father's clerk. She pushed the door open with her foot and went inside. Walter looked up from his desk, peering at her over the top of his steel-rimmed spectacles. His hazel eyes lit with a smile, and he rose to his feet, brushing a lock of dark hair from his forehead with an ink-stained hand. 'Miss Rosina.' He picked up a small package wrapped in brown paper. 'Happy birthday.'

'How kind of you to remember, Walter.' She dropped her armful of presents on the desk. 'You really shouldn't have.'

'It's not much, I'm afraid.'

She accepted the gift, fingering it gently as she tried to guess what was inside. 'I wonder what it could be.' She teased the paper apart, and her eyes widened in surprise. 'Oh, Walter, you really shouldn't have.' She held the gold breastpin up to the light. 'This must have cost you a week's wages.'

'Do you like it? I could always change it if you didn't.'

'I love it. What can I say? I just love it. Will you put it on for me?'

As he took it from her, she noticed that his hand shook slightly and she gave him an encouraging smile. She had always liked Walter. He might be a little dull, but he was a kindly, serious sort of fellow who worked hard keeping the books and doing whatever it was that he did to keep the *Ellie May* in business. Such matters were as much a mystery to Rosina as the stars and planets in the night sky, and Papa always said that she need not bother her head about such things. She lifted her chin, pointing to the neck of her blouse. 'Just there, if you please, Walter. I can't do it without a mirror.' His face was close to hers, and he was biting his lip as he concentrated on fastening the brooch to the material.

A bloom of perspiration stood out on his forehead. 'There, it's done.' He took a step backwards, taking a hanky from his pocket and mopping his brow. 'I – I didn't catch you with the pin, did I?'

'No, of course not. I'm afraid I would have screeched if you had, Walter. I'm not very brave. But the gold pin is beautiful and it was such a kind thought.' She seized his hand and held it briefly against her cheek. 'If I had a big brother, I would want him to be just like you.'

A dull flush rose from his starched white shirt collar to his thin cheeks. 'I'd better help you upstairs with your parcels.'

'I can manage, thank you. But there is something you can do for me, Walter.'

'Anything, Miss Rosina. You know that.'

'I saw Caddie Trigg just now. She's in desperate need of some money, and I told her you would give her an advance on Artie's wages.'

He shook his head. 'I'd like to oblige, but I can't very well, not without the captain's approval.'

'Oh, come now, Walter. Don't be mean. The *Ellie May* will dock soon and you'll be paying Artie off, so what difference does a couple of hours make?' She smiled up at him, fluttering her eyelashes. He appeared to be struggling with his conscience, and she pressed home her advantage. 'Please, Walter. It is my birthday, after all.' He ran his finger round the inside of his collar, and she saw that his shirt cuff, although spotlessly clean, was frayed, and there were shiny patches on the sleeves of his jacket where he rested his elbows on the desk. She suffered a pang of guilt as she realised that he had spent his money on her present, and yet he could not even afford a new shirt. She knew that she had placed him in an awkward position, for which she felt sorry, but she was even sorrier for Caddie. 'Please, do this for me, Walter. I'll tell Papa it was all my idea, and that I made you do it.'

A reluctant smile lit his face. 'All right, I'll do it just this once, and only because it's your birthday.

But I won't allow you to take responsibility for my actions.'

Rosina gathered up her parcels. 'Don't worry about Papa; I can wind him round my little finger.' She picked up the apple that the costermonger had given her and placed it in Walter's hand. 'There, that's for you. You really are a splendid fellow, Walter.' She blew him a kiss as she left the office, closing the door behind her. She hurried down the narrow passage that led to the kitchen, and her footsteps echoed on the bare floorboards.

Bertha looked up from her ironing as Rosina breezed into the room. 'Well, you look pleased with yourself, young lady.'

'I've had a lovely time. Just look at all the presents that people gave me.' She went to put them on the table, but Bertha shook her head.

'Don't clutter me table, Rosie. Can't you see that I'm ironing your best frock?'

'Oops, sorry.' She scooped the gifts onto the seat of a chair. 'I can't believe how kind people have been to me today.'

'You're spoilt, you are.' Bertha thumped the flat iron down on the voluminous skirt of Rosina's Sunday best gown. 'I don't hold with spoiling children.'

Rosina crept up behind her and gave her a hug. 'Woof, woof. Your bark is worse than your bite, Bebe, you old fraud.' She kissed Bertha's wrinkled cheek. Her skin was as tough and leathery as Papa's old sea boots, but despite her grim appearance Rosina knew that she had a heart as soft and squishy as a marshmallow. It was Bertha who had nursed her through the miserable childish ailments that had kept her confined to her bed for weeks at a time. It was Bertha who had bathed the scrapes on her knees when she had fallen over on the cobblestones, playing tag with the neighbours' children amongst the cranes, barrels, sacks and anchor chains on the wharf. It was Bertha who had always stood up for her when she was in trouble with Papa. She gave her another hug. 'Don't be cross, Bebe. I've had a lovely day and I saw all our old friends in Ratcliff Highway.'

'I can see that. But I've told you a hundred times not to go roaming round the Highway on your own. It ain't safe.' Bertha tested the heat of the flat iron by spitting on it. 'You're a young woman now, not a little girl in short petticoats.'

'Don't fuss, Bebe. We lived there once, remember? No one in the Highway would harm me.'

'I know where you was raised. I was with your sainted ma even before you was born and with her when she died.' Bertha put the rapidly cooling iron back on the fire, and picked up the one that had been heating over the hot coals. She held it close to her cheek, judging the temperature before she set about ironing the fine cotton poplin. 'And you might think they're all kind and friendly, but there's plenty who ain't. There are evil men who prey on young girls like you. There's opium dens and houses of ill repute down Ratcliff Highway. It ain't safe, I tell you, Rosie.'

Rosina snatched up the silk scarf that fat Freda had given her, and she wound it around Bertha's neck. 'There, this will suit you much better than it does me. I want you to have it.'

Bertha's face crinkled into an unwilling smile. 'You always could get round me with your soft-soaping ways.'

'You're still my Bebe, the kind and lovely Bebe who tucked me up in bed every night and told me stories about fairies and princesses.'

'Get on with you, you minx.' Bertha unwound the scarf, but she did not take it off. 'Get out of me way and let me finish me chores afore the captain gets home. A fine welcome it would be if he found me doing the ironing, instead of having a hot meal ready and waiting for him.'

'I'll call out when I spot the *Ellie May*'s sails coming upriver.' Rosina scooped up her belongings and took them upstairs to the parlour. She laid her gifts out on a side table, displaying them for her father to view when he had had time to settle in at home. Untying the ribbons on her bonnet, she took it off and went to sit on the seat in the oriel window overlooking the wharf and the river beyond. Through the forest of masts she could see past Watson's Wharf and the Standard Wharves where ships from foreign ports unloaded their cargoes of fruit and vegetables, wines, spirits and tea. It all sounded so romantic to Rosina's ears: she had never been further afield than the creeks and salt marshes of Essex, and probably never would. If she had had the luck to be born a boy, she could have sailed with Papa as mate on the *Ellie May*. But if she had been a boy she would not have been able to wear pretty things like her lovely new bonnet. She fingered the smooth satin ribbons and sniffed the silk forget-me-nots; they had no smell, of course, but it was fun to imagine that they were real, and that she had picked them fresh from a country garden, the like of which she had seen on picture postcards and in magazines. A movement below caught her eye, and looking down she saw Caddie standing on the wharf, with eighteen-month-old Alfie straddled on her hip, and Ronnie, who was little more than a year older, clinging to her skirt as she peered into the distance. Following her gaze, Rosina spotted the unmistakeable tan sails of a Thames barge coming upriver. Even before she could read the lettering on the bow, she knew that it was the *Ellie May*. With a cry of delight, she jammed her bonnet on her head and leapt to her feet. She ran downstairs, tying the ribbons beneath her chin.

The office door was open and she beckoned to Walter. 'She's home, Walter. The *Ellie May* has just arrived in port.'

He rose from his seat behind the desk. 'I'm coming. I'll just get my cap.'

'Don't be so formal, Walter,' Rosina said, struggling to contain her impatience. 'You don't need to wear a cap in order to welcome home the *Ellie May*.'

'The captain wouldn't appreciate it if I turned up improperly dressed.' He took his peaked cap off the hat stand and put it on.

'Oh, really! You are so – so proper!' She bit her lip, realising by his downcast expression that she had hurt his feelings. She was sorry for her hasty words, but sometimes he was so maddening that she couldn't hold her tongue. It wouldn't have been so bad if he fought back, but he always seemed to be in total command of his feelings. He gave her a brief nod as he strode out of the house and onto the wharf. Rosina followed more slowly, wondering if Walter had ever done anything spontaneous in his whole life. In the two years that he had worked for her papa, she had never known him to be anything other than polite, punctilious and hardworking. She had seen occasional flashes of humour in his eyes, but she had never heard him laugh, or even chuckle. He could not be more than twenty-two or twenty-three, but to her it seemed that, nice though he might be, he was tumbling headlong into middle age. She broke into a run, and by the time she reached Caddie's side she had forgotten all about Walter. She waved frantically to her father as he steered the barge alongside another vessel. Artie leapt off to make it secure. He looked up and smiled as Caddie shrieked his name, with the infants' shrill voices piping 'Dada, Dada'.

'I'm so glad he's home. I miss him something horrible when he's away.' Caddie kept waving as though she was afraid the barge might sail away again. 'Isn't my Artie just the most handsome fellow you've ever seen, Miss Rosie?'

Rosina murmured something that passed for agreement. Handsome wasn't the word she would have used to describe Artie. He was not very tall; in fact, he was quite short and stocky. His face was tanned by the sun, wind and salt air from the estuary, but his features were unremarkable. She would have said he was plain, but pleasant-looking. Caddie, on the other hand, obviously saw something quite different. Judging by the rapt expression on her face, she was seeing a prince amongst men. Artie leapt from barge to barge until he reached the ladder on the quay wall; he shinned up the steps as nimbly as a circus performer heading for the high wire. He enveloped Caddie in an embrace that almost squashed Alfie, who howled in protest. Artie kissed him on his downy head and then he lifted Ronnie up in his arms, chuckling and tickling him until the little boy let out a peal of laughter. In spite of herself, Rosina felt a lump in her throat as she watched the family walk off towards the lodging house, where they lived in two small rooms on the first floor. It was touching to see them in such a loving relationship and so happy together. She moved to Walter's side, suddenly stricken with conscience. 'I didn't mean to offend you, Walter.'

'That's all right. You're entitled to say what you think.'

'Well, you are very proper – but that's a good thing. It wouldn't do if everyone was like me and said the first thing that came into their head.'

'No, ma'am.'

She turned to stare at him, but his generous mouth curved into a grin and his eyes twinkled in a way that invited an immediate response. She tucked her hand in the crook of his arm. 'Why, Walter, I believe there's a little devil hiding somewhere inside that serious head of yours after all.'

He stiffened and his smile faded. 'Excuse me, miss. The captain wants me to go on board.'

She followed his gaze and saw her father making imperative gestures with his hand. 'You'd best go then, and see what he wants.' She waited impatiently for Papa to come ashore; it was, after all, her special day. She paced up and down on the cobblestones, stopping occasionally to acknowledge birthday greetings from the dock workers. She had known most of them since she was a child, and she made polite enquiries as to the health of their wives and numerous children, but all the time she kept an eye on the deck of the *Ellie May*, where Papa and Walter were deep in conversation. When they finally came ashore, she ran to her father and flung her arms around his neck. 'It's good to have you home, Papa.'

He gave her a perfunctory peck on the cheek. 'Hello, Rosie.'

'Is that all you've got to say to me?' She let her arms fall to her sides, staring into his bewhiskered face. 'Papa?'

'Don't pester me now, girl. I've got a lot on me mind.' He walked away from her, heading towards the wharfinger's office.

She ran after him. 'But what's the matter? Why are you so angry?'

'I'm going to make an official complaint about that bastard, Ham Barnum.'

'Captain Barnum? What has he done now?'

He stopped outside the office door, staring down at her with a frown puckering his forehead into deep lines. 'He's crossed me once too often. Go home, Rosie. Wait for me there. This hasn't anything to do with you.' He stormed inside and slammed the door.

'Well!' Rosina stared after him. He hadn't even noticed her new bonnet, and, worse still, it was apparent that he had completely forgotten that it was her birthday. Something must have gone badly wrong. She turned to look for Walter; he would tell her the truth. He was talking to a group of men, but he broke off as she approached them. 'Walter, what is going on?'

'It's not for me to say, miss.'

'If you don't tell me, I shall scream.' She opened her mouth as if to carry out her threat. She had no intention of doing so, but she knew it would have the desired effect on him. Walter was so easy to manipulate. He took her by the arm and led her back towards the house.

'It's a matter between Captain May and Captain Barnum. It seems as though they've fallen out again, and this time it's serious. You'll have to ask your father to tell you the rest. That's all I know.' Walter opened the door for her. 'It would be best if you were to wait at home.'

'Stop treating me like a child. You were talking to Papa; he must have told you what happened.'

'You're placing me in an awkward situation.'

'Oh, come on, please tell me. I promise I won't let on to Papa, but I'm dying with curiosity. Please, Walter.'

His lips twitched as if he was trying hard not to smile. 'You'll get me the sack.'

'Please, please tell.'

'They were racing to get the best cargo. The captain said that Barnum took his wind and drove him onto a mudflat. Luckily the tide was coming in and they soon floated off, but it cost him the cargo he had aimed for, and he says Barnum got it by cheating. He's gone to complain of malpractice to the wharfinger, and he intends to take the case to the Watermen's Company. I can't tell you more, miss. That's all I know.'

Rosina had to be content with that until her father came home, but by this time she was ready and waiting with a jug of hot buttered rum to soothe his temper, and his slippers were warming by the range. Even though it was mild outside, Papa always suffered from cold feet, more so when he was tired after a long and trying voyage. She had his favourite pipe already filled with baccy, and she had placed his chair by the fire. Bertha had cleared away the ironing and was laying the table for supper, which was to be boiled mutton and caper sauce. Rosina lifted the saucepan lid and sniffed appreciatively; it was one of Papa's favourite dishes, and was to be followed by spotted dick and custard – a sure winner. Bertha was probably the best cook in Wapping, if not the whole of London.

Captain Edward May stormed into the kitchen, kicking off his sea boots so that they flew up in the air and one of them landed on the table.

Bertha scowled at him, but she said nothing as she picked up the muddy boot and placed it close to the range. Rosina knew better than to make a fuss. She poured the toddy into a rummer. 'Welcome home, Papa.'

Edward shrugged off his pea jacket and dropped it onto a chair. His scowl lightened as he took the glass from her. 'Thank you, Rosie, love.'

She waited in silence, watching the colour return to his pale cheeks as he gulped the drink. The tension seemed to leach from him and his shoulders sagged. Bertha said nothing as she busied herself slicing a freshly baked loaf of bread. Rosina smiled and refilled his glass. 'Sit down, Papa. Bertha has made your favourite supper.'

'And I'm a brute for taking me megrims out on you, my pet.' Edward put the glass down on the table and held out his arms. 'Come here, Rosie. Let your old dad give you a birthday kiss.'

She walked into his arms and he kissed her on the forehead, on the tip of her nose and on both cheeks, in the way he had greeted her ever since she could remember. She kissed his cheek and his mutton-chop whiskers tickled her nose. He smelled of the river, of salty mud, a faint hint of pipe tobacco and buttered rum. She smiled up into his weathered face. 'It's good to have you home, Papa.'

'And leave your blooming temper outside the door next time,' Bertha said, obviously judging that the time was right to have her say. 'What sort of greeting was that for a girl on her eighteenth birthday?'

Rosina felt her father's muscles tense and she held her breath. One day Bertha would go too far, but today was not going to be that day, as her papa let out a shout of laughter and sat down on his chair, pulling her onto his knee. 'Trust Bertha to put a man in his place. I've been captain of the ship all week and now I must bow to petticoat rule. Happy birthday, poppet.'

'You never bowed down to nothing in your life, old man.' Bertha waved the bread knife at him. 'And if you've had an up and downer with that Ham Barnum again, then shame on you for bringing it into the home.'

'I don't wonder that no man ever offered to marry you, you old harridan,' Edward said conversationally. 'You keep your place, madam. If you wasn't such a good cook I'd have sent you packing years ago.'

'And I'd have gone, if it wasn't for the little lamb.' Bertha huffed her way over to the range and stirred the caper sauce. 'Serve you right if it was burned black as your heart.'

'Stop it, both of you,' Rosina said, stifling a sigh of relief. When Papa and Bertha insulted each other, things were normal. It was only when they were coldly polite that she ever worried. She wriggled off his lap and handed him the pipe. 'I bought you some of your favourite baccy, Papa.'

He smiled. 'I'll enjoy a pipe after supper. Now tell me if you got that bonnet you were hankering after.'

'Papa!' Rosina pursed her lips in a mock pout. 'I was wearing it when I met you on the quay.'

'I'm sorry, poppet. I was so fired up against that villain Ham Barnum that it escaped my notice. I've filed a complaint against him at the wharfinger's office and I'm going to take it up with the Watermen's Company. I'll have their solicitors on him and that will take the smile off the bastard's face. If he wants war, then war he shall have.'

# Chapter Two

Rosina cleared the table, taking the dirty plates into the scullery and piling them on the wooden draining board.

'You go on up, ducks,' Bertha said as she squeezed into the small room holding a steaming kettle. 'I'll see to the dishes.'

'But, Bebe, I always help you clear up after supper.'

'Not on your birthday you don't. Upstairs you go. Chop-chop.'

Rosina was not going to argue. She hurried through the kitchen, pausing in the narrow hallway as she saw a splinter of light beneath the office door. Walter must be working late yet again. She sometimes wondered if he had a home to go to, but that was his business. She barely gave it another thought as she ran lightly up the twisting staircase to the parlour at the front of the house. The fragrant scent of pipe tobacco wafted out through the open door and she could see her father's outline as he sat on the window seat, puffing away on his pipe. He looked relaxed and contented after the excellent meal that Bertha had prepared. When Papa became agitated, as he did rather too frequently these days, she feared for his health. It was not good for a man of his age to get overexcited; it was well known that Mr Barton Medley, the owner of the flour mill downriver, had suffered similar fits of temper and had expired from apoplexy in the middle of a dinner party. But Papa seemed peaceful enough now, and she smiled as she entered the room.

'Shall I light the lamp, Papa? It's getting too dark to see.'

'Leave it a while, Rosie. I like to sit here and watch the dusk creeping along the river.'

She drew up a chair to sit beside him. 'You mean you like to keep an eye on your old boat. You can't bear to let her out of your sight.'

Edward puffed a plume of smoke out of the open window. 'There are still river pirates about, in spite of the efforts of the police to round the villains up and put them behind bars. They come out at night like sewer rats, crawling all over the vessels moored alongside the wharves and stealing anything that they can lay their thieving hands on. I know what I'd do with the buggers if I was to catch one of them.'

Rosina laid her hand on his arm. She could feel the tension in his muscles and a vein was throbbing in his temple. She knew that she must change the subject or he would get worked up again. 'Would you like to see my presents, Papa?'

'Of course.' He patted her hand. 'Pay no mind to me, poppet. I'm just a grumpy old man.'

'And I love you, Papa.' She leapt to her feet and went to the side table to fetch a handful of the gifts she had received. If she could just keep his attention until it was too dark to see outside, then they would enjoy a peaceful evening. She tickled his nose with the parrot's feather. 'Old Jamjar gave me this. I'll get Walter to fit a pen nib on the end for me.'

'Very pretty, dear. But if you visited the bird shop, it means that you went to Ratcliff Highway today. You know I don't like you wandering around that place on your own.'

'Papa, you're as bad as Bebe. I really can take care of myself.'

'You're too trusting, Rosie. You're just like your dear mother. Ellie always saw the good in people – she was a saint.'

'That I am not,' Rosina said, chuckling. 'I think I take more after you . . .' She broke off. He was no longer listening to her. His attention was fixed on something he could see from the window. 'What is it, Pa? What do you see?'

'There he is, the blackguard. Look at him, strolling along as though he hasn't a care in the world.' Edward leapt to his feet. 'I'm going to have it out with Ham Barnum, once and for all.' He stormed out of the parlour.

'Oh, Lord!' Rosina ran after him, but she was hampered by her long skirts and he was out of the house before she had even reached the front door. She almost collided with Walter as he stepped out of the office.

'What's going on?'

'Pa's gone chasing after Captain Barnum. I'm afraid he's raring for a fight. We've got to stop him.'

'Stay here. I'll go.'

'No. I'm coming too.' Rosina followed him, quickening her step to keep up with his long strides. The lamplighter had just finished his rounds and he walked past them with a cheery nod. In the flickering gaslight, Rosina saw her father disappearing into the Black Eagle pub. As they reached the entrance, Walter stopped and caught her by the hand.

'Let me go in, miss. It's not a fit place for a young lady.'

'Oh, Walter. Not you too!' Rosina jerked her hand free and marched into the taproom. A wave of noise hit her and the fuggy atmosphere, thick with tobacco smoke and the mixed fumes of beer and strong spirits, almost took her breath away. The punters were mostly men: dockers, sack-makers, seamen and labourers; the only other females present were the kind that Bertha described as 'loose women' and a few who might once have led decent lives but were now shambling, snuff-stained wrecks who had succumbed to the temptation of jigger gin and grog.

'Please go home,' Walter hissed in her ear.

Ignoring his plea, she pushed through the crowd, following the sound of raised voices. She could hear her father shouting at Ham Barnum even before she had managed to squeeze through the forest of burly men, who had formed a ring around them like onlookers at a bare-knuckle fight in the street.

'You're a lying, cheating bastard.' Edward squared up to his opponent, fisting his hands.

Captain Ham Barnum was taller by a good head, and broad-shouldered into the bargain. He stood his ground, folding his arms across his chest. 'Take care, old man. I don't let anyone accuse me of cheating. You were beaten fair and square.'

'Says you, mister!'

'Says I. You're a poor loser, sir.'

'Only when I'm cheated out of winning a race and you stole my cargo, Barnum. What's more you saw to it that the one I got was rotten with mould. I'll be lucky if I can get half its worth.'

'Hit him, guvner.' A voice from the crowd called out.

'Settle it like men.'

'Fisticuffs, outside.'

'No!' Rosina's clear treble shrilled above the

deep bass of the men's voices. 'Pa, leave him be, and come home.'

Captain Barnum turned his head and gave her an appraising stare. 'Well, now. If it isn't your girl, Captain May. And a pretty little thing she is too – just like her mother . . .'

With a mighty roar, Edward lunged at him, butting Barnum in the ribs and knocking him to the floor. He went down on him, flailing his fists and landing punches wherever he could find a sensitive spot. Momentarily winded, Barnum gasped for breath, and then, recovering quickly, he twisted his body so that Edward was now helpless on the ground. He pummelled him mercilessly, much to the enjoyment of the crowd. They roared their approval, smacking their clenched fists against their hands and cheering as each blow landed.

'Stop them,' Rosina screamed. 'He'll kill my pa. Walter, do something.'

Walter took off his glasses. 'Hold these for me.' He dived into the fray, but Barnum punched him in the face and tossed him aside with an angry roar. He went back to throttling Edward, who had turned blue in the face.

'You're killing him,' Rosina cried, wringing her hands. 'Someone stop them, please.'

Walter scrambled to his feet, wiping a trickle of blood from his lip. He hooked his arm around Barnum's neck, dragging his head backwards so that he was forced to loosen his grip. Edward lay on the floor with his eyes closed, gasping for breath. Rosina threw herself down on her knees beside him. 'Papa, speak to me.'

'I'll kill him next time.' Barnum struggled to get free but the landlord came from behind the counter, rolling up his sleeves.

'Not in my pub you won't, Captain Barnum. Leave him to me, lad.' He pushed Walter aside, and grabbing Barnum by the collar and the seat of his pants he frogmarched him out of the building.

Walter bent down to help Edward to his feet. 'Let's get you home, Captain.'

'What are you all staring at?' Rosina demanded, turning on the crowd. 'The show is over, no thanks to you. I'm ashamed of you all, standing by and watching two old men fighting each other.'

'Who are you calling an old man?' Edward muttered as Walter led him outside. 'I'll have a little more respect from you, my girl. And what d'you think you're doing, Walter? Bringing her into the pub like that. It ain't no fit place for a young lady.'

Rosina handed Walter his spectacles. 'I made him bring me. Anyway, Pa, you should be grateful to him. Captain Barnum would have killed you if Walter hadn't pulled him off.'

'Bah!' With an irritated twitch of his shoulders, Edward stamped off in the direction of home.

'They'll kill each other one day,' Walter said, wiping the blood from his cut lip on the back of his hand.

Rosina took a hanky from her pocket and handed it to him. 'Here, use this.'

He stared doubtfully at the scrap of cotton lawn with her initials embroidered in one corner. 'Bloodstains will ruin it.'

'Don't be silly, Walter. You probably saved my pa's life tonight, so why should I worry about a mere handkerchief? Come on, let's go home and I'll put some salve on those cuts and bruises. You'll have a real shiner by morning.'

'It's all right. I'll see to it when I get back to my place.'

As they walked slowly back towards the house, Rosina shot him a curious glance. 'You are a puzzle, Walter. You must have worked for Papa for at least two years, and yet I know little or nothing about you.'

'There's not much to know, miss.'

'I'm sure that's not true. For example, where do you live? I've never thought to ask you before.'

'Not far away.'

'That's no answer. Why are you being so mysterious? Do you live with your family? Or are you secretly married and have ten children?'

'I have a room in a lodging house in Angel Court. I have no family and I'm not married.' He stopped outside the front door. 'There is no mystery.'

'What a pity. There's nothing I like better than a good puzzle. Goodnight, Walter.'

He hesitated. 'I'm sorry your birthday was spoilt.'

'It would have ended up much worse if you hadn't been there to stop the fight.' She reached up and kissed him on the cheek. He was standing with his back to the street lamp and she could not make out the expression on his face, but when he did not immediately make a move to leave, she gave him a gentle push. 'Go on home, Walter. I'll lock up, so there's no need for you to worry on that score. I'll see you in the morning.'

'Goodnight, miss.' He began to walk away but she called out to him.

'Walter. Thank you so much for the breastpin. I love it.'

He glanced over his shoulder, and she thought she saw the shadow of a smile on his face before he disappeared into the darkness.

Having locked up and made everything secure, she was halfway up the staircase when Bertha appeared on the landing. She was dressed for bed in a voluminous white calico nightgown and her hair was confined in a mobcap. In the flickering candlelight, she looked like a rather substantial ghost. 'What's going on? I've just seen his nibs go into the parlour. If I didn't know better, I'd say he'd been in a fight.'

Rosina hurried up the stairs. 'It's all right, Bebe. Papa got in an argument with Captain Barnum in the Black Eagle, but it's all settled now.'

'It will never be all right between them two.' Bertha gave her a searching look. 'And what was you doing in the Black Eagle? I'll have a few words to say to the captain on that score.'

She made a move towards the parlour, but Rosina caught her by the arm. 'Not now, Bebe. I'll explain everything in the morning. Go to bed, there's a dear.'

'All right, but you haven't heard the last of this.' Bertha mounted the staircase that led to her bedroom at the rear of the second floor. The treads creaked beneath her weight and the candle smoked, leaving the scent of hot wax in its trail as she took the light with her. Left in the dark, Rosina went into the parlour. To her intense relief she found her father slumped on the window seat, scowling like a grumpy school-boy, but he seemed to have suffered nothing worse than a bruised neck and hurt pride.

'You should have let me teach him a lesson,' he grumbled, with his pipe clenched between his teeth. 'I could have beaten Ham Barnum with one arm tied behind my back.'

'Of course you could, Papa. But what good would that serve? You may not get on well with Captain Barnum, but he is our neighbour. I've grown up with Sukey and her sisters, and I may not like Mrs Barnum very much, but she's always been civil to me.'

'I know, poppet. But I could wish that you had picked another friend. Ham and I have old scores to settle.'

She went to sit beside him on the window seat. 'Why do you hate him? What did he ever do to you that made you bear such a grudge?'

Edward took the pipe from his mouth and tapped it on the windowsill, watching the ash fly up in the air and float away on the gentle breeze. 'It's not something that I like to talk about, but I think you're old enough to understand, Rosie.'

'Understand what, Papa?'

'We were boyhood friends, Ham Barnum and I. We went to the same school and we served our apprenticeships working for the same barge owner, old man Carpenter. He had a beautiful daughter and we were both sweet on her.'

Rosina's breath hitched in her throat. 'Mama?'

Edward patted her hand, smiling. 'Yes, your dear mama. Ellie was the loveliest girl for miles around.'

'And you both fell in love with her?'

'I did, for certain. I can't speak for Barnum. He was always ambitious, and, when he had finished his apprenticeship, he moved to another and bigger company. He went to live away from Black Eagle Wharf, and by the time he returned a few years later I was courting Ellie. But Ham still fancied her: he turned her head with his smooth talk and he showered her with presents. He convinced her father that he was a better man than I, and he asked for Ellie's hand in marriage.'

'But she married you, Pa. She must have seen him for what he was.'

He barely seemed to hear her. 'She was so young and trusting. A sweet and guileless girl.' Edward stared down at his pipe, twisting it between his fingers and frowning. 'It wasn't her fault, poppet. Ham flattered and cajoled her into thinking that he adored her, and then he took advantage of her innocence. He persuaded her to go on a day trip to Southend. He said they had missed the train home, but I know that he planned her seduction. He convinced her that spending the night together was all right because they were soon to be married. I could have killed him – but he seemed intent on standing by her and the wedding date was fixed.' The stem of the pipe snapped in two between Edward's taut fingers. A speck of blood oozed from a small cut on his hand but he did not seem to notice the pain. His voice broke as he continued. 'He was married all along, Rosie. He had a wife in Kent, and a child. It all came to light when his father-in-law turned up at the church to denounce him. There she was, in her wedding finery, my little Ellie, broken-hearted.'

'But that's terrible. Why did he pretend that he was free to marry her?'

'Ellie's father owned four sailing barges, a couple of lighters and some wherries. Ham had married a penniless girl, and I think that he had simply grown tired of her. He saw that Ellie was not only desirable, but whoever married her would inherit her father's business. He had ruined her reputation, and that made it almost impossible for old man Carpenter to object to the match. He would have gone through with the bigamous marriage if the truth had not come out. Barnum walked away without so much as an apology for the hurt he had caused.'

'No wonder you hate him, Papa. But you still loved Mama, and you married her.'

Edward tossed the broken pipe out of the window. 'Not immediately, poppet. Ellie was naturally distraught and her father was beside himself with rage. He sent her to the country for a while, to get her away from the gossips. But in the time she was absent he suffered ill health, and he seemed to have lost interest in the company. I was master of the *Ellie*, and I did what I could to keep the business going, but he was in financial straits, and the bank foreclosed on him. He was forced to sell all the vessels, but one. In the end, I went to the village near Colchester where Ellie was staying with an elderly aunt, and I brought her back to London.

We were married shortly afterwards and we took rooms above the milliner's shop in Ratcliff Highway. Bertha had worked for the Carpenters for years and she came to join us to look after your mother while I was away on the river.'

'I don't remember my grandfather. Did he get better?'

'He was a broken man, Rosie. When my blessed Ellie lost her life so soon after you were born, he simply gave up and died. He left this house to you. You will inherit the property on your twenty-first birthday, together with the ownership of the *Ellie May*.'

She stared at him, too stunned to take it all in at once. 'I don't understand. Why did he not leave the house and the ship to you?'

'Your grandfather wanted you to be secure. He had seen his daughter's life torn apart by a ruthless man, Ham Barnum, and he wanted you to have some independence. He knew that I could be trusted to keep the business going, and that I had your best interests at heart. In three years' time you will be a woman of property, my dove.'

'Why did you keep all this from me until now, Papa?'

'No one knows any of it, except for Bertha and me, and now you, of course. I didn't want fortune hunters chasing after my girl. Heaven knows, the business is struggling and Ham

Barnum is largely to blame for that. He's never forgiven me for marrying Ellie. I just thank God that you have a young man like Harry Gostellow, who is wealthy enough in his own right not to be interested in your small inheritance.'

'No, Papa, I won't have that. Harry is just a friend. You mustn't start reading anything else into what is little more than an acquaintanceship. I like Harry, he's very entertaining, but that is as far as it goes.'

'It may be so on your part, poppet.' He reached over to clasp her hand. 'But I've seen the way the young fellow looks at you. I'm just surprised that you didn't ask him round to supper tonight.'

'Harry was out of town on business, Pa. And as he's obviously forgotten that it's my birthday, I'm very glad that I didn't invite him.'

Edward squeezed her hand. 'I didn't mean to upset you, my dear. And I wouldn't have told you about your mother and Ham Barnum, but perhaps it's best out in the open.'

She rose to her feet. 'I'm glad you've confided in me at last.' She leaned over to kiss his forehead. 'It's been a long day and I'm tired. I think I'll go to bed now.'

'I'll stay up a while longer.'

'Goodnight, Papa. You will be all right on your own, won't you?'

'I will, Rosie. You get your beauty sleep, and

I'll find my second-best pipe and smoke some of that fine baccy that you gave me.'

'Will you promise me one thing, Papa?'

'If I can, darling.'

'That you'll let bygones be bygones, and stop this feud with Captain Barnum, for all our sakes.'

Edward shook his head. 'I don't know that I can make such a promise. He has much to answer for.'

'I'm sure that my mother would not have wanted all this ill feeling between you.'

'I know that too, but she is in heaven, and every time I see that man I am in hell.'

Next morning, after Bertha had dragged every last detail concerning the events of the previous night out of her, Rosina was glad to escape from the kitchen before her father put in an appearance. There would be a few harsh words bandied about when Bertha got her hands on him, and home truths would be flying around like mad magpies. She did not want to be caught in the middle of a heated argument. It would cool down as quickly as it had erupted, but Rosina had witnessed too many spats between Papa and Bebe to want to endure another one. Oddly enough, they never bore a grudge against each other, and even seemed to get some grim satisfaction from their verbal battles. There was no understanding some people. Rosina went to find Walter.

As usual he was seated behind his desk in the counting house. He rose to his feet when she entered the room. 'Good morning, Miss Rosina.'

She could not repress a gurgle of laughter. 'Oh, Walter! What a lovely black eye.'

'It looks worse than it is.' His swollen lips twitched and he grimaced with pain.

'I'm sorry. I didn't mean to be unkind, but it really is a shiner.'

'How is the captain?'

'I haven't seen him yet this morning, but he wasn't badly injured, thanks to you. I think his pride was hurt more than anything.'

Walter picked up a sheaf of papers. 'I need to see him urgently.'

She knew by his tone of voice that something was wrong, and a cold shiver ran down her spine. 'What is it?'

'It's nothing for you to worry about, miss. But I do need to speak to the captain.'

'You're as bad as the rest of them. You all treat me like a child.'

The shuttered, stubborn look that she had come to know so well made Walter's face an impassive mask. 'It's business, miss.'

'And the *Ellie May* will be mine when I'm twenty-one. Papa told me so last night, and I mean to start taking an interest in how it runs. So you see, Walter, it is my business.'

'Harry Gostellow has refused the cargo. I met

him on the wharf early this morning and I was with him when he examined the hay. He said it had been affected by a mould which makes it unfit for animal fodder and causes disease in humans. He said it must be taken away and destroyed.'

'The whole cargo?'

'I'm afraid so.'

'Is it completely valueless, Walter?'

'Unscrupulous dealers might buy it at a knock-down price and sell it for bedding, or even for fodder, but it is unfit for anything. I'm only surprised that Captain May did not see it himself.'

She had never before heard Walter utter anything close to a criticism of her father and a shiver ran down her spine. 'And Captain Barnum's cargo – is that diseased too?'

Walter shook his head. 'No, it is perfectly clean.'

'But my papa accepted the rotten hay. He should have known better, or else he was tricked into taking the unsaleable cargo.' She paced the floor, wringing her hands. It was simply not possible that Papa, with all his past experience in the trade, could have been fooled into taking on a worthless cargo. She had been aware that his health was failing, but surely not his judgement? She turned to Walter, who was standing quietly watching her with a guarded expression in his eyes. 'Don't just stand there, Walter. You must have a fair idea of what happened. Tell me what you think.'

'I think that this is a matter for your father, miss. It really is none of your concern.'

'How dare you! It is my business, and I think I know who is to blame for this disaster.' She slammed out of the office, intent on sorting things out with Captain Barnum.

Walter followed her. 'Just wait a moment.' He laid his hand over hers as she was about to open the front door. 'Please calm down and think it through. You'll only make matters worse.'

'You don't know what I have in mind.'

'I think I do, and I'm telling you again, that you won't win with Captain Barnum. And your father won't thank you for interfering.'

She pushed his hand away, meeting his eyes with a determined lift of her chin. 'Thank you, Walter. You've said your piece, now stand aside and let me do this my way.'

For a moment she thought he was going to do as she asked, but he folded his arms across his chest and leaned his shoulders against the door, making it impossible for her to leave the house. She stamped her foot. 'Let me out, Walter.'

'This isn't the way.'

'And who are you to tell me what to do?'

Walter closed his lips and said nothing.

She angled her head. 'Please, Walter.'

'Rosie.' Her father's voice from the top of the stairs made her spin round to face him as he came down them, plodding like an old man. 'What's all the noise about?' He stopped short when he saw Walter's face, and he laughed. 'Good God, man. You look as though you've done a few rounds in the ring.'

'He got that black eye on your account, Pa,' Rosina said, stung by the unfairness of her papa's laughing at Walter's misfortune.

'And so he did, poppet.' Edward modified his tone and the laughter faded from his eyes. 'But that don't answer my question. Why are you two going at each other like a pair of turkeycocks? I could hear you all the way upstairs.'

Walter stepped away from the door. 'It was nothing, sir. But I need to speak to you urgently.'

'I'm stiff and sore all over thanks to that brute Barnum. Can't it wait until I've had my breakfast?'

'No, sir. I don't think so.'

'All right, if I must. We'll go into the office. Rosie, love, go and make your poor old pa a cup of tea, if you please. I can't seem to catch me breath this morning. In fact, I think I must have caught a chill from those damnable Essex marshes.'

By the time she had fetched the tea, Rosina had calmed down considerably. She did not dare let on to Bertha about the spoiled cargo; she would leave that to Papa. But, as Bertha always said, there's more than one way to skin a cat. With that thought uppermost in her mind, Rosina fetched her new bonnet and her best shawl, put on her white crocheted gloves, and she set off for the Barnum's house just a hundred yards or so along Black Eagle Wharf. It was identical in size and architecture to her home, but the Barnums were considerably more affluent and a great deal of money had been spent on the decoration and furnishings.

Rosina had abandoned the idea of speaking directly to Captain Barnum. Although she did not want to admit it, she knew that Walter had been right – if she tried to interfere, she would only make matters worse. Instead, she had decided to pay a call on Sukey to see if she knew anything about the ill-fated race and the rotten hay. She quickened her pace, smiling as she acknowledged the greetings from the men working on the wharf, and received a nod and a wave from the wharfinger himself as he came out of his office. She had barely reached the lodging house where Artie and Caddie lived when the sound of a horse's hooves striking the cobblestones at a gallop made her stop and turn to see who could be so foolhardy as to ride along the narrow wharf at such a breakneck speed. She leapt for safety into a doorway as the rider drew his mount to a slithering halt, just feet away from her. The horse's hooves struck sparks from the cobbles. For a terrifying moment, it seemed as though the rider had lost control, and all she could see was flailing legs and hooves as the animal reared above her. She closed her eyes, expecting the worst.

# Chapter Three

'Good morning, Rosie. I must say that's a dashing bonnet you're wearing today.'

She opened her eyes and found herself looking up into Harry Gostellow's boyishly good-looking face. She leaned against the doorpost, fanning herself with her hand. 'You stupid idiot, Harry! You frightened me half to death.'

He leapt from the saddle and tossed the reins to a small urchin who was gaping at him open-mouthed. 'Hold my horse, boy, and there's a penny in it for you.' He turned to Rosina, sweeping his top hat off his head with a bow from the waist and a rueful smile. 'I'm sorry. I didn't mean to scare you. I just saw you in that charming bonnet and I had to hasten to your side to tell you how stunning you look.'

'You ought to know better than to gallop that poor animal along here.' She went over to the horse and stroked its muzzle. 'Poor old Nero. He's in a lather and all because you wanted to compliment me on my bonnet. For shame on you, Harry.' She took a halfpenny from her reticule and pressed it into the boy's hand. 'Walk the horse slowly, and the nice gentleman will give you twopence when he returns.'

'Why, Rosie, I believe you like Nero better than you do me,' Harry said, grinning.

'Indeed I do. Horses have much more sense than men.' She tempered her words with a smile, and walked on.

'You are a hard woman to please.' Harry caught up with her, measuring his pace to match hers. 'Where are you going on this beautiful morning?'

'I'm going to see Sukey Barnum. Aren't you supposed to be at work?'

'But I am at work, or rather, I have been working. My father sent me to inspect the cargoes of hay that arrived in port last night.'

Rosina stopped and stared up into his face. She had heard the serious note creep into his voice, and she saw confirmation of her concern in his eyes. 'Is it true then?'

'It's serious, I'm afraid, Rosie. Captain Barnum's cargo is perfectly fine, but the hay your father carried is diseased. I can't offer him a penny for it.'

'I see.' She looked away, biting her lip. Of course she knew this already, but it seemed so final coming from Harry. She knew nothing of their finances – Papa and Walter dealt with all that – but to lose money on a whole cargo must be serious indeed.

'I am sorry. It's rotten bad luck.'

'Papa will make up for it, I'm sure. Don't give it another thought.'

'But I do, Rosie.' He clasped her hand. 'I don't like to think of you going without.'

'I don't lack for anything. My pa sees to that.'

'I would give you the moon and the stars too, if I had my way.' Harry pressed her hand to his heart in a theatrical gesture.

He looked so absurd that Rosina giggled in spite of herself. 'And yet you forgot my birthday. That's not a good start.'

'No! Damn me, when was it?'

She was not going to let him off so easily. She pulled her hand free and continued on her way towards the Barnums' house. 'I shouldn't have to remind a man who wanted to give me the moon and the stars.'

He hurried after her. 'No, really. That's not fair. You should have dropped a hint – reminded me, or something.'

She stopped outside the Barnums' door. 'It's all right, Harry. It really doesn't matter, but it was yesterday as it happens.' Satisfied that he was genuinely racked with guilt, she patted his cheek with her hand. 'You'd best get back to work before your father realises what a long time you've taken.'

'I'll make it up to you. Let me take you out for supper tonight, and maybe the theatre or a music hall.'

She rapped on the door knocker. 'That would be nice, but Papa won't let me go unless Bertha chaperones me.'

'Oh God, no. She doesn't approve of me, Rosie.'

The door opened and the Barnums' maid gave them an appraising glance. 'Well?'

'Will you tell Miss Sukey that I'm here to see her, please, Gertie?'

'I suppose so.' Gertie closed the door again.

'I'd sack that stupid girl if I was Barnum,' Harry said crossly.

'My goodness, you are crotchety this morning.'

'I'm sorry, Rosie. I'll be all smiles if you'll promise to come out with me this evening? You can bring the old watchdog if you must.'

'Thank you, Harry, but not tonight. Papa will need me at home. Maybe another night, if he gives his permission.'

'I'll call on you tomorrow. Will you be at home?'

'I might be. You'll have to try your luck, won't you?'

Gertie opened the door. 'You'd best come in,' she said in a grudging tone.

Rosina stepped over the threshold and Harry followed her into the entrance hall. She shot him a sideways glance. 'I thought you had to get back to the office.'

'I do, but I think a courtesy call on Captain

Barnum might be in order, and then perhaps I could walk you home.'

The roguish twinkle in his eyes did not escape Rosina, neither was she entirely immune to Harry's charms, but she also knew that he was an outrageous flirt and not to be taken seriously. 'So you suddenly need to see Captain Barnum. Isn't that a coincidence?'

Gertie gave a loud cough. 'What's it to be then? Who's seeing who?'

'I would like to see Miss Sukey,' Rosina said firmly. 'It seems that the gentleman has difficulty in making up his mind what he is doing and where he is going.'

'I say, Rosie. That's below the belt. I have to see Barnum or his mate to arrange for another cargo of hay. The horses in London gobble the stuff up at an alarming rate.'

'I'll take you up to the parlour, miss. But if he wants to see the master, he'd best go to the boat as that's where he'll find him.' Gertie looked from one to the other, and seeing that she had their full attention she warmed to her theme. 'Mr Barker, the mate, come to the door early this morning. Blooming river pirates have been at it again, says he. Why, they've even stole the bloody compass and all the charts. Them's his words not mine, miss. What shall us do, Cap'n? says he. They've stripped the poor bitch bare as a tart's arse.'

'Thank you, Gertie,' Harry said, frowning. 'I think we've got the picture.'

'Who's there, Gertie?' Sukey Barnum appeared at the top of the stairs. Her face lit up with a smile when she saw Rosina. 'Rosie, I thought I heard your voice. And Harry too.' A coral blush coloured her cheeks as she picked up her skirts and ran down the stairs to greet them.

Harry doffed his hat with a flourish. 'Good morning, Miss Sukey.'

'I was just going to show 'em into the parlour, miss,' Gertie said, eyeing Sukey warily.

'No you weren't, you fibber. I heard you telling them my dada's business. Go about your work, girl.' Sukey tucked her hand through Rosina's arm. 'I have a birthday present for you, even if it is a day late. But I had to persuade Dada to give me some money. Luckily he was in a good mood yesterday before the thieves stripped the *Curlew* of everything that wasn't bolted to the deck.' She turned her head to cast Harry a flirtatious glance beneath her golden eyelashes. 'Will you join us, Harry?'

'Sadly, I must leave you, ladies. I need to see Captain Barnum rather urgently.' Harry made a move towards the door. 'I'll see myself out.'

Rosina glanced at Sukey's eager face and then at Harry, who had stopped in front of a wall mirror to put his hat on at exactly the right angle. The thought flashed through her mind that it was hardly the action of a man in a hurry. 'Harry, wait.'

He patted the crown of his hat, adjusted the angle and turned to her with a pleased smile. 'I do like this topper. I must order another just like it.'

Rosina giggled. 'And they say that women are vain.'

'Don't be mean to Harry,' Sukey protested. 'I think he looks quite dashing.'

'Thank you, ma'am.' Harry inclined his head in her direction. 'You see, Rosie. Some people appreciate me.'

'Oh, poor Harry,' Rosina said in mock sympathy. 'You're so misunderstood.'

'Well, I think he looks most handsome today.' Sukey tossed her curls. 'And much too smart to be going on board dirty old sailing barges.'

'Thank you, Miss Susan. But I really must be going. I need to sort out this business with the hay. We're a load down and I need to send another barge to fetch a full cargo.'

Rosina spotted an opportunity for her father to recoup his losses. She moved to Harry's side. 'I'm coming with you.' She turned to Sukey with an apologetic smile. 'We will have to postpone our chat until later.'

Sukey pursed her lips into a pout.

'I say, Rosie.' A perplexed look crossed his face, and Harry frowned. 'I mean, I know you're worried about your father, but there's nothing you can do. You're not thinking of making a scene, are you?'

'Of course not. You said you needed another cargo of hay. If Captain Barnum can't take the *Curlew*, I'm sure my pa would be only too pleased to have the work. The *Ellie May* only needs to be unloaded, and she could be ready to sail on the next tide.'

'I don't know about that,' Harry said, shaking his head. 'The first thing Captain Barnum did when he docked yesterday was to go to the office and sign up for another cargo. It could be difficult.'

'But not if he can't honour the deal, Harry.'

'Hold on, there,' Sukey protested. 'That doesn't sound very fair.'

Rosina spun round to face her. 'Well it wasn't very fair when your dada cheated in the race and set my papa up with a load of rotten hay. I'm truly sorry, Sukey. I hate their silly feud as much as you do, but I must do something. I'll go and speak to Mr Gostellow myself if it will secure the cargo for the *Ellie May*.'

'Well!' Sukey stamped her foot. 'Some friend you are, Rosina.'

'I am your friend, you know that. But I have to look after my papa, just as you would look after yours.'

'But my present for you . . .'

'Will be lovely, Sukey. And I'll come back later to receive it.' Rosina turned to Harry. 'Are you ready?'

'I don't know what Barnum would have to say about this,' Harry said, eyeing her doubtfully. He opened the door and stood back to allow her to pass. 'I know that you're concerned about your father, but you should leave business matters to those who know what they're doing.'

'By that I suppose you mean that I should leave it to the men, who are so much the cleverer sex.'

'I say, Rosie. I don't think your papa would like you using that word.'

She shot him a sideways glance. 'What word, Harry?'

'You know perfectly well what word – the word that ladies do not use.' With an embarrassed twitch of his shoulders, Harry began walking towards the *Curlew*. 'I have business to do.'

She broke into a run to keep up with him. 'Precisely so. You need to keep your father's warehouse filled with hay or he will have nothing to trade.'

'It would take almost as long for the *Ellie May* to be unloaded and made ready to sail as it would for Barnum to refit his ship.'

'I'll fetch Artie Trigg and I know the stevedores will work twice as hard if I ask them nicely. We can do it given half a chance.'

'I'd have to square it with the old man first, Rosie.'

'Oh, Harry. Don't you ever take any responsibility for anything? Stand up to him for once.'

'It really isn't up to me. Captain Barnum has a legal contract . . .'

'A contract which he is unable to honour. That must cancel out any agreement he had with your father.'

'Well I'm blowed.' Harry stopped suddenly, pointing to the *Ellie May*, which was tied up alongside the *Curlew*. Artie was standing in the stern directing the men who were using the umbrella cranes to unload the spoiled cargo of hay onto a lighter. Rosina could see Walter standing outside the wharfinger's office, talking to the dock foreman. She picked up her skirts and ran towards him. 'Walter, what's happening?'

He gave her a lopsided smile, wincing as the cut on his lip cracked open. 'There's been a slight mishap to Barnum's boat.'

'I know. I've just come from his house. But how did you find anyone to take the spoiled cargo?'

'It's going to be taken with the city's rubbish and dumped.'

'It must be costly. Can we afford it?'

'Let's just say that Mr Gilks of Duke's Shore Wharf owes me a favour. Don't worry, Miss Rosina. It's all taken care of.'

'Now look here, my good fellow.' Harry strode up to Walter, sticking out his chin like a pugilist about to start a fight. 'You seem to be taking a lot on yourself for a mere clerk. I can't allow you to interfere in my business.'

'No, sir,' Walter said equably. 'But your father can, and he did. I went to the office first thing this morning. Mr Gostellow's main concern is filling the warehouse with enough hay to feed the work horses in the city. I suggest it ought to be yours, too.'

'Infernal cheek.' Harry's face flushed dark red and he clenched his fists.

Rosina laid her hand on his arm. 'That's wonderful, Harry. I'm so grateful to your father. And it really serves Captain Barnum right for cheating in the first place.' She turned to Walter. 'Well done. I can't thank you enough.'

'Don't thank me, miss. It was the river pirates who made it possible.'

'And I suppose a fellow like you approves of such villainy?' Harry said angrily.

Rosina could see that this argument might escalate into a full-blown row. 'Now, Harry . . .'

Walter held up his hand. 'I think sometimes a man has to take direct action even though it goes against the grain.'

'Bah! You're just a jumped-up little pen pusher. What would you know about anything?'

Behind his spectacles, Walter's eyes held a

steely glint and Rosina saw, for the first time, a stubborn set to his jaw. Harry was spoiling for a fight, and she did not want to see Walter's other eye blackened and swollen. She moved to place herself squarely in between them. 'That's enough of that, gentlemen. Harry, I'd like you to walk me home if you will.'

'Of course.' He glanced over his shoulder at the ragged urchin who was patiently walking Nero. 'Bring my horse here, boy.'

The boy broke into a run, his bare feet skimming over the rough cobbles as he led Nero towards them. Rosina held her breath as the horse broke into a trot. There was an eager look of anticipation on the child's face that went straight to her heart. His stick-thin body looked so frail against the well-muscled, sleek body of the animal that was undoubtedly housed and fed better than the boy's whole family. Her hand flew to her mouth as he stumbled, but somehow he managed to regain his footing. One slip beneath those flailing hooves would cause terrible injuries or even death. She clutched Harry's arm. 'Take the reins, Harry. The child is not strong enough to hold such a mettlesome animal.'

Harry snatched the bridle from the boy's hand. He tossed a penny into the air and the boy made a dive for it: he would have tumbled over the edge of the wharf into the water if Walter had not caught him.

'Ta, mister.' The urchin closed his fist around the coin and backed away, as if afraid that someone might steal his money.

'Harry, I promised him twopence.' Rosina held her hand out to the child. 'Wait, boy. I think the gentleman has something more for you.'

Reluctantly, Harry took another penny from his pocket. 'I say, Rosie. You'll bankrupt me and spoil the brat.'

'Give him the money and don't be so mean.' She raised her eyebrows, waiting for him to throw the coin and nodding with approval when he did. 'There, that didn't hurt, did it?'

'You don't understand these people, Rosie,' Harry said, scowling. 'The boy will squander the money on raw spirits or tobacco.'

'Or maybe he will waste it on luxuries like bread and dripping, or a decadent meat pie.' Walter's lip curled in contempt.

'Did I ask for your opinion?' Harry rounded on him angrily. 'Get back to work, fellow.'

'Harry, that's no way to speak to Walter. Walk me home and let's have no more of this bad feeling between you.' She turned to Walter with a grateful smile. 'You've done so well today. I can't thank you enough.'

'I don't know why you're thanking him,' Harry grumbled as they walked slowly towards home with Nero following them on a loose rein. 'You shouldn't be too familiar with servants, Rosie. They'll only take advantage of you.'

'Walter isn't a servant. He's my pa's right-hand man. I don't know what we'd do without him.'

'He's probably fleecing your papa left, right and centre. I know his type, Rosie. He tries to act like a gentleman but don't be fooled by that. My father keeps a pretty tight rein on the clerks in our office. He don't stand for any old nonsense from them and they know their place.'

'I'm sure they do,' Rosina said sweetly. 'Thank you for walking me home, Harry.'

They had reached the house and Rosina was about to go inside when he caught her by the hand. 'Will you allow me to take you to supper tomorrow night, Rosie?'

'I'll have to ask Papa.'

'Then I'll call on you tomorrow morning.'

'All right, Harry.'

He hesitated. 'Perhaps I should speak to your father now.'

'I don't think that's a very good idea in the circumstances. He'll be anxious about the cargo and I expect he's still out of sorts with Captain Barnum.'

'This damned silly affair between them is getting out of hand.'

'It's not really your business, Harry.'

'It is if it affects trade. My old man won't stand for too much of it, Rosie. You can pass that message on from me, as a friendly warning. I wouldn't like to see your papa put out of business, but that's what will happen if he can't settle things with Captain Barnum.' Harry put his foot in the stirrup and mounted his horse. 'I'll see you tomorrow.' He tightened the reins so that Nero performed a caracole, and he doffed his hat, bowing from the saddle.

Rosina laughed at his antics. Really, she thought as she watched him urge the horse into a canter, Harry Gostellow was a dreadful show-off, but she was genuinely fond of him.

The interior of the old house felt cool and slightly damp after the warm sunshine outside. She went straight to the kitchen where she could hear Pa's deep tones and Bertha's higher-pitched voice; it sounded as though they were arguing, but that was nothing new.

'Ah, there you are, poppet.' Edward turned to her with a welcoming smile as he struggled into his reefer jacket, hampered by a fit of coughing.

'What did I tell you, you old fool,' Bertha said crossly. 'You're not fit enough to go out on the river so soon.'

'Hold your tongue, you old harpy. It's none of your business.'

Rosina looked from one red face to the other, sighing. 'Are you two fighting again?'

'Me? Fight with her?' Edward snatched his cap from the table and rammed it on his head.

'Miss Spinks forgets that she's a servant in this house.'

Bertha folded her arms across her ample bosom, squinting at him through narrowed eyes. 'A servant gets paid for her labours. You ain't paid me nothing for the past ten years or more.'

Rosina could see that this argument was getting out of hand. 'But Bebe, dear, you're more like one of the family than a servant.'

'Yes, a nagging old aunt,' Edward muttered.

Bertha shook her fist at him. 'A woman what brings up a man's child and waits on him hand and foot for no wages is usually his wife.'

'I'd as soon sleep with a mop stick soaked in vinegar as share my bed with you, you nagging old crow.'

Rosina threw up her hands. She was used to their bickering, but this was getting them nowhere and there were more important matters to discuss. 'Stop it, the pair of you.'

'This is the day he likes me,' Bertha said, tossing her head.

'She started it, the sour old spinster. Treating me like a schoolboy.'

'That's enough.' Rosina clapped her hands together. 'Quite enough.'

'He'll die of lung disease if he risks them bad airs from the Essex marshes in his poorly state.' Bertha slumped down on the chair by the range, putting her feet up on the brass rail. 'But don't no one listen to me. I'm just the slave round here.'

'Bah! I feed you, don't I, woman? I clothe you and keep you in boots the size of herring boxes, don't I? If I don't take the *Ellie May* downriver there'll be no food in the larder, no coal for the fire and no roof over our heads. And that bloody Barnum will have won. I ain't allowing him to beat me for a second time.' Edward stamped out of the kitchen.

'Oh, Bebe. How could you?' Rosina cast a reproachful glance over her shoulder as she hurried after her father. She followed him into the office. 'Papa, maybe Bertha is right. Perhaps you ought not to sail today.'

'Nonsense, Rosie.' He picked up a dog-eared ledger and flipped through the pages. 'I'm quite well, apart from the wretched cough, and that's common enough amongst men who breathe in the dust from hay. It will pass, but more important, I've got a cargo and I took it from Barnum.'

'Oh, Pa. Aren't you ever going to put an end to this feud?'

'It's between Barnum and me, poppet. It don't concern you.'

'But it does concern me, Papa. It affects all of us, and one day I'm afraid that one of you will come off the worse for it.'

He brushed her cheek with paper-dry lips. 'It'll

be him that gets the worst of it then, my duck. He took advantage of your mother and he abandoned his wife and child – I'll see him in hell before I shakes the bugger's hand. Begging your pardon for the language, poppet. But thanks to the river pirate, I got my chance to get one over on the swine.'

She could see that nothing was going to stop him, and Rosina managed a wobbly smile. 'You will take care, won't you, Papa?'

'Of course I will. The river is my friend and he won't let me down. Haven't we been working together for forty years or more? Don't worry about me, Rosie. I'll be home again in a few days with a cargo of good hay this time.'

'I'll come and see you off.'

'No, ducks. You know I can't stand the sight of a woman left on the quay wall waving her handkerchief, all sad and lonely-looking. You go and make my peace with old Bertha. She's a good sort really.'

'I don't know why you're so mean to her.'

'She don't take it seriously. She enjoys a good spat just the same as I do.' He pinched her cheek. 'When I get home we'll have supper at the Turk's Head, and we'll take old grumble-gizzard with us. That should sweeten her temper.'

Rosina walked with him to the street door. 'Papa, Harry asked me out to supper.'

Edward shook his head. 'Not while I'm away,

poppet. He's a fine young man, but I wouldn't want him to get the wrong idea. If he wants to pay court to my daughter, then he has to ask my permission first.'

She felt the colour flood to her cheeks. 'It's just an evening out, Pa. I like Harry, but there's nothing more in it.'

A glimmer of a smile lit Edward's pale blue eyes. 'I think I know the signs when a man is besotted by a woman. Be guided by me.' He pulled his cap down to shield his eyes from the sun, and strode off towards his ship.

Rosina could see Walter, a tall slim figure amongst the burly stevedores and dock labourers. The unloading appeared to be complete and the lighter was being rowed away from the wharf, taking the rotten cargo of hay to be loaded onto another vessel downstream. Caddie was standing outside the wharfinger's office clutching Alfie by the hand while Ronnie toddled in and out between the working men, who gave him the occasional word of encouragement and a pat on the head. Rosina smiled to herself, remembering the days when she had been not much older than young Ronnie Trigg, and the kindness that had been shown to her by the tough men who worked the docks. It had been like having a dozen or more uncles who watched out for her, keeping her out of danger from the moving cranes and the bales of hay, barrels and sacks that were being unloaded. A labourer caught hold of Ronnie by the seat of his pants and lifted him onto his shoulder. He restored him to his mother, tipping his cap, and grinning. No wonder Caddie looked so pale and tired these days, Rosina thought, with a rush of sympathy. She could not imagine what it must be like to be tied down with two tiny tots and another expected within the next month or so. Poor Caddie! She would call on her later that day, after having made her peace with Sukey.

Rosina was about to go back into the house when she heard shouting. There was no mistaking the tones of Ham Barnum. Without stopping to think, she raced across the wharf, pushing her way through the interested crowd of men who had gathered to watch the spectacle of two well-known skippers haranguing each other. The ill feeling between Ham and Edward was legendary along the wharves of Wapping and Shadwell. She reached Walter first, but he caught her by the arm, preventing her from intervening between the two angry captains who were squaring up to each other.

'Let me go, Walter.'

'You'll only get hurt if you get in the way.'

'I said, let me go. My pa is a sick man. This has got to stop.'

Walter lifted her bodily and placed her behind him.

'You old bastard,' Ham roared. 'I'll wager you had something to do with my ship being ransacked.'

'Take that back, you black-hearted fiend, or do I have to make you?'

'Just try it, old man.' Ham pointed to his chin. 'Let's finish what we began last night.'

'I could put out your lights with one hand tied behind my back.' Edward danced about on his toes, but was overcome by a fit of coughing.

Walter stepped in between them, holding up his hands. 'Now, gentlemen. Can't we settle this in a friendly fashion?'

Ham pushed him aside. 'Get out of me way, scribbler. This is men's business.'

'Stand aside, Walter.' Edward managed to catch his breath. 'This is between me and him, the cheating old sod.'

With an infuriated roar, Ham lunged at Edward, but Walter deflected the blow with his arm. 'I don't want to knock you down, Captain Barnum. But if you continue in this manner, I may have to.'

A gasp of indrawn breath seemed to suck in all the air around Rosina. All eyes were on Ham Barnum, as the audience waited for his response to this challenge. She held her breath as he stared at Walter, clenching fists like bunches of bananas. Ham's thick bull-neck had turned brick red and the colour flooded his lined face, clashing horribly with his ginger hair and whiskers. For a moment she thought that he was going to pound Walter into mincemeat, but Barnum was staring at Walter with a look of puzzlement on his face and his mouth worked silently. A ripple of anticipation ran through the onlookers. Rosina could see the men fisting their hands, as if ready to leap into the fray, but it never happened.

Barnum turned away from Walter, pointing a shaking finger at Edward. 'I'll remember this, May. Next time it will be just you and me, but I choose not to mash your ugly face into pulp with women present.' He turned on his heel and barged his way through the crowd. 'Barker. Where's that bloody man? Do I have to do everything myself?' He stamped off in the direction of the ship's chandler.

'Are you all right, Papa?' Rosina clutched her father's arm, alarmed by his sudden pallor. 'Won't you come home and rest for a while?'

Edward shook his head. 'I'm fine, Rosie. The damn fellow is a coward. Did you all witness that?' He turned to his audience, but they were dispersing beneath the stern gaze of the dock foreman and the wharfinger. Edward shrugged his shoulders. 'Well, I always knew he was lily-livered.'

'That was so strange,' Rosina said, staring at Barnum's retreating figure. 'I thought he was going to kill you, Walter. And then he just stopped, for no apparent reason.'

'Perhaps he was too gallant to hit a man wearing spectacles.'

'I think you actually scared him.' Rosina eyed him curiously. She felt as though she was seeing a different person to the quiet, self-effacing young man she had always known.

'Don't talk nonsense, poppet.' Edward snatched a sheaf of papers from Walter's hands. 'Ham Barnum just knew when he was going to be beaten. If it wasn't for that bout of coughing, I'd have laid him out for the seagulls and rats to pick at.' He beckoned to Artie, who was saying his goodbyes to Caddie and the children. 'Hurry up, Trigg, or we'll miss the tide. Walter, take my girl home and keep an eye on her. If young Gostellow comes sniffing around while I'm away, you send him packing.'

'Pa, please,' Rosina said, feeling the blood rush to her cheeks. 'I'm not a child any more.'

'No, Rosie. And that's the problem. There's plenty of bilge rats that would take advantage of two women living on their own and unprotected. Walter, I'd be obliged if you'd stay on late in the office for the next few nights until I return. I'll make it worth your while.' Edward climbed stiffly down the ladder and dropped onto the deck of the barge.

Rosina could have wept with embarrassment,

but she met Walter's sympathetic eyes with a straight look and a lift of her chin. 'Walter, if you dare breathe a word of this to anyone, especially Mr Gostellow, I will never, never speak to you again as long as I live.'

# Chapter Four

Bertha was busy preparing steak and kidney to go in a pudding. She brushed aside Rosina's attempts to apologise for her father's ill temper. 'Get on with you, girl. As if I takes any notice of what your dad says to me. Haven't I put up with his tantrums for nigh on twenty years?'

'You're a saint, Bebe. I can't think of anyone else who would stand for such treatment.'

Bertha cut a kidney in half with a surgeon-like incision and she chuckled. 'Never you mind your cajoling ways, missy. Haven't you anything better to do than stand round getting in me way?'

It was the equivalent of telling her to go out and play, and Rosina had to conceal a smile. As far as Bertha was concerned, she would always be a little girl. It was sometimes annoying, but it was also comforting. 'I thought I'd go and see Sukey.'

'Just keep out of old Barnum's way then.'

'Don't worry, I will.' She picked up her reticule and left the kitchen, tiptoeing along the hallway. She hesitated outside the office door, peering inside. Walter was sitting at the desk with his head bent over a ledger. She had no intention of asking his permission to go out visiting, and if she decided to accept Harry's invitation to supper, then Walter would just have to acknowledge the fact that she was her own mistress. He did not look up, and she left the house, closing the door quietly behind her.

There was frantic activity aboard the *Curlew*. She saw Barker standing on deck, issuing instructions to the men from the chandlery as they carried new equipment on board. It seemed that the river pirate had done his work well, but it was strange that he, or they, had picked upon Captain Barnum's vessel and left the *Ellie May* untouched. Whatever their motives, she would have liked to thank them for giving Pa a chance to recoup his losses. Perhaps the thieves also bore a grudge against Barnum? She quickened her pace – it was too nice a day to bother her head about matters that really did not concern her. As she was about to walk past the house where Caddie and Artie lodged, she decided to call in there first. She needed to make certain that Caddie was not too distressed about the unexpectedly quick turnround of the *Ellie May* that had deprived her of her husband's company. It was the least she could do in the circumstances.

The front door was open and the smell of

boiled beef bones and cabbage water wafted from a room at the back of the ground floor. She wrinkled her nose as she headed up the stairs to the first floor. She could hear a child crying and a woman's raised voice coming from a room on the top floor. Somewhere in the house a door slammed and a man was shouting. She could not make out the words, but it was obvious that he was angry about something. A woman screamed and then there was silence.

Rosina shuddered: this was not a nice place to live. The paintwork was peeling; there were holes in the floorboards and cracks in the plasterwork. She went to Caddie's door and knocked.

'Come in, it's not locked.' Caddie's voice from inside was almost drowned by the wailing of the children.

Rosina opened the door and went inside. She remembered the room as being sparsely furnished, but now it looked barely habitable, the only pieces of furniture being a deal table and two beechwood chairs. The floorboards were scrubbed as clean as bleached bones but were bare of any covering, not even a piece of drugget or a rag rug. She was certain that there had been a picture on the wall above the mantelshelf, and a rectangular clean patch on the stained wallpaper confirmed that something had once hung there. Caddie was sitting on the window seat watching helplessly as the two little boys fought over a slice of stale-looking bread.

'Are you all right, Caddie?' It seemed a silly question, since Caddie had obviously been crying.

'N-not really,' Caddie said, sniffing. 'Ronnie, give your brother a bit of bread.'

Ronnie crammed the last morsel into his mouth and gulped it down whole, causing Alfie to roar with rage. Rosina scooped him off the floor and cuddled him. 'There, there, Alfie. I've got something you'd like.' She sat down at the table, setting him on her knee and she opened her reticule. She tipped the sugared almonds out of the poke. Ronnie leapt up from the floor and tried to climb onto her knee so that he could reach the table.

Caddie laughed in spite of herself. 'Now, boys, behave yourselves.'

Rosina bit one of the sweets in half and gave them a piece each, making sure that Alfie only had the sugary outer shell. 'Chew it carefully; we don't want you to choke.'

'I'm sorry, miss. They ain't usually so badly behaved,' Caddie said tiredly. 'They're hungry, that's all.'

Rosina looked at her aghast. 'When did you last have a proper meal, Caddie?'

'Dunno. Days ago, I think. I never had a chance to ask Walter for an advance on Artie's wages, and then he weren't due for none – there being no cargo to sell.'

'Oh, dear! I'm so sorry. ' Rosina broke another sugared almond in half and fed it to the boys. 'Haven't you any money at all, Caddie?'

'No, miss. And nothing in the cupboard neither.'

'This is terrible. I really had no idea that you were so dreadfully hard up.' Rosina set Alfie down on the floor. 'This can't go on. I'll speak to Walter and tell him to give you an advance on Artie's next wage.'

'Thank you, miss.' Tears spilled from Caddie's eyes. 'You're too kind.'

'Nonsense. I can't bear to see you and the little ones living like this. I know it's none of my business, but how did things get so bad?'

'It's not my place to say, miss.'

'Come now, I won't have that. Your Artie works for my papa and I'm sure he would be horrified if he could see you in such a poor state.'

'Artie don't bring home so much in the way of wages since the captain and Captain Barnum have been competing for the trade. Artie says that Captain Barnum always wins and that he cheats, but I know nothing of such matters. All I know is that we've been living on half pay for months.'

Rosina stood up, automatically brushing the

creases from her full skirts. 'This is shocking. I had no idea that things were so bad, but trust me, Caddie. I'll speak to Walter as soon as I get home and he'll give you some money.' The contents of her reticule were still laid out on the table and she picked up her purse. It was suspiciously light, but tucked in its silk lining she found a silver sixpenny bit. She pressed it into Caddie's hand. 'There, that will buy you some bread and milk for the children, and you must come to supper at my house this evening.'

'Ta for the money, but I don't think it would be fitting for us to impose on you. Ta, all the same.'

Rosina frowned. 'I can't see the sense of that, considering it was our fault that you had no money this week. You must come, Caddie. The children will enjoy it, I'm sure, and Bertha loves little ones. She'll be delighted to see you.'

Caddie bent her fair head, seemingly lost for words. Slightly embarrassed, Rosina scooped the rest of her belongings back into the reticule. 'I'll be off then, Caddie. Come to the house at six o'clock and I'll make sure that Walter sees you right.'

She was glad to get away from the lodging house with its unpleasant smells and depressing atmosphere. Even though she was well aware that poverty was a fact of life for many this part of London, it was still a shock to see someone quite close to her suffering in this way. As she walked briskly towards the Barnums' establishment, the image of the bare room and Caddie's hungry children haunted her thoughts. It occurred to her that her own life had been sheltered and cushioned from reality by the combined efforts of Papa and Bertha. They were not wealthy like the Gostellows, but Papa had always said they were comfortably off, and she had never thought to question the fact. She had always had everything she wanted, within reason. She had nice clothes, a room all to herself filled with pretty things and relics of her childhood: a wooden rocking horse, a doll with a waxen head and glossy black hair, picture books and novelettes, fashion magazines, and, her favourite, a musical box that played the 'Blue Danube', which had belonged to her mother. Her safe, secure world was rocking on its axis – it was not a pleasant experience.

She entered the Barnums' house with a feeling of relief that here, at least, things were normal. Gertie, although her usual sullen self, seemed plump, well fed and smart in her cotton print gown and starched white apron. While she waited in the front parlour for Sukey, Rosina looked around with pleasure at the floral wallpaper, the tasselled velvet curtains and the gleaming mahogany furniture polished to a mirror sheen and scented with beeswax. The mantelshelf groaned with ornaments: two pot dogs glaring at each other from opposing ends, a spill jar, a brass clock, and china figurines of shepherds and shepherdesses. Papa would have said it was a vulgar show of new money, but it was solid and comforting.

The door burst open and Sukey flounced into the room, pouting and tossing her golden curls. If she had been a bird, Rosina thought, stifling the desire to giggle, Sukey would have been ruffling her feathers. Rosina held out her arms. 'I am so sorry. I was hateful to you earlier. Am I forgiven?'

Sukey's mouth curved into a smile. 'Of course you are. It was a silly old argument anyway and nothing to do with us.'

'Just because our fathers choose to squabble like two schoolboys, there's no need for us to fall out, is there?'

'Certainly not. It's time they put all that behind them.' Sukey reached up to the mantelshelf and picked up a small package. 'And now I can give you your birthday present. I'm sorry it's a day late.'

Rosie held out her hand. 'It's never too late to receive a present. I wonder what it is?'

'Open it, silly. There's only one way to find out.'

The tissue paper wrapping came away with a couple of tweaks of Rosina's eager fingers to reveal a small box. Inside was a silver bracelet and she gasped with pleasure as she took it from its case. 'It's beautiful. Thank you so much, Sukey.'

'I thought you'd like it, and you have hardly any jewellery.' Sukey did a twirl, holding out her skirts. 'Our dada is always buying us presents. Do you like my new gown?'

Rosina dropped the bracelet back in the box, her delight in the gift dulled by Sukey's careless comment. She knew that no malice was intended, but it still hurt just a little to know that she was pitied for not owning as many trinkets as the Barnum girls. She managed a smile as she fingered the material of Sukey's new gown. 'It's really lovely. And it's silk.'

'Of course it is. Dada wouldn't have me wear anything else.' Sukey executed a half- turn. 'And it's got the latest bustle. What do you think of that?'

It was hard not to be a little envious. Rosina gazed down at her skirts, that were plain by comparison to the lavish amount of trimming on Sukey's elegant gown. She smiled and nodded, she hoped enthusiastically. 'It's splendid.' It was splendid; in fact it was gorgeous, and she would have given her right arm to possess such a magnificent dress. It was the most delightful shade of violet blue, but, if she were being honest, it swamped Sukey's pale complexion and made her look quite sallow. Such a rich colour would have suited her much better – after all, it was almost the same colour as her eyes and everyone knew that brunettes could get away with vibrant shades much better than insipid blondes.

Sukey was looking at her with a worried frown. 'You do like it, don't you?'

Rosina instantly hated herself for being so mean and she clasped Sukey's hands. 'It is the most beautiful gown that I have ever seen, and you look lovely in it.'

A rosy blush coloured Sukey's pale cheeks. 'Thank you, dearest Rosie. I knew you would tell me the truth. Mary said it made me look peaky, the spiteful little cat. Anyway, she's only sixteen so what does she know about fashion?'

'What indeed?' Rosina said, with heartfelt sympathy. Sukey's younger sisters – staid, bookish Mary and precocious, spoilt Lillian – made her glad that she was an only child.

'I must go upstairs and change back into my morning dress before Mama catches me. I'm not supposed to be wearing this until we go out to tea with the Jones-Hardings on Thursday afternoon.'

'I didn't know that your mama knew the Jones-Hardings.' Rosina tried once again to stifle feelings of envy. The Jones-Hardings were almost as wealthy as the Gostellows, even if they had made their money in the rag and bone trade.

'My mama makes it her business to befriend the wives of rich merchants, particularly if they have eligible sons.' Sukey nudged Rosina in the ribs with a saucy wink. 'She has her sights set on taking tea with the Gostellows next. I think she sees me and Harry as a pair. What do you think, Rosie?'

Rosina shrugged her shoulders. She wasn't sure that she liked the idea, and she was quite certain that he'd never looked twice at Sukey – at least, not in a lover-like way. 'He's a good catch, if you're interested in finding a rich husband.'

'And you're not, I suppose?'

'One day I'll marry for love, not money.'

Sukey let out a peal of laughter. 'How romantic. But it wouldn't hurt if the man in question was well off, now would it?'

'I just said . . .'

'I know what you said. I think you're sweet on Harry yourself.'

'I am not. I like Harry, but just as a friend, that's all.'

'Then you wouldn't mind if he came courting me?'

'Well, we certainly aren't going to fall out over a man.' Rosina picked up a satin cushion and threw it at Sukey. 'Isn't it bad enough that we've had to put up with our fathers feuding like a couple of moody old Sicilians all these years?'

Sukey caught the cushion and threw it back, but she was laughing so much that her aim was wide of the mark, and as the door opened the missile hit Gertie full in the face. She took a step backwards, spluttering with rage. 'Miss Sukey! You could have had me eye out.'

'Nonsense, Gertie. How many times have I told you to knock before you enter?'

'Is there a war on?' Harry strolled into the room, picking up the cushion and holding it in front of him like a shield. 'Is it safe for a fellow to come in?'

Rosina was nearest to him and she snatched it from his grasp. 'Not unless you tell us the password, Harry.'

Sukey waved her hand at Gertie, who was hanging about in the doorway intent on following the conversation. 'Go about your business, girl.'

Gertie shut the door with unnecessary force.

'That girl ought to be sent straight back to the foundling home,' Sukey said, frowning.

'The password, Harry,' Rosina insisted, smiling. 'You can't stay unless you say it.'

'Well, now. How about Cremorne Gardens?'

'Cremorne Gardens!' Rosina and Sukey breathed the words in unison.

'That's what I said.' Harry took the cushion from Rosina and dropped it onto the sofa. 'I thought a trip to Cremorne tomorrow evening, for the three of us, would be just the thing. What say you?'

Rosina glanced at Sukey. Cremorne Gardens was famous for its al fresco entertainments. She had heard that there were concerts, ballets, fireworks and balloon ascents. The gardens were reputed to be magnificent and brilliantly illuminated by hundreds of gaslights. There were equestrian events, puppet shows, music and dancing, and, it was rumoured, a great deal of loose and lewd behaviour by drunken and debauched men and women, which was the main reason why Rosina and Sukey had never been allowed to go there.

'Do you really mean it, Harry? Would you take us there for supper and dancing?' Rosina held her breath. She wouldn't mind in the least if Sukey were to come too; after all, they would chaperone each other. It would be perfectly respectable, and terribly exciting.

'Of course I do. I wouldn't have suggested the outing if I did not intend to do it. What do you say, ladies? Will you accompany me?'

Sukey clapped her hands. 'Yes. Oh, yes, Harry.' Her smile faded and she sat down on the nearest chair in a flurry of silk and a swirl of lace-trimmed petticoats. 'There's only one problem. My father would never allow it.'

'Nor mine, either,' Rosina said, frowning. But she so wanted to go. She met Harry's eyes and saw that he was looking at her with a twinkle. She smiled. 'But if they didn't know about it, then they couldn't object, could they?'

'They'd never let me out of the house.' Sukey's bottom lip trembled ominously. 'If I tried to slip out unnoticed, my beastly sisters would sneak on me.'

'And Bertha is only deaf when it suits her.' Rosina did not mention Walter, but she had a suspicion that he might be following Pa's instructions to work late so that he could keep an eye on her. Prisoners in Newgate had more chance of escape than she did.

'Don't worry, ladies.' Harry puffed out his chest. 'I intend to do this properly. I'll speak to Mrs Barnum and ask her permission to escort you to my home for dinner, Miss Susan. And then I'll speak to Bertha and give her the same story. I don't think they'll object to the pair of you being entertained by my parents.'

'Oh, Harry. You are wonderful,' Sukey said, fluttering her eyelashes and blushing.

Rosina was doubtful. 'You'll have to work hard to convince Bertha.'

'Don't worry,' Harry said with a confident smile. 'I know how to turn on the charm. She'll say yes, you can count on that.'

*

'Certainly not,' Bertha said, wagging her finger at Rosina. 'I promised your papa that I would look after you while he's away, and look after you I will.'

'But Sukey will be going with us, and Harry is going to take us there and bring us safely home.' Rosina's heart sank as she saw the stubborn set of Bertha's jaw. That was a bad sign. She tugged playfully at her apron strings. 'What harm could come to us in the Gostellows' mansion?'

'It's not you being there that worries me. I'm coming with you to see that there's no hanky-panky on the way there or on the way home.'

'As if either Sukey or me would allow such a thing! Shame on you for thinking so, Bebe.'

'It's not you two innocents that worries me, it's the young gentleman in question. If his intentions are honourable, then that's fine, but if they ain't – then he'll have me to deal with.' Bertha heaved her large body from the chair by the range. 'Your pa would never forgive me if I was to let you go out with a young man without a proper chaperone.'

'But Sukey will be coming too. Won't you just think about it, please, Bebe?'

'Don't pester me, girl. I got the meal to finish preparing, and you shouldn't have invited Caddie and her nippers to supper without asking me. What if there weren't enough food to go round?'

Rosina gave her a hug. 'You always cook enough for an army, and I'll bet poor Caddie has never tasted anything like your steak and kidney pudding. She's close to her time, poor thing.'

'Well, I suppose we must look after her. But don't make a habit of it, Rosie. This ain't a soup kitchen.'

'No, I promise I won't.' Having skilfully changed the subject, Rosina tried not to look too pleased with herself. Given time, she could usually twist Bertha round her little finger. She had until tomorrow evening – a lot could happen in twenty-four hours.

But Bertha remained adamant, and, next evening, Rosina was beginning to despair.

'I'm coming with you, and that's final.' Bertha rammed her bonnet on her head and tied the ribbons under her several chins. 'I'm sure that the Gostellows won't mind if I wait for you in the servants' hall.'

'But, Bebe, wouldn't you rather sit by the fire and rest your weary bones? You're always saying that your bunions begin to play up at this time of night.'

'I don't care. I got to do me duty and I'm coming with you.'

Rosina glanced at the kitchen clock. Harry would be arriving in less than half an hour and there seemed to be no way of deflecting Bertha from her purpose. She hadn't wanted to involve Walter, but she was desperate, and she knew that he was her last chance. 'Bebe, I don't want to put you to so much trouble. If it's the return journey that is worrying you so much, why don't I ask Walter to meet us at the Gostellows' house and keep us company on the way home? You know you can trust dear old Walter. Papa certainly does.' She held her breath, watching Bertha's expression carefully. As she had hoped, there was a flicker of uncertainty in her grey eyes.

'Well, I suppose that would do: so long as Walter promised to see you safely into the house. I am a bit tired after having them dratted kids running wild in me kitchen last evening. You was such a good child at that age, but poor Caddie has no control over them boys. Goodness knows how she'll manage when the next one is born.'

'So is it all right if I go and ask Walter?'

Bertha nodded and slumped down on her chair. 'You can ask him, but I ain't taking off me bonnet until he tells me hisself that he'll do it.'

Walter was tidying up the office in preparation for the close of business that day. Rosina went in with her fingers crossed behind her back. This was not the perfect solution, but it would have to do. They would just have to make certain that they returned from Cremorne

Gardens in good time to be waiting outside Harry's house when Walter came to meet them. 'Walter,' she said sweetly. 'I have an enormous favour to ask of you.'

'And he really believed you?' Sukey was seated next to Rosina on the deck of the steamer bound for Cremorne Pier.

'He's a simple soul,' Harry said, spreading his arm along the back of the seat so that it rested against Rosina's shoulders.

She allowed the intimacy without comment. After all, the steamer was packed with people all out for an entertaining evening at the gardens. There was much chatter and laughter, and, as far as she could see, quite a lot of what Bertha would call 'lewd behaviour'. Some of the young women on board allowed quite blatant intimacies to take place as they cuddled close to their gentlemen friends. Rosina was not sure that she ought to allow Harry to call Walter a simple soul, but she decided to let it pass. She leaned back against his arm, feeling the warmth from his body against her shoulders. It was not an altogether unpleasant experience. 'We must be back before midnight, Harry,' she murmured. 'I told Walter to wait outside your house and that we would be travelling home in a hackney carriage.'

'Just like Cinderella,' Sukey giggled. 'You

know, having to leave the ball at midnight or the coach would turn back into a pumpkin and be driven by white mice.'

Harry gave her an indulgent smile. 'And which one of you beauties is going to play the part of Cinderella, I wonder?'

Rosina barely heard Sukey's pert reply; she was more interested in the sights and sounds of the river that was almost as busy with traffic in the evening as it was in the daytime. Barges, wherries and lighters plied their trade along the piers and wharves. The sound of the water smacking the bottom of the boat like an angry mother spanking a naughty child was all but drowned out by the chug-chugging of the engine and the piercing blast of the steam whistle warning other craft to get out of the way. A cacophony of hooting and tooting, accompanied by the shouts of watermen, filled the air. The muddy waters of the River Thames glowed bronze in the last rays of light as the sun plummeted towards the west in a great fireball. As the steamer ploughed upriver, the stench of the manufactories in the East End was less pungent, and the smell of hot engine oil was mixed with the cheap scent, pomade and body odour of the closely packed passengers. By the time they reached Cremorne Pier, Rosina was intoxicated with anticipation and excitement. The steamer bumped against the wooden stanchions and there was a frantic scurry as people snatched up their belongings in their hurry to get ashore.

As Harry handed her onto dry land, Rosina gasped in wonder at the flickering gaslights that illuminated the gardens. Coloured lanterns hung from the trees which lined the avenue leading to the famous crystal platform. She could hear music wafting through the foliage and the babble of voices interspersed with laughter. She felt as though she had left smoky, dirty old Black Eagle Wharf and landed slap bang in the middle of fairyland. Harry paid the one shilling entrance fees at the kiosk, but Rosina was barely aware of anything except the magical, musical atmosphere heightened by the dazzling gaslight.

'Isn't this fun?' Sukey's voice rose with excitement as she clutched Harry's arm. 'This was such a good idea, Harry. You were so clever to think of it.'

'The evening has only just begun.' Harry offered Rosina his other arm with a self-satisfied smile. 'Tonight, ladies, I trust you will be hugely entertained. We'll visit the sideshows and I believe there is a ballet this evening. I've booked a supper box for later on, and we can sit and watch the dancers on the crystal platform while we eat.'

'And we can dance too? We can't come to Cremorne without dancing, Harry.' Sukey tugged at his arm to attract his attention. 'You will waltz with me, won't you, Harry?'

'Of course I will. We'll dance the night away.'

A chill breeze rustled through the fresh young leaves on the trees and Rosina shivered. 'Don't forget that we have to be home by midnight.'

Harry threw back his head and laughed. 'Don't fret, my lovely. I will look after you.'

She had to be content with that, although a small voice was nagging at her conscience. She had lied to Bertha and to Walter. Papa would be furious if he knew what she had done.

'Oh, just look at that,' Sukey cried, pointing to a huge, hexagonal pagoda. 'Isn't that the most amazing sight you've ever seen?'

Rosina pushed her feelings of guilt to the back of her mind. This truly was an enchanting place – she would worry about the consequences later, much later. They visited sideshows and shooting galleries. They watched a comic ballet performed in one of the theatres, followed by the ascent of a hot air balloon. The gardens were crowded with revellers and some of the entertainers moved amongst them, dressed in costume, some wearing masks, inviting them to come and watch their plays and the fireworks display that was to be held later in the evening.

Harry escorted them to the refreshment room and bought them lemonade, while he drank several glasses of claret.

'Don't look now, Rosie,' Sukey said, leaning over and whispering behind her hand, 'but that man at the next table has been staring at you for the past five minutes.'

Unable to resist the temptation, Rosina glanced over her shoulder. The man raised his glass to her and winked. She turned away hastily. 'Just ignore him, Sukey. He's very rude.'

Harry slipped his arm around Rosina's shoulders with a proprietorial air. 'Take no notice of the masher, Rosie. No one will bother you while you're with me.'

Sukey downed her lemonade and put her glass down with a thud. 'Don't mind me, Harry. I suppose I'm just the chaperone here.'

'Not at all,' Harry said with a tipsy grin. 'I count myself a fortunate fellow to have two such lovely ladies on my arm.'

Rosina wriggled free from his casual embrace and she stood up. 'Perhaps we'd better go to supper now, Harry. It's getting late.'

'She's such a spoilsport,' Sukey said, cuddling up to him.

Really, Sukey was such a flirt. Rosina eyed her impatiently: Sukey was her best friend, but she was making a show of herself with Harry.

He rose, smiling smugly as he helped Sukey to her feet. 'Come, my dear. Rosie's right. I think we should eat, and then we'll dance.'

The man at the next table stood up as Rosina

went to pass him and he barred her way, bowing from the waist. 'Allow me to introduce myself, ma'am.'

'This young lady is with me, sir.' Harry turned to face him, but his scowl melted into a grin. 'I say, it's Rivers, isn't it? We met once at the City of London club.' He held out his hand. 'Harry Gostellow, of Gostellow and Son, Hay and Provender Merchants.'

Rivers eyed him speculatively. 'I do vaguely recall you, sir.'

'Well, it's good to meet you again. May I introduce you to my companions, Miss Rosina May and Miss Susan Barnum?'

'Delighted, ma'am.' Rivers took Rosina's hand and raised it to his lips. 'Roland Rivers at your service.'

He had been drinking – she could smell wine on his breath – but he did not appear to be drunk. He was obviously a gentleman and good-looking too, although her taste ran towards men with dark hair like her own, rather than silver-blond as this young man's was, and his light blue eyes were the colour of a winter sky. She snatched her hand away, feeling the blood rush to her cheeks.

He turned to Sukey and kissed her hand. 'Miss Barnum.'

Harry stepped in between them. 'Perhaps we'll meet up again at the club, sir. But as to the present, I've booked a supper booth, so I'm afraid we must bid you goodnight.'

'I'd say this fellow don't deserve you, ma'am.' Roland tipped his hat to Rosina with a disarming smile. 'And I call it rather greedy of a man to hog the attention of two such lovelies for the evening.' He sauntered off into the crowd.

'That fellow's father owns a fleet of merchantmen,' Harry said grandly. 'He's as rich as Croesus, but don't take his attentions too seriously. I don't think he'll bother you again.'

'He was very good-looking,' Sukey whispered. 'And well spoken too.'

'I'm hungry,' Rosina said loudly. 'Supper would be lovely, Harry.'

The supper booths were arranged in tiers overlooking the crystal platform where couples were dancing to the strains of a fifty-strong orchestra. Rosina could not but be impressed when Harry ordered the half-crown menu and a bottle of champagne. The food was brought by a blue-coated waiter and she forgot all about the impertinent Roland Rivers as they ate, listening to the music and watching the dancers swirling about on the platform in a kaleidoscope of colour. Harry kept their glasses filled and ordered a second bottle of champagne. Rosina was rather cross with Sukey, who had quickly reached the giggly stage and did not seem to know when she had drunk enough. Rosina was feeling a bit merry by this time, but she was careful to sip the bubbly rather than to drink it down like lemonade as Sukey had done.

After they had enjoyed strawberry ice cream for dessert, Sukey rose rather unsteadily to her feet and laced her arms around Harry's neck. 'I want to dance. You promised me that we could dance after supper.'

He steadied her with his hands spanning her tiny waist. 'Well, it would be churlish to break my promise.' He turned to Rosina with an apologetic grin. 'Would you object to my dancing with Sukey?'

'Not at all. I'm quite content to sit and watch you.'

'Come then, Sukey. Let's show the rest of them what we can do.' Harry led her out of the booth.

Rosina leaned over the balcony, resting her chin on her folded arms. The sky was dark but the innumerable gaslights flooded the crystal platform with so much light that it might have been midday.

'Would you like to dance?'

A disembodied voice from the next booth jerked her out of her reverie. She turned her head and saw Roland Rivers leaning over the balustrade.

'No, thank you,' Rosina said stiffly.

He disappeared and she breathed a sigh of relief. At least he took no for an answer. But her relief was cut short as the door to the booth opened and he walked in without waiting to be invited. She leapt to her feet, angry at the intrusion. 'Please leave at once, sir. I don't think you ought to be here.'

'Come now, I only want to enjoy your company. You need not be afraid of me.'

'I am not afraid of you, Mr Rivers. But I am asking you to leave.'

He took a step closer. 'And what if I refuse?'

'I'll call out to my friend.' He was so near to her that she could feel his hot breath on her cheek, but the table and chairs blocked her exit.

Rivers glanced over her shoulder at the dance floor where couples were whirling round to the strains of a Viennese waltz. 'I don't think he will be able to hear you, my dear.' He traced the outline of her cheek with his finger.

'You are no gentleman, sir.'

'Isn't that fortunate for me?' Before she could protest, he had taken her in his arms and claimed her lips in a kiss that was both shocking and exciting. No man had ever had the temerity to go any further than giving her a peck on the cheek; nor had any held her in such a crushing embrace. She struggled but he was much the stronger: she could barely breathe, and for a moment she thought she was going to faint. Then, suddenly, she was free. She clutched the balustrade for support, staring in disbelief as a masked man, dressed like storybook illustrations of a pirate with a scarlet bandanna tied around his head and gold earrings in his ears, seized Rivers by the collar and the seat of his trousers and pitched him over the balcony.

# Chapter Five

Rosina gripped the rail and leaned over the balustrade, half expecting to see Roland Rivers stretched out on the ground in a pool of blood.

'He hadn't far to fall,' her rescuer said, laughing. 'We're only on the first tier, and there's a nice soft flowerbed down below.'

It was true: Rivers had fallen onto soft earth and crushed a bed of red and white geraniums. He was already scrambling to his feet and brushing himself down, much to the amusement of the passers-by. 'You could have killed him,' Rosina said, slightly dazed by the sudden turn of events. 'Or he might have fallen on another person and killed them.'

Behind the mask his eyes shone with laughter. 'You have a tender conscience for one who was being molested by a complete stranger, or am I mistaken?'

'No, sir. You are not mistaken, and I thank you for intervening.'

He bowed from the waist. 'May I claim my reward?'

'R-reward?'

'A dance. Just one waltz with a beautiful girl would be reward enough.' He held out his hand.

She hesitated. He looked so handsome and so dashing in his costume – like a romantic figure from a novelette. He must be an actor or one of the characters from a sideshow, but he had just saved her from a most embarrassing situation. She laid her hand in his. 'Just one waltz then.'

She did not want to admit that, apart from her recent fleeting encounter with Rivers, this was the first time she had ever been held in any man's arms other than those of her father. She had shared dancing lessons with Sukey and her sisters, but thus far she had not had the opportunity to put them into practice. Beneath the canopy of black velvet sky the crystal platform was ablaze with light; the air was filled with music and laughter. The sensation of being held so close to a man who was unrelated to her was strange and oddly thrilling. At first, as she concentrated on her steps, Rosina could not bring herself to look him in the face. The mask made him seem mysterious and intriguing, but she could not bring herself to look him in the eye. The top of her head just reached the level of his chin, and she found herself staring at the open neck of his frilled shirtfront, which revealed a tantalising glimpse of a muscular chest and smooth, tanned skin. Hanging round his neck, he wore a small heart-shaped medallion on a fine gold chain.

'It is rather a fine medallion, isn't it?' His voice held a hint of laughter.

She looked up and saw that he was smiling. 'Are you an actor, sir?'

'As you see, I'm a pirate.'

His laugh was infectious and she found herself joining in. Suddenly it seemed as though anything was possible. 'All right, I believe you.'

'Are you going to tell me your name?'

'Rosina May.'

'That's a beautiful name, just like its owner.'

'Now you're flattering me.'

'No, I'm simply telling you the truth.'

She was saved from the embarrassment of answering as the rhythm of the waltz changed to that of a polka, and he swept her into the fast movement so that her feet barely touched the ground. As they moved together as one in time to the music, she found the courage to raise her eyes to his face. There was something so different about him and yet there was a hint of the familiar. She felt as though she had known this enigmatic stranger for years, although they had only just met. As the polka ended, the orchestra stopped playing for a moment to allow the dancers who wanted to leave the floor time to tear themselves away and seek refreshments. She knew that she ought to have gone too, but she felt so comfortable in his arms and he showed no sign of letting her go. She was vaguely aware that Harry was glaring at her from the other side of the platform, and that Sukey had her hands entwined around his neck, clinging to him with the tenacity of ivy.

'You haven't told me your name,' Rosina murmured, looking deeply into his eyes that were a shade that was neither green nor brown, flecked with golden glints when he smiled. He was smiling now.

'My name is Pirate.'

'Now you're teasing me.'

Before he could answer, Harry came striding towards them. Sukey was still clinging to his arm and she had to run to keep up with him. He did not look pleased. 'Who the devil are you, sir? It seems to me that you are being a great deal too familiar with this young lady, who is in my care.'

'Harry!' Rosina twisted round to glare at him. She felt her partner's arms tighten around her and she leaned against him. Ignoring Harry's furious expression, she was barely conscious of anything but the thrill of being supported by strong arms; the heat of his body permeated through his thin cotton shirt and the muslin of her evening gown; the scent of him filled her nostrils and was more intoxicating than a glass of sherry wine. Spice, cloves, lemons and – Indian ink. She found herself sniffing the air like a hungry hound. How could a pirate, or an actor, or whatever he was, smell of Indian ink? Without thinking, she caught hold of his hand and turned it palm upwards – his fingers were ink-stained, long and supple – she had to suppress the urge to raise them to her lips and kiss each one in turn.

'What the devil are you doing, Rosina?'

Harry's sharp voice brought her back to earth with a bump. But instead of answering him, she turned her head to look up into the pirate's face. 'You are a scholar, sir?'

His lips twitched and the martial gleam in his eyes was wiped away by a glimmer of amusement. 'Alas, no. As you guessed, I am an actor, and the ink stains were caused by writing out playbills.'

'He looks like a real pirate,' Sukey said, giggling. 'I think he looks quite dashing.'

'He looks like a bounder to me.' Harry extended his hand to Rosina. 'Come, Rosie. Allow me to escort you back to our booth, away from this charlatan.'

The pirate fingered the wooden dagger that was lodged in his wide leather belt. 'I could challenge you to a duel for that, sir.'

Rosina shot him a quick glance, and saw to her relief that he was laughing. His teeth flashed white against his dark skin, and, when he lowered his gaze to smile at her, she felt herself go quite weak at the knees. She summoned up all her self-control and laid her hand on Harry's arm. 'This is ridiculous, Harry. This gentleman and I were dancing. There's no harm in that, is there?'

'We were dancing too, Harry.' Sukey tugged at his arm. 'Let's go back to the booth. I would love a glass of champagne.'

'We will all go back to the booth,' Harry said firmly. 'But not you, sir. Haven't you got a play to act in, or a charade, or something?'

The pirate inclined his head, and his gold earrings flashed in the gaslight. 'I have business to conclude, but first I would like to claim this last dance with Miss May.'

The orchestra had already begun to play a lively gallop, and before Harry had a chance to protest further the pirate had whisked Rosina onto the dance floor amongst the throng of dancers. She caught a glimpse of Harry escorting Sukey in the direction of their supper booth, but at this moment she cared about nothing except the thrill of dancing with the handsome stranger. The gallop was followed by a stately quadrille and then a waltz. There was no need to talk as she floated in his arms, looking into those mysterious eyes behind the black mask. Suddenly the sky was filled with a million coloured stars and an explosion of sound and light. The dancing stopped while everyone craned their necks to watch the firework display. He was holding her hand and they were standing so close together that she was certain she could hear his heart beating. The firework display ended with a huge starburst and a succession of loud explosions. The noise seemed to awaken Rosina from her dream. She snatched her hand free. 'It must be getting late. I really must go.'

'It's not yet midnight. Can't you stay a bit longer?'

'I must be home – I mean, I have to be somewhere at midnight. It's terribly important that we're there on time.'

'Where exactly is home?'

'Black Eagle Wharf. I doubt if you would know it.'

'I'm a river pirate, am I not?'

'Now you're laughing at me.'

'No, I would never laugh at you, Rosina.' He drew her into his arms and kissed her so softly and tenderly that she opened her lips with a sigh of delight, giving herself up to the strange and wonderful sensations flowing through her veins. It was over too soon, leaving her desperate for more, but he drew away from her, laying his finger on her parted lips. 'I will see that you get home safely.'

'Y-you will?'

He tucked her hand in the crook of his arm. 'Let's go and find your friends.'

By the time they reached the supper booth, Sukey and Harry had drunk a whole bottle of champagne between them. Sukey was hiccuping and giggling and Harry had reached the belligerent stage of intoxication.

'So, there you are,' he murmured thickly. 'I ought to give you a good hiding, mister.'

Stepping in between them, Rosina laid her hand on his arm. 'Have you any idea of the time, Harry? No? Well, it's almost midnight. We're supposed to be back at your parents' house before midnight. Have you forgotten that Walter is going to meet us there?'

'Walter!' Harry's lip curled scornfully. 'That scribbling Pharisee! Well, I can sort old Walter out.'

'Oh, Lord. I shall be for it if we're late. My papa will kill first me and then you, Harry.' Sukey hiccuped again and covered her mouth with her hand.

'We'll get a hackney carriage then. Don't worry, ladies. Harry Gostellow will look after you.' Harry took a step towards the door, staggered, and sat down heavily.

'Oh, dear! He really is rather drunk,' Rosina said, turning to the pirate. 'You said you would help us, sir. I should be so obliged if you would.'

He kissed her hand. 'It will be my pleasure.' He turned to Harry. 'If you can walk as far as the jetty, I have a boat tied up alongside.'

'You have your own boat?' Rosina stared at him in surprise.

He smiled. 'I'm a pirate, aren't I? I just take what I fancy.'

'I say,' Sukey giggled. 'That sounds terribly exciting.'

'He's a gigolo,' Harry said, glowering. 'Don't take any notice of him. If I wasn't a trifle bosky, I'd sort the fellow out.'

'I'm sure you would,' the pirate said equably. 'But we need to get to the pier, old chap. Can you walk?'

Staggering to his feet, Harry focused his eyes with difficulty. 'Of course I can walk. Been doing it since I was an infant, haven't I? Lead on Blackbeard, or whatever your name is.'

They reached the pier just as midnight struck. By this time, Rosina was in a reckless mood, and she was past caring whether she would get into trouble once she reached home. All that mattered was here and now. She never wanted the journey back to Black Eagle Wharf to end. The pirate led them to a small steam launch moored at the end of the pier. It looked suspiciously familiar, rather like the wharfinger's private launch, but then all boats looked much the same to her anyway and what did she care if he'd stolen it? The mystery only added to the excitement of the night. He held her hand just a little longer than was necessary as he helped her aboard the craft. In the moonlight, his eyes were dark pools, shining like the ripples on the inky surface of the river. His hand was smooth and warm. She wanted to hold on to it forever, but he squeezed her fingers gently and moved away to start the engine. She went to sit beside Sukey, who had curled up like a child and fallen asleep with her head resting on her arms. Harry had slumped down on a seat with his chin on his chest and was snoring loudly.

Rosina closed her eyes and allowed the cool breeze coming upriver to fan her hot cheeks. In her mind's eye she was still dancing with the pirate. She could still feel his arms around her, and the scent of him was in her nostrils. She knew that if she lived to be a hundred, she would never forget this magical evening. With Sukey and Harry asleep, it seemed as though she and her pirate were the only two people in the world as the steam launch chugged its way downstream. She did not care that they were going to be almost an hour late, or that Walter would be cross and would question her as to why she was not waiting outside the Gostellows' mansion in Wellclose Square. She did not want the night to end. But all too soon she recognised the wharves close to home and the steam launch glided into a small space between a wherry and a lighter at the tunnel pier. She shook Sukey awake and then Harry. He sat up with a grunt of surprise. 'Is it morning, Mother?'

'Oh, Harry! Don't be such an idiot,' Rosina said, giving him another shake. 'You're drunk and now we've got to find Walter. I'll have to tell him everything. If he's been waiting outside your parents' house for over an hour, he's not going to believe that we've been inside at a supper party, and not had the courtesy to let him know that we were going to stay late.'

'Damn it!' Harry struggled to his feet. 'Apologies for the language, Rosie. But I'm stiff as a board and my head aches like the devil.'

'Serves you right then.' Rosina bundled up her skirt in preparation for ascending the steep ladder. 'Help Sukey, and I might forgive you.'

Sukey moaned. 'I feel sick, Rosie.'

'Take some deep breaths and think of something else,' Rosina said, trying not to sound impatient. 'We're going to be in trouble enough when we get home, without you spoiling your nice new dress.'

'Oh, heavens! Don't say that, Rosie.' Sukey's eyes filled with tears. 'I wish I'd never agreed to this silly escapade.'

Rosina watched the pirate leap onto the wooden deck of the pier and make fast. Sukey might be sorry that she had come, but for herself she would gladly take any punishment that Papa or Bebe might hand out. She held her hands out to him, shivering with the thrill of his touch as he helped her from the boat. He held her, clasping her hands to his chest and looking deeply into her eyes. 'This is where we say goodbye, Rosina, my beautiful rose.'

'No, don't say that. It sounds so final. We've only just met.'

'And will not meet again.'

'Never?'

He raised her hands to his lips and kissed each one in turn. 'Never. I don't exist. Not in your world.'

'Then I want to be in yours. Tell me your name at least. Give me something to remember you by.'

'Leave her alone.' Harry caught Rosina by the arm and pulled her away. 'Are you mad, Rosie? We're well over an hour late. We have to get back to Wellclose Square before your friend Walter rouses the whole house.'

'Yes, Rosie. Do hurry,' Sukey cried. 'Look, there's a hansom cab dropping someone off at the mouth of the tunnel. We can cram into it if the cabby will take three instead of just two.'

Rosina nodded dully. 'You're right, of course.'

Harry took off his hat and waved it, shouting to attract the cabby's attention. Rosina turned to say a last farewell to the pirate, but he had gone. It seemed as though he had vanished into thin air. The sensation of loss was so intense that it was all she could do not to break down and weep. She allowed Harry to help her into the cab for the short journey through the dark streets to Wellclose Square. She barely noticed the wild scenes that flashed past them as drunken men and women lurched out of public houses laughing and singing. Prostitutes solicited from doorways and there seemed to be fights on every street corner. The cabby urged the horse on with a flick of his whip. Wellclose Square seemed like a quiet oasis away from the seething nightlife of the Ratcliff Highway and its environs. Harry leapt out of the cab first and paid off the driver. He lifted Sukey down first and then Rosina. She looked around with a sinking heart. There was no sign of Walter waiting outside the house. A clock on the church in the centre of the square struck two. She imagined the scene at home. Walter must by now have roused the whole of Black Eagle Wharf. The men would be out looking for the missing girls and the police were probably involved as well.

'So, he didn't wait then.' Harry mounted the steps to his front door. 'Stay here while I go inside. If he's raised the alarm then all hell will be let loose in the house.'

The sound of running footsteps made Rosina glance over her shoulder. 'Harry, wait. I think he's coming.'

Sukey slumped down on the steps holding her head in her hands. 'I can't stand this. I wish I'd never come.'

'It is Walter.' Rosina ran to meet him. 'Oh, Walter, I was never so glad to see anyone in my whole life.'

He stopped, holding his side and panting. 'I – I thought I'd missed you and I ran all the way back to Black Eagle Wharf.'

'Well, fellow,' Harry said, folding his arms across his chest. 'As you can see, we're here waiting for you.'

Rosina cast him a reproachful look. Poor Walter had been doing them a favour and Harry was being so disagreeable. She patted Walter's arm. 'I'm so sorry you were put to all that trouble.'

He took off his spectacles and wiped them on his shirt tail, which had worked its way loose. 'It's all right, miss. No harm done.'

'Look at the state of you, man!' Harry shot him a scornful glance. 'I suggest you tidy yourself up before I allow you to escort the young ladies to their respective homes.'

'Harry, don't be so – so pompous!' Rosina stared at him aghast. This was a side of him that she had not witnessed before the events of this evening. Perhaps it was the drink that had made him behave so, but whatever it was, she did not like him much at the moment. She turned to Walter. 'I'd be most grateful if you could find us a cab, Walter.'

'Of course, miss.' He tipped his cap and hurried off in the direction of the Highway.

'And as for you, Harry,' she said angrily, 'this was all your idea and you should be grateful to

Walter for helping us out. I think you ought to apologise to him for being so grumpy.'

'Me, apologise to a mere clerk? I think not.'

'If that mere clerk had raised the alarm, or knocked on your parents' door and demanded to know where we were, then you would be in serious trouble with my papa and with Captain Barnum. You might think you own us all because our fathers depend on yours to give them trade, but you are mistaken. My father could find business anywhere along the Thames.' She hooked her arm around Sukey's shoulders and helped her to her feet. 'Come, Sukey. It's time we went home.'

'I say, don't be like that, Rosie.' Harry hurried down the steps to stand at her side. 'I didn't mean to offend you, or the clerk fellow come to that. Perhaps I'd better come home with you. I can explain to your housekeeper and to Mrs Barnum that our party went on later than expected. I'll write a note of apology as from my mother tomorrow and send it round, if you like.'

'Oh, dear.' Sukey leaned her head against Rosina's shoulder. 'I'm in for it. I just know it.'

'You'll do no such thing,' Rosina said hotly. 'We'll do as we planned, and there's no need for you to forge your mother's signature, Harry. I won't hear of it.'

'Well, all right, if you're sure. But I'll call round tomorrow to make certain that you're not in trouble.' He waved to attract the driver of an approaching cab, but his gesture proved unnecessary as it drew to a halt and Walter leapt out onto the pavement.

'I was lucky,' Walter said, holding the door open. 'There was one passing at just the right moment.'

The door of the Barnums' house was opened by Gertie, who was dressed for bed in a calico nightgown with her hair tied up in rags, but had obviously been asleep at her post. She blinked at them like a sleepy owl as Sukey went indoors, scolding Gertie for not remaining awake.

Rosina heaved a sigh of relief as the door closed. 'It doesn't look as though she was missed.' She leaned on Walter's arm as they walked on towards home. 'Let's hope it's that easy for me.'

'I wouldn't worry on that score, miss. Bertha trusts me to bring you home safely, and she thinks that Gostellow is a gentleman.'

She was quick to hear the note of disapproval in his voice. 'That's not fair, Walter. Harry is a gentleman. He just had a little drop too much champagne and he was cross with . . .' She broke off in mid-sentence. She had almost mentioned the fascinating man who called himself 'Pirate', but that would never do. Neither Walter nor her papa would understand, or approve. She bit her lip, hoping that he had not noticed, or at least would not question her. 'You go on, Walter,' she said, as they reached the door to her house. 'I'm quite safe now.'

'I'll just see you inside, miss.'

She hesitated with the latchkey in her hand. 'I really do appreciate what you've done for me tonight, Walter. And I'm so sorry that Harry was rude to you.'

His back was to the street light and the glass of his spectacles was acting like a mirror – all she could see in them was her own anxious face.

'It's quite all right, miss. No harm done.'

'You are a good friend to me, Walter.'

'I hope so, miss.'

She turned the key in the lock and the door groaned on its hinges. She stifled a giggle as she stepped inside. 'I hope Bebe didn't hear that.'

Walter stood in the doorway, silhouetted against the light. 'I'll see you in the morning.'

'It is the morning.'

'Then I'll see you later, miss.'

As he turned to go, Rosina was awash with guilt. Dear, solid, dependable Walter. She called his name and he stopped, turned to look at her. 'Miss?'

She flung her arms around his neck and kissed his cheek. 'Thank you, dear Walter.'

She closed her eyes. For a wonderful, intoxicating moment, she could smell spices, lemons and above all, Indian ink. She dropped her hands to her sides and took a step backwards. Of course she could smell Indian ink – it clung to Walter like a London particular. He spent half his life writing in dreary old ledgers and account books. If he cut himself, he probably bled black ink. The smell had fooled her tired brain into linking it with the man she had only met a few hours ago, and with whom she had fallen desperately in love.

'Goodnight, Walter.' She closed the door and locked it.

She went into the kitchen, and taking a spill from the jar on the mantelshelf she stuck it in the glowing embers of the fire, watching the tip turn red and then burst into flame. She lit a candle and tossed the spill into the fire. What a night it had been – her head spun with the sights, sounds and the memory of a man's arms holding her as they danced. She crept upstairs to her room and slipped off her dress, letting it fall to the ground in a heap of crumpled muslin. She stepped out of it and unlaced her stays, tossing them onto the chintz-covered chair on which her doll, Dorcas, sat with her frilled skirts spread out around her and her dark, painted eyes staring blindly into space. Taking off her undergarments, Rosina stood in the flickering candlelight, staring at her reflection in the cheval mirror that had once belonged to her mother. She ran her hands lightly over her breasts and down the smooth curve of her belly to her thighs. Suddenly her body, which had never been of much interest to her in the past, became a mysterious entity filled with strange sensations and longings for which she had no name. She closed her eyes and her head was filled with the image of a handsome man wearing a mask; she could recall every second of their brief time together. She parted her lips and she could taste his kiss. She opened her eyes and realised that she was blushing. Her whole body was tinged with pink at the wild thoughts running through her head.

Rosina snatched up her cotton lawn nightgown and slipped it over her head, covering her shameless nakedness. She climbed into bed and lay down, pulling the coverlet up to her chin. She closed her eyes, but she knew then that she would not sleep. She could still hear the strains of the orchestra playing a waltz, then a polka, a schottische and a quadrille. She was floating in his arms and they were the only two people on the crystal platform – if only she knew his name. The music played on and on, they were whirling round and round – he was repeating her name over and over again. He was shaking her by the shoulder – she opened her eyes and found herself staring up into Bertha's wrinkled face.

'Wake up, sleepyhead. Half the morning has gone already,' Bertha said, chuckling. 'My goodness, you must have had a good time at the

Gostellows' last night. I never heard you come in.'

Rosina raised herself up on her elbow and yawned. 'Walter brought me home.'

'I should hope so. I wouldn't have let you go if he hadn't offered to bring you home safely.' Bertha grunted as she bent down to retrieve Rosina's discarded clothing. 'You should pick up your own things, miss. Not leave it to poor old Bertha. Me back's killing me this morning.'

Rosina swung her legs over the side of the bed. 'I'll do it. I was tired. I'm sorry, Bebe.'

'Well, lambkin, you don't get asked out to dinner at a rich man's house very often. I suppose I shouldn't grumble. Come downstairs and have your breakfast and you can tell me all about it. I want to know every detail.' Bertha waddled to the doorway. 'Your papa will be so pleased that young Gostellow is taking such an interest in you. I know it's looking ahead, but it would be a fine match.'

'Don't get your hopes up. I think Harry was more interested in Sukey than in me.'

'Then the man is a fool. But I think you're being too modest. Who would give that whey-faced girl a second glance when they could choose my girl, with her raven hair and violet-blue eyes?'

Rosina hurried to the washstand and poured cold water into the bowl. 'That's soft sawder and you know it, Bebe. Sukey is twice as pretty as me

116

and as lively as a cricket. Gentlemen adore her and I wouldn't be at all surprised if Harry wasn't knocking on her door this very minute.'

'Well, that's odd, ain't it? Because young Mr Gostellow has been sitting in my kitchen for the past ten minutes waiting for you, missy.' Bertha gave a throaty chuckle. 'You hurry up and get dressed and come downstairs. He don't want to chat to an old woman like me.' She winked at Rosina as she left the room and the stairs creaked beneath her heavy tread.

'Bother, bother, bother!' Rosina dashed cold water on her face and rubbed it with a towel until her skin glowed with colour. She dressed hastily, her fingers fumbling with laces and buttons, and she prayed silently that Harry would not say anything to make Bertha suspicious. Having brushed her long hair, tugging at the tangles until it hung about her shoulders like a dark cape, she twisted it into a heavy knot at the nape of her neck and secured it in a snood. Smoothing back the stray tendrils that curled around her forehead, she took a quick look in the mirror, and, satisfied that at least she looked reasonably presentable, she went downstairs to the kitchen.

Harry leapt up from his seat by the range. 'Good morning, Miss Rosina. How splendid you look this morning.'

'She missed out on her beauty sleep because of you, young man,' Bertha said severely. 'It were good of your parents to entertain her and Miss Barnum, but don't make a habit of it. Late nights are bad for young girls.'

Rosina cast her eyes up to heaven. 'Thank you, Bebe. I'm sure Harry doesn't want to hear all that.'

Harry took her hand and raised it to his lips. 'On the contrary, I agree entirely with Miss Spinks. Your welfare should always come first with me.'

'There, what did I say?' Bertha lifted the singing kettle from the hob. 'Wasn't I right, Rosie?'

Rosina felt the blood rush to her cheeks as Harry gave her a quizzical look. 'Is this a social call, Harry? Or did you have business with Walter?'

'A bit of both, but mainly I wanted to speak to you, Rosie.'

'Not until she's had her breakfast, young sir.' Bertha poured boiling water into the teapot.

'I'm not hungry,' Rosina said hastily. There was something in Harry's expression that sent chills running down her spine. His lips were stretched in an urbane smile but there was a disturbing light in his eyes and she sensed trouble. She needed to get him away from Bertha before he said anything out of turn. 'I was going to call on Sukey this morning. Would you like to walk with me, Harry?'

'Delighted.'

'What about your breakfast?' Bertha demanded, barring her way. 'And you ain't going nowhere without a bonnet and gloves. You was raised proper, Rosie, and don't you forget it. Your mama was a real lady and she'd be turning in her grave to see you go out hatless and without gloves.'

Rosina snatched her bonnet and mittens from the dresser and put them on. 'There! Are you happy now, Bebe?'

Bertha stuck out her bottom lip. 'I still say you ought to have something inside you before you go out gallivanting.'

'I will eat later. I promise you.'

Harry opened the door. 'Don't worry, Miss Spinks. I'll take good care of her.'

As she walked past the office door, Rosina could see Walter in his customary seat behind the large oak desk. He looked up and smiled. She waved to him but she did not stop. Outside on the cobblestones, she turned to Harry. 'Well? What is so urgent that it couldn't wait?'

Harry held his bowler hat in his hands, his knuckles whitening. 'I wanted your reassurance that what happened last night would not be repeated.'

'I beg your pardon?'

'And so you should, Rosina. The way you behaved with that – that charlatan was beyond belief.'

'How dare you!'

'I do dare, my dear girl. I dare because I care about you. And I believe I have your father's blessing in paying court to you, Rosina. Do you understand what I'm saying?'

'If speaking to me like a stupid child is your idea of paying court, then I'm sorry for you, Harry.'

He caught her by the hand. 'Don't be angry with me, Rosie. I know I'm not putting this very well, but I – love you. And I want you to be my wife.'

She stared at him in disbelief. Suddenly it seemed as though he was speaking in a foreign tongue. Nothing made sense. 'We hardly know each other. You can't possibly want to marry me. And I'm sorry, but I don't love you.'

'That doesn't matter in the slightest. You will come to love me when we are married. I want you, Rosie. I could look higher for a bride, but I want you.'

'You're saying that I'm beneath you socially, but you'll marry me anyway?'

He squeezed her hand. 'My dear, I wouldn't have put it like that. But you've bewitched me. I can't get you out of my thoughts, and last night, when that oaf was making up to you – I could have killed him. He was just playing with you, Rosie. He was amusing himself at your expense.'

'I don't believe you.'

'You will never see him again. I'm asking you – no, I'm begging you to consider my proposal. I know it's sudden, but you need not answer me immediately. You need time to think it over, I realise that.'

'But Harry . . .'

He leaned towards her so that his face was close to hers. 'I'd advise you to think carefully before you refuse me, my dear. Your papa relies on me to put trade his way. He's made bad decisions lately and lost a lot of business. If I were his son-in-law I could save him from himself. But if I were to go against him – you wouldn't want to bring about his downfall, now would you?'

# Chapter Six

Rosina took a step backwards, staring at Harry in disbelief. The man who was glowering at her was so unlike the good-natured, easy-going person she had always thought him to be. 'Are you threatening me?'

The anger died from his eyes and he smiled sheepishly. 'No, not at all. I'm just pointing out that I could be instrumental in restoring your father's flagging fortunes.'

'You're making it all up. My papa works hard and his business might have hit a bad patch, but it will soon recover. You're just exaggerating the case to scare me into accepting your proposal.'

'Would I be so base?' Harry laid his hand across his heart with a comical twist of his lips. 'Come now, Rosie. Surely you don't believe such a thing of me?'

'I don't know. You've got me all confused, Harry. I wish you'd say no more on the subject. I can't marry you, and that is that.'

'You need time to consider my offer. I understand, my dear. And perhaps I should have proposed to you in a more romantic manner. I would have done so last night had that clown dressed as a pirate not intruded on our party.'

Rosina shook her head vehemently. 'No, Harry. The man who was masquerading as a pirate has nothing to do with my decision, and I won't change my mind. I'm sorry.'

'I'm disappointed, of course, but I won't give in so easily.' He offered her his arm. 'Will you allow me to escort you to Miss Barnum's house? I need to see the captain on a business matter.'

'All right, as long as you promise not to mention marriage ever again.'

In the Barnums' morning parlour, Sukey sat on the edge of her chair and clapped her hands. 'Oh, Harry. That would be delightful, wouldn't it, Rosie?'

Rosina shot him a reproachful glance. He might have warned her of his intention to ask them both to tea at Gostellow House. If she refused it would look churlish and Sukey was so eager to accept that her heart went out to her, and she could only echo her friend's reply. 'Yes. Delightful.'

He chortled triumphantly. 'I knew you would agree. The fact is that if we're to get away with last night's escapade, you will need to have met my parents. It wouldn't do at all if it came out that they did not know you, when we were all supposed to have dined together.' He slanted a glance at Rosina. 'Who knows, we might even have another outing. We could visit the Crystal Palace or even Cremorne Gardens again, if you so wished.'

She searched his face to see if he was joking, but Harry's expression was innocent of mockery. Forgetting everything that had passed between them, Rosina allowed herself to dream. This might be her only chance to see him again – the mystery man who had quite literally swept her off her feet into that first waltz. She realised that they were both staring at her, waiting for her answer, and she shrugged her shoulders. 'I wouldn't mind. It might be fun.'

Sukey leapt up from her chair, and seizing Rosina round the waist she danced around the room. 'We got away with it last night, Rosie. We could easily do it again.'

'Shall I tell my mother that you accept her invitation to afternoon tea?' Harry smiled indulgently as Sukey twirled away from Rosina and collapsed onto a chair.

'Yes, please.' Sukey clasped her side, giggling. 'Now I've got a stitch, and it's all your fault, you bad man.'

'Rosie?' Harry turned to her with a question in his eyes.

Slightly dizzy, her thoughts filled with the prospect of seeing the pirate again, she smiled and nodded. 'Thank you, yes.'

'Splendid. I'll come for you at three o'clock this afternoon. Now I must go about my business. Good day, ladies.'

As the door closed behind him, Sukey let out a squeal of delight. 'Isn't that exciting, Rosie? He must like me after all. I used to think it was you he wanted, but he made such a point of asking me to meet his mother; maybe there's hope for me. What do you think? After all, you know Harry much better than I.'

'I think he would be a fool if he did not see what a wonderful girl you are.'

'And do you think his mama will approve of me?'

'How could she not, Sukey?'

The Gostellows' mansion was set in the middle of a terrace of five-storey town houses. The red bricks had long ago been dulled to dark brown by soot and city dirt. The carved oak front door had developed the patina of age, but the brass door furniture was polished to a high shine, and the lion's head door knocker almost growled at them as they waited on the top step. An aged retainer opened the door, shielding his rheumy eyes against the sunlight with a gnarled hand.

'About time too, Potter,' Harry said impatiently. He stood back to allow Rosina and Sukey to enter the entrance hall. 'Show the ladies to the drawing room.'

Rosina could feel Sukey shivering, and she gave her arm an encouraging squeeze. Despite the warmth outside, the house had a morgue-like chill. Potter hobbled across the black and white marble floor, and his hands shook as he reached out to grasp the porcelain doorknobs. He looked so old and frail that it seemed wrong to allow him to wait on them. Rosina had to curb the desire to rush over and help him, but she thanked him kindly as he opened the double doors and ushered them into the drawing room. It took her eyes a few moments to become accustomed to the gloom. The heavy velvet curtains were half drawn across the tall windows, and the ornately carved mahogany furniture loomed up out of the shadows like predatory monsters.

'Mother,' Harry said, approaching the pale-faced woman who was reclining on a sofa in front of a desultory fire. 'May I present Miss Rosina May and Miss Susan Barnum?'

Margaret Gostellow raised a lorgnette to her eyes and looked them up and down: for all the world, Rosina thought, like an auctioneer inspecting a couple of pieces of sale goods. She curtsied, as it seemed the correct thing to do in the circumstances. With a nervous giggle, Sukey copied her.

'Please be seated,' Margaret said in a weak voice. 'You're making my neck ache with staring up at you.'

Harry pulled up two chairs. 'You mustn't tire yourself, Mother.'

Sukey gave him a grateful smile and sat down, but Rosina did not feel comfortable in this oppressive atmosphere and she remained standing.

'It's all right, Harry. I'm feeling quite well this afternoon.' Ignoring Sukey, Margaret gave Rosina an appraising look. 'So you are Ellie Carpenter's daughter.'

'You knew my mother, ma'am?' Rosina's knees seemed to have turned to jelly at the unexpected mention of her mother's name, and she sank down onto the chair.

'We were at school together.' Margaret smiled for the first time. 'It seems like yesterday when we were pupils at Miss Harbutt's Academy for Young Ladies.'

'I never knew her.'

'She was a lovely girl. It was such a shame that she became entangled with the wrong sort of man, and then she married beneath her station. I believe she was quite happy with your father, although, naturally, we did not see much of each other after the wedding.'

Rosina opened her mouth to defend her father, but Margaret seemed to have lost interest in her. She raised her lorgnette again to peer at Sukey. 'And you, Miss Barnum. You are welcome in my house. I don't hold the sins of the fathers against the children.'

Harry coughed and cleared his throat. 'I don't think we need to go into that, Mother.'

Sukey's lips trembled. 'I – I don't understand.'

'Doesn't the child know about her father's reputation, Harry?' Margaret's eyebrows formed twin arcs of surprise. 'Well, it would all have come out in time, I suppose.'

Sukey leapt to her feet. 'Perhaps I should not have come? I don't know what you're talking about, ma'am. But I can't stay here and listen to bad things about my dada.'

'Oh, sit down, you silly girl. It's ancient history, and it really doesn't concern you.'

'Mother, please,' Harry said hastily. 'Can we change the subject?'

'You're so sensitive, Harry. You poor dear boy, I'm afraid you inherited that trait from me.'

Rosina could see that Sukey was close to tears. In a protective gesture, she slipped her arm around her friend's shoulders. 'I'm sorry, ma'am. But if Sukey is not welcome here, then I cannot stay. It was good of you to invite us to tea, but in the circumstances I think we should leave now.'

'Mother, I think you spoke out of turn,' Harry said, frowning. 'Miss Barnum is a guest in our house.'

'Don't fuss, my boy. You'll bring on one of my heads.' Margaret raised a shaking hand to her brow. 'I'm a semi-invalid, as you can see, young ladies. My constitution is delicate and I have to be careful not to overexert myself. You will stay for tea and we will talk about other things. Ring the bell for Watson, please, Harry.'

Rosina and Sukey exchanged wary glances, but Harry gave them an encouraging smile as he moved to the fireplace and tugged at the bell pull. 'Do sit down, ladies. Watson will bring tea directly.'

Reluctantly they obliged him. Margaret flashed him a doting glance. 'I am so lucky to have a son like Harry.' She turned to Rosina with narrowed eyes. 'Now, my dear, tell me all about yourself.'

Rosina hesitated, not knowing where to begin, but before she could gather her thoughts Margaret had begun asking her questions about her home, her education and her father's business prospects – all of which she answered to the best of her ability. It was, she thought, almost as painful as having her teeth pulled out, one by one. She could have cried with relief when Watson entered the room bearing a tray of tea, which she placed on a table behind the sofa. She was followed by Potter, staggering beneath the weight of a tray laden with plates of tiny sandwiches, toasted muffins dripping with butter, and a selection of fancy cakes. Rosina held her breath, waiting for him either to collapse or to drop his burden on the carpet, but somehow he managed to place the tray safely on the table.

'That will be all, Potter,' Margaret said wearily. 'Watson, you may serve our guests, but I will just take tea.' She turned to Rosina with a feeble smile. 'I have little appetite, my dear. My husband says that I eat like a bird.'

'I – I'm sorry, ma'am.' Rosina could think of nothing else to say as she found herself involved in a delicate juggling act, attempting to balance a bone china plate on her lap and a cup and saucer in one hand, while selecting delicacies from the dishes offered to her by Watson. Margaret sipped her tea and continued the relentless interrogation. Rosina could only wish that Harry's nosey mother would show more interest in Sukey. In the end it was Harry who put a stop to the ordeal by placing his teacup and saucer firmly down on a side table and rising to his feet.

'You must not overdo things, Mother. You know what the doctor told you.'

'You're right, of course, my dear boy.' Margaret signalled to Watson, who had been hovering by the door. 'You may clear, Watson.'

Realising that they had been dismissed, Rosina leapt to her feet. Then, remembering her manners, she thanked Mrs Gostellow for her hospitality. Margaret gave her a wan smile, and she beckoned to Harry.

He hurried to her side. 'Yes, Mother?'

'She might do, my boy,' Margaret said,

nodding her head in Rosina's direction. 'With judicious coaching, I think I could make something of her.'

A dull flush suffused his face. 'Try to get some rest, Mother.'

'Anyone would think that I was invisible,' Sukey whispered in Rosina's ear. 'Miserable old bat.'

Rosina stifled a giggle. 'Shh! She'll hear you.'

'I don't care. She's ignored me completely. I was never so humiliated in all my life.'

Rosina sighed. 'I wish she'd ignored me.'

'And I never got to taste one of those scrumptious-looking pastries.'

'I wonder if all that food will go to waste?' On a sudden impulse, Rosina went over to the tea table where Watson was stacking what remained of the food on a tray. There were enough cucumber sandwiches left to give Caddie and her children a good meal, to say nothing of a plate of cakes covered in fondant icing and choux buns oozing with cream. 'Excuse me, Miss Watson,' she whispered, 'but is that food going to be thrown away?'

Watson opened her eyes wide with surprise. 'I suppose so, miss.'

'I know a poor family who would be so grateful for it.'

'I dunno, miss. No one's ever asked to take their tea home with them before.'

'What's the problem, Watson?' Harry had come up behind them.

Rosina glanced nervously at Mrs Gostellow, but she was reclining against the arm of the chaise longue with her eyes closed, and her hand clutched to her forehead as though she was suffering from an acute headache. 'I'm sorry, Harry. It was my fault. I just wondered if I could take what was left of the food to a poor family who live near me.'

'What a strange request.' Harry stared at her for a moment, and then he smiled. 'What a kind girl you are, to be sure. Watson, tip the lot in a paper bag and bring it to the front entrance.'

Watson bobbed a curtsey. 'Yes, sir. Right away, sir.' Picking up the tray, she hurried from the room.

'I'll just make sure that Mother has everything she needs,' Harry said, as he ushered Rosina and Sukey out of the drawing room.

They stood in silence, waiting for him to re-join them. Rosina stared up at the two huge crystal chandeliers that must hold enough candles to last an ordinary family for a year at least. Sukey had a dazed expression on her face as she gazed at the heavily embossed red and gold wallpaper and the gilt-framed oil-paintings that adorned the walls of the sweeping staircase. They both turned with a start as Harry breezed out of the drawing room. 'It is a fine house, isn't it?'

'It is a magnificent house, Harry,' Sukey said in

an awed tone. 'And your mother is an extremely handsome lady.'

Rosina said nothing. She had not forgotten Mrs Gostellow's last remark, and was wondering whether the comment 'she might do' was a reference to her or to Sukey, but before she could frame the question tactfully Watson came hurrying along the hall towards them. She thrust a bulging paper bag into Rosina's hands. 'Cook's put a couple more buns in, miss. They was going stale anyway.'

'Thank you so much, Miss Watson.' Rosina said, smiling. 'Please thank Cook too.'

'It's just Watson, miss.'

'Really, Rosie. That was so embarrassing,' Sukey hissed, as Watson bustled away into the depths of the house. 'Don't you know how to behave in front of servants?'

'Maybe not, but they're human beings just like us, aren't they?'

'Treat them like equals and they'll get above their station, that's what my mother says.'

'Where's Potter?' Harry tugged at the nearest bell pull. 'Really, that old man should have been pensioned off years ago. I suppose I'll have to open the door myself.' He strode across the floor and wrenched at the door handle. 'I'll have words with father about the old fool.'

'You simply can't get good servants these days, Harry.' Sukey shot a triumphant glance at

Rosina, as if to say that she at least was used to dealing with menials. She picked up her skirts, stepping daintily out into the sunshine. 'Are you coming, Rosie?'

Rosina could not bear to be in the gloomy house one moment longer; she hurried past Harry and ran down the steps to the pavement.

'I think that went well,' Harry said, closing the door behind him. 'Mama certainly took a liking to you, Rosie. And you too, Sukey.'

'What did she mean by saying "she might do"?' Rosina demanded, unable to keep silent a moment longer.

He smiled and shrugged his shoulders. 'My mother is not a well woman. You mustn't mind what she says.' He lifted his hand to hail a passing cab. 'It will be my pleasure to see you home, ladies.'

'Oh, Harry. You are so gallant,' Sukey said, smiling coquettishly.

The hackney carriage took them as far as the entrance to the wharf and they walked the rest of the way, coming to a halt outside Sukey's house. Harry kissed her hand. 'That was delightful, Miss Susan. Thank you for your company.'

'Thank you, Harry. But I wish I knew what your mama meant when she spoke about my dada.'

'It was unimportant, and certainly nothing over which you should bother your pretty head.'

'Oh, Harry. You do say the nicest things.'
Sukey smiled up at him, blushing furiously.

Rosina wondered if he was aware of the havoc
he was creating by toying with Sukey's tender
feelings. Did he realise that she had a huge crush
on him, which might just possibly be real love?
Or was he such an incorrigible flirt that he could
not help himself when it came to a pretty girl?
She would have to put Sukey straight one day,
but not right now. She tugged at his arm. 'Harry,
I'm going home.'

He turned to her with a disarming smile. 'Of
course, my dear. I'll escort you to your door.'

'There's no need, really. It's just a short
distance.'

'Nevertheless, I will see you safely home.'
Harry doffed his hat to Sukey, and tucked
Rosina's hand in the crook of his arm.

'You are not being fair to Sukey,' she said hotly
as they strolled homewards.

'I don't know what you mean.'

'Yes, you do. You know perfectly well that
Sukey likes you, and you were openly flirting
with her, even though you had proposed marriage to me, making it plain that you wouldn't
take no for an answer.'

'I was just being civil to her, Rosie. My feelings
for you must be so obvious that I did not want
her to feel slighted. And, as I said before, I did
not mean to pressurise you, my dear.'

'Really? That's not how it seemed to me, Harry.'

He patted her hand and smiled. 'I laid my heart open to you, Rosina. If I was too pressing it was only because of my sincere regard for you.'

'Did I imagine that you threatened to put my papa out of business if I did not accept your proposal of marriage?'

His face crumpled with consternation. 'What I meant to say was that if we were married, then naturally I would do everything I could to promote your father's business interests.'

'That wasn't how it sounded.'

'I apologise most humbly.' Harry stopped walking and he clasped her hands in his, crushing the paper bag filled with leftovers from their tea party and covering his fingers with cream. 'Damn. I'd forgotten that you were intent on feeding the poor.'

'It's the cake and sandwiches for Caddie and her children,' Rosina said, suppressing a giggle. 'Perhaps I shouldn't have asked for them.'

Harry licked his fingers, smiling ruefully. 'Oh, Rosie, what do I care about a few rotten cakes? You could turn my house into a soup kitchen for all I'd care, if it made you happy.'

'Harry, please don't say any more.'

'I have to, my sweet. I want you to accept my apology for the way I behaved to you. I must have been carried away by the passion burning in my heart. I confess that I was eaten up with jealousy after that – that creature took such an obvious interest in you at Cremorne Gardens. You can hardly blame me for that, my love.'

She hesitated. He seemed so humble now, quite different to the devil-may-care, self-confident Harry Gostellow she thought she knew. She could almost believe him, but that did not alter her feelings. She drew her hands away gently, and with a smile. 'Oh, Harry. What am I to do with you?'

'Marry me, Rosie. I know that both our families would approve of such a match.'

She angled her head. 'Is that what your mother meant when she said "she might do"? You didn't answer my question when I asked it before.'

'Mother took an instant liking to you, as I knew she would. I had no idea that she was acquainted with your mama, but that is all to the good. Won't you give me a chance, my dear girl?'

'Harry, please . . .'

'I know you need time to think it over. That's quite all right with me. I won't press you on the subject.'

'How many times must I refuse you, Harry?'

'It's what young ladies always do. I understand that, my dear.'

'I don't want to give you false hope.'

'But you will think about it?'

His eyes pleaded with her and she could not find it in her heart to disappoint him yet again. She lowered her gaze. 'I will think about it, Harry.'

He raised her hands to his lips. 'Oh, Rosie, my dear girl. I know I've rushed matters. That's me all over – when I want something I can't help myself, I just go out and get it. No, don't say anything. Let us continue as good friends, for the time being at least. I meant it when I suggested that we have another outing. We'll do it properly this time, with your father's permission. We'll make it a foursome with Susan and a most eligible gentleman of my acquaintance. We'll even take your watchdog, Walter, with us if that would make you feel better.'

She felt herself weakening. Perhaps she had misunderstood him in the first place. What harm could there be in a well-chaperoned visit to the pleasure garden? And it might be her only chance to meet the pirate again. The sound of his voice, the thrill she had felt when he had held her in his arms, were all beginning to seem like a dream. She had to find out if he was real or just a figment of her imagination. She smiled at Harry's eager expression. 'Well, if my papa agrees, and if Walter can come too, then I suppose it would be all right.'

'I'll make the arrangements straight away.'

'And it would be nice to see the Crystal Palace,

or to go to Cremorne Gardens again. I did love the fireworks and I would love to see another ascent of a hot air balloon.'

'Anything you want is—'

He was interrupted by a cry from above them. Rosina looked up and saw Caddie leaning out of the window, waving frantically. 'Help me, miss. Help.'

'Oh, Lord. Whatever can have happened?' Rosina ran into the building. She could hear the children screaming as she raced up the stairs. Imagining all manner of terrible accidents that might have befallen them, she burst into the room. But nothing could have prepared her for the sight that met her eyes. Ronnie and Alfie were huddled together, sobbing hysterically. Caddie was collapsed on the window seat and her skirts were stained red with blood. Her ashen face contorted with pain as a fresh spasm racked her distorted body. 'Miss Rosina, it's me baby, coming afore its time.'

Harry entered the room just seconds behind Rosina. He took in the scene with a gasp of horror. 'Oh, dear. Oh, I say.'

Caddie held her hands out to them. 'Help me, for the love of God.'

Curbing the desire to run away, Rosina grabbed Harry by the arm. 'Fetch Bertha. She'll know what to do.'

He nodded dumbly, backing towards the open

door. 'Yes, all right. Oh, I say. Not too good with blood and such, Rosie. Think I might be sick.' He bolted out of the room as though the devil were at his heels.

'I'm sorry, miss,' Caddie whispered. 'It come all of a sudden.'

Rosina had only the haziest idea of how babies came into the world, and the sight of so much blood terrified her. She knew that many women died in childbirth, and she had not the slightest idea what to do, but she forced herself to sound calm. 'What can I do to help?'

'Look after me nippers, miss.'

Praying that Bertha would arrive soon, Rosina knelt down on the floor beside Ronnie and Alfie. They threw their arms around her and buried their faces in her skirts, sobbing. 'Hush, now. Everything will be all right, but you must be quiet. Your poor mama doesn't feel very well.'

'They're hungry, miss,' Caddie murmured feebly. 'They've had nothing to eat since last night.'

Rosina remembered the bag of food that she had tossed carelessly on the table as she entered the room. She manoeuvred the children into a position where she could reach up to get the bag. 'Ronnie, Alfie, if you stop crying, you shall have some lovely cake.'

It worked like magic and two small, tear-stained faces looked up at her as if she had said something wonderful. She placed the paper bag in between them and they fell on its contents like ravening wolf cubs.

Caddie let out a low, agonised moan. Rosina rose to her feet and paced the floor, wringing her hands. She resisted the temptation to cover her ears and shut out Caddie's cries as she tried hard not to panic. She wished that there was something she could do to ease her friend's pain, but she simply did not know what. After what seemed like hours, but could only have been minutes, she heard the sound of footsteps on the stairs. 'Bebe. Up here – come quickly.'

But it was Walter who came through the door. He paused for a moment, taking in the scene. In two strides he was at Caddie's side, and, taking her hand in his, he held it, speaking to her in the soothing tones he might have used to calm a terrified child. 'Don't be afraid, Caddie. Bertha has gone to fetch Mrs Wilkes, the midwife. They'll be here soon.'

'I can't afford to pay her,' Caddie whispered. 'Just take care of me little ones.'

'You mustn't worry about anything, Caddie.' Walter lifted her up in his arms, ignoring her feeble protests, and he carried her into the adjoining bedroom. Through the open door, Rosina saw him lay her gently on an iron bedstead covered with a patchwork quilt. He perched on the edge of the bed, holding Caddie's hand and keeping up a one-sided conversation. The boys were too busy stuffing cake and sandwiches into their mouths to take much interest in what was happening to their mother, and for that Rosina was grateful. Caddie's groans were muffled and it sounded as though she was growing weaker. Rosina had never felt so helpless in her whole life, and she could have cried with relief when Bertha and Nora Wilkes hurried into the room. Bertha's face was crimson with exertion and she was breathing heavily, but she went straight to the bedroom with Nora following close on her heels. They sent Walter out and closed the door.

He looked down at his blood-stained jacket with a rueful grin. 'It looks as though I've murdered somebody.' Stripping it off, he laid it over the back of a chair.

'You were wonderful, Walter,' Rosina said sincerely. 'I was so frightened, but you seemed to know exactly what to do. I hope Caddie will be all right.'

Walter bent down to separate Ronnie and Alfie who were fighting over the last iced bun. He broke it in two and gave them a piece each. 'You mustn't worry. She's in good hands now.'

'She was in such pain. What happens if she . . .?'

Rosina could not bring herself to put her fear into words.

He gave her an encouraging smile. 'She's young and strong and she's borne two children already. She'll be all right, you'll see.'

Between them they managed to keep the small boys entertained for more than an hour, despite the sound of Caddie's anguished moans coming from the bedroom. Walter was on all fours pretending to be a horse and giving the boys turns at riding on his back when they heard a faint, mewling cry. Rosina leapt to her feet, waiting for what seemed like an eternity, and then the bedroom door opened and Bertha emerged holding a tiny scrap of red-faced humanity wrapped in a strip torn from a sheet. 'It's another boy,' she said, smiling tiredly.

The door was slightly ajar and Rosina could see Nora bending over the bed. Cold fingers of fear clutched at her heart as she sensed that all was not well. 'What about Caddie? Is she all right? May I see her?'

Bertha thrust the baby into her arms. 'Best take the nippers home, Rosie. Caddie's in a bad way.'

Rosina stared down at the wrinkled face of the baby. 'She won't – she's not going to . . .'

'Not if we've got anything to do with it she won't, but she needs rest and quiet. She won't be in a fit condition to feed this one for a while. We'll need to find a wet nurse for him.'

Rosina shot a sideways glance at Walter, feeling the blood rush to her cheeks. Such intimate subjects were not usually spoken of in mixed company, especially if the man was unmarried.

Walter did not seem at all embarrassed. 'Gladys Smilie has a new addition to her brood,' he said in a matter-of-fact tone. 'Maybe she'd look after the baby until Caddie regains her strength.'

Gladys laid her own infant down in its cradle, and she took Caddie's baby in her arms. 'Well now, of course I'd be glad to look after the baby until his ma gets better. I've enough milk for two hungry mouths, heaven knows. Has he got a name?'

Rosina shook her head. 'I don't think so.'

'Well, never mind.' Gladys sat down on the sofa, holding the baby and soothing his cries by allowing him to suck on her finger. 'You can tell poor little Caddie that I'll look after her baby, but as to the two older ones, I'm sorry, dear. I got me hands full with me own nippers. We're cramped enough living behind the shop and the kids sleep top to toe as it is. I really can't take the boys in as well, even though I'd love to oblige.'

Rosina felt the two small hands tighten their grip on her fingers and she smiled down at Ronnie and Alfie. 'No matter, Mrs Smilie. The boys can come and stay with me and Bertha until their mama gets better.'

'Well said, dearie.' Gladys began to unbutton her blouse as the baby, apparently realising that there was no milk issuing from her finger, began to roar its disapproval.

'We'd best go then,' Rosina said hastily. 'Come, Walter. We'll take the boys home.'

'Of course.' He took some coins from his pocket and laid them on the kitchen table. 'To help with expenses, Mrs Smilie.'

'Ta, ducks. I won't say no.' Gladys beamed at him. 'We does quite nicely in the shop, but there's always something wanting with six growing nippers in the house.'

As they went out through the shop, Sam Smilie gave the boys a small bar of chocolate to share between them. Walter broke off two pieces and gave them one each.

'Ah,' Sam said, smiling. 'I see you got a way with young 'uns, Walter.'

'Not really,' Walter replied. 'It only takes a bit of commonsense.'

'Don't be so modest.' Rosina took the boys by their sticky hands. 'Walter has been marvellous, Sam. I don't know what I would have done without him today.'

Sam nodded. 'I hope young Caddie gets well soon. Poor little thing, there's nothing of her at the best of times. She ain't as robust as my Gladys.'

As soon as they were outside the shop, Ronnie began to whimper, and Walter lifted him onto his shoulders and strode on ahead, making Ronnie laugh by bouncing him up and down. Not to be outdone, Alfie clamoured for similar attention, and Rosina lifted him up in her arms. Walter was already far ahead, and she searched for something to distract Alfie, who was beginning to grizzle. The *Curlew* was making ready to sail and she walked to the edge of the wharf. 'Just look at that fine boat, Alfie,' she said, pointing. 'That barge belongs to Captain Barnum, but your papa will be coming home tomorrow on a boat just like that one. Won't that be exciting?' She was about to move on when Ham Barnum looked up and saw her.

He came thundering along the deck, shaking his fist. 'I want a word with you, young lady.'

'What is it, Captain Barnum?'

'Don't put on that innocent air with me, girl. You keep away from my daughter, d'you hear me?'

Rosina shifted Alfie to her other hip. 'I hear you, Captain. And so does everyone else in Black Eagle Wharf.'

'Then hear this. I'll not have you leading my girl into bad ways and keeping her out until all hours. I've only just found out that she went off gallivanting to Cremorne Gardens with you and that counting-house clerk. I won't have her reputation sullied by the likes of you. I've kept things friendly with you up till now, but I can see that you're as bad as that father of yours. Keep away from Sukey, or it will be the worse for you.'

# Chapter Seven

Walter might not have heard what Barnum was saying, but he could not have been deaf to the angry pitch of his voice. Retracing his steps, he hurried to Rosina's side, setting Ronnie down on the ground. 'That's no way to speak to a lady, Captain Barnum.'

'Are you addressing me, mister?'

'If you have anything to say, you'd best say it to me. Permission to come aboard, sir?'

'I've got plenty to say to you, scribe. Although it's a sound thrashing that you deserve. But it will have to wait.'

'I don't know what you're talking about, Captain Barnum.'

'Bah! It's her I blame for all this trouble, the little trollop. I haven't got time for this right now. We're sailing on the tide.' Barnum turned on his heel and stomped along the deck, shouting instructions to Barker.

Walter looked as though he was about to leap on board the barge, but Rosina laid her hand on his arm. 'Ignore him, Walter.' Despite the fact that she was trembling with suppressed anger, she was not going to let Walter see how much Barnum's words had confused and upset her. Her main concern at this moment was for Caddie's children, and she caught Ronnie by the hand. With a huge effort she managed to keep her voice calm. 'Come away, Walter. He's all bluster and hot air. Don't stoop to his level.'

'I won't allow him to speak to you in that manner.'

'Thank you, but I can stand up for myself. I'm just sorry that Sukey is in trouble because of me.'

'If anyone is to blame, it's Harry Gostellow, for taking you to a place like Cremorne Gardens. I'll see you safely home. My business with Barnum can wait.' Walter took a wriggling Alfie from her arms and hitched him onto his shoulders. 'It's your turn for a ride now, matey boy.'

'How did you know we went to Cremorne Gardens?' Rosina stared at him nonplussed.

'You told me so yourself.'

'I'm sure that I did not.'

Ronnie tugged at Rosina's hand. 'Daddy not coming.' His small face had puckered up again as though he was about to cry.

'Daddy's coming home tomorrow, Ronnie,' Rosina said gently. 'But for now you and Alfie can come back to my house and Bertha will make you a nice dinner.'

'Mummy,' Ronnie whispered anxiously. 'Want my mummy.'

Rosina shot a worried glance at Walter. 'What on earth do you say to two little fellows in these circumstances?'

'As little as possible, Miss Rosina.' He bounced Alfie up and down on his shoulders, making him chuckle. 'Let's get these two home.'

She fell into step beside him, allowing Ronnie to run on ahead. 'Walter, if you don't stop calling me Miss Rosina I'll – well, I'll be very cross. Surely we know each other well enough by now for you to call me Rosie?'

Alfie chose that moment to push Walter's cap down over his eyes, knocking his spectacles sideways. Walter laughed, setting them straight, and taking off his cap he put it on Alfie's head. 'You young monkey.'

'Did you hear me, Walter?'

'I heard you, Rosie.'

She chuckled. 'That's better. After last night, I feel I owe you so much, and you've come to my rescue yet again. You're a good friend, and you're right about our trip to Cremorne Gardens. I didn't want to lie to you, but I had to convince Bertha that we were dining with the Gostellows.'

'Which was obviously complete fiction.'

'I know, and I'm sorry that we involved you.'

'It's over and done with now.'

'Harry said I may ask you to join us on our next trip. It will be all above board this time.'

'You heard what Barnum just said. Would you

risk your reputation by going on another outing with Gostellow?'

They had reached the house, and she stopped, puzzled by the harsh note in his voice. 'I'm not afraid of Captain Barnum, but if Sukey doesn't want to disobey her pa that's up to her. What's the matter, Walter? Don't you approve?'

'It's not up to me to approve or disapprove.' He did not look at her as he set Alfie down on the ground.

'Oh, Walter, you're being stuffy again. I thought we could speak as friends.'

'We can, of course.'

'I am sorry that I lied to you. It won't happen again.' She opened the door, and without waiting to be told Ronnie and Alfie scampered off in the direction of the kitchen.

'I'd best get back to work.' Walter was about to enter the office, but he hesitated, turning to her with an anxious look in his eyes. 'Be careful, that's all I can say.'

Rosina bit her lip. The last thing she wanted to do was to fall out with him. He had proved a staunch ally, and she did not want him to think badly of her. 'Wait a moment, Walter. It's not how it looks. I mean, it is quite proper for me to go out with Harry, providing we are chaperoned. His intentions are honourable: I can assure you of that.'

His expression was guarded. 'What are you saying?'

'Harry has asked me to marry him.' If she had slapped Walter in the face he could not have looked more shocked. When he made no comment on her announcement she was torn between disappointment and embarrassment. 'It would be a very good match. Aren't you pleased for me? Say something, Walter.'

'Did you accept his proposal?'

The cold tone in his voice chilled her to the marrow. A spurt of anger rose in her throat, almost choking her. She did not know whether she was annoyed with herself for telling him, or cross with Walter for receiving her news in such a cool manner. 'I'd best see to the boys.' Turning on her heel, she left him standing in the hallway. It had been a mistake confiding in him. A big mistake. Walter Brown was an old misery – perhaps he wanted to see her dwindle away into a sad spinster? At least Harry wanted to spend the rest of his life with her. Maybe she ought to reconsider his offer? After all, she had promised him that she would think it over. She hurried towards the kitchen where it sounded as though the boys were up to no good.

They had climbed onto the table looking for more food. Rosina knew next to nothing about looking after small children, but she remembered that Bertha used to give her bread soaked in warm milk, sprinkled with a little sugar. She made some for them and was gratified when they demolished it in seconds and asked for more. They seemed to have forgotten about their mother for the moment, and Rosina was relieved not to have to answer any awkward questions. As soon as they had eaten, she took them upstairs to her own room and put them to bed. She sat with them until they fell asleep. She smoothed their damp curls back from their foreheads and tucked the sheet up to their small chins. Poor little mites, she thought, sadly. What if they were to lose their mamma now? She went downstairs, praying silently that Caddie would have the strength to survive.

When Bertha returned, half an hour later, Rosina took one look at her face and was alarmed by her serious expression. 'Oh, Bebe. She's not . . .?'

Bertha slumped down on her chair by the range. 'She's very weak, but we've done all we can for her. Nora says she's seen worse.'

'You look tired, dear Bebe. I'll make you a pot of tea.'

'Ta, love. That's just what I need. As if things wasn't bad enough, we had a bit of a to-do with the blooming rent collector. He come demanding the rent and the poor soul hadn't got a penny to her name. Nora and me sent him off with a flea in his ear, but he'll be back tomorrow.'

'Papa and Artie should be home by then. Poor Caddie. We can't leave her alone in those dreary rooms, Bebe. We must bring her here and look after her.'

Forgetting their differences, Rosina went straight to Walter to ask for his help. She did not have to ask him twice. He organised the construction of a makeshift stretcher, using a piece of canvas and two spars donated by Higgins, the sailmaker. With Sam Smilie's help, he dismantled Caddie's bed and they reassembled it in the attic room at the top of the Mays' house. One of the sailmaker's apprentices staggered over with a pile of pillows and bedding and went back to fetch the truckle bed for Ronnie and Alfie. With their combined efforts, Caddie was brought to the house and put to bed.

When Rosina took her up a cup of tea she was horrified to find her lying pale and lifeless with tears running down her cheeks. 'There, there, Caddie, dear. Please don't cry.' She propped her up on the pillows and supported her while she sipped the hot, sweet tea.

'My baby,' Caddie sobbed. 'My baby.'

Rosina put the cup down and hugged her. 'Your baby is safe and well and being cared for by Gladys.'

'I want to hold him. You aren't lying to me, are you? He is all right?'

'He's a fine, healthy boy. And he has no name yet. What are you going to call him?'

Caddie managed a watery smile. 'He must be

named after his dad. I wanted both Ronnie and Alfie to be called Arthur, but my Artie wouldn't have it. What? says he. Call them poor little tykes after me? Not likely! But this time I won't be overruled.'

'And it's a fine name, Caddie.'

'Now I want to see me boys. Please let me see them, Rosie.'

'You can see them when they wake up from their nap. Artie will be home tomorrow and you must get some rest. You don't want him to see you in a state, now do you?'

Caddie laid her head against Rosina's shoulder. 'I'm sorry. I – I just can't seem to stop c-crying.'

Rosina stroked her hair and made sympathetic noises, but she was at a loss to know what to do for the best. She stifled a sigh of relief when she heard Bertha's heavy tread on the stairs.

'Now, now, what's all this?' Bertha demanded as she wheezed into the attic room. 'I've got something here what will make you sleep, young lady.' She produced a brown medicine bottle from her pocket, uncorked it and poured a few drops of dark liquid into a teaspoon. 'Move away, Rosie. I'll take over now.'

Caddie took her medicine like an obedient child and lay back against the pillows, closing her eyes.

'Will she be all right?' Rosina whispered as they made their way downstairs.

'She will, so long as she don't start bleeding all over again. Nora said she'll look in later, but we've got to keep her quiet.'

'Thank goodness Papa and Artie will be coming home tomorrow,' Rosina said with feeling.

Rosina was too busy looking after Ronnie and Alfie to be worried when the *Ellie May* did not arrive on the morning tide. But as midday approached she was beginning to feel anxious. She had allowed the boys to go upstairs to see their mother, but Caddie tired easily, and Rosina took them into the kitchen where Bertha was preparing their dinner.

'For the love of God, get them kids out of me way,' Bertha said as Ronnie tugged playfully at her apron strings. 'Heaven knows, I like nippers, but I can't make a pot of oxtail stew with them under me feet.'

'All right, Bebe, we'll go and see Uncle Walter.'

'Huh!' Bertha said, wiping her brow with the back of her hand. 'Uncle Walter indeed. Don't you get too familiar with that young man, Rosie. I seen the way he looks at you.'

'Walter?' Rosina gurgled with laughter. 'You're imagining things, Bebe. Walter is just a friend.'

'Men are never just friends. You keep him in his place, and concentrate on them as is in your station of life, so to speak.'

'I suppose you mean Harry?' Rosina caught Alfie by the hand. 'Stop matchmaking, Bebe. I'll make up my own mind about Mr Gostellow.'

Bertha looked up from chopping vegetables and her eyes were alert with curiosity. 'Has he proposed then?'

'Never you mind.' Rosina made a grab for Ronnie as he was about to head for the stairs. 'Come with me, boys. We'll leave Miss Crosspatch to get on with our dinner.'

She would tell Bertha everything, of course, but not yet. As she went towards the office, she could hear raised voices. She realised that it was Walter and Harry, and they seemed to be having an argument. They stopped mid-conversation as she entered the room. Ronnie and Alfie made a dash for Walter and clung to his legs, demanding sweets.

'Rosie, darling.' Harry took her hand and brushed it with his lips. 'How lovely you look this morning.'

Despite the fact that she had decided to reconsider his proposal, his proprietorial attitude struck a false chord. He was acting as though they were already engaged. She snatched her hand free, feeling the ready colour rise to her cheeks as she met Walter's questioning gaze. He looked away before she could speak, and he appeared to be more interested in feeding the little boys with broken biscuits than in what she might have to say. Really, she thought, men could be such infuriating creatures at times. Harry was assuming too much, and Walter was being difficult again. She would not let either of them see that she was ruffled by their differing attitudes. She managed a smile. 'Good morning, Harry. Good morning, Walter. I thought I heard raised voices. Is there anything wrong?'

'Nothing to bother your pretty head about, my dear,' Harry said. 'It was just business.'

'But the business is my concern, Harry. One day, when I reach my majority, it will be mine.'

'And when we are married I shall take all that responsibility from your delicate shoulders.'

'Harry!' She shot a covert glance at Walter, but he did not seem to be listening. She lowered her voice. 'I haven't accepted your proposal yet.'

'And I will continue to live in hope, but until then I intend to spoil you as you deserved to be spoiled. In fact, my love, I was just making arrangements with Walter for our next trip to Cremorne Gardens, since you enjoyed our last outing so much.'

'Oh, really? And what does Walter have to say about that?' She raised her voice so that Walter could not fail to hear, unless he had been struck deaf, which he quite obviously had not, as he looked up with a carefully guarded expression on his face. 'What do you have to say, Walter?' She could not quite keep the edge from her voice.

He shrugged his shoulders. 'Perhaps you should ask your father first. It's not up to me, Miss Rosina.'

So, he had reverted to being cold and formal. She bit back a sharp retort. When they had worked together to help Caddie it seemed as though their differences had been forgotten. Now it appeared that they were still very much on Walter's mind. She would not let him see that she was upset, and she turned to Harry. 'I'll speak to Papa when he comes home. I'm sure he'll agree. Now, if you'll excuse me, I'm going to take the children to see Sukey. Ronnie, Alfie, come along.'

'I have business in Watson's Wharf. I'll accompany you, if I may?'

'Of course, Harry.' Rosina shot a sideways glance at Walter, but he was making the children laugh by pulling funny faces at them. 'Come along, boys. Uncle Walter has more important things to do than play with you.'

Walter gave her a direct look, but he made no response. She took the children by the hand and led them from the office with Harry following close behind.

'When may I call on your father?' He fell into step beside her. 'Don't look alarmed, my dear. I only mean to ask his permission to take you on the next outing.'

'Harry, I wish you would not speak to me in

159

front of other people as though we were already engaged.' Rosina bent down to pick up Alfie and she hoisted him onto her hip.

'Surely you don't count your father's clerk, Rosie? Walter is an employee, a mere servant. What he thinks doesn't matter.'

'Not to you, maybe, but it does to me. Walter is my friend, Harry.'

'And yet you were quite happy to trick him into thinking that we had dinner at my parents' house the other night, just so that you could accompany me to Cremorne Gardens. You used him as a decoy, Rosie. Now, I could be wrong, but I don't think that's the way to treat a friend.'

It was too painfully true, and Rosina could not look at him. Nor could she think of a suitable reply. She was saved from answering by Ronnie, who tripped and would have fallen if she had not held on to his little hand, jerking him to his feet. 'You're all right, Ronnie. We're nearly there.'

'You haven't answered my question, dearest. When may I call on your father?'

'Perhaps tomorrow, Harry. His mood will depend on whether or not he has had a good trip, and if you have another cargo for him.'

Harry stopped as they reached the Barnums' front door, and he smiled at her, gently pinching her cheek. 'What a good little businesswoman you will make, my pet. Of course I'll have another cargo for your father – a hundred cargoes if it pleases you. I'll call on him in the morning, and I'll bring a formal invitation from my mama, asking you both to dine with us.'

'Don't go too fast, Harry. You won't push me into making a decision.'

He reached across her to rap on the door knocker. She could feel his warm breath on her cheek as he looked deeply into her eyes. 'I will wait forever, if necessary. But I pray it won't be that long before I can make you mine. I have a fancy for an autumn wedding and a honeymoon in Italy.'

The door opened and Gertie looked them up and down. 'Yes?'

'Goodbye, Harry.' Rosina did not wait for Gertie to ask her into the house; she pushed past unceremoniously, dragging the children with her. Harry was going altogether too fast for her. The idea of being engaged was not unappealing, but the thought of getting married so soon was frankly terrifying. She breathed a sigh of relief as Gertie slammed the door, shutting Harry out.

'Some folks has got no manners,' Gertie muttered.

'I beg your pardon?' Rosina drew herself up to her full height, but it was difficult to appear haughty with two small children clinging to her, and wiping their noses on her skirt.

'I suppose you wants to see Miss Sukey?'

'Yes, please.'

Gertie eyed the boys warily, as though they were two small animals that might suddenly turn nasty and bite her. She jerked her head in the direction of the front parlour. 'She's in there with her sisters.' She hurried away into the dim recesses of the house.

Rosina tapped on the door and went inside. Sukey was sitting on the sofa next to Mary, who as usual had her head stuck in a book. Sukey leapt to her feet, almost tripping over Lillian, who was kneeling on the floor playing with a small tortoiseshell kitten. Ronnie broke away from Rosina and hurled himself at the kitten: it took fright and climbed up the curtains.

Sukey clapped her hand over her mouth. 'Oh, my goodness. If it tears Mama's best velvet curtains there'll be hell to pay.'

'You shouldn't say "hell" – it's not ladylike,' Mary said primly.

Lillian scrambled to her feet and shook the curtain, but the kitten clung on, sticking its claws into the material and mewing piteously.

'Stop that,' Sukey cried, catching hold of Lillian by the shoulders and dragging her away. 'You're frightening the poor thing. Leave it alone and it will come down.'

Mary stared at Alfie and Ronnie, who were huddling together with their thumbs stuck in their mouths. 'Where did you get those dirty little children, Rosie? They haven't even got shoes on their feet.'

Rosina knelt down and wrapped her arms around the boys. 'Not everyone is lucky enough to be able to afford shoes, Mary. These are Caddie's children and she was taken ill yesterday. We're looking after them all until her husband returns tonight on the *Ellie May*.'

'Our dada doesn't like yours,' Lillian said, giving the curtain a sly shake and receiving a cuff round the ear from Sukey for her pains. 'Ouch, you beast. That hurt.'

'It was meant to,' Sukey said smugly. 'And you oughtn't to be rude to a guest. What Dada thinks about Captain May is none of your business.'

'They are dirty little children,' Mary said, eyeing them dubiously. 'I daresay they have fleas and head lice.'

'Indeed they have not.' Rosina clutched them to her bosom, hoping that they were not infested; she had not thought to check them. She hugged them both as they began to snivel. 'When Artie comes ashore he'll take them home, but until then I have to look after them.'

Sukey leaned over to whisper in Rosina's ear. 'I need to speak to you, urgently. But not in front of my sisters, the little sneaks.'

Rising to her feet, Rosina patted the boys on their heads. 'Perhaps Lillian will be kind enough to play with you for a while. I want a few words with Sukey.'

'I'm not playing with them and getting fleas,' Lillian said, pouting. 'Mama wouldn't like it. She wouldn't want them in the house, come to that.'

'Shut up, Lily.' Mary closed the book she had been reading with a snap. 'I suppose that means you two have got secrets to share. Come here, you little urchins, and I'll show you some pictures in a book. It will be good practice for me, for when I become a teacher.'

'Heaven help her pupils,' Sukey said, pulling a face. She opened the door. 'We'll only be gone for a couple of minutes. Don't you girls dare do anything that will upset Mama. And get that kitten down from the curtains, Lily, before it ruins them.' She led Rosina into the hallway and closed the door behind them.

'What is it?' Rosina asked, although she knew the answer before Sukey had said a word as she recalled the stern warning from Captain Barnum. 'Is it to do with your papa?'

Sukey nodded vigorously. 'He's forbidden me to have anything to do with you, Rosie. Gertie went and told him that I'd come in late, and he made me tell him the whole thing. He's cross with me, but he's furious with you. I didn't want him to blame Harry, so I said that we had dinner with his parents and then we left for Cremorne Gardens.'

'But, Sukey, surely your father wouldn't believe that we went to that place on our own?'

Sukey blushed and looked away. 'I'm afraid I told him that we went with Walter. I'm sorry, but I couldn't think of anything else on the spot: besides which, Gertie saw Walter when you and he accompanied me home that night. I'm so sorry, dear. I didn't want Dada to think badly of Harry.'

'I'm sorry too.' Rosina clasped Sukey's hands. 'I should never have encouraged you to disobey your father.'

Sukey's eyes gleamed with mischief and a dimple hovered at the corner of her mouth. 'I wouldn't have missed it for anything. I had a simply wonderful time, and Harry was so dashing and handsome. I think he likes me, Rosie. And I certainly like him.'

Rosina couldn't bring herself to tell Sukey that Harry had proposed marriage. Sukey seemed so convinced that he reciprocated her tender feelings; it would be too cruel to tell her the truth. But it would also be unkind to allow her to labour under a delusion. Rosina bit her lip: she did not know what to say.

'Do you think he likes me, Rosie? Do you think he will take us to Cremorne Gardens again?'

'But, Sukey, what if your father found out?'

'Pooh! I'm not afraid of Dada – well, not much anyway. And I would just have to make sure that he didn't find out. I would love another chance to get closer to Harry. Will he ask us, do you think?'

'You would risk everything, just for an evening out with Harry Gostellow?'

'Oh, yes.' Sukey's eyes shone. 'Wouldn't you risk everything for the man you loved?'

A vision of the pirate flashed through Rosina's mind. She could hear his voice and feel his arms around her as they danced on the crystal platform. She could smell the scent of roses and jasmine, heavy in the night air, and see the gaslights shining through the green leaves of the trees. 'Yes, I would. If I truly loved a man, I would do anything to be with him.'

'Then will you arrange it? I don't want to ask Harry for fear of being thought forward, but you could do it.'

'Your father told me to keep away from you. I daren't come to the house when he is at home.'

'No, we must arrange some way of getting messages to each other. This is so exciting, just like one of Mrs Gaskell's novels. Not that I have much time for reading, but Mary is so bookish and she reads to us most evenings. Some of it's a real bore, but I do love the romances.'

'I'll ask Harry to call on you,' Rosina said, thinking quickly. 'Your parents would hardly object to his calling on you, now would they?'

'Absolutely not! Mama would be beside

herself with joy if she thought I might hook a rich husband.'

A sudden commotion inside the parlour caused Sukey to fling the door open. 'What's going on? Oh, dear!'

Rosina hurried into the room and found Ronnie sobbing hysterically as blood oozed from a scratch on his cheek.

'It wasn't my fault,' Lillian said, pouting. 'He pulled the kitten's tail and it scratched him. Serves the little beast right.'

Rosina dabbed Ronnie's cheek with her hanky. 'I think I'd better take them home.'

'I'll ring for Gertie to see you out,' Sukey said, reaching for the embroidered bell pull.

'There's no need to disturb her.' Rosina picked Ronnie up and cuddled him. 'Let's go to Mr Smilie's shop and see if he's got some sweeties that will make you feel better. We can take a look at baby Arthur and then we can tell your mama we've seen him and he is thriving.'

'You'd better not come here again,' Mary said solemnly. 'Our dada said he would tell Gertie to slam the door in your face if you came knocking on it.'

'Hush, Mary.' Sukey's fair eyebrows knotted together in a frown. 'That's not very polite.'

'It's true though,' Lillian added gleefully. 'Our dada said he would sink the *Ellie May* and laugh as it went down to the bottom of the river.'

'Lillian!' Sukey hurried Rosina and the children out of the parlour. 'I am so sorry. They shouldn't have repeated what they heard. I'm sure that Dada says things he doesn't mean.'

'I expect he does.' Rosina laid her hand on Sukey's shoulder. 'But it doesn't affect our friendship, does it?'

'Never,' Sukey said, kissing her on the cheek. 'Friends forever, Rosie May.'

'Friends forever, Sukey Barnum.' Rosina was still smiling as she walked the boys to Sam Smilie's shop. He gave them twists of barley sugar and she was able to reassure herself that baby Arthur was doing well with Gladys as his wet nurse. When they arrived home, Rosina took the boys up to see their mother, and she was able to tell Caddie that her baby was being well looked after.

Caddie's thin cheeks flushed a delicate shade of pink as she cuddled Ronnie and Alfie in her arms. 'Is there any sign of the *Ellie May* yet, Miss Rosina?'

'Not yet, Caddie. But there are a couple of hours until high tide. I'm sure she'll haul into sight very soon, and then you'll have your Artie back home with you.'

Caddie closed her eyes, but a smile played about her pale lips. 'Yes. Everything will be all right when Artie gets home.'

Later that afternoon, while the boys took a nap

on the truckle bed in Caddie's room, Rosina went to the office to look for Walter, but he was not there. Mindful of Bertha's strict rules about how a young lady should dress when she went out of doors, she went into the kitchen and fetched her bonnet and gloves. Bertha was asleep in her chair by the range, and Rosina moved stealthily so as not to wake her. The heat of early morning had become oppressive as the day had worn on. A hot wind sent eddies of dust spiralling into the sulphurous air, and rattled the stays on the ships moored alongside. The sky was heavy with storm clouds that seemed to hover just above the rooftops, colouring the waters of the Thames slate grey. She saw Walter standing on the wharf. He was staring eastwards, and, as she followed his gaze, Rosina let out a gasp of horror. She hurried to his side. 'Walter, is that the *Ellie May*? Surely, it can't be?'

He glanced down at her, his jaw set in a tense line, his face ashen against the yellow-ochre sky. 'I can't be certain, but it looks like her.'

Her fingers curled round his arm, digging into his flesh through the thick folds of his pea jacket. 'What can have happened? Please say it isn't the *Ellie May*. Not coming home in a dreadful state like that.'

As the vessel came nearer, her worst fears were realised. The barge had a broken main mast and a gaping hole in the stern just above the water line. Rosina clung to Walter's arm, peering into the gathering gloom as huge drops of rain began to tumble from leaden clouds. She could just make out a familiar figure at the wheel – there was no mistaking Papa – and she uttered a cry of sheer relief. 'He's all right, Walter. Whatever went wrong, at least Papa was not harmed.'

Walter gently disengaged her hand from his arm. 'Rosie, run to the wharfinger's office and ask him to muster some men to help. It looks as if there's been a terrible accident.'

She stared up at him, barely able to see for the rain lashing in her face. 'But Papa is all right – you can see him at the wheel.'

He pointed to a shape lying beneath a piece of tarpaulin. At first she thought it was a bundle of rope or a pile of sacks, but then she saw a clawed hand sticking out from beneath the rough cover. 'Oh, my God,' she cried, clapping her hand to her mouth. 'It can't be – not Artie.'

'Don't look, Rosie.' Walter turned her gently towards the wharfinger's office. 'Get help.'

# Chapter Eight

She was soaked to the skin, but Rosina was impervious to the cold and wet as she stood on the edge of the wharf watching the men lift Artie's body onto the same makeshift stretcher that had carried Caddie from her lodgings such a short time ago. The summer storm had already passed overhead. The sun was fighting its way through a featherbed of clouds, but the vagaries of the weather meant nothing to her compared to the unfolding tragedy aboard the ill-fated *Ellie May*.

Walter was on deck in deep conversation with her father, and she had to wait until they climbed the ladder to join her on the wharf. She wanted to fling her arms around her father, but Edward's face was grey and he appeared to be dazed and disorientated: he seemed suddenly to be an old man.

'Papa?' She took a step towards him, but there was no recognition in his eyes as he glanced at her and then turned his head away. It was like looking into the face of a stranger, and cold fingers of fear clutched at her heart.

Walter was close behind him and he gave her a sympathetic smile. 'Your father has had a bad shock, Rosie. Take him home. I'll see to everything out here.'

She linked Pa's hand through her arm, speaking to him in the tone she might have used for Ronnie or Alfie. 'Come with me, Papa. Let's go home.'

He did not reply but he allowed her to lead him into the house. His clothes were sodden, and she could feel him trembling violently, or perhaps he was simply shivering: she could not tell which. Bertha was dozing in the chair by the fire, but she awakened with a start as they entered the kitchen. She leapt to her feet with a cry of dismay. 'God above! What happened?'

Rosina helped her father to the chair that Bertha had just vacated. 'I don't know exactly, Bebe. There must have been some sort of collision on the water, and Artie . . .' Her voice broke on a sob. 'Oh, poor Caddie. Who is going to tell her?'

'Do you mean he's . . .'

'He was lying on deck covered with a tarpaulin. Oh, Bebe, it was awful. All I could see was his poor hand, all blue and stiff.'

'He was a good man. God rest his soul!' Bertha rolled up her sleeves. 'But it's no use dwelling on what you can't alter, and we've the living to think of. The main thing is to get your pa out of them wet duds, and you too, missy. You won't help anyone if you goes down with the lung fever. I'll look after the captain; you go and change your clothes.' She reached for the brandy bottle, which she kept for emergencies on the mantelshelf. Without bothering to fetch a glass, Bertha pulled the cork and held the bottle to Edward's blue lips. 'Here, guvner. Take a sip of this.'

Opening his mouth obediently, Edward drank the liquor. Almost immediately, spots of colour appeared on his cheeks. He stared up at Bertha, shaking his head. 'It all went wrong. Terrible accident, but it weren't no accident after all. Rammed me, he did. The bugger rammed me broadsides.'

'Don't talk, guv. Drink some more and then we'll get you out of them wet things.' Bertha straightened up, glaring at Rosina. 'What? Are you still here? I thought I told you to go and change into some dry clothes. And fetch your pa's dressing robe while you're about it.'

Rosina did not argue. She felt as she had when she was six years old and had fallen over the edge of the wharf into the river. Luckily, the tide had been on the turn and the water was shallow, but she could still taste the stinking mud that had got into her mouth and ears and even up her nose. As she hurried upstairs to do Bertha's bidding, she could almost feel the sting of the cane across her backside – the punishment for playing too close to the water's edge.

After taking her pa's robe down to the kitchen, Rosina returned to her bedroom, and stripping off her wet clothes she rubbed herself dry with the towel from her washstand. Caddie was uppermost in her thoughts now that she knew her pa was safe and being cared for. How would she break the news that Artie was dead? Coming so quickly after the traumatic birth of young Arthur, the shock might be too great for Caddie to bear. Rosina's fingers fumbled with the buttons at the front of her clean blouse and she realised that she was crying. She dashed the tears away on the back of her hand. She must not let Caddie see her with red eyes, or she would know instantly that there was something dreadfully amiss. She would have to tell her what had happened – but not just yet.

She went downstairs and found that the kitchen was filled with people. It seemed as though the whole of the wharf community had gathered to offer their support in a time of trouble. Sam and Gladys were seated at the table with Mr Cotton, the wharfinger. The two apprentices, Bob and Fred, were propping up a wall and the dock foreman stood on his own, cap in hand. Higgins was standing with his back to the fire with Charlie, the landlord of the Turk's Head. They had all brought small gifts: pipe tobacco from Sam, a bottle of brandy from Mr

Cotton, a poke of tea from Higgins, and a quart of ale from Charlie. Her father was seated on the chair by the fire, but Bertha had somehow managed to get him out of his wet things and into his robe. He seemed to have recovered somewhat and was responding to the questions that were being flung at him.

Bertha stood behind him with her arms folded across her bosom. Rosina had a sudden vision of her as a guard dog ready to defend its master, and she had to stifle a hysterical giggle. There was nothing remotely funny in the situation, and even though the conversation was largely concerned with the tragic events, everyone was speaking at once, making it sound as though there was a party in progress. Rosina made her way over to Gladys, who was cradling Arthur in her arms. 'I'm glad you brought the baby, Mrs Smilie. I think Caddie will need to have all her children with her at this terrible time.'

'Have you told her, ducks?'

'No. Not yet.'

Gladys placed the baby in Rosina's arms. 'Best do it soon.' She glanced over her shoulder as Ronnie and Alfie appeared in the doorway. She jerked her head in their direction. 'You know what they say about little pitchers having big ears, and we don't want them blurting it out.'

'Will you come with me, Mrs Smilie? I don't think I can do it on my own.'

Gladys patted her on the shoulder. 'Of course you can, ducks. You've always been a good friend to young Caddie. You can do it.'

The atmosphere in the kitchen was thick with tobacco smoke as the men puffed away at their pipes and Mr Cotton smoked a fat cigar. Gladys gave her a meaningful look, jerking her head in the direction of upstairs, and Rosina knew that she must take the boys back to their mother. She was trying to persuade them to go with her but they were reluctant to leave the gathering; they were stubbornly clinging to a chair when Walter entered the room. She cast him a mute plea for help, but it was a little galling when the boys obeyed him instantly, flinging their arms around his neck and demanding to be carried up to the top of the house.

'You have a way with them, Walter,' Rosina said grudgingly as they reached the door to Caddie's room.

He smiled, setting the boys down on the floor. 'Would you like me to come in with you, Rosie?'

She shook her head. This was something she must do alone. 'No. Thank you anyway, Walter. I'll try and break it gently.'

'I'm sure you'll find the right words.'

'How did it happen, Walter? I'll have to tell her something.'

'They were caught in a storm downriver. I couldn't get the full story out of your father, but it seems they were in collision with the *Curlew*.

The mast broke and Artie was hit by a falling spar. It was instantaneous – he wouldn't have known anything about it. You can tell Caddie that he didn't suffer.'

'Dada.' Ronnie began to snivel. 'I want Dada.'

Squaring her shoulders, Rosina took a deep breath. 'I'd best get this over before Caddie realises that something is wrong.'

'I'll wait here,' Walter said gently. 'Call out if you need me.'

They were all sobbing broken-heartedly: Caddie, Ronnie and Alfie. The baby was crying too, although he could not possibly have understood what was going on. Rosina had done everything she could to lessen the blow, but now she felt that Caddie needed time alone with her babies, and she slipped out of the room. She had forgotten that Walter had promised to wait; she did not expect him to be there, but when she saw him she burst into tears. He took her in his arms, allowing her to sob against his shoulder until she had spent her grief. Feeling a little embarrassed, she drew away from him, wiping her eyes on the handkerchief that he had produced from his breast pocket. 'I – I'm sorry, Walter. I didn't mean to cry all over you.'

He smiled. 'That's all right. My jacket was too large for me anyway. It will fit much better now you've shrunk it for me.'

This drew a gurgle of laughter from her. 'You are a fool, Walter.'

'That is true.'

She gave him a watery smile. 'No it's not. You are a good, kind man, and I don't know what we would do without you.'

'Is Caddie going to be all right?'

'I don't think she'll ever get over Artie's loss, she loved him so much, but she has her children. I suppose that must be some comfort to the poor soul.'

'Come to the counting house with me,' Walter said in a low tone. 'I need to talk to you.'

Downstairs, the noise from the kitchen seemed to be growing louder, but it was quiet in the office. Walter closed the door and motioned her to take a seat.

'What is it, Walter? What is so urgent that it can't wait?'

'I didn't want to tell you in front of the nippers, but Caddie's landlord has rented her rooms out to another tenant.'

'That's dreadful. Artie would have been able to pay the rent if – if . . .'

'No, I'm afraid he wouldn't.' Walter pulled up a chair and sat down beside her, taking her hand in his. 'You see, when the collision occurred, the *Ellie May* was holed above the water line. She didn't sink, but she did take on a lot of water and the cargo is ruined. There will be no money from this trip, Rosie. The repairs will cost a small fortune and business has been bad lately, as I think you know. I'm afraid that there are no funds to pay for the shipwright's work.'

She stared at him, uncomprehending at first, until the full import of his words struck home. 'You mean – we're ruined?'

'The outlook isn't good, but perhaps Captain May could find someone in the city who would lend him the finance to repair the boat. I would help if I could, but I have no income other than from my work here.'

'Papa will do it, Walter. I know he will. Once he has got over the shock of the accident, and poor Artie's death – I'm sure he will be able to sort things out.'

'Let's hope so.'

'Papa can do anything when he sets his mind to it. And when it comes to repairing the damage to the *Ellie May*, he knows all the shipwrights in Wapping and Shadwell and probably as far away as Bow Creek. My papa will make everything come right.'

'I'm sure you're right. I'm sorry if I worried you.'

'You told me the truth, and for that I'm very grateful. Bebe and Papa are inclined to treat me like a child. They don't realise that I'm quite grown up now.'

'Yes, indeed you are.' He smiled wryly as he

rose to his feet. 'If you'll excuse me, I'd best take another look at the damage.'

Rosina stood up, holding her hand out to him. 'Just tell me one thing, Walter. Are you certain that it was Captain Barnum's ship that rammed the *Ellie May*?'

'That's what your father told me.'

'I can't believe that Captain Barnum would do such a dreadful thing.'

'There's no proof that it was deliberate, Rosie. It happened in foul weather. Perhaps it was an accident.'

'If that was so, then where is Captain Barnum now? If he had seen Artie hit by a falling spar, wouldn't he have stopped to help?'

'There will be an inquiry. We will have to wait until then to find out what really happened during that storm.'

'But do you think that it was deliberate?'

'Barnum has a lot to answer for. I'll find out, one way or another; I promise you that. I will seek out the truth, and if Barnum is to blame, then I'll see that he pays for his actions.'

She had never seen him so angry and she laid her hand on his arm, touched by his loyalty to her father. 'It's not your problem, Walter. But I thank you with all my heart for being so loyal to Papa.'

He nodded, but he did not look her in the eye. 'I have much to do, and I want to make sure that they treat Artie's remains with respect. They've left his body in the wharfinger's office until he can be taken to the dead house.'

'We can't allow them to take Artie to that awful place. He ought to be laid out at home until the funeral.'

'Caddie has no money. He will have to be buried by the Parish.'

'No! No, I won't have it. Artie must be brought here to rest until he can have a proper funeral. I'm certain that Papa will pay for it. I'll go and ask him now. Will you come with me, Walter?'

Once they knew of Caddie's dire circumstances, everyone in the kitchen agreed that it was only right and proper that Artie should be brought to the captain's house until he could be laid to rest in the graveyard. Edward nodded in agreement, although privately Rosina thought he had drunk a little too much brandy to understand fully what was being said. Bertha suggested that Nathaniel Jones, the undertaker in Nightingale Lane, might be directed to make the necessary arrangements. Higgins took off his cap and passed it around.

'It's good of you, neighbours,' Edward said, getting to his feet with a bleary smile. 'But I will take care of the funeral expenses. Nothing is too good for Arthur Trigg. But as to that black-hearted villain Barnum – I'll take him to court and I'll ruin the bugger.'

'Sit down,' Bertha hissed, giving him a gentle push so that he fell back on his seat. 'There ain't no call to use that sort of language in front of your daughter and Gladys Smilie.'

'Beg pardon, ladies.'

Rosina hooked her arm around his shoulders. He seemed to have shrunk inside his dressing robe, and she could not bear to see him looking so shamefaced. 'It's all right, Papa. We understand.'

Walter cleared his throat. 'I'm sure we all feel the same, but the damage to the *Ellie May* can be repaired. It's Caddie who needs our help right now.'

Higgins slapped him on the back. 'Well said, young Walter. We'll make certain that Artie Trigg is sent off in style.'

Rosina was powerless to put a stop to the enthusiastic arrangements that were being made for what threatened to be the grandest funeral since that of Prince Albert. Coins clinked into the cloth cap, but she could see that they were only coppers. A funeral would cost a great deal more than the money being raised in the whip-round. She sent a mute plea to Walter, but he raised his finger to his lips. It was not until everyone was filing out, refreshed and glowing from supping ale and brandy, that she had a chance to speak to him. 'What are we going to do?' she whispered. 'There's not enough there to pay for the coffin, let alone the funeral.'

Walter glanced at the plateful of pennies, halfpennies and farthings on the kitchen table with a rueful smile. 'You're right, but don't worry about it. I'll think of something. Artie will have his send-off, and Caddie will be proud of him.' He left the kitchen in the wake of Fred and Bob, who were more than a little inebriated, and being scolded by both Cotton and Higgins as they staggered out of the house.

Edward had fallen asleep with his head lolling to one side and his mouth open. Bertha covered him with a blanket. 'Best thing for him, if you ask me. How is Caddie?'

Rosina began picking up mugs and tumblers and putting them on a tray ready to take into the scullery to wash. 'She took it badly, of course.'

'A nice cup of tea will help,' Bertha said, placing the kettle on the hob. 'And you can tell Caddie that Artie will be brought here to lie in the parlour.'

'We have no money, Bebe. Walter told me that the cargo was ruined and the *Ellie May* is in need of major repairs. What's more, Caddie and the babies are homeless.'

Looking thoughtful, Bertha picked up the teapot. 'We can't turn them out on the street, that's for certain. It would mean the workhouse for Caddie and her nippers.'

'They could have the attic room, and I could help her look after the little ones.'

'When your pa gets back to his old self, he'll know what to do for the best. In the meantime, you go up and see how that poor girl is getting on. We'll leave the worrying to the men, while we get on with the work, as usual.'

That night, unable to sleep, Rosina sat on the window seat in her bedroom, gazing down at the badly damaged hull of the *Ellie May*. Walter had already made enquiries at Etheredge's barge repair yard in Limehouse, and even the rough estimate was terrifyingly high. There had been little else to be done that day. The undertaker had arrived to collect Artie's body, and, in the morning, he would be brought home in his coffin to lie in the parlour until the funeral. Walter had volunteered to make the necessary arrangements with the vicar, and Gladys had promised to help out with food for the wake. As she looked out of the window at the row of buildings strung together in higgledy-piggledy fashion, Rosina felt a surge of gratitude towards their neighbours, knowing that they would share their last crust and give their last penny to a friend who was in need. Caddie would not lack for moral support to get her through the first painful weeks of her widowhood. Her future might be uncertain, but at the moment she was sleeping with the aid of a generous dose of laudanum, obtained from the chemist with some of the money collected from the neighbours. The children had been worn out by all the excitement, and, knowing nothing of their father's fate, they had fallen asleep almost as soon as their heads touched the pillow.

Rosina shifted her position as painful cramps made her leg spasm. Walter had been so supportive, but she had seen little of Harry that day. It had been late in the afternoon when he had finally arrived at the house. He had spent some time in the counting house with Walter and then he had paid his respects to her papa. Harry had asked for his condolences to be passed on to Caddie, then he had kissed Rosina on the cheek and apologised for having to return to the office where he had urgent business. It had not been a very romantic meeting, and she couldn't help thinking that if he had really cared for her, there would be no business so urgent that it could have taken him from her side in a time of trouble.

Over supper, after Bertha had managed to persuade Edward to go to his bed, she had lectured Rosina on the advantages of accepting Harry's proposal. Once he was in the family, she had said, it would be in his interest to pay for the repairs to the *Ellie May*. After all, the vessel would come to Rosina one day, and with Harry's business sense, they might even have the beginnings of a fleet of sailing barges. He was a handsome young man, of good family – she would be a fool to turn down such an offer. And she owed it to her papa, since he was not in the best of health, and might be glad to swallow the anchor and live ashore.

The weight of responsibility was heavy on Rosina's shoulders. Until now she had been so carefree and life had seemed wonderful; now, suddenly, she felt as though everything was slipping away from her. The security that she had always known was threatened by dire circumstances. She had never seen her papa at such a low ebb, and if they could not afford the repairs on the barge, he would lose his business. They would be ruined. Maybe Bertha had been right, and she ought to accept Harry's proposal of marriage. Perhaps she had imagined herself to be in love with the mysterious pirate in whose arms she had felt so wonderfully alive. In those few magic hours she had experienced feelings that were exciting and thrilling, and also a little wicked. It could have been temporary insanity that had caused her to fall in love with a masked man about whom she knew nothing. It all seemed so far away at this moment – like a dream. But Harry was real, and Harry had said that he loved her and wanted to make her happy. If she accepted him Sukey would be upset, but she would get over it in time, and her mama would make certain that she was introduced to suitable young men.

Rosina leaned her hot forehead against the cool

windowpane. It was quite dark outside, except for the yellow pools of gaslight shining on the cobblestones and reflecting in oily puddles on the water below. What was that? She was suddenly alert, startled out of her reverie as she spotted a male figure emerging from the shadows. The man slid down the ladder onto the deck of the *Curlew*. Captain Barnum's vessel had returned soon after the *Ellie May*, apparently with very little visible damage. He had sent Barker with a message of condolence for Caddie, but there had been no admission of culpability or sympathy for what had happened to Pa's boat. Rosina held her breath. Was this the real pirate at work? She waited, uncertain as to what to do. Should she run outside and raise the alarm? There could be several of the robbers working in a gang, although there did appear to be only one. Straining her eyes, she peered into the gloom. She could just spot the odd movement on deck. She was certain now that the thief was working alone. If Papa had been well, she would have woken him. He would have known what to do. But he was far from well, and the pirate might move on to the *Ellie May* when he had done with Barnum's ship. Acting on impulse, she pulled her skirt over her nightgown and wrapped a shawl around her head and shoulders. She crept out of her room, taking care to miss the floorboard that creaked, and hurried downstairs, letting herself silently out of the house. Her intention was to raise Mr Cotton, the wharfinger, but to get to his house she would have to risk being seen in the light from the street lamp. She hesitated on the doorstep, clutching her shawl about her and shivering violently. Whether it was from the cool night breeze or simply fear, she did not know, but now she wished that she had stayed in the safety of her room. If only she were braver. Perhaps it would be better if she went back inside and closed the door. After all, what did it matter if the *Curlew* was stripped of all the expensive new items that Captain Barnum had bought to replace the stolen equipment? It would simply serve him right. She hesitated, torn between a longing for her nice warm bed and the fear that the pirate might rob the *Ellie May* of anything of value that had been left on board.

Steeling herself, she closed the door quietly behind her and crept out onto the pavement, keeping as much in the shadows as possible. The umbrella cranes loomed above her like leviathans constructed in wire and steel. Her heart was pounding so fast that she could hear the blood drumming in her ears. She had reached the circle of light. She must enter it or retreat. If she ran fast, she might make it unseen. She had to get to Mr Cotton's door in order to raise the alarm. She took a deep breath and ran. Her bare feet slipped on the cobblestones; she stumbled, twisting her ankle. She could not save herself and she landed spread-eagled on the ground. Temporarily winded, she lay there for a moment, gathering her wits and fighting for breath. She scrambled to her feet: there were only a few yards to go, but a sharp pain in her ankle made her falter. She could hear footsteps coming up behind her. She turned – too late. A hand clamped over her mouth as she opened it to scream.

'Don't be frightened. I won't hurt you.'

The deep, slightly gruff voice was achingly familiar and the tension leached out of her body. His arms were banded around her so that she could not turn round. If she had not recognised his voice, then the telltale fragrance of spices, cloves, lemon and Indian ink would have been enough to give him away. 'I'm taking my hand away,' he murmured. 'Don't cry out. You remember me, don't you, my beautiful rose?'

His beautiful rose! She felt tears of joy spring to her eyes. She nodded soundlessly and he took his hand from her mouth. She turned in the circle of his arms. 'I remember you, pirate.'

His eyes shone with golden lights behind the mask he wore, and he drew her into the shadows. 'You shouldn't be wandering about at this time of night. It's dangerous.'

'And you shouldn't be stealing from the boats of honest, hardworking river men.'

'Barnum is not in that category.'

'You know Captain Barnum?'

'I know that he ruins lives.'

Rosina pulled away from him. It was too dark to see his face clearly, and the mask made it virtually impossible to read his expression, but she was quick to hear the bitter note in his voice. This was no ordinary thief. Even if she had not known that before, she sensed it now. This was a man with a personal grudge against Captain Barnum. 'Who are you?' she demanded.

'I am a pirate. I told you that before.'

She was getting angry now. He was playing with her. 'Stop that! It was romantic and mysterious in Cremorne Gardens, but now you turn up quite literally on my doorstep. Who are you? And what has Captain Barnum done to make you hate him so?'

'One day I will tell you everything – but not now.'

'Why not now? I could raise the alarm and have you arrested. Give me one good reason why I should let you get away with acting like a common thief.'

He took her in his arms, holding her so tightly that she could hardly breathe. His lips were so close to hers that she could almost taste his kiss. She ought to struggle. She ought to slap his face. She ought to tell him that she was not one of those free and easy girls who allow men to take liberties with them. But she did none of those things. A shiver of pure pleasure ran up her spine as his hand caressed her hair. She parted her lips and closed her eyes. Nothing mattered at this moment: she did not care who he was, or why he had come here tonight. He was here and she was in his arms, being kissed fervently and passionately. She gave herself up to the delicious sensations that were rippling through her entire being. Her senses soared to the skies and she was weightless, floating in his arms and responding to his kisses with a passion that she could never have imagined. She wanted the moment to go on forever. But he drew away from her, tempering her loss with butterfly kisses on her lips, the tip of her nose, and on her forehead. 'You must go home,' he whispered. 'Go now, before the constable comes this way on his beat.'

Dazed, she stared up into his inscrutable face. 'H-how do you know so much of what goes on here? Where do you come from, pirate?'

'It doesn't matter. But you mustn't be seen with me, and I have to go now.'

He took her by the hand and led her back to her own house. Questions buzzed round in her head like a swarm of honey bees. They had met only once before and yet he knew where she lived. She must have told him during those magical moments when they were dancing together on the crystal platform, or perhaps on the way home in the stolen launch. She had thought then that he might be an actor from the theatre at Cremorne, or a performer from one of the many entertainment booths. Now she knew that he was a genuine pirate, a thief and a renegade, and yet she did not care. 'Must you go so soon?'

'I've stayed too long, my rose.'

'But we will meet again?'

He took her hand and kissed it. 'You must forget me, Rosina. I'm a phantom. I'm not real.'

'Oh, but you are real to me, pirate.' She clung to his hand, raising it to her cheek. 'I wish you would tell me your name.'

He shook his head. 'No, I cannot. Not yet.'

'But you will? One day I will know your name?'

'Just remember that there is someone who truly loves you. I can't reveal my identity to you, even though I would dearly love to tell you who I am. But, whatever happens, be sure that no matter what trouble may befall you, your pirate will not be far away. I cannot tell you more, but I love you, and I will always love you.'

'Oh! Y-you love me?' Rosina clasped her hands to her burning cheeks. He had said the words that she most wanted to hear, and she closed her eyes, barely able to contain her joy. 'And I love you too,' she whispered. But when she opened her eyes – no one was there. He was gone and she was alone.

# Chapter Nine

The news that Barnum's vessel had been robbed for a second time flew round Black Eagle Wharf like St Elmo's fire, but, as he was not generally liked, no one seemed to be sorry for him. Not only had the pirate stripped everything of value from the *Curlew*, but it was thought that he had poured lamp oil over the cargo, rendering it as worthless as the hay in the *Ellie May*'s hold. Edward knew nothing of this. His weakened constitution had made him vulnerable to infection, and he had succumbed to a recurrence of the lung fever. They could not afford to send for a doctor, and Bertha had taken it upon herself to nurse him back to health. She had soaked a blanket in a solution of Calvert's Carbolic Acid Disinfectant Powder and water, and hung it in front of the door to Edward's sickroom. This, she said, would prevent the spread of the sickness, and Rosina must not enter the room until her father was out of danger.

For two days and two nights Bertha had barely left the sickroom, but on the third morning she told Rosina that she had given the captain a dose of laudanum to make him sleep. His fever, she said, had abated enough to allow her to leave him for a while so that she could rest, but Rosina was still forbidden to enter his room. When she objected, Bertha pointed out that even if she was not afraid of catching the sickness herself, she might very well pass it on to Caddie and the children. When Bertha laid down the law, it was not to be flouted, and Rosina had to resign herself to doing as she was told and executing the mundane household chores. There was a pile of dirty linen in the scullery waiting to be taken out to the copper in the yard to be boiled clean, but she had only a hazy idea how to go about this, and so the pile had grown steadily higher. Rosina had never had to fend for herself, and Bertha had been adamant that young ladies did not need to learn even the most basic rules of cookery.

When the children had clamoured for breakfast, Rosina had been horrified to discover that the bread had gone mouldy, and the dripping had been used up: even the tasty brown bit at the bottom had been licked clean by a hungry Ronnie. There was nothing left in the larder other than a heel of cheese that the mice had nibbled, and a spoonful of tea that she had saved to make a brew when Bertha awakened from her nap. In the end, there was nothing she could do except take the boys to Gladys, who gave them food and invited them to stay and play with her own children. Rosina returned home determined to make sense of the housekeeping, a skill which had so far eluded her.

She listened outside her father's bedroom door, but his breathing was even, if a bit wheezy, and he seemed to be sleeping. She went up to the attic to check on Caddy, who was scarily silent now that the initial torrent of tears had stopped flowing. She lay in her bed, staring up at the ceiling while her restless fingers plucked at the coverlet. Poor Caddie. Rosina felt for her in her loss, and could think of little to comfort her, except to remind her that she needed to be strong for the sake of her children. The painful subject of the funeral had to be broached at some time, but perhaps not at this particular moment. Rosina did not know how to tell Caddie that her husband's coffin was resting in the parlour, and that the neighbours had been filing in to pay their respects. Walter had made all the arrangements for the interment, which was set for the next day. She would have to prepare Caddie for the ordeal, but one look at her ashen face and hollow cheeks convinced Rosina that it was best to leave it until the evening. She left the room, closing the door softly behind her.

Downstairs in the kitchen, she searched in the dresser for a bottle of ink, pen and paper. She sat at the table staring at the blank sheet on which she intended to write a shopping list. But the scent of the Indian ink brought back memories of the pirate, and she slipped into a daydream, reliving the last precious moment that they had shared. In spite of the circumstances, there had been a small part of her that had remained untouched by the tragic events of the past few days. It seemed to her as though she was leading a double life, and there was another and happier world, which she could enter at will. When she retreated into her memories of the gaslit fairyland that was Cremorne Gardens, she was deliriously happy dancing with her pirate; but sadness overcame her as she remembered her last meeting with him and their inevitable parting. The secure world that she had always known might be crumbling around her, but the dark man in the mask was constantly in her thoughts. The memory of his kisses lingered on her lips and in her heart. Would she ever see him again? She simply did not know. He had told her he loved her, and it was that thought that kept her going when everything about her seemed to be tumbling into chaos.

It was Walter who had been her silent saviour. She trusted him implicitly, never questioning his actions or making any demands on his time. She knew instinctively that he would do everything that was required of him, and more. Dear, reliable Walter. He was her rock, and as faithful as a much loved family dog – always there, and expecting nothing in return for his loyalty other than a kind word and a smile.

She came back to earth with a jolt. This was getting her nowhere and daydreaming would not put food on the table. She must not allow a recurrence of this morning's breakfast fiasco. The children needed proper food and so did Caddie if she was to regain her strength. She threw the pen down, rising to her feet. Taking the cocoa tin from the mantelshelf, she tipped the contents onto the table. She counted the pennies with a sinking heart: she had no idea how much it cost to buy food, candles, lamp oil and coal, but it was obvious that what few coins were there would not buy very much. She decided that she must pay a visit to the grocery emporium in Wapping Street. After all, it couldn't be too difficult to buy and prepare food. Bertha did it all the time. She took the wicker shopping basket from the scullery, put on her bonnet and gloves, and set off with a determined step.

Mr Hodge, the grocer, greeted her with a cheery smile. He was busy serving a customer, giving Rosina time to wander round the shop and examine the stock. When she was a child, she had been fascinated by the sacks filled with flour, sugar, rice, currants, raisins and potatoes, standing proud against the oak counter like a row of soldiers on guard duty. There were metal-lined tea chests that had come from Assam, Darjeeling and China, and boxes of broken biscuits exuding a tempting, sugary smell that mixed with the fragrance of tea, bacon and candle wax. The counter was stacked with round cheeses, slabs of yellow butter and legs of ham glistening with sugar and studded with cloves. Everything, including the tins, packets, jars and bottles on the shelves, was marked with the price. It was only then that she realised how little she could purchase and how much they needed.

Mr Hodge finished serving a plump matron with a pound of streaky bacon and a half-pound of cheddar cheese, and he turned his attention on Rosina. 'Good morning, Miss May. And how may I assist you today?'

'Um, I'd like a . . .' She glanced round at the goods displayed on the shelves behind the counter and a feeling of panic assailed her. What did one need to make a proper dinner? Everything was so expensive. She wished that she had paid more attention when out shopping with Bertha. 'I'd like a pound of wheatmeal biscuits, please. And two ounces of tea.' She thought hard, fingering the coins in her purse. 'And half a pound of bacon.' She pointed to the cheapest cut, which seemed to be mostly fat, but would probably be just as tasty as the more expensive kind. She watched nervously as Mr

Hodge weighed out the items and wrapped them in brown paper bags.

'Will that be all, Miss May?'

'Some potatoes, please.'

'How many pounds would you like?'

She had no idea. 'Er, ten.'

'Ten pounds of potatoes it is then.' Mr Hodge began tipping potatoes into the large brass bowl of the scales.

'No, I think I might not be able to carry all those. Perhaps half a dozen potatoes would be better.'

'Certainly.' The urbane smile on Mr Hodge's face did not falter as he tipped most of the potatoes back into the sack. 'And where is Miss Spinks today. Is she unwell?'

'No, she's quite well, thank you. I'm just doing the shopping for her.' She did not want the whole of Wapping to know their business. 'How much is that, Mr Hodge?'

She went home with an empty purse, and when she spread out her purchases on the kitchen table she realised that she had omitted to buy such staples as bread, butter and sugar. There had been no money left to buy candles and lamp oil, but she decided that she would think about it later. In the meantime, she needed to speak to Walter.

She found him in the counting house with his head bent over a ledger. He looked up when she entered the room, but there was a strained look about his eyes when he smiled at her. 'Good morning, Rosie.'

'Is it, Walter? Yes, I suppose it is a lovely day, but I've just been shopping in the High Street, and I really had no idea how much food costs. It's really shocking.'

His lips twitched. 'I'm sure no one would argue with that statement.'

'I need some more housekeeping money.'

'I'm afraid there is nothing left in the cash box.'

She stared at him in horror. 'Nothing? Oh, come, Walter. There must be something. We've never been that short of money before.'

'I've been going through the books, but things couldn't be worse.'

Rosina sat down as her legs went weak at the knees. 'Are you telling me that we're bankrupt, Walter?'

He set his pen down on the inkstand. 'It looks very like it. There are a few debts that I can call in, and there will be enough to settle the funeral expenses, but with the boat laid up and your papa ailing, there is no way that we can continue in business. I cannot commission the shipwright to make the necessary repairs to the *Ellie May* unless we can raise the funds to pay for it.'

'Oh, my goodness. What will we do?'

He rose to his feet. 'Don't look so worried. Leave it to me, and I'll see what I can do.'

Looking up into his earnest face, she was slightly reassured. 'I trust you, Walter. If anyone can save us, I know it will be you. And when Papa recovers his strength, things will be as they always were.'

'Be sure that they will,' Walter said, smiling. He took his cap from the peg behind the door, and put it on his head. 'I'll be back soon.'

'Thank you, Walter.'

He tipped his hat, but he was not smiling as he left the room. She heard the front door open, followed by the murmur of male voices, and just as she was about to leave the office, Harry entered. Before she could protest, he wrapped his arms around her and kissed her on the lips. 'My darling, how are you today?'

She pulled away from him. 'Harry, don't.'

'Don't what, my love? We're on the brink of announcing our engagement, so why can't I kiss my bride-to-be?'

'You presume too much. I haven't accepted your proposal. Besides which, my papa is ill in bed, and I really cannot think about anything as serious as marriage at the moment.'

'But, my darling.' Harry took her hand in his. 'Now is the perfect time for you to consider my proposal. Your father's business is ruined. I'm sorry to put it to you so bluntly, but he cannot trade with the *Ellie May* laid up and the repairs are going to be costly.'

'I know all that, Harry. I'm not a child. But my papa will find a way.'

'He's an old man, Rosie. Old and sick. I am young and healthy and, above all, I have the money to save the *Ellie May* and to keep your father in business. Just say the word and I will make funds available. You need never worry again.'

She did not doubt his sincerity, and once, not so very long ago, she had thought him charming and attractive, but her last encounter with the pirate had changed everything. She was fond of Harry, but to pledge her life to him was another matter, even if it meant that she would be able to save Papa's beloved boat and protect his livelihood. She gazed down at her small hand as it lay in his, and she remembered how it felt when the pirate held her thus. There was no comparison. But she might never see him again. Hadn't he warned her of that? She raised her eyes to meet Harry's expectant gaze. He was so confident that she would say yes. She attempted a smile; but she really wanted to cry. 'Will you give me a little more time to think about it?'

He raised her hand to his lips and kissed it. 'My darling girl, of course you may have more time, but please, don't keep me too long in suspense. I want to tell the world, and in particular my mama, that we are to be joined in matrimony.'

The mention of Mrs Gostellow sent a shiver

down Rosina's spine that was not at all pleasurable. 'She doesn't like me, Harry.'

'Of course she does. She thinks that you are delightful, and extremely pretty. Mama is certain that she can mould you into the perfect wife for an up and coming young man like me.'

Rosina closed her eyes, trying to blot out an image of Mrs Gostellow training her like a puppy-dog. 'Really?' she murmured weakly. 'How – splendid.'

'I can see that you are touched, my love. As any young girl would be when honoured with the attentions of a woman like my mama.' Harry kissed her lightly on her closed eyelids. 'It will be a union quite literally made in heaven, my pet. As soon as Captain May is well enough, I will ask him for your hand in marriage.'

Her eyes flew open. 'I haven't said yes.'

He touched the tip of her nose with his forefinger, smiling into her eyes. 'But you will, my sweet. I know you will. Even if you hated me, which I know you do not, you would not be so foolish as to pass up the opportunity to save your papa's business and make him a very happy man.'

'Would you really pay for the repairs to the *Ellie May*?'

'Of course I would.'

'And what about Captain Barnum? You seem to encourage him to compete with my papa.'

Harry shrugged his broad shoulders. 'That is good business, my dear.'

'Is it good business to abet two old men in a lifelong feud that is becoming dangerous in its intensity?'

'You worry too much, my darling. What happened on the river was an accident caused by the bad weather. I'm certain that Barnum would do nothing to endanger his own vessel.'

'But it was my papa's boat that was holed, Harry. And he was convinced that Captain Barnum was to blame.'

'My love, you must put all these thoughts out of your pretty little head. These are men's matters and should not concern you.'

She bit back an angry retort. 'You're forgetting that it is my business, Harry. One day the *Ellie May* will be mine.'

He laid his hand on hers. 'Ours, my love. As I've said before, when we're married, it will be ours.'

A vision of her life as Mrs Harry Gostellow flashed through her mind. She saw herself in the Gostellows' dark drawing room, working away at her embroidery under the eagle eye of her mother-in-law, while Harry and his father ran the company.

He raised her hand to his lips. 'Oh, my darling, I can see that the whole idea overwhelms you, but I can assure you that you will be a fitting wife for a Gostellow, and you will prove my mama wrong when she says that I ought to look higher for a bride.'

She snatched her hand away. 'Thank you, Harry. I'll remember that. Now, I really must go back to the kitchen. Gladys will be bringing the children home soon and I have the dinner to prepare.'

'What?' Harry frowned. 'No, this won't do at all, Rosie. Where is that servant woman? Cooking is her job, not yours.'

'Bebe is not a servant,' Rosina said indignantly. 'She is part of our family, and she is worn out with nursing my papa. And I can cook, or at least I will have a good try at it, so there.' She brushed past him and walked out of the office, not caring if he took offence at her abrupt departure. How dare he call her beloved Bebe a servant? She went into the kitchen and slammed the door. If he followed her now, she would give him a piece of her mind that he would not soon forget. But she heard the front door close with an emphatic bang, and she guessed that he had gone off in a mood like a sulky schoolboy. She shrugged her shoulders and set about peeling potatoes – at least she knew how to do that. Having put the saucepan on the range, she went outside into the yard intending to light the fire under the copper. But the kindling was damp and she was having difficulty in using the old-fashioned tinderbox.

She had used the last of the vestas to coax the fire in the kitchen range into life this morning. That was another item which she had omitted from her shopping list. She stood back, wiping her damp forehead on the back of her hand. Who would have thought that it was so difficult to light a fire? She sniffed the air – something was burning. The acrid smell was coming from the house. She ran through the scullery into the kitchen. The air was blue with smoke and there were hissing noises coming from the pan on the range. She covered her mouth with her hand, and with streaming eyes made her way to the range. The pan had boiled dry and the potatoes were reduced to a black smelly mess in the bottom; when she tried to lift it she burned her fingers on the handle. She let it go with a yelp of pain and the saucepan fell to the ground. Tears ran down her cheeks as she surveyed the damage to the pan, and the mess of scorched potato that had splattered all over the flagstones.

She had not heard the door open, and she turned with a start at the sound of Bertha's voice. 'Gawd almighty! What have you done, girl?'

'I was trying to make dinner, but it all went wrong.' Rosina sank down on a chair, covering her face with her hands.

Walter had followed Bertha into the room. He took a cloth from the table and stooped down to retrieve the smoking saucepan. 'There's not much damage done.' He hurried through to the scullery and Rosina heard the hiss of cold water hitting the hot metal.

'Pans cost money,' Bertha said crossly. 'And what's all this?' She snatched up the bag of biscuits and poked her finger into the fatty bacon. 'Did you waste our last few pennies on this rubbish, Rosina May?'

Tears spilled from her eyes and Rosina nodded wordlessly. 'I was going to cook dinner.'

'What sort of meal would you make out of biscuits and fat bacon? I thought you had more sense.' Bertha pushed the food away with a disdainful snort. 'I can't leave you on your own for one moment.'

'I'd say that she was trying her best.' Walter came back into the room empty-handed. 'I'm afraid the pan is ruined, but it's not the end of the world. And if you've never taught her how to do things, how can you expect her to manage on her own?'

Bertha puffed out her chest and her cheeks flushed wine red. 'Don't you speak to me like that, young man. I've brought Rosie up since she was a baby, and I don't need you telling me what I should or shouldn't do.'

'I'm sorry if it offends you, Miss Spinks, but I'd say that you're not being fair to her.'

Rosina leapt to her feet. 'Stop it, both of you. I've made a terrible hash of things and it's all my fault. Now we've no food and no money either. Tell me off if you want to, Bebe, but I was just trying to do my best.'

Bertha's face crumpled and she flung her arms around Rosina. 'Oh, my pet. I'm sorry. I'm just tired and I shouldn't have spoken to you like that. Walter is quite right.'

'I'm pleased to hear you say so,' Walter said, grinning. 'Was that an apology, Miss Spinks?'

'Certainly not.' Bertha tossed her head. 'I got nothing to apologise for.'

'How is Papa?' Rosina asked, changing the subject. 'Is he any better?'

'I've done all I can, ducks. I think he's on the mend, but he could do with seeing the doctor.'

'There's no money left,' Rosina said, shaking her head. 'None at all.'

'Not quite.' Walter took a leather pouch from his inside coat pocket and placed it on the table. 'There is enough there to pay the doctor, and also the funeral expenses.'

Bertha picked up the pouch, weighing it in her hand. She raised her eyebrows, staring at Walter. 'This feels like a lot of money. Where would you get so much?'

'Bebe! That sounds so ungrateful.' Rosina linked her hand through Walter's arm. 'Well done, my good friend. I know that I can always rely on you, Walter.'

'I hope so, Rosie.'

'Rosie? Remember your place, young man. It's Miss Rosina to you.'

Bertha's voice was severe, but Rosina saw that she was smiling, and she allowed herself to relax. 'I'd say it doesn't matter where the money came from. Perhaps we could use some of it to buy proper food, Bebe?'

'Yes, indeed. But I'll tell you what to buy this time. And you can take Walter with you to make sure that you don't spend it on chocolate or iced buns.'

'May I see Papa first?' Rosina clasped her hands together, casting a pleading look at Bertha. 'May I? Please.'

Bertha nodded her head. 'All right, but if he's asleep, don't wake him. And don't get too near the bed.' She turned to Walter. 'And you, young man. Go and fetch Dr Wilkinson. He can see young Caddie while he's about it, and maybe give her some tonic that will set her back on her feet. It's not good for a young woman to turn her face to the wall. I've known some do that and simply fade away.'

Dr Wilkinson came and was full of praise for Bertha's nursing. He prescribed a restorative draught for Caddie and lung tonic for Edward, together with rest and quiet. Peace of mind and a good diet were necessary, he said, for the recuperation of invalids who had suffered from lung fever. The captain must be kept quiet and not troubled with business matters until he was fully recovered. Furthermore, a fresh egg whipped up in sherry might be beneficial, and would tempt a jaded appetite. The doctor refused a cup of tea, but accepted his fee, and went on his way.

'Whatever we do,' Bertha said, nodding her head wisely, 'we must not let your papa attend the funeral. You heard what the doctor said, Rosie. Your papa must not be excited in any way.'

It seemed that the whole of Black Eagle Wharf, and many people from the wharves in the Upper Pool, had crowded into St John's church on the corner of Bird Street and Green Bank. Caddie was supported on one side by Walter and on the other by Rosina. Gladys had stayed at home to look after the children, but the shopkeepers, dock workers, sailmakers and other tradesmen had all closed down for an hour or so out of respect for Arthur Trigg. To her surprise, Rosina saw Sukey and Mrs Barnum sitting in the front pew, together with Mary and Lillian. She had not expected them to come, but at least Captain Barnum had had the good grace to stay away. She stifled a sigh of relief: it was going to be difficult today, what with poor Caddie still very weak and only having risen from her sickbed to attend the funeral. Then there was Papa, who had insisted on coming, even though the doctor had told him not to exert himself for a while at least. She had tried her best to persuade him to stay in bed, but Papa was stubborn at the best of times and he had dragged himself to the church, even though it was obvious to all that he was far from well. He had said that Artie was his shipmate and he would pay his last respects to him, even if he was to die in the attempt. Rosina was secretly afraid that this might turn into fact, but she said nothing. Once Papa had made his mind up, nothing would deflect him from his course. She slipped her arm through his as they sat side by side in the pew opposite Mrs Barnum and her daughters. She was proud of the fact that Papa had acknowledged Mrs Barnum with a curt nod; at least he was gentlemanly enough not to blame her for her husband's ill doings.

Hearing slow, measured footsteps, she turned her head to see the coffin being carried up the aisle by the pall-bearers. Rosina's hand flew to her mouth and she gasped in horror as she realised that one of them was Captain Barnum. Her fingers closed on her father's arm. She prayed silently that he would not say anything, but he was staring straight ahead. She caught Walter's eye and saw that he too was looking anxious. She bit her lip, willing the pall-bearers to place the coffin on the bier and make their solemn retreat before her papa had spotted his old enemy. Bertha was sitting on Edward's right, and up until this moment she had been quietly mopping her eyes, but Rosina's worst fears were realised when she sat bolt upright, staring at Barnum who was about to make his way to his seat next to his wife. Bertha leaned across Rosina to nudge Edward. 'Look who's here.'

Edward looked at Barnum – looked away – and then stared at him as if he could not believe his eyes. He leapt to his feet, pointing a shaking finger. 'You! May God strike you down for this act of blasphemy, you villain.'

Rosina tugged at his arm. 'Papa, please sit down.'

'Leave me be, child.' Edward shook her hand off, and he made his way to the end of the pew, staggering slightly, but seeming to gain strength from his anger. 'You killed that young man as surely as if you had shot him through the heart, Ham Barnum.'

Barnum faced him angrily. 'Keep quiet, old man. This is a holy place.'

'And you desecrate it with your presence.' Edward swayed on his feet, and he clutched the carved end of the pew for support. 'Get out now.'

The vicar hurried towards them, his surplice flapping like the wings of an agitated seagull. 'Gentlemen, please. This is neither the time nor the place. Please remember where you are.'

Caddie rose to her feet, trembling visibly. 'Is it true, Captain Barnum? Did you kill my Artie?

Did you leave me widowed with three babies to bring up on me own?'

'Certainly not.' Barnum went red in the face, running his finger round the inside of his shirt collar. 'This old man is deranged by the fever. He doesn't know what he is saying.'

A murmur of consternation rippled through the congregation. Moving to Edward's side, Walter laid his hand on his arm. 'Please, Captain May. Calm yourself, sir. This is not doing anyone any good.'

Edward's eyes blazed angrily and he pushed Walter away. 'It's none of your business, Brown. This reprobate has much to answer for. And I won't have him casting a shadow over the funeral of a good man who would still be alive today if it weren't for his lack of seamanship.'

'What?' Barnum's voice thundered around the vaulted ceiling, echoing like the voice of doom. 'Say that again, and I'll forget that I'm in the house of God.'

'I'd say you've both forgotten where you are, and what a solemn occasion this is.' The vicar placed his arm around Caddie's shaking shoulders. 'Think of this poor young woman, gentlemen. If you are not God-fearing men, then at least think of how you would feel if she was your daughter.'

'Don't bring my family into this, Reverend.' Barnum turned his back on the vicar and he caught Edward by the lapels of his jacket. 'Sit down, you old fool. Sit down and shut up.'

Edward brought his fists up, breaking Barnum's grip, and if Walter had not seen it coming and grabbed his right arm, he would no doubt have landed a well-aimed punch on Barnum's florid nose.

'Papa, please.' Rosina clutched his other arm, as pandemonium broke loose in the church. The men, who had been sitting in shocked silence, suddenly rose to their feet in one body. As if by general consensus, they divided into two factions, each one surrounding the angry captains, and they carted them unceremoniously down the aisle and out of the church. Rosina would have followed them, but Caddie collapsed in her arms, swooning. Bertha slithered to the end of the pew and produced a vinaigrette from her reticule, which she wafted under Caddie's nose.

'Please, Walter,' Rosina said urgently. 'Go and make sure that my papa is all right. He's still weak as a kitten from the fever.'

'Weak as a lion,' Bertha said proudly. 'He's a match for old Barnum any day.'

Walter glanced anxiously at the vicar. 'Will you carry on without them, Reverend?'

'I think we must. I have a wedding at midday, and a christening at one o'clock.'

Walter strode off down the aisle and the vicar went to stand by the coffin, clearing his throat. 'Dearly beloved . . .'

'Well, I'm not staying if my husband is not welcome in the house of God.' Mrs Barnum rose to her feet, and the stuffed bird on her over-decorated hat wobbled as if it were about to fly away. 'Come, girls. We won't stay where we are not wanted.'

Mary and Lillian jumped up, seemingly only too eager to follow their mother out of the church, but Sukey stopped by Rosina with an apologetic smile. 'This is a poor show, Rosie. I am so sorry.'

'And I too,' Rosina whispered. 'We mustn't let this come between us, Sukey.'

'Sukey Barnum.' Mrs Barnum's stentorian voice echoed round the church. 'Come away from that person. We are not speaking to the May family from this day forward.'

'Sorry,' Sukey murmured, putting her head down as she hurried to join her mother and sisters.

Caddie buried her face in her hands, sobbing loudly.

'Do you wish me to continue, ma'am?' The vicar drummed his fingers on the coffin lid as he looked at the empty pews. 'In the circumstances, maybe . . .'

Rosina could see that Caddie was close to hysteria and complete collapse. Anger roiled in her stomach. Papa and Captain Barnum were behaving like horrible, spoilt children. She gave

Caddie into Bertha's arms and she stormed down the aisle and out into the hot June sunshine. The scene outside made her even angrier. Walter was standing in between her papa and Captain Barnum, doing his best to keep them from attacking each other, but the rest of the men had formed a circle and were actually egging them on to fight. 'How could you?' she cried. 'Hasn't poor Caddie suffered enough, without grown men acting like children? Get back inside, all of you, this minute. Papa, I'm ashamed of you. And you too, Captain Barnum. Have you no respect for the dead?'

# Chapter Ten

Shamefaced and muttering their apologies, the men shuffled back into the cool interior of the church.

Ham Barnum adjusted his necktie, glowering at Edward. 'We'll sort this out at a later date, old man. But don't think I'll forget this insult.'

'I only spoke the truth.' Edward leaned heavily on Walter's arm. 'I'll get you one day, Barnum.'

'Ham, come away from that wretched man.' Mrs Barnum shooed her daughters into a waiting hackney carriage. 'I won't stay in this place a moment longer. And I'll have words to say to you when we get home, sir.'

'That's right, Barnum,' Edward jeered. 'Petticoat rule, old man.'

Scowling, Barnum silently followed his wife into the carriage and slammed the door.

'And I meant what I said, Papa.' Rosina took him by his other arm. 'That was a disgraceful show. You must apologise to poor Caddie.'

'I will, poppet. But I'll get that brute if it's the last thing I do.'

'And that's just what it will be if you don't stop fighting him, Papa.'

The altercation with Barnum seemed to have breathed new life into Edward. Despite his constant coughing and breathlessness, his recovery from the bout of fever was rapid. There was a martial gleam in his eyes, and a purpose in his step as he set about trying to raise the money to repair the *Ellie May*. Accompanied by Walter, he went out every morning, returning later in the day in such a state of exhaustion that he had to go to his room to rest. Bertha nagged him incessantly, arguing that a wooden box would be his next mode of transport if he did not take things more easily, and Rosina begged him to heed Bertha's good advice, but Edward was stubborn and refused to listen. He seemed to be obsessed by two ambitions, the first being the repairs to his beloved barge, and the second to get even with Captain Barnum. Rosina was powerless to do anything, even though she longed to be able to help. She had tried to see Sukey, hoping that between them they could persuade Captain Barnum to put an end to the feud, but her efforts had been in vain. When Gertie answered the door, she had been ruder than ever, and she seemed to take malicious delight in sending Rosina away, informing her that it was 'The missis's orders – no vagrants, no tradesmen and definitely no Mays to be allowed in.'

Rosina had to leave without seeing Sukey, and there seemed no way of contacting her. She hoped she might come across her when out walking, but, when she did see her, Sukey was always accompanied either by her mother or her sisters. The feud between their two fathers was now affecting both families and its continuance upset Rosina greatly. Bertha was as implacable in her attitude as Edward, and ready to range herself against the whole Barnum household. Rosina knew she could expect no sympathy from that quarter. It was Caddie who comforted her, saying that Mrs Barnum was not a bad sort when she forgot to stick her nose in the air and pretend to be better than she was. She was certain that Mrs Barnum would relent when she realised that she was making Sukey unhappy. Rosina was doubtful, but she was also relieved to see that Caddie was slowly recovering from the initial shock of her bereavement. Although, sometimes, in the night when she awakened in the middle of a dream about her pirate, Rosina could hear muffled sobs coming from the attic room. Her heart went out to poor Caddie in her grief, but she knew that only time would heal the terrible wound caused by Artie's untimely death. At least Caddie had gained enough physical strength to have baby Arthur back in her keeping.

Two weeks after Artie's funeral, Rosina sat in the chair by the range, cradling the sleeping baby in her arms, while she watched over Ronnie and Alfie eating their bread and scrape. Caddie was outside in the yard doing the washing, and Bertha was upstairs cleaning the parlour. Papa had gone to the bank in a last attempt to effect a loan and Walter was also out of the office. She would not have blamed him if he had looked for work elsewhere – with the best will in the world, he could not be expected to exist without pay. She knew that Walter had no close family, but she wondered if he had friends who were helping him out financially. She knew so little about his private life, and almost nothing about his past.

She rubbed her cheek against Arthur's downy head, inhaling the delicious baby smell of him. He was so small and helpless; Ronnie and Alfie were equally vulnerable and in need of protection. There were so many people who were relying on Papa and his ability to resume trading on the river. If he could not do so, then the future looked bleak for all of them. She was painfully aware that Caddie's greatest fear was of being forced to go into the workhouse. Rosina was determined that as long as she had a breath left in her body that would never happen, but it was becoming more and more difficult to be positive.

The money that Walter had secured, presumably from unpaid debts, had long since run out and their only income was obtained by pawning their belongings. The first thing to go was the clock from the mantelshelf above the kitchen range. The pair of Staffordshire dogs from the parlour had been next; Papa had been upset to see them go because they had been a wedding present, but the cash had paid for coal and candles. The picture of Highland cattle had fetched enough to pay the butcher for beef bones for soup, and a sack of potatoes. The pewter candlesticks had paid for a small bag of coal, and bread and milk for the children; if there was to be any supper tonight, she must find something else of value to take to the pawnbroker's shop.

'I want more,' Ronnie said, eyeing the crust that Alfie was chewing. 'I'm hungry.'

Rosina's stomach was rumbling; she had given her slice of bread to the children. 'Drink your milk, Ronnie. Then you and Alfie can go out in the yard and play with that India-rubber ball that Walter gave you.'

Alfie stuffed the last piece of bread into his mouth and clambered down from his chair. 'Play ball, Ronnie.'

Arthur opened his blue eyes and Rosina hitched him over her shoulder, patting his back. She rose to her feet. 'Out you go, boys. Go and find Mamma.' She opened the door and shooed them out through the scullery into the back yard.

Caddie peered at her through a cloud of steam that was billowing from the bubbling copper.

She smiled as her sons darted past her in a race to get the ball. 'They're growing so fast, Rosie. Ronnie will soon be out of petticoats, although I dunno where I'm going to get the money to buy him new clothes.'

'We'll worry about that when the times comes,' Rosina said with more confidence than she was feeling.

'He's asleep, the little lamb,' Caddie said, smiling fondly at the sleeping baby. 'It's ever so good of you to help me with the nippers. I'm sure you got better things to do than to mind someone else's baby.'

'He's a little darling, and I love him, but I do have a few things to attend to.'

'Of course you do. Put baby in his bed. He should sleep for an hour or two and I'll listen out for him.'

Rosina carried Arthur back into the house and was about to mount the stairs when the front door opened. She spun round, hoping to see her father, but it was Walter who entered. He came towards her, taking off his cap, and an appreciative smile lit his eyes. 'You look so comfortable with a baby in your arms, Rosie.'

'Comfortable isn't the word I would have used, Walter. I think young Arthur needs changing. He's a bit damp.'

'Let me take him.'

'You? What do you know about babies?'

'Not very much, but I like the little chaps.' He took Arthur from her and cradled him in the crook of his arm. 'See! Nothing to it.'

'You wait until he opens his mouth to cry.'

'Then I will hand him back to you immediately. Where do you want me to put this young fellow?'

'I was taking him to Caddie's room to put him down for a nap.' She held out her arms. 'Shall I take him now?'

'No. Let me carry him upstairs.'

'Walter, I didn't know that you were so domesticated.'

'There are a lot of things about me that you don't know.' He mounted the stairs.

She was about to follow him when Edward entered the house, slamming the door behind him. 'Papa?' She hesitated, glancing up at Walter.

'It's all right, Rosie,' he replied in answer to her unspoken question. 'I think I can manage to make this chap more comfortable and put him to bed.'

She went slowly towards her father. 'Papa?'

Edward shook his head. 'The old fool of a bank manager wouldn't listen to me. He was polite enough, but he said he wasn't in the shipping business, and he inferred that I was past me prime, the cheeky bastard – begging your pardon, poppet.'

She kissed him on his whiskery cheek. 'Go

upstairs to the parlour, Papa. I'll bring you a nice cup of tea.'

'I need something stronger than tea.'

Rosina said nothing. She knew that the last drop of brandy had been drunk after the funeral. She watched her father as he climbed slowly up the stairs. His shoulders drooped and he had the look of a beaten man. She bit back the tears that stung her eyelids, and she went into the kitchen to make a pot of tea. The tea leaves had been used so many times that they were almost transparent, the children had drunk the last of the milk for breakfast, and there was no sugar. At least the coal had lasted long enough to keep the kettle simmering. She made a brew and was pouring the straw-coloured liquid into a mug when Bertha bustled into the kitchen.

'What's going on, Rosie? I was cleaning your room when I heard footsteps on the stairs. And blow me, if it wasn't young Walter going up to Caddie's room with the babe in his arms.'

'Papa came home just as I was taking Arthur upstairs for his nap and Walter offered to take him for me.'

Bertha puffed her cheeks out. 'Well, it ain't proper for a young man to go into a woman's bedroom. I'll have words to say to Walter when he comes back downstairs.'

'Oh, please, Bebe. Leave Walter alone. He's been so good to us through all our troubles.'

'Huh!' Bertha picked up the teapot. 'Men are all the same if you ask me.'

Rosina did not ask her. She hurried out of the kitchen with the mug in her hand, and went upstairs to the parlour.

Edward was sitting on the window seat, staring down at the bustling activity of Black Eagle Wharf. He turned his head as she entered the room. 'It's no use, Rosie, dear. I have to be honest with you. I don't see any way out but to sell the old girl.'

'But that's terrible, Papa. You can't even think of selling the *Ellie May*.' Rosina deposited the mug on the table and went to sit by his side. She took his hand in hers: it felt unnaturally cold and clammy. 'Don't upset yourself, Papa. I'm certain there must be another way.'

'That old girl is part of me, Rosie. To sell her will be like cutting off my own arm, but I can't let her disintegrate into a hulk.'

'Are things so bad? Surely there must be someone who could lend you the money?'

'I've exhausted every avenue, poppet. It's sell the *Ellie May* or face bankruptcy.'

Rosina gazed out of the window at the stricken vessel moored alongside the wharf. She could see Captain Barnum on board the *Curlew* and Barker making ready to sail. Harry was there too and he looked up, as if he sensed that she was watching him. He waved and smiled. Now he was heading this way. She looked at her father, who seemed to have shrunk to half his normal size since his illness. He had almost certainly lost weight, and his complexion was unnaturally pale for a man who had spent most of his life braving the elements. She could not bear to see him suffering so, even though he was putting a brave face on things. There was one solution and one alone. The fate of the *Ellie May*, of Papa and Bertha, of Caddie and her babies, and even Walter, was in her own small hands.

She rose to her feet, dropping a kiss on her father's lined forehead. 'Don't worry, Papa. Things will turn out well, you'll see.' Picking up her skirts, she ran downstairs to open the door to Harry.

'My dear, you look ravishing as usual.' He doffed his hat and the sun glinted with coppery lights on his dark auburn hair. 'Absolutely stunning, in fact.'

'You are such a flatterer, Harry.'

Hand on heart, he smiled. 'I only speak the truth. Do I dare hope that you wanted to see me?'

She glanced over her shoulder. Caddie and the children were still outside in the yard, but now Bertha was sitting in the kitchen like a big fat spider in its web, just waiting to grab her and make her tell everything. She knew that she really ought to fetch her bonnet from the kitchen, but if she did that Bertha would want to know where she was going, and why. She stepped outside and tucked her hand in the crook of his arm. 'Will you walk with me, Harry? I have something to say to you.'

'Of course, my darling. Anything you wish.'

She glanced upwards, knowing instinctively that Walter would be standing in the attic room, looking out of the window. He shook his head and held his hands out to her as if begging her not to proceed with her intention. As always, he seemed to know what was in her heart and her head. She looked away, ignoring his unspoken plea. 'Let's walk this way,' she said, pointing in the direction of Union Stairs. She did not want to have the whole of Black Eagle Wharf watching them when she told Harry that she would marry him.

When they reached the top of Union Stairs Harry stopped, turning to her and taking both her hands in his. 'Well, then, my love. Are you going to put me out of my misery?'

She could not meet his intense gaze and she stared down at the oily brown water lapping at the steps. Fronds of green slime clung to the stones, and pieces of flotsam danced on the surface of the water. The air was heavy with the stench of boiling animal bones and hooves from the glue factory, and the choking acetic smell from the brewery downriver, where vinegar was being produced by the barrel. A couple of mudlarks were wading knee deep, stooping now and then to snatch up lumps of blue-black coal and dropping them into rush baskets slung round their skinny necks. She felt a gentle pressure on her fingers as Harry squeezed her hands. 'My love? Don't keep me in suspense.'

She raised her eyes to his face. 'Do you still want to marry me, Harry?'

'More than anything in the whole world, my darling.'

He seemed so sincere, so solid and reassuring. The future of those dearest to her depended on her answer. 'Then I accept.'

Careless of the men working on the docks, the crane drivers leaning out of their cabs, and the mudlarks who were whistling and shouting words of encouragement, Harry seized her in his arms and claimed her lips in a fervent kiss. 'Oh, my darling,' he whispered, holding her so close that she could scarcely breathe. 'You've made me the happiest man in Wapping. No, the happiest man in the whole of London.'

He took off his hat and tossed it up in the air, catching it with a deft movement, but still managing to keep one arm round her waist. 'Hurrah!'

'Give her a smacker, guv,' one of the mudlarks shouted.

Harry laughed and put his hand in his pocket. He pulled out a handful of coins and tossed them into the river. The two boys dived beneath the water liked a pair of cormorants and came up, coughing and spluttering.

'Really, Harry,' Rosina said, feeling a blush rise to her cheeks as the men on the quay wall shouted encouragements to him. 'You're embarrassing me.'

He kissed her again to a round of applause from the onlookers. 'I want the whole world to know that you have agreed to be mine at last, Rosie.'

'I – I thought perhaps we could keep it a secret for now.'

'What? I've never heard such a nonsensical idea. Why would we need to keep our love a secret?'

She started walking in the direction of home and Harry lengthened his stride in order to keep up with her. 'Darling, have I said something to upset you? I didn't mean to – it's just that I'm so happy. Do stop, Rosina. Tell me what's bothering you.'

She did not stop, but she slowed down a little. 'I'm sorry, Harry. You haven't upset me. It's just that I – I'm afraid of what people might say if we announce our engagement too soon.'

'Bother what people say. I don't give a tinker's cuss what people say, except my mama, of course. Father will be delighted that I've had the sense to pick such a jewel of a girl, and he's shrewd enough to realise that we will all benefit from the union.'

'You make it sound like a business deal.'

'You're the one who thinks that people will say you married me for my money, my pet.'

'I didn't say that.'

'My darling, you are as transparent as a pane of glass. You think they will say that you married me in order to get the wretched boat repaired. Well, I say let them talk. I'm marrying you because I adore you and I hope that you feel the same way about me.' He drew her into a doorway, holding her hands and looking deeply into her eyes. 'Do you love me, Rosie?'

She was trapped. She could neither break away from him, nor could she admit that her heart belonged well and truly to another. His eyes pleaded with her to tell him what he wanted to hear. She recalled the warm feelings that she had for him before she had fallen under the spell of the pirate. She could have loved him well enough if she had not met the man who haunted her waking thoughts and her dreams. Harry could be such a dear when he was not being patronising, controlling and utterly bossy. At this moment he looked like an eager child, and she would not have hurt him for the whole world. She reached up and brushed his lips with a kiss. 'Need you ask? You silly boy.'

He drew her into his arms and kissed her long and hard, seemingly more than satisfied with her answer. 'Now we will go and see your papa,

Rosie. I will ask him formally for your hand in marriage. And, this afternoon, I will make arrangements for the boat to be taken downriver to Etheredge's wharf, where it will be repaired in the shortest possible time.'

'Are you sure you want to do this, Harry? I don't want you to feel that repairing the *Ellie May* is a condition for my accepting your proposal.'

He kissed her again. 'Silly goose. I don't think that for one moment. Put your mind at rest, my love. I intend to build my own business empire and the *Ellie May* is just the beginning. We will soon have a fleet of barges to transport hay to the city. We will feed all the horses in London, and fill all the palliasses in the workhouse. One day, my angel, we will be rich.' He slipped his arm around her waist. 'We'll go and see your father now, and I will beg him for your hand in marriage – on bended knee, if necessary.'

Edward stared at Harry as he listened to his impassioned request for his daughter's hand in marriage, and then his face slowly creased into a smile. 'Well, blow me down. This is a splendid surprise. Of course I'll give you my blessing, Harry. My dearest wish is to see my Rosie happily married to a fine young man like yourself. You couldn't have pleased me more.' He took Harry's outstretched hand and shook it vigorously, pumping it up and down until he was breathless. He sank back onto the window seat, breathing heavily.

'Are you all right, sir?' Harry asked anxiously.

'Papa, you must not overdo things.' Rosina knelt down at his side. 'Remember what the doctor said.'

Gasping for breath and laughing at the same time, Edward patted her on the head. 'My dear girl, give your old father a hug and a kiss. I'm so happy for you.'

Rosina did as he asked. It filled her heart with joy to see him so pleased with their announcement. She knew then that she had done the right thing. Marrying Harry was the only way to look after those whom she loved best in the world: well, not quite all those she loved, but to fall for a man in a mask must count as a childish dream. She was a grown-up now, and, as the Bible said, she must put away childish things. She would have a husband who loved her and a new family to learn to love. Her optimism faltered as she pictured Mrs Gostellow's hawk-nosed beauty, cold as a marble statue. It might be a bit more difficult to grow to love her, but she would do her very best.

Harry helped her to her feet, kissing her on the lips, even though her papa was in the room. 'The first thing we will do, when I've seen to the business matters, is to find a jeweller's shop and I'll buy you a diamond ring. You shall have the biggest and the best ring in all Hatton Garden, my love.'

'Of course she should,' Edward said, beaming. 'My girl deserves only the best. I'll not argue with that, Harry.'

'I hate to leave you at this propitious moment in our lives, my angel,' Harry said, kissing Rosina's hand, 'but I must go back to the office now. I need to talk money with my father, who keeps a rather tight hold on the purse strings, but I'm sure I won't have any trouble in persuading him to finance the repairs to our boat.'

'But I thought that was all settled?' Rosina stared at him, appalled. It had never occurred to her that Harry's father might not agree to his plan.

'As good as, my darling.' Harry kissed her on the tip of her nose. 'It's man's talk, and you mustn't bother your beautiful head with sordid money matters.'

'Quite right,' Edward said, nodding in agreement. 'I have every faith in you, my boy.'

Harry smiled as he picked up his top hat and kid gloves. 'I'll go now, but I'll return as soon as I can.' He was about to leave the room, but he paused in the doorway. 'There's just one thing though, Captain. If we're to merge the businesses, we won't be needing the services of your clerk, Brown. Have I your permission to tell him so?'

'But that's not fair,' Rosina cried. 'You can't do that to Walter. He's a good and loyal employee.'

'My love, this is between the captain and me. It's not personal, it's just business.' Harry strolled over to Edward, lowering his voice. 'Have I your permission to give him notice, sir?'

'No,' Rosina cried. 'I won't allow it. Walter has stood by us throughout our troubles. Why, if it hadn't been for him calling in some debts, we wouldn't even have been able to afford Artie's funeral.'

'Debts?' Edward raised his eyebrows so that they almost disappeared into his hairline. 'What debts? I don't recall that we were owed any money.'

'I – I don't know. He didn't say.'

Harry patted her hand. 'I daresay you misunderstood him, my love.'

'I did not misunderstand him.' Rosina stamped her foot. They were both regarding her with affection and amusement, as if she were a precocious child who had interrupted an adult conversation.

'There were no outstanding debts,' Edward reiterated patiently.

'And if there were no debts to be collected,' Harry said, frowning, 'the question is – how did the fellow come by such a large amount of money? Could it be that he has been feathering his own nest all these years, Captain? Have you ever checked the accounts, sir?'

'That is monstrous.' Rosina stared at him aghast. 'Harry, how can you accuse Walter of dishonesty?'

'My darling, I did not. I merely suggested that it might behove your papa to look into his business matters a little more closely.' Harry turned to Edward with an urbane smile. 'Or perhaps you would like me to do it for you, Captain?'

'Papa!' Rosina held her hands out to him. 'This is madness.'

Edward tugged at his beard and the frown lines deepened on his forehead. 'I trusted Walter implicitly. Perhaps I should have been more particular when it came to checking his work.'

'It would have been so easy for a person in his position of trust to alter a set of figures here and there, and to keep back monies for himself.' Harry folded his arms across his chest, eyeing Edward severely. 'I think we both know what has been going on, sir. Have I your permission to sack the scoundrel?'

'No, Papa. Please think again,' Rosina cried in desperation. 'At least give Walter a chance to defend himself.'

'You are too generous, Rosie. You have your mother's loving and trusting nature, and therefore you are very easily taken in by an unscrupulous rogue.' Edward pushed her away gently. His breathing was becoming laboured, and he clutched his throat.

'Papa, are you unwell?' Alarmed by his sudden pallor, Rosina laid her hand on his shoulder. 'Shall I fetch the doctor?'

'He needs rest, my love.' Harry said calmly. 'Don't worry, sir. Leave everything to me.'

Rosina cast him a furious glance. 'You take too much on yourself, Harry. Papa hasn't agreed to this injustice.' She turned back to her father. 'Please, Papa. Don't allow this to happen. Let Walter speak for himself before you judge him so unfairly.'

Edward rose slowly to his feet. 'Hush, daughter. You don't know what you're talking about. This is men's business, and I've been a fool, taken in by young Walter's pleasant manner and quiet ways. I took him on out of the goodness of my heart, knowing nothing of his background, and asking no questions. This is how he's repaid me.'

'Quite right, sir. He has betrayed your trust. How else could a mere clerk come to have such a large sum of money?'

'Certainly not from the meagre salary that I can afford to pay him.'

'Then have I your permission to send him off without a character?'

Rosina clutched her father's hand. 'Papa, no!'

Edward drew his hand away, silencing her with a stern look. He turned to Harry, nodding his head. 'Sack him, Harry. Tell him that I never want to see his face again. And he should think himself lucky that I don't put the matter in the hands of the police.'

# Chapter Eleven

'Harry, wait.' Rosina ran downstairs after him, but he ignored her pleas to stop. He strode into the office and slammed the door. She threw herself against it but the key rasped in the lock. She beat on it with her hands. 'Let me in. Please don't do this. Walter, make him let me in.'

'Whatever is going on?' Bertha emerged from the kitchen, wiping her hands on her apron. 'Good heavens, girl. Is the house on fire?'

Ignoring her, Rosina continued to hammer on the door. 'Harry! Walter! Let me in.'

'Stop that.' Bertha pulled her away and dragged her, protesting loudly, down the hall and into the kitchen. 'Calm yourself, Rosie. What's upset you so?'

'It's awful, Bebe.' Rosina paced the floor, wringing her hands. 'I don't know how it happened, but suddenly they think that Walter is to blame for everything. Harry has convinced Papa that Walter has been stealing money from him, and he's going to send him off without a character. Oh, Bebe, it's so unfair. Walter has done nothing wrong.'

'Can you be sure of that, ducks? He did come up with a fair old sum of money for poor Arthur's funeral. I don't wonder that the men folk think it's a bit odd.'

'Not you too! Has everyone gone mad?'

Taking her by the shoulders, Bertha guided Rosina to a chair and made her sit down. 'Now, listen to me, my girl. Sometimes you've got to let other people make the decisions. Your pa may be a stubborn old man, but he's not stupid, and Harry Gostellow is no fool.'

'I know that, but to accuse poor Walter . . .'

'If Walter is innocent, then it will all come out. Your Harry is a fine young man, and he's well off. Be thankful that you've hooked a rich husband, Rosie.'

'What?' Rosina stared at her, shocked into forgetting Walter's plight. 'H-how did you know that I had accepted Harry's proposal?'

Bertha dropped her gaze. 'Well, I . . .'

'You were eavesdropping again.' Springing to her feet, Rosina pushed her away. 'How could you, Bebe?'

'Don't get on your high horse with me, young lady. I brought you up from a baby, remember? It was me who wiped your snotty nose when you was a nipper, and me who sat up all night with you when you had the measles, mumps and scarlet fever. You wouldn't be here today if it wasn't for your Bebe.'

'I know, and I'm sorry. But you really shouldn't listen at keyholes.'

'And how else am I to know what's going on in this house?'

'It doesn't matter now. I must find out what's happening.' Rosina made for the door but Bertha jumped up with amazing agility for a big woman, and she barred her way.

'Leave it to Harry. Ain't you just got yourself engaged to him? Wait until you got that golden wedding band on your finger afore you begin setting him to rights.'

In spite of everything, Rosina could not suppress a gurgle of laughter. 'Bebe, you are a wicked woman.'

'No, ducks. I'm just sensible and I knows what men are like. You got to handle them right if you wants them to do as you say.'

'I just want Walter to be treated fairly.'

'If he ain't guilty, then he's got nothing to worry about.' Bertha put her arm around Rosina's shoulders. 'If you marry young Gostellow you'll save us all from the workhouse. You won't get another chance like this, Rosie. There's not many girls from Black Eagle Wharf what could do better, not even young Susan Barnum.'

The mention of Sukey's name sent a cold shudder down Rosina's spine. Sukey had been sweet on Harry: she would not take kindly to the news of the engagement. If only there was a way to see her before she heard about it from someone else.

'That's a good girl,' Bertha said, stroking Rosina's cheek. 'I knew you'd see sense, just as your mama did all those years ago.'

Rosina stared at her, momentarily forgetting everything else. 'What do you mean?'

'I – er – well, nothing.'

'You can't leave it like that. Tell me what you meant, Bebe.'

Bertha slumped down on a chair with a sigh. 'I suppose it doesn't matter if I tell you now. It was a long time ago.'

'Tell me what?'

'Well, your mama was a lovely girl, sweet and good-natured, but she liked her own way. She fell head over heels in love with a man, and it was almost the ruin of her.'

'Do you mean Captain Barnum? Papa has told me about him, but he didn't say that she loved him.'

Bertha nodded. 'She really did love him, Rosie. Oh, I know your papa likes to believe that Ham Barnum was completely to blame, but I think he genuinely loved her too. They were going to elope, but it all went wrong.'

'But Papa said that he was entirely to blame.'

'It was put about, by your grandpa, that Ham was the villain of the piece. That he took Ellie to

Southend for his own pleasure, not caring about her reputation. But that wasn't quite true. Your ma was desperate to be with him, and she didn't care a jot for what other people thought.'

'And Captain Barnum really loved her?'

'In my opinion, yes. From what I saw then I'd say he was as much in love as any man could be. Anyway, they went off together telling everyone it was just a day trip. When they didn't return that evening, your grandpa and your dad went chasing after them, and they brought poor Ellie home next day in disgrace. Ham said he wanted to make an honest woman of her. Your grandpa didn't have much option but to agree, and the wedding was all set. Then it turned out that Ham was married after all. You know the rest.'

Rosina closed her eyes, trying to imagine her mother as a young woman hopelessly in love with the wrong man. It was not a difficult leap of imagination. 'So she married my papa.'

'Your pa had loved her for a long time, but she only had eyes for Ham. She was broken-hearted when she discovered the truth. I don't think she cared what happened to her then, but she knew that her reputation was ruined. She didn't have much of a choice but to accept your pa.'

'And my grandfather agreed to the match?'

'The scandal was out. Your grandpa would never have agreed to it in normal circumstances, but he knew very well that no respectable man would want to marry poor Ellie. I think it broke his heart to see his one and only daughter marry beneath her, but I think, in the end, she was happy enough with your pa.'

'And she died giving birth to me. I killed my poor mamma.'

Bertha grasped her hands so tightly that Rosina felt her knuckles crack. 'Don't never say that. Your ma died of the milk fever just a few days after you was born, but that weren't no fault of yours, and she loved you with all her heart. Do you know the first thing she said when she saw you? No, of course you don't. Well, she took one look at your little red face, and she said, "Oh, my beautiful little rose." She looks up at me with tears in her eyes and smiles. I never seen her so happy. "That's what we'll call her, Bertha," she says. "My little Rose. I'll call her Rosina after my grandmother, God rest her soul."' Bertha's eyes filled with tears and her voice broke on a sob.

Rosina was crying too, her heart wrung out with sympathy for the star-crossed lovers, and for her own lost love. He had called her his beautiful rose, using the same words that her mother had spoken all those years ago. The coincidence was almost too painful to bear. She laid her head against Bertha's shoulder and sobbed.

'What's wrong? What's happened?' Caddie rushed into the kitchen and fell down on her knees beside them. 'Why are you crying?'

Rosina wiped her eyes on the back of her hand. She rose unsteadily to her feet. 'It's all right, Caddie. Nothing for you to worry about. Bebe was just telling me about my mother. You see, I never knew her. And now I'm about to be married, Bertha was just telling me things I didn't know before.'

'Married?' Caddie's dull eyes lit with enthusiasm. 'You dark horse, Rosie. You never said nothing about getting married.'

Bertha wiped her eyes on the corner of her apron. 'Well, you know now. Miss Rosina is going to marry Mr Harry Gostellow. She's going to be a lady, so you be respectful, Caddie.'

'Bebe, no! Don't say things like that to Caddie. Nothing is going to change. We'll still be a family, and I'll be able to take care of you all.'

'I knew it was too good to last.' Caddie's face crumpled and tears ran down her cheeks. 'You'll marry him and me and the nippers will be cast out on the streets. It'll be the workhouse for us.'

'No one is going to the workhouse,' Rosina said firmly, rising to her feet. 'Not you, nor your babies, do you hear me, Caddie? If the Gostellows won't look after my family, then I won't marry their son.' She took a deep breath. Caddie and Bertha were staring at her open-mouthed. She tossed her head. 'I mean what I say and I'm going to begin by telling Harry so.' She left the room determined to speak firmly to him.

She was still seething inwardly about his cavalier treatment of Walter, and that was another matter on which she meant to challenge him.

The office door was open but Walter was nowhere to be seen. Harry was standing behind the desk rifling through a sheaf of papers.

'Where is he?' Rosina demanded. 'And what are you doing, Harry? You've no right to go through my father's papers.'

'Sweetheart, I've just earned every right to take an interest in the company. Without my financial help, the company does not exist. Your father will be bankrupt in days if I don't step in and pay a few of these outstanding accounts.'

She felt her confidence dissipating like morning mist over the river. 'Outstanding accounts?'

'Sailmakers, chandlers, sackmakers – the list is almost endless. It seems that your friend Walter has been juggling their accounts for months; paying off a bit here and there, but never settling the whole amount. I hope that is enough to convince you of his dishonesty.'

'Th-there must be some other explanation, Harry. Did you give Walter a chance to defend himself?'

He came out from behind the desk and laid his hands on her shoulders. 'My darling, your loyalty is touching, but misplaced. Now, we'll have no more talk about Walter Brown. I want you to fetch your bonnet and shawl, and we'll go to Hatton Garden to buy that diamond ring I promised you.'

'Bother diamonds!' Rosina cried angrily. 'You're not my husband yet, Harry. And you had no right to treat Walter like a common criminal.'

'But he is a common criminal, my love.'

'That is unjust and untrue.' She turned on her heel and made to leave the room, but Harry caught her by the arm.

'Where are you going?'

She shook free from his grasp. 'I'm going to right a terrible wrong.'

'Rosina, I forbid you to go chasing after that person.'

Picking up her skirts, Rosina ran from the office and out through the open front door. She glanced over her shoulder to see if Harry was following her, but he had stopped in the doorway with a look of sheer bafflement on his face. 'If you don't come back at once, I won't take you to choose a ring.'

His voice had the plaintive sound of a seagull mewing overhead. Rosina was too angry and upset to take any notice. Diamond rings seemed unimportant at this moment. A great injustice had been done and she meant to address it as best she could. She slowed her pace as she came to the end of Black Eagle Wharf, aware that she was receiving curious looks from the dockers who were unloading a barge loaded with barrels. Her hair had escaped from the confines of the chignon at the nape of her neck, and it fell in dark skeins around her shoulders. She realised that she must look a strange sight, wandering the wharves unaccompanied and dishevelled like a common street woman. She squared her shoulders and quickened her pace, heading towards Angel Court, where she knew that Walter had lodgings. She had only a vague idea of its location, but she knew that it was somewhere between the High Street and Great Hermitage Street.

The alleyways and courts were dark, dingy places where she would never normally have ventured on her own, but she was driven by her need to speak to Walter. In this maze of narrow canyons between soot-blackened warehouses and crumbling tenements, the people lived in a twilight world where the sun's rays were unable to penetrate, even at midday. Rosina almost tripped over the feet of a man who was sprawled in a doorway, either dead drunk, or he could have been a genuine corpse; she did not stop to find out. She hurried on, dodging the clutching fingers of hollow-eyed street urchins, whose ragged clothes barely covered their skeletal frames. She had no money, but she knew they would have torn the clothes from her back if she had stopped to speak to them. They hunted in packs, like wolf cubs, waiting to attack a drunken sailor or a person stupefied by opium. Rosina knew that Bertha and her papa had done their best to shelter her from the ugly truths that lurked in the shadows, and, even though she had seen much of the sordid side of life when growing up in the Ratcliff Highway, she was shocked by what she now saw, and not a little frightened.

She broke into a run, her breath torn from her in ragged sobs, as a feral dog leapt out of a doorway barking ferociously and baring its teeth. The stench of overflowing privies and unwashed bodies was making her feel sick, and she slipped and slid on the detritus underfoot. Her heart was beating so fast that she was deafened by the blood pounding in her ears, but she had come too far to turn back. Just as she thought that she was completely lost and would never find her way out of this terrible place, she saw the name 'Angel Court' scrawled in red paint on a wooden sign, hanging by a single nail. She stopped, holding her side as a painful stitch made her double over, gasping for breath. It was then that she realised she had come on a fruitless mission: she had been so fired with righteous indignation that she had not given a thought to Walter's address, other than that he lived in Angel Court. But she could not go home without seeing him. Rosina forced her feet to take her into the dark alley. The tall, blank-eyed buildings loomed above her. She thought she saw movements in the shadows, but she could not be sure if it was her imagination or whether danger lurked behind every shuttered window and closed door. The narrow court opened into a cobbled square lined with seemingly derelict houses. The filthy window-panes were cracked or broken into jagged shards. Paint peeled in scabby strips from woodwork and the square was criss-crossed with washing lines, where ragged garments hung liked tattered pennants. Rosina shuddered. 'Walter.' She murmured his name and the sound echoed round the square. She raised her voice. 'Walter.' She stifled a gasp of fear as a man lurched out of the shadows. 'Walter!' Her voice rose to a scream.

The man leered at her. 'I'll be your Walter, missy.'

Sick with terror, she backed away from him. 'No, you're mistaken, sir.'

'Sir, is it? Have we got a lady here in Angel Court? I never had the pleasure of a lady afore.'

'And you won't now, Hawkins. Get away with you, scaring a young girl out of her wits.'

Rosina spun round with a cry of relief as Walter emerged from a doorway.

'Oh, it's you she's come for, is it, Walt?' Hawkins backed away. 'I didn't know she was your trull.'

'Mind your tongue, man.' Walter took Rosina by the arm. 'What are you doing in this place, Rosie? You shouldn't be here.'

'Walter, I was never so glad to see anyone in my whole life.' She leaned against him, weak with relief. 'How can you bear to live in this dreadful place?'

'You'd better come inside for a while, and then I'll take you home.'

She allowed him to lead her into the tenement building. She wrinkled her nose at the nauseating odour of damp rot, rodent droppings and human excrement. 'This is horrible, Walter. How can you stand it?'

'It's all I can afford.'

Following him up a narrow staircase where the plaster had come off the walls in great chunks, leaving the laths exposed like the ribs of a human skeleton, Rosina could barely repress a shudder of revulsion. She had never been in such a terrible place and it was hard to believe that human beings dwelt here. Walter opened a door on the first landing and ushered her into his room, which was little better than a cell. The only furnishings were a single iron bedstead, a chest of drawers and a chair. It was bare of any ornament or anything that might have made the room comfortable, but at least it was clean.

'So this is where you live.' Rosina ignored his offer of the chair and she walked round the room, forgetting her distress in her curiosity about the conditions in which he lived. 'Have you been here long, Walter?'

'It doesn't matter. What is more important is why you risked your safety by following me here. You shouldn't have come, Rosie.'

'I had to. I couldn't bear to think of you being so unfairly treated. Harry had no right to take matters into his own hands.'

'He said that you have agreed to marry him. Is that true?'

She couldn't meet his eyes and she turned away. 'Yes.'

'And do you love him?'

With anyone else she could have lied, but not to Walter. She took the offensive. 'I don't see that that is any of your business.'

'I should have committed highway robbery rather than allow you to give yourself to a man you don't love.'

She spun round to face him. 'How dare you say such things to me? I only came here because I thought you were unjustly treated, but you have no right to question my decision.'

'I am your friend, Rosie. And ever will be. You must believe that.'

There was no mistaking the sincerity of his words or the genuine contrition in his expression and her anger melted away. 'I do believe it, just as I know that you did not cheat my papa.'

'That means more to me than anything.'

'Will you be all right? Will you be able to find another position without a reference? Perhaps I can persuade Papa to give you one when he has calmed down a little.'

'One day I'll prove my innocence, but you mustn't worry about me. I'll find work somewhere. Now I really should take you home.'

'Yes, of course.' For some strange reason, she did not want to leave immediately. She had this unexpected glimpse into his private life: this room was his home, and it was just possible that she might learn a little more about the real person. 'Have you no one you could turn to, Walter?'

He shook his head. 'We'd better go. Your father will be worried about you.'

She had spotted a framed daguerreotype on the chest of drawers, half hidden behind an enamel jug and wash basin. She could not bear to leave without taking a peek, and she moved swiftly to examine the likeness. A young woman with dark hair and eyes, a handsome face rather than a pretty one, gazed out of the tortoiseshell frame. 'Is this your mother?'

'She died a long time ago.'

'And your father?'

'He is dead too.'

She replaced the frame, and was about to turn away when a glint of gold caught her eye. The temptation was too great, and she picked up the gold chain, dangling it between her fingers. From it hung a heart-shaped medallion, so similar to the one that the pirate had worn that her heart missed a beat. 'Is this yours?'

Walter stood very still, his expression unreadable. 'No.'

'Then how did you come by it? Did you steal it?'

'Of course not.'

On closer examination, she realised that the medallion had two initials inscribed on its face – *WB*. 'If you didn't steal it, and it isn't yours, then whose is it? And whose initials are these?' She closed her fingers around the precious metal and felt it absorb the warmth from her hand. She was certain that this had hung around the pirate's neck, and just holding it like this made her feel close to him again. 'Tell me, Walter. I must know.'

He was standing very still. His back was to the light and she could not read his expression but she sensed that he was keeping something from her. Was it possible that he was acquainted with the man she loved? She hardly dared to breathe as she waited for his answer. 'Tell, me, please, Walter.'

'My mother's name was Winifred. The medallion belonged to her.'

'WB, of course, Winifred Brown. Then it is yours.'

'No. It's not mine. It belongs to my – brother.'

'Your brother? But you said you had no family.'

'I don't like to speak of him.'

She clutched the medallion to her bosom. 'Why not? Why don't you speak of him? I must know.'

'He is not a good man. He breaks the law.'

'Your brother is a river pirate?' She read her answer in his silence. 'He is the pirate who stole from Captain Barnum. Isn't that the truth, Walter?'

Walter turned away. 'I am not proud of his actions.'

'But that is how you got the money to pay for the funeral, isn't it? Your brother stole from ships moored alongside the wharves, and he gave you the proceeds from selling stolen goods. Am I right, Walter? Is that the way it happened?'

'It's better that you don't know about these things, Rosie. Don't ask questions that I cannot answer.'

'I promise I won't give your secret away. You know you can trust me, just as I trusted you. I knew you weren't capable of stealing from my papa.'

'Thank you for that.'

He had turned slightly and she studied his profile silhouetted against the dim light from the window. 'I see the likeness now. He was always masked but I always felt so comfortable in his company. Did your brother tell you that we met, Walter? Did he speak of me?'

Walter nodded, seemingly unable to answer.

Rosina rushed to his side and clasped his hand in hers, raising it to her cheek. 'Tell me what he said. Did he say nice things about me, Walter?'

'Of course he did. A man would be a fool if he didn't see your worth, Rosie.'

She rubbed his hand against her cheek, closing her eyes and inhaling the familiar scent of Indian ink. 'So that is why you reminded me so much of him.' She examined his fingers, studying the dark stains on his skin. 'I love the smell of Indian ink – it will always remind me of you, and – your brother. I don't even know his name.'

'It is better that you don't know his name. Believe me; it's for your own good. Now I must take you home, Rosie. This has gone far enough.'

She clung to his hand. 'No, I won't go without knowing his name. I love him, Walter. I fell in love with him when we first met at Cremorne Gardens.'

Walter's stern expression melted into a smile. He raised her hand to his lips and kissed it. 'And he loves you. But it cannot be, you know that. He is a felon. If he's caught he could be hanged for his crimes. You must forget him.'

'No, I could never do that. I don't care what he's done – I love him with all my heart. You will tell him that, won't you, Walter?'

He dropped her hand as if her flesh had burned his fingers. 'Nothing can ever come of it.'

Tears spilled from her eyes. She nodded,

wordlessly. It was true, nothing could ever come of her impossible love for a man on the wrong side of the law. She had promised to marry another, and her family were depending upon her to provide for them. She had accepted Harry's proposal of marriage and she was morally bound to him.

'Don't cry, Rosie.' Walter wrapped her in his arms, holding her close to his chest. 'He didn't mean to make you sad. He only wants your happiness, as I do.'

She drew away from him, swallowing a sob and sniffing. 'I know it's hopeless, but it will give me some comfort just knowing who he is. If he's your brother, Walter, then he can't be all bad.'

'Oh, Rosie.' Walter's voice cracked with emotion. 'I'll always be somewhere close by, if you have need of me.'

'I believe you, and I'm truly grateful. I think you should keep away from Black Eagle Wharf for a while, but I'll miss you terribly. Now I'll have to hold the two of you in my heart. You and your wicked brother.' She managed a wobbly smile as she held out her hand with the medallion in the palm. 'You'd better give him back his talisman, and with it my love.'

Walter stared at it as it lay in the palm of her hand. 'He would want you to keep it, Rosie. Wear it close to your heart and remember that he loves you dearly.'

'Oh, Walter.' Lost for words, Rosina clutched the precious golden object in her hand, and then she slipped the chain over her head, tucking the medallion into the neck of her blouse. 'Tell him, I'll wear it always. Tell him that if things were different . . .' Her voice broke on a sob, and she could not continue.

'Come, we really should go now.' Walter's voice was gruff, but he made no move to comfort her. 'It's getting late. I must get you safely home.'

His matter-of-fact tone brought her back to stark reality; she ought not to have come here and there would be untold trouble at home if anyone found out. She brushed the tears from her eyes, and her hands flew to her tumbled locks. She looked round for a mirror; there was none in this austerely masculine room. 'I can't go home looking like this.'

Walter smiled. 'You look wonderful with your hair hanging loose about your shoulders.' He picked up a strand and let it run through his fingers. 'It's like silk. You have beautiful hair.'

She felt herself blushing at the unexpected compliment. 'I do believe that's the nicest thing you've ever said to me, Walter.'

'I may not have spoken them, but the words were always in my thoughts.'

'You and your brother are so alike. I can't think why I never noticed it before.' She smoothed her hair back from her forehead. 'That will have to do, and I'll hope to sneak indoors without anyone seeing me.'

'You must never again venture here alone, Rosie. This is a shockingly rough area.'

She took one last look round the room. 'I know where you live now, and when I feel low I can picture you and your brother here together. You can't imagine what a comfort it is to me, just having a link with him through you.'

Outside in the small square, Hawkins was leaning against a wall smoking a clay pipe. He took it from his mouth and grinned when he saw Rosina. 'Given him a good time, have you, ducks? Put me on your list for when you come here again and you'll find out what a real man can do for you.'

'Shut up, Hawkins,' Walter snapped. 'That's no way to speak to a lady.'

'Since when did ladies come a-calling on gents in Angel Court?' Hawkins spat in the gutter and his throaty laughter followed them into the narrow alley.

'I'm sorry about that,' Walter said apologetically. 'He's a foul-mouthed fellow, but he's not as bad as he makes out.'

Rosina tucked her hand in his arm. 'Never mind him. I'm glad I came, Walter. I feel so much happier now that I know who my pirate is. I couldn't have wished for him to have a better brother than you.'

He patted her hand, saying nothing, but she was not deceived by his silence. She had felt the quiver of emotion run through him, and she realised that, until this moment, she had never felt closer to Walter, or felt that she had a better understanding of him. Not so long ago she had thought him stiff and starchy to the point of boredom – now she knew better. He might not have the dash and panache of his brother, but Walter was not as dull as she had first thought. They walked on companionably, arm in arm, towards Black Eagle Wharf.

When they reached Union Stairs, Walter stopped. 'I had better not come any further. I'm too well known round here, and it's better that you're not seen with me.'

'I understand. And I'll be fine from here.' She reached up and kissed his cheek. 'Goodbye, my dear Walter.'

He nodded abruptly and turned on his heel, but Rosina caught him by the sleeve. 'Please tell me his name. I know I may never see him again, but I would dearly love to be able to put a name to his face.'

The late afternoon sun slanted off Walter's spectacles, making it impossible for Rosina to read the expression in his eyes. He hesitated; she thought that he was going to refuse her request, and then he seemed to relent. 'Will. His name is Will.'

Rosina opened her mouth to repeat the magical name, but the blast of a steam whistle from a launch at the bottom of Union Stairs made her start, and look round. The boatman threw a line ashore, and a dock worker scrambled to catch it and loop it over a bollard. She turned back to speak to Walter, but he had gone.

# Chapter Twelve

Bertha pounced on her the moment Rosina put her foot inside the house. 'Where have you been, you bad girl? And just look at you – wandering about the streets looking like a common flower seller. Where's your bonnet and gloves?'

Rosina had been thinking up excuses all the way from Union Stairs, but, looking at Bertha's angry face, she knew that she would spot an untruth immediately. 'I – I – went for a walk.'

'Balderdash! You've been up to something, my girl, but there ain't time to go into that now. Upstairs with you and wash your hands and face. You've got to change into your best gown and Caddie can do something with your hair. You look like you've been dragged through a hedge backwards.' Bertha shooed her towards the staircase. 'Hurry up. Don't dawdle.'

'What is all the fuss about?'

'You rushed off and left Mr Harry standing there like a lemon. He was going to take you to buy the ring and yet you rushed off goodness knows where. Whatever got into your head, Rosina?'

'I – I needed time to think.'

'You ought to be considering your man, not running wild about the neighbourhood.'

'Was he very angry?'

'He was mad as fire, and so was your pa. It brought on one of his breathless attacks and he's had to go for a lie down on his bed. You've upset everyone by your thoughtless behaviour. You bad, bad girl.'

'I'm sorry you were upset, but I'm not doing anything until you tell me what's going on.'

'Mr Harry will be here shortly. He's going to take you to meet his parents, and your pa is invited too. I've got to get him up and dressed in his Sunday best, so you get on up them stairs, Rosie. This is your chance to shine in society. We'll all be made if you get in with the nobs.'

There was no escape now; she had made her own bed, as Bertha was so fond of saying, and she would have to lie on it – with Harry. Rosina went slowly up the stairs to her bedroom with a panicky feeling in the pit of her stomach. She had thought she could go through with the engagement, but that was before she discovered that her pirate was Walter's brother. Will had become flesh and blood, a real person, instead of the shadowy romantic figure who was never far from her thoughts. She would have to tell Harry that she could not be his wife, but she would wait for the right moment.

She slipped off her blouse and stepped out of her skirt. It was stiflingly hot in her bedroom and flies buzzed tiredly against the windowpanes. She could not bear to see them trapped and she opened the window, watching them drop downwards and then soar up and fly away. They would probably end up on the wrong end of a fly swat, but at least she had given them a brief moment of freedom. The air was unnaturally still and the sails of the moored vessels hung limply against the ships' masts. The sky had a sulphurous yellow tinge, and the gathering clouds promised a thunderstorm later. Rosina went to the washstand and poured water from the flower-patterned jug into the china bowl. She felt hot and sticky, and perspiration pearled on her skin. She splashed the cool water on her face, shivering as it trickled down her neck. The medallion felt cold as it nestled between her breasts. She closed her fingers around it, conjuring up a vision of Will's smiling face. 'Will,' she whispered over and over again. As her lips formed the single syllable, it was as if they were preparing to receive his kiss. She was startled out of her reverie by a rap on the door. She reached for her wrap. 'C-come in.'

Caddie hesitated on the threshold. 'Bertha said I was to come and help you dress.'

'Oh, it's you.' Rosina sank down on the edge of the bed.

'Is everything all right, miss?'

'Caddie, since when have you started calling me miss?'

'Bertha said I was not to be familiar now that you're going up in the world.'

'That's nonsense, and I won't have it. We're friends, aren't we, Caddie?'

'I'd like to think so.'

'It is so, and always will be. But I would be grateful if you'd help me dress and put up my hair. I suppose I must look my best for Harry's dreadful mama.'

'I'll see what I can do.'

Rosina sat on the stool in front of her dressing table. She stared in the mirror, watching Caddie's nimble fingers fashion her long hair into sleek coils. 'Where did you learn to do hair like that?'

'I weren't always a wife and mother,' Caddie said, smiling. 'I was lady's maid to a merchant's wife in Islington afore I met Artie. Started as a tweeny, I did, when I was ten, and worked me way up.'

'You certainly have got a magic touch.' Rosina watched appreciatively as her hair was arranged into an elaborate coronet.

'Now, if you had some pearls or fancy combs, I could make you look like a queen.' Caddie stood back to admire her work. Her eyes lighted upon the medallion and a puzzled frown creased her brow.

'What are you staring at, Caddie?'

'Nothing. I mean, I ain't seen that piece of jewellery before.'

'It was given to me by a friend.'

'You're blushing, Rosie.'

Their eyes met in the mirror, and Rosina realised that she simply had to tell someone about Will or she would burst. She had not intended to say so much, but once started, she found that she could not stop. Caddie sat down on the bed, listening open-mouthed. Rosina eyed her nervously. 'No one else knows any of this, Caddie. I want you to promise me that you won't breathe it to a soul.'

Caddie's blue eyes were huge in her pale face. 'Cross me heart and hope to die.'

'I'll never see him again. I thought about breaking off my engagement to Harry, but if I do that then Papa will lose the *Ellie May* and we will have to leave this house. I'll try to be a good wife to Harry, I really will.'

'It won't be easy, not if you're in love with someone else.'

'I have no choice, Caddie. And Harry must never know.'

'Then you'd best take that thing off.' Caddie rose to her feet and picked up the gown that Bertha had laid out on the bed. 'Here, step into it, and I'll do you up.'

Rosina took a deep breath while Caddie did up

the tiny pearl buttons down the back of the bodice. As she surveyed her reflection in the mirror, she realised that Caddie had been right. The gold chain and pendant were exposed for all to see by the low neckline of the afternoon gown. 'I said I would never take it off.'

'Then you'll have a lot of explaining to do.' Caddie angled her head. 'Unless – have you got a locket? I'm sure if you had one large enough, that little medallion would fit inside nicely, and no one would know the difference.'

Rosina flung her arms around Caddie and hugged her. 'Why didn't I think of that?' She went to the dressing table and opened a small casket, which held the few items of jewellery in her possession. She poked around with her forefinger until she found what she was looking for; and she held it up with a triumphant smile. 'This is the only piece of jewellery I have that belonged to my mother.' She prised the locket open and handed it to Caddie. 'See, there is a watercolour portrait of both my parents.'

'You look just like your mum,' Caddie said. 'And the captain looks so different without his whiskers.' She almost dropped it as a shout from downstairs made them both jump.

'Rosina, your young man is here.' Bertha called. 'Did you hear me?'

'Give it to me, please,' Rosina said, holding out her hand. 'Go down and tell Bebe I'm nearly ready. It won't take me a minute to put the medallion inside the locket. Go, now.'

Harry's dour expression lightened as he looked up and saw Rosina coming down the stairs. He held out his hands. 'My darling, you do me proud.'

She descended slowly, holding her head high and forcing her lips into a smile. 'I must apologise for this afternoon, Harry.'

'I forgive you, Rosie. But you must never do that again. Now we are officially engaged, you are not to wander round the streets alone. You must be accompanied at all times.'

Biting back an angry retort, she drew her hands away. 'What possible harm can come to me round here? I've walked out on my own ever since I can remember.'

'But you were just a child. Soon you are to be a married woman, and you will have risen in society. Ladies do not wander the street unaccompanied.' Harry glanced at Caddie, who was standing at the foot of the stairs. 'You, Trigg, what is your position in this household?'

'Harry!' Rosina stared at him, shocked and surprised by his tone of voice. 'You can't speak to Caddie like that.'

'Hush, my dear. Leave this to me.' Harry beckoned to Caddie. 'No offence meant, Trigg. I'm a blunt man when it comes to business matters. Are you employed by Captain May?'

Caddie bobbed a curtsey. 'No, sir. I – I just live here.'

'Then may I suggest that you earn your keep by acting as lady's maid to Miss Rosina? I will pay you a suitable wage and then you need not feel as though you are taking advantage of the captain's hospitality.'

'Please, Harry.' Rosina caught him by the arm. 'You're embarrassing both me and Caddie. There's no question of her being a servant in my father's house.'

'Isn't there?' Harry looked up as Edward came slowly down the stairs, followed by Bertha. 'Captain May. I've made the suggestion that Trigg should be employed on a regular basis as lady's maid to my fiancée. Rosina seems to think this is in bad taste. What do you think, sir?'

Edward tugged at his necktie. 'Dashed uncomfortable things, neckties. Don't like dressing up like a tailor's dummy.'

'Papa. Please tell Harry that you are the head of the household, and that you make decisions here.'

'Rosie, dearest.' Harry took her by the hand. 'I would have thought that Trigg would infinitely prefer working as your maid to the alternative of the workhouse.'

'The workhouse!' Caddie's knees buckled and she collapsed on the bottom stair tread, burying her face in her hands. 'For the love of God, sir. Not the workhouse.'

'See what you've done.' Rosina shot him a furious look. She rushed to Caddie's side, placing her arm around her shaking shoulders. 'Don't worry, there's no question of you ever going to the workhouse. You are safe here with us.'

'I'll be your maid, miss,' Caddie said, sniffing. 'I'll work for nothing so long as you let me and me babies stay with you.'

Edward made his way past them. 'I can't pay you, my dear. But if young Harry has a mind to, then I'd say you should take it and be grateful.'

'Maybe he'd like to pay me too,' Bertha muttered, helping Rosina to raise Caddie to her feet. 'It's years since I had any wages.'

'We already have a housekeeper,' Harry said stiffly. 'But I'm sure that Captain May will keep you on after Miss Rosina and I are married. Naturally we will be living with my parents in Wellclose Square.'

'But Harry, this is my home.' Rosina cried angrily. She had not considered the practicalities of being married into the Gostellow family, and now she was really worried. Panic seized her and she was tempted to run up to her bedroom and lock the door, but Harry had taken her firmly by the hand and he drew her gently away from Caddie.

'Silly goose, of course we'll live in the mansion with my parents. You wouldn't expect me to live here, would you?' He turned to Caddie. 'Fetch Miss Rosina's mantle and gloves, please, Trigg. My father's carriage is waiting in the High Street, and I suggest we leave before it starts to rain.'

The first clap of thunder rolled around the darkening sky just as the carriage pulled up outside the Gostellows' mansion in Wellclose Square. The matched pair of bays snorted and reared in the shafts, and the coachman leapt off his seat to hold their heads. A footman ran down the steps to open the carriage door. Harry climbed out first and he helped Rosina to alight. He smiled down at her as he led her up the steps and into the house. 'Welcome to what will soon be your home, my lovely bride-to-be.'

A flash of lightning illuminated the gloomy hallway for a brief second and Potter loomed from behind a marble pillar, making Rosina jump.

'May I take your mantle, miss?'

Rosina shrugged the garment off and handed it to him. 'Thank you, Mr Potter.'

'It's just Potter, miss.'

'You have so much to learn, my darling.' Harry chuckled as he handed his top hot and gloves to the butler. 'Are my parents in the drawing room?'

'They are, sir.' Potter hobbled over to Edward to relieve him of his hat and coat.

'Come and say hello to your future in-laws, my

darling.' Harry offered her his arm. He glanced over his shoulder at Edward. 'You know my father, sir, but I do not believe you have ever met my mama.'

Edward cleared his throat, running his finger round the inside of his starched collar. 'No. I've not yet had that pleasure.'

Rosina shot him an encouraging smile, but she suppressed a shudder as they entered the drawing room. She felt a definite chill, even though it was hot and sultry out of doors. Margaret Gostellow was lying on the chaise longue in front of a roaring fire. She might never have moved since the last time Rosina had seen her, except for the fact that she was now wearing an ivory satin gown lavishly trimmed with Brussels lace and pearls. She stared at Rosina through a lorgnette, her hooded eyes registering nothing except the faintest hint of surprise. 'I see that you can look presentable when you make the effort. I'm agreeably surprised.'

Rosina bit back a sharp retort. 'Good evening, ma'am.'

Harry leaned closer to Rosina, lowering his voice. 'Mama meant it as a compliment, my love. She speaks her mind, but you'll soon get used to that.'

Margaret eyed him with an ominous frown. 'If you have something to say, Harry, say it so that we can all hear.'

'Mama, may I introduce Captain Edward May?' Harry gave Edward a gentle shove towards the chaise longue. 'Captain May, my mother, Margaret Gostellow.'

Edward bowed from the waist. 'Charmed to make your acquaintance, ma'am.'

A flash of lightning illuminated the shadowy room just long enough for Rosina to realise that a man was sitting in a wing-back chair, smoking a cigar. He rose to his feet, moving towards them and exhaling a cloud of blue smoke. 'So this is your intended, my boy?'

'Yes, Father. May I present my fiancée, Rosina May?'

'How do, my dear?' Harold Gostellow breathed cigar fumes into her face as he kissed her on the cheek. 'What a little beauty, Harry, my boy. You show excellent taste in women as you do in horseflesh.' He winked at Rosina and guffawed. She saw that he had long yellow teeth, rather like one of his horses. She was not absolutely certain, but she thought that his free hand had strayed to touch her bottom, although with a bustle at the back of her gown it was not possible to be completely sure. Bobbing a curtsey, she backed away. 'How do you do, sir?'

Harry did not appear to have noticed his father's raffish behaviour and he smiled as he motioned Edward to step forward. 'Of course you know my future pa-in-law, Father. Captain May.'

'Good evening, Ed, old boy. Bad do about your boat, but if you're in need of work I might be able to find you something suitable to a man of your talents.' Harold slapped him on the shoulder, causing Edward to cough. 'No need to thank me, old chap.' Harold signalled to the butler, who was drooping quietly in the shadows. 'Potter! Fetch the brandy decanter and three glasses.'

'Come here, my dear.' Margaret's voice quavered as she beckoned to Rosina. 'Come over here where I can see you more clearly.'

Rosina went to stand by the chaise longue. 'Yes, ma'am.'

'Sit down, child. You're making my neck ache.'

Rosina perched on the edge of a chair opposite her prospective mother-in-law.

'So, my boy has asked you to marry him?'

'Yes, ma'am.'

'I can't say that I was surprised, or that I was best pleased. I had hoped that Harry would pick a girl of good family, similar to my own. My father was a magnate, you know.'

Harold, apparently overhearing this remark, gave a loud snort. 'He was a bloody dustman, just the same as I was when I started out. Made a fortune out of other people's rubbish, did old Ezra Huggins.'

'Don't pay any attention to him.' Margaret

fluttered her fan, casting a furious look at her husband. 'My papa was a public servant, overseeing the refuse disposal of the city. He was a hygienist.'

Doing her best to ignore Mr Gostellow's loud guffaws, Rosina made an effort to sound impressed. 'I didn't know that, Mrs Gostellow.'

'Well, he was. And he left this house to me, together with the money that set my husband up in business. I was quite a catch, I can tell you. And I was considered to be a beauty until ill health forced me to retire from polite society.'

'I'm sorry to hear it, ma'am.'

'But you will be a comfort to me, I hope, Rosina. You will keep me company during the long winter days when I am too fragile to venture out of doors, or to receive guests. I'm sure we will do very well together, once you have learned to be a lady.'

Rosina was saved from replying by Harry who strolled over to them clutching a glass of brandy in his hand. 'How are you two getting along? Splendidly, I hope. I told you that you would love her, Mama, just as I do.'

'She's very pretty, Harry. I'm sure she will learn to be a good wife, given time, and the benefit of my knowledge and experience.'

Harry leaned over and kissed his mother on the forehead. 'She could not fail to benefit from your patronage, dearest Mama.'

'My darling boy.' Margaret aimed a triumphant glance at Rosina. 'See how he idolises his mama, Rosina. I hope that when you have sons they appreciate you as Harry does me.'

Rosina felt herself blushing. She had not given motherhood a thought. In fact, she had only the haziest idea what constituted the intimate side of matrimony, and this had been gained from whispered conversations with Sukey, who had quizzed her newly married cousin, Jane, about what actually happened in the marriage bed. They had concluded that Jane had made up most of it to shock them, and that she was not a reliable witness, since she had insisted that she kept her eyes tight shut and had thought about chocolate cake and ice cream during the whole beastly business. Although, Sukey had said, on reflection – Jane had been married for nearly a year with no sign of a happy event, so she might have been telling the truth. It was a well-known fact, according to Miss Carmody, who had taught French at the dame school attended by Sukey and her sisters, that if one did not enjoy marital relations, then a baby would not be the result. Unfortunately Miss Carmody had been sent away in disgrace shortly after this conver-sation, and so the girls had not been able to question her further.

'See how she blushes, mama. Isn't she a dear?' Harry sipped his brandy, smiling his approval.

Margaret's lips curved, but her eyes were cold as agate as she stared at Rosina. 'So where is this ring then? I thought you were taking her to buy one this afternoon, Harry.'

He gulped down the remainder of his drink. 'I, er – we didn't get round to it, Mama.'

'And diamonds are a shocking price. Your father is not a generous man, and I doubt if he would sanction such a gross extravagance.' Margaret tugged at the ring on her engagement finger, working it round until it came off in her hand. 'This is the engagement ring that he bought me, all those years ago. Hold out your hand, Harry.'

With child-like obedience, Harry held out his hand and his mother placed her ring on his palm, closing his fingers round it with a sigh. 'There, give her that, my dear boy. And I hope it brings Rosina as much happiness from her marriage as mine has to me.'

Harry opened his hand and stared doubtfully at the small stone. 'But you have not been happy, Mama. You are always telling me so.'

She smacked him with her furled fan. 'Silly boy. You know I like to tease you. Give it to her now.'

Rosina clenched her hand into a fist. She did not want his mother's ring. The thought of wearing it made her feel physically sick. She shook her head. 'Really, ma'am. It's too much to ask you to part with something so precious.'

'Rosie's right, Mama. You must not part with your engagement ring.' Harry tried to give it back, but Margaret thrust his hand away.

'You will displease me greatly if you don't put my ring on her finger. I can feel an attack of palpitations coming on. You know that I must not be upset.'

Harry gave Rosina a pleading look. 'My darling? It means so much to Mama.'

Reluctantly, Rosina held out her left hand, suppressing a shudder as Harry slipped the ring on her finger. If he had clamped an iron manacle on her she could not have felt more disturbed and ill at ease.

'What's this then?' Harold peered over his son's shoulder. 'Doing the right thing by the little lady, eh? Congratulations, old fellow.' He slapped Harry on the back. 'Now, as her future father-in-law, allow me to be the first to kiss the bride-to-be.'

Before Rosina had a chance to move out of reach, Harold seized her round the waist and drew her to him, planting a wet, slobbery kiss on her lips, and taking rather more pleasure in it than was appropriate.

'Put her down, you lecherous beast,' Margaret said, raising her voice to a point where the crystals on the chandelier tinkled in unison. 'The girl may be common but she is not a maidservant with whom you can take liberties.'

'Come now, ma'am,' Edward said, tugging nervously at his whiskers. 'I'm sure that it was just a mark of fatherly appreciation. My girl is precious to me and I would take it badly if a man was to show her any disrespect.'

Harold thumped him on the back with a cheerful grin. 'And none was meant, old chap. Can't a man show appreciation for his son's choice of bride in his own front parlour, Maggie?'

'Drawing room, Harold.' Margaret's winged brows knotted together in a frown. 'You are showing me up, as you always do. Common born and common to the grave, that is you, Harold Gostellow.'

'I was good enough to make an honest woman of you, madam. I didn't see suitors queuing up outside your father's door, even though you was the dustman's only daughter and had expectations.'

She rose from the chaise longue with a rustle of silk petticoats. 'The whole city knows that I married beneath me. My father was a great man and you drove one of his scavenger carts.' She almost spat the words at him. 'You were the common dustman, taking the city rubbish to his dust mound.' There was a horrified silence.

Rosina moved closer to her father, clutching his arm. She longed to take the ring from her finger and throw it back at Harry's mother, but she could see that he was upset by this extremely public show of animosity between his parents. She glanced anxiously at Harold to see how he had taken the insult, but he threw back his head and roared with laughter. 'She's a one, is my missis. A veritable hell-cat when she's got the wilds.' He hooked his arm around his wife's waist and planted a kiss on her cheek. 'There's one for you, old girl. Just so's you don't feel left out.'

'Beast!' Margaret took a swipe at him with her fan, but he ducked and she missed. 'Uncouth brute!'

He chucked her under the chin and nipped smartly out of the way before she could retaliate. 'Uncouth I may be and I admit I'm a self-made man, but there's no shame in that, is there, Ed, old chap?'

Edward swallowed hard and his beard moved up and down, seemingly of its own accord. 'It's true that hard work pays, Harold.'

'Father, I . . .' Harry began, but the timely arrival of Potter, announcing that dinner was served, put a stop to the cut and thrust.

Margaret pushed her husband out of the way and she took Edward's arm. 'We will lead the way into the dining room, Edward.' She glanced over her shoulder. 'Harry, escort your fiancée. I don't trust your father to lead her anywhere, unless it was into the broom cupboard. And don't deny it, Harold. I know all about your little antics with the maidservants.'

'Well, if you wasn't always pleading your delicate constitution when it comes to your conjugal duties, then maybe I wouldn't have to seek my rights as a husband elsewhere.' Harold strode on ahead, his footsteps echoing angrily on the marble-tiled floor of the entrance hall.

Rosina tugged at Harry's arm. 'It might be best if Papa and I went home now. Considering the circumstances.'

Harry stopped, halfway across the hall. 'Mother! Father! Rosina is embarrassed by your behaviour, so much so that she wants to go home.'

Margaret stopped and pointed a shaking finger at her husband as he disappeared into the dining room. 'It's all his fault. I can't be held to blame for his lack of breeding.' She fixed Rosina with a gimlet eye. 'You must not be upset by our trivial disagreements, my dear. I am, as you see, outnumbered by men and I need a female ally in my house. You will dine with us and there will be no further outbursts, I can assure you of that. Do you hear me in the dining room, Harold? Or are you in there taking liberties with Watson?'

Watson came running from the dining room, adjusting her white mobcap. 'I'm going for the soup, ma'am.'

'Harold, you licentious libertine.' Margaret marched into the dining room, leaving Edward standing open-mouthed, staring after her. Her scream of rage was followed by the sound of breaking china.

Rosina looked up into Harry's troubled face. 'Is it always like this?'

'Oh, no,' he replied, without the flicker of a smile. 'Sometimes it's much worse.'

'I think that we ought to leave,' Edward said, shuddering at the sound of another piece of crockery shattering against a wall.

'No, please.' Harry slipped his arm around Rosina's shoulders. 'Just wait a minute and they'll calm down. It will be as though nothing has happened, I promise you.'

Watson came hurrying towards them carrying a tureen. 'Soup,' she said tersely as she headed into the dining room, adding over her shoulder, 'if there's any plates left to serve it.'

'Come,' Harry said, squeezing Rosina's hand. 'It will be all right, believe me.'

She allowed him to lead her into the dining room, where their feet crunched on broken shards of china, and the host and hostess were already seated at opposite ends of the rectangular dining table. Potter was calmly setting out fresh soup plates and Harold rose to his feet, smiling. 'Pray be seated.' He raised his glass. 'Margaret, my love, let us toast the happy couple.'

She bared her teeth in a smile and raised her glass. 'To my darling boy and . . . I'm sorry, my dear – your name has slipped my mind.'

Harry pulled out a chair for Rosina. 'You know very well, Mama. Don't tease her.'

Margaret pulled a face. 'To whatever-her-name-is, as well. Oh, do serve the soup, Potter. I'm famished.'

Harold tucked a starched white table napkin into the top of his waistcoat and picked up his soup spoon, waving it at Edward. 'Well, I call this very sociable. We won't talk business in front of the ladies, but I'll be blunt, old boy. With your boat out of action I daresay your pockets are to let, so to speak.'

Edward choked on his soup. 'I – well, to be frank, things are a bit tight at the moment.'

'Say no more. Come to the office in the morning and I may be able to help you out, just until that boat of yours is shipshape and Bristol fashion again.'

'Do shut up, Harold.' Margaret glared at him and pushed her plate away. She turned to Rosina with a martyred expression. 'My digestive system is so delicate that the slightest upset robs me of my appetite. I daresay that I will fade away one day, and I doubt if anyone will even notice.'

'Don't worry, old girl. I'm sure they'll take you away on one of your pa's old dustcarts.' Harold winked at Rosina and continued to dip large chunks of bread in his soup, spilling most of it down his front.

'Sticks and stones, Harold,' Margaret said,

sipping her wine. 'You shall not provoke me. Remember that we have guests, and that this evening is to celebrate the betrothal of our son to . . .'

'Rosina, Mother.'

'Yes, to be sure. Potter, more wine if you please.'

The Gostellows did seem to have called a truce to hostilities during the long drawn-out meal, but Rosina could not relax and she barely tasted the excellent food. Her nerves were stretched as tight as violin strings, and she was heartily relieved when the time came to leave. Harry insisted on accompanying them home, and, having waited for Edward to enter the house on Black Eagle Wharf, he took Rosina in his arms and kissed her. His breath smelt of wine and cigar smoke, and his hands strayed to cup her breasts.

'I must go in, Harry. Papa will think it unseemly if I linger outside with you.'

'We are engaged, my darling.' Harry kissed her again, probing her mouth with his tongue and sliding his fingers down the front of her bodice.

She laid her hands flat against his chest in an effort to push him away. 'Goodnight, Harry.'

'Don't go in yet.' His voice was thick with desire and he tightened his arms around her waist. 'Just one more kiss, Rosie.'

She closed her eyes and allowed his embrace but she did not return his kiss. 'No, Harry.' She pushed harder as his fingers found the locket. 'That's enough, really.'

'Not nearly enough for me, as you will discover when we are married.' He chuckled deep in his throat, but he held the locket in the palm of his hand and he stared at it, a frown replacing his smile. 'Dare I ask whose likeness is enshrined in this gold case?'

'My mother and father, of course. Who else?'

'It could be another lover.'

She was quick to hear the note of jealousy in his voice, and Rosina snatched the locket from his grasp with a nervous giggle. 'Don't be absurd, Harry. You know that there is no one other than you.'

'Do I, my love? I rather thought you took a shine to that pirate fellow we met at Cremorne Gardens. He hasn't bothered you since, has he? Because I would take a pretty dim view of it if he had.'

'Don't be silly. Of course he hasn't. He was a perfect stranger.'

'And what about the scribbling Pharisee, Walter? You went rushing after him this afternoon instead of accompanying me to Hatton Garden to choose the ring. I forgave you, but I think it's pretty odd behaviour.'

'Harry, this is ridiculous. Why are you questioning me like this?' Rosina backed into the doorway. 'It's late and I'm tired.'

He laid his finger on her lips. 'Hush, my love. I didn't mean to upset you. Just remember one thing, Rosie. I love you and I am a very jealous man. I forbid you to have anything to do with Walter.'

'That is so unfair. Walter is just a friend, and he has been a good friend too.'

'Too good in my opinion. I'm telling you, Rosie. If I see him sniffing round here again I won't be responsible for my actions.'

'You can't mean that, Harry. Walter might come to see my papa. He might have work on the wharf. You can't stop him working.'

'Can I not? If he puts a foot on Black Eagle Wharf, I'll set the police on him. I'll have him arrested for embezzling your father's money, and he'll spend a very long time in prison.'

# Chapter Thirteen

It was sad to see a steam tug towing the *Ellie May* downriver to be beached and repaired by the shipwright. Rosina perched on the window seat in the parlour watching its slow progress. She was glad that her papa was not here to witness the event. He had gone out early that morning to keep his appointment with Harold Gostellow, and he had been in a high state of anticipation as to the nature of the employment he might be offered. Bertha had been equally excited, suggesting that Mr Gostellow might need a right-hand man to assist him in running his business. After all, who knew more about the hay trade than one who had worked in it for so many years? The captain might even end up as a partner in the firm, now that the two families were to be united by marriage. Rosina had said nothing; she suspected that her future father-in-law did not give much away, and she hoped that Papa would not be disappointed.

It was proving difficult to remain dry-eyed as the poor old *Ellie May* slid away from the wharf with her masts down, giving her the appearance of a mortally injured bird. Rosina sniffed and swallowed hard; she should be happy that the boat was going to be repaired and refurbished, and she should be grateful to the Gostellows for putting up the necessary money, but a nagging doubt lingered in her mind. She was prepared to place her whole future in Harry's hands, but she did not trust his father, and it was not just his roving eye and wandering hands that had coloured her judgement. As to Margaret, her future mother-in-law, the mere thought of her sent shivers down Rosina's spine. She stared at the diamond ring on her finger with a sick feeling in the pit of her stomach. Perhaps she could persuade Harry to replace it with a ring of her choosing. A piece of glass would do just as well if it was bought as a love token and not as a symbol of ownership.

She turned her head to stare out of the window as she heard a man's voice raised to a shout. She saw Captain Barnum standing on the edge of the wharf gesticulating at the fast-disappearing *Ellie May*. She could not hear what he was saying, but she could tell from his expression that he was enjoying the spectacle. Suddenly his attention was focused in a different direction. Rosina craned her neck, but it was not hard to guess who was on the receiving end of Barnum's taunts.

'Papa.' As he came within her range of vision, Rosina knew by the hunch of his shoulders and plodding gait that something was wrong. It was not the walk of a jubilant man. She leapt to her feet, tripping over her long skirts in her haste to get down the stairs. Without bothering to put on her bonnet, she ran out into the hot July sunshine. Captain Barnum had been joined by Sukey and her sisters, and they were laughing as he pointed at Edward's dejected figure. As he drew nearer, Rosina could tell from his dull eyes and down-turned lips that her papa was not a happy man. She hastened to his side. 'Papa, what's the matter? What went wrong?'

Edward shook his head. 'It was humiliating, poppet. I'm a man cut down to size.'

Barnum strode towards them. 'I see your old hulk has been towed away. Has she been taken to the match factory then? I suspect that is all she's worth now.'

'Stow your gaff, Barnum. I ain't in the mood.'

'Things going bad for you, are they, May? I'm sorry to hear it.'

'No you ain't, you two-faced river rat. You're enjoying me suffering, and you're the one who caused it in the first place.'

'Best be careful what you say, old man. I could have you up for slander.' Barnum waved his hand to encompass the dockers who had stopped work to watch and listen. 'I have plenty of witnesses.'

'You have now, you lily-livered coward. But

where were the witnesses that night on the river when you rammed my boat? None – and why? Because you made certain that there was none.'

'That is slander. It was an accident and your man wasn't keeping a proper watch, so you'd best keep your trap shut, May.'

'I've sent a letter of complaint to the Wharfingers' Association. You'll be lucky if the Watermen's Company renew your licence, Barnum. I'll see you out of business, you bastard.'

'You'll be too busy defending yourself in court to care what happens to me. I'm accusing you of setting the river pirates to steal from my boat.'

'What? That's ridiculous.'

'Is it? Then tell me why it is that they chose the *Curlew* to rob, and none other?'

'How should I know?'

'You know because it was you who instigated the thefts. Twice I've had my vessel stripped of everything that wasn't nailed down, and your boat ain't been touched. I call that pretty strong evidence as to who's behind the robberies.'

Edward took a menacing step towards Barnum, who fisted his hands as if ready for a fight.

Rosina sprang between them. 'Stop it, both of you. This is no way to behave.'

'Yes, Pa. Come away.' Sukey tugged at her father's coat tails. 'Don't lower yourself to speak to that family. They're no better than the river pirates.'

'Sukey!' Rosina stared at her in horror. 'I thought you were my friend.'

'Yes, I was your friend, but you were not mine.' Sukey pointed to Rosina's left hand. 'You stole my beau. He was mine but you bewitched him, you crafty cow.'

'Don't lower yourself by speaking to the trollop,' Barnum said, pulling Sukey away. 'Go home to your mother, girl. This is man's business.'

'Sukey,' Rosina pleaded. 'Let me explain.'

Sukey's lip curled and her blue eyes narrowed. 'You don't love Harry. You just want him for his money. I'll never speak to you again as long as I live, Rosina May.' Turning on her heel, she tossed her blonde curls and stalked off towards home.

Mary shot a venomous look at Rosina. 'Traitor!' She marched off after her sister, dragging Lillian by the hand. Lillian turned her head and stuck her tongue out, crossing her eyes and blowing a raspberry. It was not a pretty sight and Rosina stared helplessly after them. Everything had gone horribly wrong. She could not blame Sukey for being upset, but at least she could have given her the opportunity to explain.

'I hope you're satisfied, girl,' Barnum said, sneering. 'You've broken my poor Sukey's heart, you hussy. But I suppose that the rotten apple doesn't fall far from the tree.'

'Now you've gone too far, Barnum.' Edward drew himself up to his full height. 'You can say what you like to me, but you don't insult my girl.'

Barnum gave him a pitying look. 'It's obvious, ain't it? Your girl has sold herself to the highest bidder in order to bail you out, you old fool. Anyone can see that.' With a scornful laugh, he strode off towards the wharfinger's office.

Rosina tugged at her father's arm. 'Don't pay any heed to him, Papa. He's just a horrid, spiteful old man. He doesn't know what he's saying.'

'Spiteful old man, am I?' Barnum stopped in his tracks, turning his head with a scornful curl of his lips. 'Well, old man I may be. But this year I'm going to win the sailing barge match, and at least your pa won't have the humiliation of losing yet again.'

'Maybe not.' Edward placed himself squarely in front of Rosina. 'But I'll be there to jeer when you come in last.'

'You'll be laughing on the other side of your face when I return with the trophy.'

'This is getting us nowhere, Papa.' Rosina tugged at his arm. 'Come home and leave Captain Barnum to crow if he so wishes, but I know who is the better man.'

Reluctantly, Edward allowed her to lead him into the house. 'I may not be able to compete this year, but I'll beat him at that match next year, Rosie. If it's the last thing I do, I'll wipe that grin off Barnum's face.'

'Yes, Papa. I'm sure you will.' As they passed the office, Rosina instinctively turned her head to look inside, half expecting to see Walter at his usual post, sitting behind the desk with his dark head bent over a ledger or a bill of lading. But, of course, he was not there and never would be unless Harry had a change of heart.

'I miss that boy,' Edward said as if reading her thoughts. 'To think that he has been systematically cheating me is like a dagger plunging into my heart. I almost thought of him as a son, and that was how he repaid me.'

'Walter is innocent, Papa. I believe that, and I think you know it, deep down.'

'I'd like to, poppet. But Harry made a good case against him.'

She could see that it was useless to argue. 'Come into the kitchen, Papa. Bertha will make you a nice hot cup of tea.'

Caddie was sitting at the kitchen table feeding baby Arthur, and the two older boys were gnawing on raw carrots. Bertha jumped up from her chair, taking in Edward's downcast expression with a glance, and without saying a word she set about making a brew of tea.

'Sit down, Papa,' Rosina said gently. 'Tell us everything.'

Edward sank onto the chair by the range. 'There's not much to tell, poppet.'

'Stop shilly-shallying, old man, and tell us.'

Bertha poured boiling water onto the tea leaves in the pot. 'Did he give you a job or not?'

'Don't bully me, woman.' Edward tugged at his necktie, loosening his starched collar with agitated fingers. 'He's given me work of sorts.'

Rosina knelt down beside him. 'Tell us the worst, Papa.'

'He gave me a job in the warehouse.'

'But, Papa, the doctor said you weren't to work with hay. It will bring on your chest complaint.'

'It was all that Gostellow had to offer, poppet. He's paying me a fair wage for my labours and we have to eat. Without the barge I have no livelihood. I can't do any better until I get my boat back.'

'Well, I call it an insult,' Bertha said angrily.

Caddie hitched Arthur over her shoulder, rubbing his tiny back. 'Mr Harry is going to pay me for being Rosie's maid. You can have all my wages, Captain May.'

'Thank you, Caddie. But we couldn't exist on what little Harry Gostellow intends to pay you. I can work in the warehouse until my boat is ready. It won't kill me.'

Rosina patted his hand, biting back tears. It was cruel of Harry's father to treat her papa like a common labourer. 'Isn't there any other way?'

'Not that I can see.'

'But he did agree to pay for the repairs to the *Ellie May*?' When her father did not answer immediately, Rosina grasped his hand, sensing trouble. 'Did he, Pa?'

'You really mustn't worry your pretty head about business, my dear. Harold agreed to advance the money, but there was a condition.'

'For heaven's sake, man. Tell us everything.' Bertha poured tea into a mug and handed it to him. 'There's no milk. I give it to the little ones.'

Edward sipped his tea and pulled a face. 'And no sugar, it seems.'

'How can I buy sugar if I don't have any money?' Bertha stood with arms akimbo. 'You might as well tell us the worst of it, old man. We're three grown women and you don't have to treat us like nippers.'

'Well, then. The truth of it is that I had to put the house up as security against the loan. Don't look so alarmed, Rosie. It's just a legal formality, and as soon as the *Ellie May* is refitted and repaired I'll be able to start repaying Gostellow with interest. This time next year, we'll be back on our feet. And you, my little Rosie, will be a married lady with a position in society.'

'But, Papa. What happens if you cannot repay Mr Gostellow?'

'That won't happen, poppet.' He set the mug down and rose slowly to his feet. 'Now, I have to get back to the warehouse and start earning my wages.'

'I never thought I'd live to see the day!'

Bertha said, throwing up her hands. 'I'd sooner take in washing than allow my master to stoop so low.'

'Shut up, you old war horse.' Edward tempered his words with a tired smile. 'There's no call for talk like that. I am the head of my household and I'll put bread on the table.'

'We're a burden to you, Captain,' Caddie said, blinking away a tear. 'My Artie would be turning in his grave if he knew what had happened.'

Edward picked up his cap and set it on his head. 'Artie was as good a man as ever sailed on the river. I doubt I'll ever be able to replace him, Caddie. But the least I can do is look after his widow and his boys. Never speak of being a burden, my dear. I'm proud to have you living under my roof.' He hurried from the kitchen, closing the door behind him.

'There goes a good and a brave man,' Bertha said, scowling. 'I'd like to wring that Gostellow fellow's neck.'

'Well, I won't have Pa treated this way,' Rosina said, snatching her bonnet off its peg. 'I'm going to speak to Harry, and if I can't get any sense out of him, then I'll go and have it out with Mr Gostellow himself.'

She found Harry in the outer office of Gostellow and Son, Hay and Provender Merchants. He was riffling through a sheaf of papers with a frown puckering his brow. He looked up as she entered, and he smiled. 'Rosie, my love, what a pleasant surprise.'

He looked so genuinely pleased to see her that the harsh words died on her lips. In her head she could hear Sukey's furious voice accusing her of being interested solely in his money. It plagued her conscience to admit that it was partly true. She forced Will's ever-present image to the back of her mind. She would never see her pirate again – Harry was her future. She would do everything in her power to make him happy, and she would never let him know that he was second best. 'Am I intruding, Harry? I don't want to get in the way of your business.'

'I would willingly put business matters aside for you, Rosie.' He came out from behind the desk, taking her in his arms and kissing her on the lips. 'Could you not bear to be parted from me, sweetheart?'

She drew away from him, struggling to find the right words. 'Of course I wanted to see you, Harry. But I need to speak to you about Papa.'

'Is anything wrong?'

'No – well, yes. Your father was good enough to find him temporary work, but I fear for Papa's health. The doctor said that he should not be exposed to hay because it brings on his chest complaint. I'm afraid that working in the ware-house will make him ill. Is there nothing else that he could do?'

'If what you say is true, then your father will not be able to work for us even when the boat is repaired. If he cannot work with hay, then we will have no further use for him or his barge.'

She stifled a horrified gasp. Why had she not thought that far ahead? She had been so busy thinking about the here and now that she had not considered the long-term aspects of her father's ill health. There were other cargoes, of course, but Papa had spent many years dealing with the farmers in Essex, building up his trade with them – to say nothing of goodwill – that to change at his time of life might prove impossible. 'Perhaps I am wrong, Harry. In fact, I think I may have been mistaken. The doctor did say that it was the mouldy hay that was the cause of Papa's problems.'

'My darling, you really should not try to understand business.' Harry slipped his arm around her waist, chuckling. 'Leave that to us men, dearest. If your father cannot work in the warehouse, which is a very responsible position, then we will find him something less taxing on his health. As to the future, I will take care of you. When we are married you will be my sole responsibility, and I will see that you never want for anything.' He kissed her firmly on the lips. 'And if Captain May is not fit enough to return to the river, then I will put another captain in charge of the *Ellie May*, and your papa will be able to hang up his sea boots and retire.'

'Please don't tell him about this conversation. He wouldn't thank me for interfering.'

'I won't breathe a word of it.'

'And you won't mention it to your papa?'

'My darling, my lips are sealed.' Harry held her even closer to him. 'You are so beautiful, Rosie. I cannot wait to make you mine.'

Attempting to pull away from him, Rosina was alarmed to find that this seemed to excite him more and his arms banded around her like steel.

'We must name the day, sweetheart. The sooner the better as far as I am concerned.'

'Yes, Harry.'

He relaxed a little, raising his eyebrows in surprise. 'Really? Do you mean it, my love?'

'Of course I do, or I would not have said so. Let us get married as soon as possible.'

'My darling, you don't know how happy that makes me.'

His mouth sought hers in a long and passionate kiss, and Rosina responded with as much enthusiasm as she could muster. Harry really loved her and she must not disappoint him. Once they were married, her papa would be certain of some kind of employment with the Gostellows, and their home would be secure. She rested her hands on his chest, gently easing away from him. She met his gaze with a determined lift of her chin: her decision was made. 'We could get a special licence and be married tomorrow, or the next day.'

'You little minx,' he said with a teasing smile. 'To know that you are so eager makes me a very happy man, but I don't want a hole in the corner affair. I want you to have the best wedding that money can buy.'

She glanced at her left hand as it rested on his expensive tailored jacket: Margaret's ring seemed to wink mockingly at her. 'I don't care about all that, Harry. But there is one thing I would like.'

'Anything, just name it.'

'I would like my own engagement ring. I don't feel right wearing one that belonged to your mother. It should be on her finger, not on mine.'

'You dear, sensitive child. You must not think that. Mama wanted you to have it and she would be mortified if I were to buy you another. You and my mama are the two women dearest to my heart, and I want you to love her as I do. We are going to be so happy together, all of us Gostellows in Gostellow Mansion.'

'Yes, Harry.' She had heard people say that they felt their heart sink, and now Rosina knew exactly what they meant. She might grow to love Harry, but the thought of living with his parents was almost too much to bear. She had to stifle the impulse to tear herself from his arms and run away from the stuffy office that smelt of money, dust and hay. She had sealed her own fate – now she must live with her promise to become Harry's wife.

'We must celebrate, darling,' Harry said, tracing the outline of her face with the tip of his finger as if committing every last detail of her features to memory. 'I will take you out to celebrate our engagement, anywhere you like.'

Her first thought was of Cremorne Gardens, ablaze with gaslights and the velvet night air filled with the scent of flowers and music. But Will would not be there, and the bittersweet memories would be too much to bear. 'You choose, Harry. But this time we will have to get Pa's permission, and I don't think he would allow me to go out unchaperoned, even if we are officially engaged.'

'Then we will go out in a foursome – that must be acceptable to him. You can ask Sukey to accompany you with a gentleman of her choosing.'

'I don't know about that. The ill feeling between our fathers has come between Sukey and me.'

Harry patted her hand. 'All the more reason for us to mend the breach, my dear. I will call upon the Barnums; there can be no objection to that.'

Rosina could hardly break a friend's confidence; she could not tell Harry that he was the main reason for her falling out with Sukey. But neither could she dissuade him from his purpose. He insisted on escorting her home, and then he went on to the Barnums' house to see Sukey. Rosina did not think that he would receive an enthusiastic welcome. She was all the more astounded, when half an hour later, looking out of the parlour window, she saw Harry and Sukey walking arm in arm along the wharf. They were headed in her direction and seemed to be on the best of terms. She hurried downstairs to open the door.

Harry doffed his hat, smiling. 'It's all arranged, my love. Sukey has agreed to accompany us on our outing. I am to make the arrangements.'

Sukey threw her arms around Rosina's neck. 'Rosie, I am so sorry. It was a foolish argument.'

Rosina hugged her. 'It was all my fault.'

'No, I won't allow that. I was in part to blame.'

Harry chuckled. 'Please, ladies. Don't fall out again over who was the most culpable. You are friends again, and that is all that matters.' He tipped the curly brim of his hat with his fingers and set it at a rakish angle. 'Now, I must get back to the office. Can I trust you two to be nice to each other?'

'Harry, you are such a tease.' Sukey flashed him a coy glance beneath her lashes.

'We will be perfectly fine,' Rosina said, taking Sukey by the hand. 'Come up to the parlour, and we can talk. Goodbye, Harry.'

'Until this evening, my dear. I will call on you after supper, if that's all right with you?'

'Of course.' Rosina gave him a cheery wave as

she dragged Sukey into the house and up the stairs to the parlour. Once they were inside, she released her hand and gave her a searching look. 'Have you really forgiven me?'

Sukey smiled. 'I hated you for a while, but then I realised that it was hardly your fault if Harry preferred you to me. I just didn't know how to make things right with you. Then Harry turned up on our doorstep, and he was so sweet and sincere that I simply melted. You are so lucky to have found such a wonderful man, Rosie. I envy you, but I am happy for you too.'

'You really do love him, don't you, Sukey?'

'Enough to want only his happiness, and if he achieves that by marrying you, then I would be a mean-spirited person if I could not be pleased for him and for you too. We've been friends for as long as I can remember, Rosie. We mustn't allow a mere man to come between us.'

Rosina threw her arms around Sukey and gave her a hug. 'No, indeed.'

Sukey broke away with a trill of laughter. 'Look at us two silly things. Scratching each other's eyes out one minute and firm friends the next.' She did a twirl, holding out her skirts. 'Do you like my new gown? Papa bought it for me. I think he felt guilty for once in his life. Anyway, now he's gone off on that silly old barge match. He'll be totally insufferable if he wins. He'll gloat over your poor pa for weeks.'

'Won't he be angry if you come out with Harry and me?'

Sukey sat down on the sofa in a swirl of pink taffeta. 'We've thought of that. Harry has a rich friend who is going to escort me. Isn't that thrilling? I might just fall in love with him, if he's good-looking as well as wealthy. Harry is going to arrange a chaperone, so it will all look splendidly respectable.'

'It seems he's thought of everything.' Rosina went to sit on the window seat. So this was how her future life was going to be, with Harry planning and organising every last detail without even consulting her.

'You might sound a bit more enthusiastic,' Sukey said with a teasing smile. 'I'd love to be cosseted and pampered by a man like Harry.'

'I'm not used to it, that's all.'

'Then you'd better get used to it, Rosie. For Harry told me that he intends to spoil you and give you everything your heart desires. You'll live in that enormous mansion with servants waiting on you hand and foot. You'll drive in a private carriage and wear silks and satins.'

'Yes,' Rosina said dully. 'I am very fortunate, I do know that.'

'I shall have to stop thinking about it, or I will become very jealous, and then we'll quarrel again. We can't have that.'

'No. We must not quarrel.'

'And I have some gossip for you. About a certain young man who used to work for your papa.'

'Walter?'

'The very same. You'll never guess who has given him a job, or where he is working now. It is such a scream, I can hardly tell you for laughing.'

Momentarily forgetting Harry and her painful conscience, Rosina was suddenly alert. 'Don't tease me. Tell me, please.'

'Pa gave Walter a job on one of his barges. I think it was because your father had turned him out on the street, so, being contrary, my pa stepped in and made Walter mate on the *Mudlark*.'

'But Walter isn't a sailor. I can't imagine that he would know one end of a boat from the other.'

'I told you it was a scream. Poor Walter won't know if he's coming or going once Captain Juggins starts bellowing orders at him. He's a foul old man who can't keep a mate for more than a couple of trips. I wouldn't be surprised if they ran aground or sank before they got as far as Barking Reach.'

The unfairness of it all! Rosina had to force herself to keep calm when she longed to leap to her feet and cry out at the unfairness of Walter's treatment. First, Harry, then Papa and now Captain Barnum – it seemed as though they had all ganged up on him, determined to destroy a good and honest man. She clenched her fists, hiding them beneath the folds of her skirt. Somehow she managed to keep her voice calm. 'Poor Walter, indeed. Has the *Mudlark* set sail, Sukey? Do you know where she is trading?'

'No, nor do I care. I take no interest in Pa's beastly business. I hate barges and boats of all kinds. I hate this smelly old wharf and I long to move away from it all. It's so – so sordid.'

'The *Mudlark* carries coal, I believe.'

'Does she? I really don't know. Let's talk about something else, Rosie. Where shall we ask Harry to take us on this outing? Shall it be the theatre? I love the theatre. Or could we go to Cremorne Gardens again, do you think? It was so wonderfully romantic; at least it was until you went off with that man in the silly fancy dress. Did you ever discover his true identity?'

Rosina shook her head. She could not bring herself to lie outright to Sukey, but neither could she tell her the truth. Will really was the river pirate and now he was on the run from the police. Piracy, whether at sea or on the river, was a serious offence, which would incur a long term of penal servitude, or even hanging. She could not endanger him by revealing his identity, even to Sukey.

'What is the matter with you today?' Sukey rose to her feet, staring hard at Rosina. 'You should be dancing for joy with Harry's ring on your finger. I don't understand you, Rosie.'

Rosina held out her hand so that Sukey could examine the diamond. 'It was his mother's ring.'

'No! Really? And she gave it to you. Oh, I think that's so romantic, Rosie. She must think a great deal of you to give you her own engagement ring.' Sukey's blue eyes brimmed with unshed tears. 'You lucky, lucky girl.'

'It's taken me by surprise. Life was so easy and settled. I thought things would never change, and then, all of a sudden, everything is different.'

'But change for the better is good. Soon you will be a married lady, and you will have to find me a rich husband. Maybe Harry's friend will be that man. I'm so excited, Rosie. It's going to be a thrilling evening.'

'Are you sure you don't know which wharf Captain Juggins's barge sails from, and when it is due in?'

'Oh, Rosie. Forget about dull old Walter for a minute. We need to discuss what we are going to wear for our night out.'

Rosina could not forget Walter. She needed to be certain that he was going to be all right working with the notoriously bad-tempered and sometimes drunken Captain Juggins. She could not imagine how Walter would take to a life of hard physical work, and she worried constantly about him. She dared not confide in Harry or even her pa; Bertha would tell her not to be a silly goose and to concentrate on her betrothed, so it was Caddie to whom she unburdened herself late that evening when Harry had left, and she was getting ready for bed.

'I know where the colliers from Whitby discharge their cargoes onto barges and lighters. It's St Hilda's Wharf. My Artie mentioned it once, although I can't think why it come up in conversation. He didn't like the coal trade – too mucky and dirty. Artie was particular about being clean and keeping hisself looking good.' Caddie's eyes filled with tears and she sniffed. 'I can take you there, if you want to go looking for Walter.'

'I do, Caddie. I must see him and make sure he's all right, but no one must know about it. Not even Bebe.'

# Chapter Fourteen

She did not recognise him at first, but when she called his name Walter looked up and smiled. His teeth flashed white in a face that was blackened with coal dust.

'Rosie!' He leapt for the ladder and his feet slipped on the slimy rungs, but he shinned up to stand beside her with surprising agility for a landsman. He tipped his cap to her and to Caddie who was standing at her side. 'You shouldn't have come here. This isn't a nice place.'

Rosina glanced nervously in the direction of the dark figures at work unloading the collier. They were too absorbed in their task to take much notice of two young women, who so obviously had no place in this man-made depiction of Hades. Clouds of coal dust filled the air as the cargo was transferred to the hold of the barge. Everything on and around St Hilda's Wharf, from the warehouse buildings to the furled sails of the ships, was covered in a film of black dust. The workers had the eerie, ghost-like appearance of dark shadows, with only the whites of their eyes and the pink tinge of their lips to make them look human. The river water lapping around the hulls was slicked with powdered coal and the seagulls wore black mantles, like lawyers in their robes. 'This is a dreadful place, Walter. I can't bear to see you brought this low.' Rosina laid her hand on his arm, but he pulled away from her.

'Don't touch me. I'm filthy.'

'It's only coal dust – it will wash off. But the slur on your good name will stick. You must clear yourself of blame, Walter. Then you can come home.'

'I will, given time. But I have to earn a living somehow, and word gets round quickly. My reputation is such that no one will employ me in a counting house.'

Caddie cleared her throat, drawing their attention to her presence. 'I wouldn't have taken you for a waterman, sir.'

'Caddie! Since when have you called me sir?'

'Since I am now Miss Rosina's maid, bought and paid for by her fiancé, Mr Gostellow.'

'Rosie? Is this true? Have you accepted Gostellow?'

She could not meet his eyes. 'I have, but that shouldn't concern you.'

He seized her hands in his, gripping them so tightly that Rosina winced. 'Were you forced into this engagement? Tell me honestly, Rosie. Do you love this man?'

'You're hurting me, Walter.'

'Answer me, Rosie.' He tightened his grip, staring into her eyes. 'Were you coerced into this match?'

She pulled her hands away, raising her chin and meeting his angry gaze with a defiant stare. 'That is none of your business, Walter. I came here to speak about you and your fate, not mine. I know what I'm doing, and it really is no concern of yours.'

Walter lowered his voice but his eyes blazed angrily. 'And what of Will? I thought you loved him. Or was the lure of money too much for you?'

Caddie's gasp was drowned by the sound of flesh on flesh as Rosina slapped Walter's face. 'That was unworthy of you, and insulting to me. I came here to make certain that you were all right, and to offer to find you more suitable work. But now I wish I hadn't come.'

'You shouldn't have come,' Walter said slowly, raising his hand to touch his cheek.

Rosina bit her lip. Her fingerprints were clearly etched in the dirt on his face, and she regretted her hasty action, but she would not apologise. 'What you said was unforgivable. Will is gone – I will never see him again. He told me that himself.'

Caddie tugged at her sleeve. 'Best come away now.'

'I'm coming.' Rosina brushed her hand away, leaving sooty marks on Caddie's arm. 'I'm leaving now, Walter. I wish things had been different, but I can see that we have nothing left to say to each other. If you see your brother you can tell him . . .'

'What shall I tell him, Rosie? What would you have me say to him?'

'Nothing. It isn't important now. Goodbye, Walter.' She turned to go, but he blocked her way.

'If you ever need me . . .'

'If I ever need you?' Rosina's voice broke with emotion. 'You didn't tell me where you were going, or what you were doing. You went away, just like your brother. I realise now that I cannot rely on either of you. Perhaps Harry was right in his accusations.'

'He was not.'

She raised her eyes to his face. This angry man was not the Walter she knew and cared for; this was a different person to the quiet, sensitive and earnest fellow she thought she knew. She angled her head, as if seeing him for the first time. 'Why aren't you wearing your spectacles? I thought you looked strange, and it wasn't just the coal dust, and now I know why.'

'I only need them for close work. They would get knocked off and broken working on the barge, or be so coated with dirt that I could barely see anyway.'

'You look so different. I don't think I know you, Walter.'

'I am the same person, Rosie. I haven't changed.'

'Yes, you have.'

'Don't marry him, Rosie.'

'Goodbye, Walter.' Slipping past him, she turned in the direction of home. 'Come along, Caddie.'

'I'm coming, but first I have something to say to Walter.'

'I can't think what you have to say to him. I'm going.' Rosina squared her shoulders and walked on, quickening her pace. Perhaps she had been mistaken in believing Walter to be innocent. Maybe he was of the criminal fraternity just like his brother. She had allowed her romantic notions to cloud her judgement, falling in love with a phantom.

She stopped at the end of the wharf, glancing down at her hands covered in coal dust, and the diamond winked at her. Marriage with Harry was the only way ahead and her future lay in the hands of the Gostellow family. She would pay a social call on her future mother-in-law, perhaps tomorrow afternoon, and she would make a great effort to get on with her. Harry had promised to take her to a theatre and afterwards to a restaurant for a late supper: she was looking forward to it immensely. If Walter didn't want her help to find a better job, that was his decision: she had done her bit. Rosina turned her head to look for Caddie. She was still talking to Walter and his dark head was bent low as if he was listening intently to what she had to say. A shaft of something very much like jealousy stabbed her in the heart, and she tossed her head. She could not be jealous of Walter – never in a million years.

'Caddie. Don't dawdle. I'm not waiting for you.' She marched off in the direction of home.

'There has been a slight change of plan,' Harry said, leaning back against the leather squabs of his father's carriage.

Sukey clapped her gloved hands together. 'Oh, Harry, how exciting. Do tell.'

'You mean we are not going to the theatre?' Rosina could not prevent a note of disappointment creeping into her voice. She had never been to a theatrical performance and she had been looking forward to their outing for days.

He smiled. 'We are going somewhere much more exciting.'

Rosina exchanged anxious glances with Caddie. It had been hard enough to persuade Pa to allow them to go to the theatre; he would not be best pleased to learn that Harry had changed his plans without first asking his permission. She was about to question him, but Sukey was agog with excitement. 'Don't keep us in suspense, Harry.'

'We are meeting my friend at Ludgate Hill station.' Harry turned to Caddie, his smile fading. 'We won't be needing your services after all, Trigg. Chapman will take you home.'

Anger replaced surprise and Rosina spoke sharply. 'Harry! Papa only allowed us to come with you if Caddie was to act as chaperone.'

He reached out to take her hand in his, squeezing her fingers and smiling into her eyes. 'I am here to look after you, my love. In a month's time we will be married and you will never need your papa's permission to do anything again.'

'But, sir . . .' Caddie began, and was silenced by a quelling glance from Harry. She subsided into the corner of the carriage with a disgruntled sigh.

'Well, I think it's a lark,' Sukey said. 'I love mysteries.'

Rosina was not so enthusiastic; somehow she did not quite trust Harry when he was in this mood. He had a reckless air about him and a glint of mischief in his eyes that made her feel uncomfortable. His hand was hot and when she attempted to pull hers away, he tightened his grasp. A small shiver of apprehension ran down her spine, but the carriage was drawing to a halt and Harry leaned over her to open the door. He leapt out, barking an order to Chapman to lower the steps.

'He is so masterful,' Sukey murmured. 'You are a lucky girl, Rosie.'

Harry held his hand out to Rosina. 'Come along, my love. Hurry up, or we'll miss our train.'

She alighted with his help. 'Train? Where are we going?'

He held his hand out to Sukey. 'Come along, Miss Barnum. We're meeting my friend inside the station.'

Caddie leaned out of the door. 'What am I to do, miss? I should come with you.'

'You take your instructions from me, Trigg,' Harry said coldly. 'You will go home and you will make some excuse to Captain May. Tell him that you were unwell, but don't you dare mention that we have changed our plans.'

'Harry, I won't budge until you tell me where we are going. And please don't speak to Caddie in that tone. She is not one of your servants.'

For a moment, Rosina thought that he was going to lose his temper, but then Harry forced his lips into a smile. 'That will all change when we are married, although I don't think I will be keeping Trigg on. We will find you a properly trained lady's maid, my love.'

Sukey tapped him on the arm. 'Harry, don't be an old crosspatch. Do tell us where we're going.'

'We're going to the Crystal Palace at Sydenham. We'll travel by train – first class, of course. Come, we haven't any more time to waste.'

Reluctantly, Rosina tucked her hand in his proffered arm. 'Go home, Caddie. You needn't wait up for me.'

'Take her back to Black Eagle Wharf, Chapman.' Harry offered his arm to Sukey. 'Now, ladies. Let's begin our adventure to deepest, darkest Sydenham and the delights of the Crystal Palace. But first we must find Roland – that is if he has not grown tired with waiting and gone home.'

'Roland?' Rosie's heart thudded against her ribs.

'You remember him, sweetheart. We met him at Cremorne Gardens. Roland Rivers – I hear that he's a great chap when you get to know him, and hugely wealthy.'

'Is he really?' Sukey's eyes lit up. 'I remember him now. He's good-looking and rich too. What fun.'

The evening had not begun well, and Rosina could not share Sukey's enthusiasm for the outing. She found it difficult to be polite to Rivers, but he either did not remember that Will had tossed him over the balcony of the supper booth at Cremorne Gardens, or he had deliberately chosen to forget the incident. He was all charm and good manners during the train journey to Sydenham and the short walk from the station to the Crystal Palace. Sukey flirted outrageously with Roland, and he did nothing to discourage her, but Rosina was uncomfortable in his presence, even though he said very little to her. It was the way she caught him looking at her that was embarrassing and unnerving – as if he could see through her pink silk gown, through her stays and her cotton lawn chemise to her bare flesh. She kept close to Harry, allowing him to slip his arm round her waist in a familiar fashion as they strolled through the magnificent gardens. If she had not felt so strained and over-anxious, she would have appreciated the setting and enjoyed the open-air concert, but worms of worry niggled her brain. There was something not quite right, although she could not quite put her finger on the cause of her anxiety. They had supper in the garden room of the palace, but she barely tasted the food. Harry, however, ate with a good appetite: he ordered champagne and claret, of which he drank many glasses, as did Roland. Under the influence of the wine, they became loud and effusive with their compliments. Harry's hand strayed to touch her thigh beneath the starched white tablecloth, and Rosina felt herself blushing. She moved her leg, frowning at him, but he merely chuckled and tightened his grip. She could not make a scene in the restaurant, and she turned away from him, sipping her champagne although she did not particularly like the taste. She glanced anxiously at Sukey, who had drunk far too much and had become giggly; she was flirting even more outrageously with Roland. He was leaning towards her, toying with the corsage of silk flowers on her bodice and allowing his fingers to stray to the swell of her breasts above the décolletage of her gown. Sukey should have slapped his hand away, but she seemed to be enjoying the sensation. Rosina could stand it no longer. She rose to her feet. 'It's getting late, Harry. I think we ought to go back to the station.'

'Put that girl down, Rivers,' Harry said, getting to his feet. 'There'll be plenty of time for spooning later.'

'What do you mean by that?' Rosina demanded.

Harry shrugged his shoulders. 'Nothing, my love. It's just a figure of speech.'

Outside, the summer evening had dissolved into a purple dusk and the lighting displays, for which the gardens were justly famed, illuminated the scene with dazzling brilliance. A burst of coloured stars followed by a loud bang brought a gasp of appreciation from the spectators who had gathered to watch the firework display.

'Oh, how lovely,' Sukey cried, leaning heavily on Roland's arm. 'We must stay and watch the fireworks.'

Rosina was torn; she would dearly love to watch the display, but Harry's arm was a little too tightly clasped around her waist for comfort. His hand was straying upwards to touch her breasts. Glancing up at him, she saw a hot look of desire in his eyes, and his breath was wine-scented and warm against her cheek. 'Oughtn't we to be getting back to the station, Harry? We might miss the last train if we don't go now.'

He pinched her cheek. 'You are such a little worrier, my pet. We will be in plenty of time to catch the last train, won't we, Rivers?'

'Absolutely, old man,' Roland said, winking.

'Don't be a spoilsport, Rosie,' Sukey giggled. 'We're having such a splendid time.' She held her champagne glass out to Roland. 'A little more, Roly. I love the bubbles, they tickle my nose.'

He laughed and refilled her glass from the champagne bottle that he had taken from their table. 'I would dearly love to tickle your pretty little nose and more, if you'll let me, Sukey.'

She sipped the champagne, slanting a coy look at him beneath her lashes. 'You are a wicked man, Roly.'

'Drink up, my sweet. Champagne makes your eyes shine like the stars above and brings roses to your cheeks.' Roland poured the bubbling wine into her glass so that it overflowed.

'I think she's had quite enough,' Rosina said, casting a pleading glance at Harry. 'We ought to get her home.'

'Of course we will, my darling. After the fireworks display has ended, I promise you that we will leave.'

She was not convinced: she had seen the look that passed between them, and she sensed that Harry was not telling her the whole truth.

A rocket whooshed up into the sky, causing Sukey to shriek with delight. She dropped her glass and clung to Roland, who immediately discarded the bottle and wrapped his arms around her. She did not look like a girl who wanted to be saved from all this impropriety, but Rosina could see that Sukey was not herself. The wine had gone to her head and she was, if Rosina were to be totally frank, drunk. She made a move towards Sukey, but Harry tightened his hold, drawing her to him and claiming her mouth in a kiss that was laced with pent-up passion. His tongue snaked in between her parted lips, exploring her mouth and shocking her with the intensity of his desire. This was not the sweetly sensual way in which he had kissed her on previous occasions and she was panicked by his unashamed lust. She pulled away from him, wiping her lips on the back of her hand.

'Harry, we are not married yet.'

Seemingly unabashed, he nuzzled her hair. 'You will not push me away then, my pet. I will teach you how to love a man so that you beg me for more.'

A series of flashes and bangs with showers of coloured sparks flying up into the air prevented any further conversation. Bats circled crazily overhead and the warm breeze was filled with the scent of roses and night-scented stock. Memories of the evening at Cremorne Gardens came flooding back, and Rosina found herself looking round and praying that her pirate would materialise from nowhere and take her away from all this. But commonsense reasserted itself and she knew that he would not come. Will was probably miles away from London by now and hopefully safe from discovery by the law. Walter would be somewhere on the river, taking the cargo of coal to its destination. Papa was at home, expecting them to return from the theatre very soon. What would he think when they did not arrive?

'Aren't you enjoying the fireworks, my love?' Harry's voice was chocolate smooth in her ear.

'I really do think we should leave now, Harry. Sukey has drunk far too much champagne and we ought to get her home.'

'Of course, darling. You are right as always.' To her surprise and relief, Harry turned to Roland. 'It's time we took the ladies home, Rivers.'

'I couldn't agree more.' Roland hitched Sukey's arm around his shoulder. She hung limply, like a puppet with a broken string. 'I may have to carry her, old boy.' He hoisted her into his arms, and grinned as he followed them towards the exit. 'She's light as a feather, but thank goodness it ain't far to the station hotel.'

'To the station hotel?' Rosina would have stopped but Harry had her in a firm grasp, and he dragged her with him as he quickened his pace.

'Just to wait for the train, sweetheart. And a pot of strong coffee will do Miss Barnum the world of good.'

She had no alternative but to walk alongside Harry, but she was determined that she would not set a foot inside the hotel. If Pa were to find out she had done such a thing, he would never forgive her and neither would Bebe. Rosina made up her mind that she would go straight to the platform and wait for the train with Sukey, even if she had to lay her down on one of the benches. As they walked towards the station, she stole a glance at Harry's profile. She was beginning to wonder if he had heard of her mother's reckless escapade with Captain Barnum, which had ruined her reputation. Surely he would not do anything that would put her in a similar situation? He loved her, or so he said, and he wanted to marry her. His intentions became crystal clear as they approached the station hotel, and he led her inexorably towards the main entrance.

Rosina dug her heels into the ground, refusing to move. 'I don't want to go to the hotel. We should get the train immediately.'

Harry came to a halt, looking down at her with

a mocking smile. 'My dear, the last train has gone. See, the station is in darkness. You can go and sit on the platform all night, if you want to, but I suggest we will be much more comfortable in the hotel.'

Roland staggered past them with Sukey in his arms. 'Can't walk much further, old chap. I hope you damn well booked the rooms.'

'Shut up, and take her inside.'

'I will sit on the platform all night then.' Rosina gave him a push that caught him momentarily off balance. She ran towards the station entrance, but Harry was at her side before she had gone more than a couple of paces. He swung her off her feet, carrying her protesting into the hotel.

The hall porter looked up in alarm as Rosina struggled and kicked, demanding to be set down. 'Ahem, begging your pardon, sir.'

'My wife is a trifle overtired,' Harry said pompously. 'Be good enough to show us into the parlour. Bring wine and brandy.'

The porter glanced at Sukey, who had fallen asleep in Roland's arms with her mouth hanging open and was snoring softly. 'And is the other young lady overtired as well, sir?'

'Show us into the parlour or I'll report you to the manager and have you sacked for impudence.'

'Follow me then, gents.' The porter ambled off down a narrow corridor. He thrust a door open and stood back, grinning.

'And don't expect a tip,' Harry said, pushing past him. He loosed his hold on Rosina so that she stumbled and would have fallen if a man had not stepped out of the shadows to catch her.

The room was dimly lit by flickering gaslight, and she could not see his face clearly, but she would know the scent of him anywhere. 'Will?' she whispered. 'Is it you?'

'It's me, Walter.' He set her on her feet. 'Are you all right, Rosie?'

Harry pushed him out of the way. 'Of course she's all right, man. Miss May is my fiancée and you can keep your grubby hands off her.'

'It's you who must keep your hands off my daughter.' Edward's voice echoed round the room.

'You libertine!' Bertha leapt up from an armchair by the empty grate and she advanced on Harry, bristling like an angry mother hen. 'You can't treat my baby girl like a common harlot. Thank the Lord that Caddie come and told us you'd changed your plans, or heaven knows what might have happened.'

'I say, Gostellow. Who are these common people?' Roland dropped the semi-conscious Sukey onto a horsehair sofa. 'This is not at all what I was expecting.'

Bertha turned on him. 'And what have you done to that poor innocent girl? Caddie, take a look at her and see that she ain't harmed.'

Dazed and unable to believe her eyes or her ears, Rosina leaned against Walter. 'I don't understand. How did you all come to be in this place? How did you know that we would be here?'

Caddie knelt by Sukey's prostrate figure. 'She's swipey, that's all. I'd say there's no harm done, not yet anyhow.'

'I never touched the girl,' Roland protested. 'It ain't my fault that she can't hold her drink.'

Walter glared at him. 'You got her drunk, and it's quite obvious what your intentions were.'

Roland backed towards the doorway, holding up his hands. 'I didn't expect this. Sorry, Harry old boy, but I didn't bargain for angry relatives wanting to make mincemeat of me.'

'I should knock you down, you rotter,' Walter said, fisting his hands and advancing on Roland.

'Leave him, Walter.' Rosina laid a restraining hand on his shoulder. 'He's not worth it.'

'Wait a moment,' Harry blustered. 'This is ridiculous. I am here with my bride-to-be. We missed the last train home and I booked two rooms for the night. Who is to say that the two ladies were not to share a bed? You can't prove me in the wrong.'

'If you think I believe that story, then you're more stupid than you look, young man.' Edward thrust his face close to Harry's. 'You were supposed to be taking care of my little girl, mister. You were supposed to love and cherish her, but you were planning to seduce her. I don't call that the action of a gentleman.'

'Come now, sir. You're making too much of this,' Harry said with a nervous smile. 'Let's discuss this like men. After all, I may have been a bit impatient, but I was only going to take what was going to be mine in a few weeks anyway.'

'You cad! You complete and utter bastard.' Edward took a swipe at him, catching Harry on the nose with his fist.

'Pa!' Rosina cried. 'Don't, please.'

Walter stepped in between them, but Harry seemed unlikely to retaliate. He covered his nose with his hands, in an attempt to staunch the freely flowing blood.

'See what you've got yourself into, old boy,' Roland said, opening the door. 'I don't want anything to do with this sort of thing. You're on your own, Gostellow.'

'You stay where you are, Rivers,' Harry mumbled through the blood-soaked handkerchief he held to his nose. 'You're in this with me. It was your idea in the first place.'

'That's a damned lie.' Roland folded his arms across his chest, leaning against the doorpost. 'But I wouldn't expect anything else from a hay merchant's son.'

'Bastard.' Harry's bloodshot eyes glared at him over the crumpled piece of cloth.

'Stop it, both of you,' Rosina cried, wringing her hands. 'You're both to blame.'

'If you wasn't so grown up,' Bertha said, wrapping her arms around Rosina, 'I'd put you across my knee and give you a good hiding for scaring us out of our wits.'

'It won't happen again, Bebe.'

'I should say it won't.' Harry mopped his swollen nose, wincing with pain. 'When we're married, Rosina . . .'

'Married?' Edward roared. 'I wouldn't allow you to marry my girl if you were the last man on earth.'

Rosina caught him by the hand. 'Papa, please. Nothing happened.'

'And you have Walter to thank for that, poppet. I'm telling you to your face, young Gostellow, I don't think much of you and I don't think you're good enough for my little girl.'

'Rosina?' Harry turned to her, his expression grim. 'What have you to say in all this? Are you going to side with your father against me? You will, after all, soon be my wife.'

A vision of her future life almost blinded her: in a split second, she knew that whatever the cost, she could not go through with marriage to a man whom she did not truly love. She shook her head. 'No, Harry. I thought that I could marry you, and I was fond of you, once. But, even for Papa, I can't go through with it. I would rather die than live in your ghastly mansion with your hateful parents. I'm sorry, Pa. I know what the *Ellie May* means to you, but I just can't marry him.'

'So that's the way it was.' Harry dabbed at his nose with the blood-stained handkerchief, his voice sounding thick and nasal. 'Well, I don't want an unwilling bride. I did love you, Rosie. More than you can imagine, but I don't want you if you're hankering after another man.' He glared at Walter. 'How she can fancy you is beyond me, you – you coalman.'

'She doesn't love me,' Walter retaliated. 'But neither does she love you. And I, for one, am glad that she has seen sense at last.'

'Hear, hear!' Caddie said, jumping to her feet. 'You tell him, Walter.'

'Are you sure, Rosie?' Bertha hooked her arm around Rosina's shoulders. 'Think hard before you throw away your one chance in life.'

'I – I'm sorry, but I can't do it.' Rosina tugged at the ring on her engagement finger. 'I can't marry you, Harry. You behaved like a cad tonight, but I know that you're not a bad man at heart. I just hope that you can find a girl who is more suited to you than I am.' She threw it at his feet but the ring rolled towards the doorway and Roland bent down to scoop it up in his hand.

'Perhaps I'd better look after this,' he said, tucking the ring in his waistcoat pocket. 'You might want it back at a later date, Miss May.'

Harry had not taken his eyes off Rosina. 'I did love you,' he said angrily. 'But I want a woman, not a silly, hysterical girl who runs to her father every time something goes wrong for her.'

'It's you who were at fault, Gostellow,' Walter said, grabbing Harry by the lapels. 'You were about to dishonour your own fiancée. You may have money but you are no gentleman.'

Harry pushed him away with a derisive snort. 'So, the scribe has feelings, has he? You're very bold now, threatening an injured man.' He clutched the blood-stained hanky to his nose. 'Going to call me out are you, pen pusher? Quills at dawn, is it?'

'Leave him alone,' Edward roared. 'Walter's been a good friend to my girl this day, and you were about to ruin her reputation. Mud sticks, mister. And Rosie is too good for you.'

'You'll be sorry for this night's work, old man.' Harry backed towards the doorway. 'Consider yourself unemployed for a start.'

'I've had enough of this,' Roland said, yawning. 'I'm going to my bed. You can sort this mess out, Gostellow.'

'Harry, please.' Rosina ran to him and caught him by the sleeve. 'I know you're angry with me, but you won't renege on your bargain with Papa, will you?'

He shook off her hand and his eyes were cold. 'That has nothing to do with you.'

'It has everything to do with me. You made a business deal with my father. Surely you won't go back on your word?'

'You plighted your troth to me, madam. You've broken your word and our engagement. I owe you nothing.'

'We might not be suited as marriage partners, but you can't use that against my pa.'

'You naïve little fool.' Harry's features twisted with anger. 'Did you really suppose that I wanted to do business with a sick old man?'

Edward lunged at him but was held back by Walter. 'Don't, Captain. He's just trying to goad you.'

'How dare you insult my pa?' Rosina said, tossing her head. 'He's a better man than you will ever be.'

'He's had his day and he's ailing. With the barge and the house on the wharf I could have made our fortune, you silly little mare.'

'And you would have married me to get your hands on the property that I will inherit when I'm twenty-one? Is that what you're saying, Harry?'

He shrugged his shoulders. 'Would you have accepted me if I'd been as poor as old Walter there?'

'I thought you loved me, Harry.'

'You've spurned and humiliated me. My mama was right: you are not a fit bride for a

Gostellow. I'm recalling the loan. If you can't repay the money within a fortnight, the *Ellie May* together with the property on Black Eagle Wharf belongs to Gostellow and Son.'

# Chapter Fifteen

Rosina spent an uncomfortable night sharing a bed with Bertha and Caddie. They both seemed to sleep well, if their combined snores and even breathing were anything to go by, but Rosina slept little. The hotel room was small and dingy; the bed was lumpy and smelled of damp and stale tobacco, as if the last occupant had been chain-smoking before he had fallen asleep. Every time she closed her eyes she saw Harry's face contorted with rage as he announced that he was recalling the loan. He had stormed out then, leaving them in shocked silence. Papa had been taken with a fit of coughing, which had laid him so low that Walter had had to help him up to the room that they were to share for the night. It had all seemed such a dismal end to what had promised to be an enjoyable evening out. Sukey had been so drunk that it was easier to leave her where she was. They had begged a pillow and some blankets from the hall porter, who had complied with much grumbling, and only after Walter had handed him a generous tip, which she knew that he could ill afford.

At the first hint of daybreak, Rosina was only too pleased to get up from the bed and slip on her creased gown. She tiptoed out of the room and made her way down to the parlour to make certain that Sukey was all right. Bertha had said she would be unlikely to remember much of what had happened last night, and Rosina could only hope that was true. The thought of explaining the reason for their overnight stay in Sydenham to an anxious and irate Mrs Barnum was worrying enough, without having to admit that Sukey had been extremely drunk and on the verge of allowing a man to seduce her. Rosina opened the door and peered into the gloomy parlour. Sukey's tousled head lay on the pillow and she was snoring softly. The air in the room was thick with dust and the odour of stale wine; Rosina wrinkled her nose in distaste. There was nothing she could do until everyone had awakened, and she felt a desperate need to breathe fresh air. She decided to take a walk to the station to check the times of the trains bound for London.

The hall porter had dozed off in his chair by the main entrance, and she crept past him. The door was unlocked and she went outside, taking deep breaths of the early morning air scented with damp earth and newly mown hay from the fields nearby. Birds trilled from the leafy boughs of the trees surrounding the hotel garden, and in the distance she could hear the clip-clopping of a horse's hooves and the rumble of cartwheels.

'Rosie! You're up early.'

She spun round to see Walter approaching her from the direction of the station. She had paid little attention to him last night, but it was a relief to see him looking his normal well-groomed self, free from the cloying mantle of coal dust that had so altered his appearance when they had last met. 'I couldn't sleep.' She held out her hand in a gesture of reconciliation, and he took it in a warm grasp.

'I spoke out of turn before.'

'I'm sorry too. I didn't mean all those things I said.'

'You had every right to be suspicious, but I would never cheat you or your father.'

'I knew that deep down, but I was so confused. And it seemed that you were deserting me, just like . . .'

'Will would have rather had his right hand cut off than leave you, but he had no choice, and I was desperate for work.'

'I know that now, Walter. But what I don't understand is how you knew where to find me.'

'Caddie told me of your proposed outing with Gostellow. She had seen through him and suspected that he was up to no good.'

'So that's why she stayed behind to talk to you. I had no idea.'

'I wasn't going to leave you unprotected and so I jumped ship. I went to the public baths to clean up before going to your house, but you had already left with Gostellow. It took me some time to convince your father that I was not the villain of the piece, but Caddie confirmed my story. We left immediately for Sydenham.'

'I trusted Harry.' Rosina sighed. 'I'll give him a piece of my mind when I see him this morning.'

'He's gone, Rosie. He left on the first train to London.'

'Oh, dear! I expect he will go straight to their solicitor and instruct him to call in the loan. What are we going to do, Walter? We will be homeless.'

'I won't allow that to happen.' He wrapped his arms around her and held her.

She laid her cheek against his shoulder, comforted by the warmth of his embrace. She felt so safe with Walter, and so at home in his arms. 'Thank you,' she murmured.

'For what?'

'Just for being you, Walter. I know I can rely on you, my dear friend.'

A cry from an upstairs window made them spring apart and look upwards. Caddie was waving frantically. 'Come quick. Your pa's been took ill, Rosie. Really ill.'

Rosina hesitated, casting a worried glance at

Walter. 'You shared his room last night; didn't you notice anything was wrong?'

'I slept in a chair and let the captain use the bed. He was wheezing a bit, but it's only what you'd expect considering he's been working in the warehouse where they store the hay.' He held his hand out to her. 'Come on, we won't find out anything by standing here.'

In the upstairs bedroom, Bertha was sitting by the bedside, mopping Edward's brow with a damp flannel. She looked up, frowning. 'It's his lung complaint come back. He's really poorly this time.'

Rosina knelt down at the bedside. 'Papa, can you hear me?'

'He's out of his head with fever, ducks,' Bertha said. 'I doubt he'll even recognise you.'

'Pa, it's me, Rosie.'

His eyelids fluttered but he did not open them. His breathing was laboured and his chest rattled ominously.

'We must send for a doctor,' Rosina said, raising his hand to her cheek. 'I can't bear to see him like this.'

'We can't afford a doctor. In fact, I dunno if we've got enough money even to get us back to London.' Bertha handed the flannel to Caddie. 'Dampen this again in the washbowl, ducks. He's burning up like a furnace, poor man. We must get him home as soon as possible.'

Rosina cast an anxious glance at Walter. 'Have we any money left?'

He shook his head. 'We weren't expecting to stay the night. I'm not even sure if I can settle the bill here.'

'This is a terrible mess. I would beg Harry to help us if he hadn't already left.'

'That young man of yours has caused enough trouble, if you ask me,' Bertha muttered. 'You should sue him for breach of promise. That would wipe the smile off his face.'

Rosina tucked her father's hand beneath the quilt and she rose to her feet. 'I don't want anything more to do with Harry. I truly believed that he loved me, and that I could make him a good wife, but I realise now that I was terribly mistaken.'

'He's a brute,' Caddie said, wringing her hands. 'I can't see nothing ahead but the bleeding workhouse. I'd rather throw meself and the nippers in the Thames than go through them grim doors.'

'That won't happen.' Rosina raised her chin, speaking with more confidence than she was feeling. 'I think I might have a solution to our immediate problem.'

Walter caught her by the wrist as she made to leave the room. 'What are you going to do?'

'First, I'm going downstairs to find out exactly how much we owe for these horrible rooms. And then I'm going to ask Mr Roland Rivers to lend us the fare home. It's the least he can do in the circumstances.'

'I'm coming with you.'

'No, Walter.' Rosie shook free from his restraining hand. 'This is something I must do alone.'

She found the hotel manager in the dining room laying up the tables for breakfast and complaining bitterly about his lack of staff. 'You'll have to wait, miss,' he said crossly, when she asked him for the bill. 'As you can see, I'm having to do the work of the idle slut of a waitress who has not bothered to turn up this morning.'

'Then I should sack her, if I were you, my good man.'

Rosina turned her head and saw Roland Rivers standing in the doorway.

'A bad master makes bad servants,' Roland drawled. 'This place is not fit to house convicts, let alone paying guests.'

The manager drew himself up to his full height, which was only up to the middle button on Roland's waistcoat. 'I'll have you know that this hotel is mentioned in Baedeker.'

'And an adverse criticism from me could have your establishment wiped off the map.'

The manager's expression changed visibly from sullen to fawning. 'Will you allow me to set you a place for breakfast, sir?'

'If the state of your kitchen is anything like the way in which you keep your public rooms, then I would rather eat in a sewer than in your dining room.'

In spite of everything, Rosina had to stifle the desire to giggle at the sight of the manager's face. Serve him right for being so horrid and for running such a disgusting hostelry. For a moment, she almost liked Roland, until she remembered the cavalier way he had treated both her and Sukey. She turned to the manager, who had assumed the look of a whipped cur. 'My father has been taken ill, sir. You must tell me how much we owe you for our night's lodging, as we need to leave on the next train for London.'

'I told you, miss. You'll have to wait until I've finished here.'

Roland drew her aside. 'Miss May, I hope you will allow me to settle your account here.'

Rosina stared at him in amazement. 'Why would you do that?'

'I am not the blackguard that you think me. I realise that I behaved like a cad to both you and your young friend, but Gostellow gave me the impression that you were ladies of – a different kind. I cannot apologise enough for the way in which I treated you.'

She eyed him doubtfully. 'Did Harry put you up to this?'

'On my honour, no. Harry had already left the hotel when I awakened this morning. My aching head tells me that I imbibed too much last night, and that I might regret some of my less worthy actions when they come to mind.'

'You didn't behave well, but you should apologise to Sukey, not to me.'

'I will grovel on my hands and knees, if necessary. Please let me make amends for my conduct.'

His guilty expression verged on the comical, and Rosina found that her lips were twitching. Despite her initial dislike of him, she sensed that Roland was genuinely sorry for his bad behaviour. But she was not going to let him off easily: he had gone along with Harry's plan to seduce two young women, and now the least he could do was to pay for their enforced stay in this horrible place. She allowed herself to smile. 'All right, Mr Rivers. I am in such a position that I can't refuse you, although under different circumstances nothing would induce me to accept such a favour.'

He bowed from the waist, clicking his heels together. 'Understood, absolutely. You are doing me a huge favour in allowing me to pay for my mistakes.'

She went to walk past him, but he barred her way. 'If you'll pardon my asking, what is wrong with your father? I overheard you telling the manager that he had been taken ill?'

'Pa suffers from a lung complaint, and he was taken poorly in the night.'

'Then he should see a doctor immediately.'

'Mr Rivers, I'll be frank with you. We cannot afford a doctor. In fact, if you had not offered to pay the hotel bill, we would have been in dire financial straits, so I thank you for your help, but as to my father's ill health, that is my concern.'

Rosina left him in the dining room, but he caught up with her before she had reached the foot of the stairs.

'Don't think that this puts you under an obligation to me, but I will gladly pay the doctor's bill, and I will hire a carriage to take you and your party back to London.'

Rosina was tempted to accept, but she could not allow herself to be put so much in debt to one of Harry's friends. She shook her head. 'That is too generous, but perhaps you could lend us our rail fare, which I will repay as soon as possible.'

'Miss May, I am a hideously and undeservedly wealthy man. I've done nothing to earn my fortune except being born into a rich family. I'm a selfish devil, who has taken his pleasure wherever he wanted, and you were the first woman who rebuffed me. I was pitched head first over a balcony on your account, as I remember it.'

'Into a bed of geraniums.'

'Yes, exactly. Ruined my Savile Row suit into

the bargain.' He held up his hands in a gesture of surrender, but his eyes twinkled merrily. 'However, I admit that I deserved it. Now I am utterly ashamed of my conduct last night, and if you won't accept my help for yourself, please take it on behalf of your sick father and the young lady whose honour I so nearly compromised.'

Rosina stared at him for a moment, thinking hard. 'All right, on one condition.'

'Absolutely anything.'

'That you must go in person to see Sukey's mother, Mrs Barnum of Black Eagle Wharf. I want you to tell her of your part in the affair, and to convince her that nothing untoward occurred.'

'Do you think that she would believe me?'

'I don't see why not. Mrs Barnum is an ambitious woman, and, although you may not think so, people in Black Eagle Wharf honour their good name as highly as any of you rich toffs.'

'I am humbled, Miss May.'

'Then you will do as I request?'

'You have my word.'

'Your word as a gentleman?'

'My word as a cad, which is much nearer the mark.' Roland lifted her hand to his lips. 'You are an amazing young woman, Miss May.'

'Save your flattery for Mrs Barnum. I can assure you that you will need to use all your wiles to charm that lady.'

*

Roland hired two carriages, one to take Edward, Bertha and Rosina, and the second for himself, Walter, Caddie and a sick and subdued Sukey, who was terrified of going home to face her mother. They arrived home in style. Roland and Sukey went off in the direction of the Barnums' house, and Walter helped Edward up to his room. Caddie volunteered to fetch the doctor, before going to the Smilies' to collect her children. Having made Edward comfortable in his bed, Bertha went to the kitchen to get a fire going in the range. Rosina paced the floor, anxiously awaiting the doctor's arrival.

'You won't do no good fretting,' Bertha said, rolling up her sleeves. 'Do something useful, girl.'

'I'm just so worried, Bebe.'

'Aren't we all?' Bertha plucked the cocoa tin from the mantelshelf and took off the lid. She tipped it up and a penny rolled into the palm of her hand. 'That's all we got in the world, but it will buy a penn'orth of laudanum for your pa.'

Rosina hesitated, looking down at her travel-stained evening gown. 'I can't go out looking like this.'

Bertha pressed the penny into her hand. 'Five minutes isn't going to make much difference. Go upstairs and put on a clean frock. Then you can go to the chemist's shop. We don't want the neighbours seeing you look like some street girl, Rosie. We may be in a fix, but we got to keep up appearances.'

'You're right, of course. I'll be as quick as I can.'

Wearing a cotton-print gown and with her hair firmly confined in a knot at the nape of her neck, Rosina felt more optimistic as she hurried out into the humid heat of midday. She ran all the way to the chemist's shop in Wapping Street, parrying enquiries from neighbours as to her father's state of health. It never ceased to amaze her how quickly news spread round the tight-knit community. She arrived home to find that the doctor was already upstairs with her pa. She would have gone straight to his bedroom but Bertha stopped her. 'Walter is with him; leave it to the men, Rosie.'

'But I want to know what the doctor has to say.'

'And you will, in good time.' Bertha handed her a wooden bucket. 'I need more water. Be a good girl and fetch some from the pump.'

Reluctantly, Rosina went out into the yard. As she worked the handle, pumping water into a wooden bucket, she glanced up at the house where she had lived for most of her life. Harry's threat to call in the loan on the property was uppermost in her mind now. With Papa so ill, and the *Ellie May* out of commission for at least another fortnight, things looked bleak. The Gostellows could have them all thrown out on the street, and there would be nowhere to go. She shuddered and jumped backwards as the bucket overflowed and water splashed over the hem of her skirt. She brushed back a stray lock of hair with her hand. What would become of them all?

'Rosie, come inside,' Bertha called to her from the scullery. 'The doctor wants to see you.'

Rosina picked up the bucket and carried it into the house, slopping water over the flagstones. The doctor was in the kitchen, and one look at his set expression made her heart contract with fear. 'What is it, doctor? Is Pa going to die?'

Bertha took the bucket from her hands. 'I'll make a pot of tea.'

The doctor set his medical bag down on the kitchen table. 'I won't take tea, thank you, Miss Spinks. I've got to visit the workhouse next, so I'll be brief.' He turned to Rosina with a tired smile. 'I warned your father, Miss May. The last time he had one of these attacks, I told him that he must not work where there was hay, particularly if it was contaminated with mould.'

'He had no choice, doctor.'

'Unfortunately, I hear that all the time. But the truth is, my dear, unless your father keeps well away from the cause of his illness, his lungs will become so congested that he is quite likely to succumb to respiratory failure.'

'You mean he will die?' Rosina held her breath.

He nodded. 'To put it bluntly, yes. His heart won't stand the strain of prolonged bouts of the disease. He needs to get away from the heat and dust of the city. He must have peace and quiet, and good nourishing food. Ideally, he should go somewhere where the air is clean and bracing, to the seaside if possible, and he should stay there until he is well enough to return to London. He must never be exposed to hay, or the same thing will happen again and again, until it proves fatal.'

'I have a cousin who lives in Burnham-on-Crouch,' Bertha said, half to herself. 'She's a widow woman now, but I ain't seen her for years.'

'Well, then, Miss Spinks. Maybe the captain could convalesce there? I believe the air is very bracing on the Essex coast.'

Rosina opened her mouth to tell him that what he suggested was impossible, but Bertha shot her a warning glance. 'Are you sure you won't have a cup of tea, doctor?'

'Thank you, Miss Spinks, but I really must be on my way.' He cleared his throat, and his thin cheeks flushed a dull red. 'I'm afraid I must request my usual fee, Miss May.'

'Of course, doctor. And thank you for coming so promptly.' Rosina hurried to the door. 'I'll go and get the money from Pa's clerk. He handles our finances.' She found Walter sitting by her father's bedside. He rose to his feet as she entered the room.

'What did he say, Rosie?'

'That Papa needs to go away, preferably to the seaside. That he must never work with hay again. And I have to pay him, Walter. Have you any money left?'

He delved into his pocket and produced a half-crown. 'This is all I have. Pay him that on account and I'll try to raise whatever is outstanding.'

She took the coin from him with a sinking feeling. She had spent their last penny on laudanum and now she had taken all that was left of Walter's money. She hesitated in the doorway. 'Thank you for everything, Walter. You've been so good about it all, and I didn't give a thought to your personal circumstances. Will Captain Juggins take you back on the coal barge?'

He shook his head.

'I'm so sorry that I put you in this position.'

Walter gave her a reassuring smile. 'You and the captain are more important to me than making money for Barnum.'

'So now you are out of work. Isn't it ironic, Walter? We'll all be out on the street together if Harry has his way.' She laughed, but there was no mirth in the sound, and her voice broke on a sob as she hurried from the room without giving Walter a chance to reply.

The doctor was waiting in the hallway and she gave him the half-crown. 'If that is not enough, you must tell me, doctor. I will pay you the remainder as soon as I can.'

He stared down at the shining silver coin in his palm. 'It is enough, my dear. I've known your father for many years, and he's a good man. I hope you will be able to find a way to get him away from London before it is too late.' He doffed his hat and went out onto the wharf. Rosina stood in the doorway watching him walk briskly in the direction of the workhouse in Old Gravel Lane. She was about to close the door when she saw Roland hurrying towards her. He was waving to her and calling her name. 'Miss May.'

'What now, Mr Rivers?' She had not meant to speak so sharply, but her nerves were stretched to breaking point and a creeping tiredness was slowly overtaking her.

'I came to enquire about your father's health. What did the doctor say?'

'That he is very poorly and needs to go away to the seaside to convalesce.'

'I am truly sorry, Miss May. Our foolish jaunt caused him to be in this sorry state. Is there anything more that I can do?'

She relented a little, touched by his obvious sincerity. 'You've already repaid us. You need not feel obligated.'

'You're too kind. I only wish that Mrs Barnum had been so generous.'

'What did you expect? You would have seduced her daughter and ruined her reputation with no qualms if your plans hadn't been thwarted.'

He pulled a face. 'I know, and now I find that I am engaged to be married.'

'You're engaged to Sukey?'

'I'm not even sure how it came about. But it was either that, or risk having my throat cut by Captain Barnum. His wife is a formidable woman too – I was lucky to escape from the house in one piece.'

'But you actually proposed marriage?' Rosina could hardly believe what she was hearing. 'How did that come about?'

'We were sitting in their parlour, taking tea. I was in a bit of a sweat, if you'll pardon the expression. Madam Barnum was eyeing me as if she wanted to disembowel me with a teaspoon, and, as I pulled my handkerchief from my pocket, your diamond ring shot out and landed in Sukey's cup of tea. The poor girl fished it out with a dazed expression, and her mama pounced upon me like a bird attacking a juicy worm. The next thing I knew, Miss Susan Barnum had put the ring on her finger and we were engaged.'

'You could have explained that the ring belonged to Harry.'

'I panicked. And if I tell the truth now I will have two angry matrons after my blood – Mrs Gostellow and Mrs Barnum. It's more than a man can stand.'

'And do you really intend to marry Sukey?'

'Certainly not! I have no doubt that she's an excellent girl, but not of my class. My father would cut me off without a penny if I were to marry beneath my station.'

'Your future outlook seems only a little less grim than mine, Mr Rivers.' Rosina was about to shut the door when he put his foot over the sill.

'I think I might leave the country for a year or two. Would you like to accompany me, Miss May?'

'You are the boldest rogue I have ever come across.'

He chuckled. 'But I am charming.'

'Go away, please. I have much more important things to worry about than what might befall you, especially since you have brought all your misfortunes on yourself.'

She pushed the door but it would not shut. She turned her head as she heard Walter's quick footsteps approaching along the hallway.

'What's wrong? Is that fellow bothering you, Rosie?'

Roland managed to stick his head round the door. 'Is that you, Walter? Let me in, old chap. I was offering my help, but Miss May seeks to punish me further.'

'Shall I shut his head in the door?' Walter asked, taking the handle from her and pushing against the door so that Roland went purple in the face.

Rosina stifled a slightly hysterical giggle. 'Best let him in. I'm afraid he will not leave us alone until he has had his say.'

'Be grateful to Miss May,' Walter said as he opened the door. 'I would have enjoyed severing your head, Rivers.'

Adjusting his collar and cravat, Roland strolled in with a nonchalant smile. 'Is there somewhere we can talk privately, old boy?'

Bertha was thumping around in the kitchen, and Rosina could hear the shrill voices of Caddie's little boys outside on the wharf. She suppressed a shiver; they had come to think of this house as their home, and now it looked as though they would have to move on yet again. Roland Rivers might think this was hugely entertaining, but what did he know of hardship and worry? He was so wealthy that he could not even begin to imagine what it was like to be poor. She was only just beginning to understand it herself. 'We can talk in the office, although I can't think what you would have to say to us, Mr Rivers.'

Roland took off his hat and followed them into the room. 'I really do want to make amends. As I said before, I feel in part responsible for Captain May's attack of ill health, and if there is anything

I can do to help, then you only have to ask.'

Walter folded his arms across his chest, glaring at Roland in a none-too-friendly manner. 'Haven't you done enough, Rivers?'

'You resent me, Walter. I understand that, but my concern for Miss May and her father is genuine.'

Walter opened his mouth to reply, but Rosina held up her hand. 'Let him have his say. Please continue, Mr Rivers.'

'Thank you, Miss May. Before we became officially engaged, young Sukey told me a little about your predicament. I understand from the rather heated words last night that the Gostellows hold a mortgage on this property and that your sailing barge is out of commission. It don't take a genius to work out that you are in a fix.'

'We don't need your help,' Walter said, bridling.

Rosina patted his hand. 'It's all right, Walter. Let me handle this.' She turned to Roland. 'My father will die if he does not get out of London. The doctor says he needs sea air and Bertha has a cousin who lives on the coast at Burnham-on-Crouch, but we have not the funds to meet his travelling expenses.'

'And I have a sudden fancy to visit the Netherlands where we do a great deal of trade. My father's ships transport grain to Holland and on the return voyage they bring cargoes of gin and wine. It seems like the right moment for me to take a prolonged business trip. I will sail from Harwich to the Hook, and could easily make a small detour to Burnham.'

'What's in it for you, Rivers?' Walter eyed him suspiciously.

'A clear conscience, my dear fellow. I may be a bounder, but I don't prey on innocent young women. And to tell the truth, I never really liked Gostellow. New money and all that.' He raised Rosina's hand to his lips and kissed it. 'I need to leave London tomorrow morning at the very latest, before Captain Barnum realises that I have no intention of marrying his daughter. If you could have your father ready to travel, I will send my coachman to pick him up.'

'And Bertha too? She really must go with my father to look after him.'

'Naturally. I would not expect him to go without his nurse.' He gazed into her eyes. 'You know, you are a remarkably beautiful young woman, Miss May, and spirited too. Had things been different, I would have pursued you with the most honourable of intentions.'

'But you could not marry a girl who was so far beneath your station in life.' Rosina struggled to maintain a straight face.

'Sadly that is true.' Roland raised her hand to his lips and brushed it with the lightest of kisses. 'Now I must depart hurriedly before I get myself into any further trouble.' He slapped Walter on the shoulder. 'We don't really know each other, and probably never will, but you look to be a decent enough sort of chap. Look after her, Walter. Rosina is a treasure amongst women.'

'I know that already.' Walter strode to the front door and opened it. 'Goodbye, Rivers. I hope your stay in Holland is a long one.'

Roland smiled and tipped his hat. He glanced cautiously up and down the wharf, as if expecting to see Captain Barnum bearing down on him with a belaying pin in his hand and a cutlass between his teeth. Seemingly satisfied that the coast was clear, he squared his shoulders and strode off at a brisk pace.

'I don't fancy his chances when Barnum discovers the truth,' Walter said, chuckling.

Rosina laid her hand on his arm. 'You should go away from here too, Walter. I don't think Captain Barnum is going to be very pleased with you either.'

'I hate leaving you like this, Rosie, but I have to find work. I'll get a job on the docks if necessary, and I'll help you in any way that I can.'

'Just look after yourself and don't worry about us. We'll be all right.'

'You are a brave girl.'

'If you see Will, remember me to him.'

'He will never forget you. I know that.'

She drew the gold chain from the bodice of her gown and opened the locket. 'I wear it close to my heart, Walter. Tell him that no matter what happens, I will wear it forever.'

He shook his head as if lost for words, and strode away towards Union Stairs. Rosina went back into the house, closing the door behind her. In the kitchen she could hear the children's shrill laughter and the lower-pitched tones of Caddie and Bertha. She went slowly up the stairs to tell her father what was planned.

Next morning, as Roland's coachman helped Edward into the brougham, Bertha clung to Rosina. 'This is all so wrong,' she said tearfully. 'We should not be parted like this. It ain't right.'

Rosina hugged her, biting back her own tears. 'It's for the best, Bebe. Papa's health is the most important thing at this moment.'

'But you and I have never spent a night apart since you was born. I hate leaving you here alone, poppet.'

'I'm not alone. I have Caddie and the babies to keep me company.'

'And what if he carries out his threat to take the house?'

'I don't think it will come to that. I'm going to see Mr Gostellow today. He's a reasonable man, and he's a businessman. The *Ellie May* will be repaired within a week or so, and hopefully Papa will be well enough to come home. We'll just have to make sure he carries any cargo other than hay in the future. We will get back on top again, Bebe. I promise you we will.'

Bertha gave her a last hug and she climbed into the carriage. She leaned out of the window, waving to Rosina and Caddie, who was standing in the doorway holding the baby with Alfie and Ronnie clinging to her skirts.

Roland had been standing back tactfully while their goodbyes were said. 'You mustn't worry about your father, Miss May. I'll see that he gets safely to his destination.'

'Thank you, Mr Rivers. I am truly grateful to you for putting yourself out like this.'

'I know; I surprise myself sometimes. Just when I think I have perfected the role of a complete and utter cad, I do something good and ruin the whole thing.'

Rosina glanced over her shoulder as she heard footsteps approaching along the wharf, and her worst fears were realised. 'You'd better leave quickly, Mr Rivers. That man striding along the wharf is Captain Barnum, and judging by the look on his face he is not best pleased.'

He leaned forward and planted a kiss on her lips. 'Farewell, Rosina. I think I have earned the right to call you that.' He leapt into the carriage. 'Drive on, Jenkins.'

The coachman flicked his whip, and the horses

lunged forward. Bertha waved her handkerchief until the brougham turned into Wapping Street.

'Was that the scoundrel who seduced my daughter?' Barnum demanded breathlessly. When Rosina chose not to answer him, he seized her by the shoulders. 'Answer me, girl.'

'Leave her be, mister,' Caddie shouted.

Ronnie raced forward and began kicking Barnum on the shins. Rosina twisted away from him and caught Ronnie by the hand. 'Now, now, Ronnie. That's not a nice way to behave. Go back to your mama.'

'I asked you a question.' Barnum raised his voice, sending a colony of seagulls mewing into the air.

'And I refuse to answer you until you stop shouting.'

He went red in the face, but he closed his lips into a tight line and glared at Rosina, waiting for her answer with his arms folded across his chest.

'Yes,' she said reluctantly. 'It was Mr Rivers; he is going away on a business trip.'

'I thought as much. I don't trust that man, making out that he's going to marry my girl, the libertine. Now he's running away, leaving her to face humiliation and disgrace. I've got his measure. Where is he going? I demand to be told.'

Rosina shook her head. 'I don't know, Captain Barnum.'

'I think you do and I want the truth. If he's

playing fast and loose with my daughter's affections I'll have him followed and dragged back so that he can be charged with breach of promise. I won't have my Sukey's good name sullied by an upper-class piece of shit.'

'You can't browbeat me, Captain. I wouldn't tell you where Mr Rivers is going, even if I knew his destination.'

'I blame you for all this,' Barnum said between clenched teeth. 'You haven't heard the last of this matter.' He stormed off along the wharf towards his house.

Rosina's legs were shaking as she went indoors. She had not thought any further than getting her papa safely away from the city, but now she realised that she must face the problems that lay ahead on her own.

'There's some tea left in the pot, although that's the last of it, and we have no coal for the fire, nor wood,' Caddie said, shooing the boys in the direction of the kitchen.

'I know,' Rosina said tiredly as she closed the street door behind her. 'I'll go through everything in the house and see what is left to pawn. We'll manage. You mustn't be afraid.' She was about to follow Caddie into the kitchen when there was a loud pounding on the front door. Slowly, with her heart thumping in time to the blows raining on the door, she walked the length of the hall to open it.

'Bailiffs, miss. We come to repossess the property on behalf of the new owners, Messrs Gostellow and Son.'

# Chapter Sixteen

'No, that's impossible. We have two weeks' grace. Go away.' Rosina tried to close the door, but the bailiff was obviously used to this reaction and he stuck his booted foot over the threshold.

'I suggest you cooperate, miss.'

'Have you got an eviction order from the court?'

'Come now, lady. Order or no order, we'll have you out of here today.'

'Go away. I'll not let you in.'

'You're only making it harder on yourself, miss.' The bailiff withdrew his foot, said something in a low voice to his companion, and they marched away grumbling.

Rosina slammed the door and leaned against it, closing her eyes as she waited for her heartbeat to return to normal.

'Was it the bailiffs?' Caddie emerged from the kitchen, cradling baby Arthur in her arms. 'It's the workhouse for us, I knows it.' She began to sob, with Ronnie and Alfie joining in.

'No. Not while I've got a breath left in my body.' Rosina snatched her bonnet off its peg and put it on, tying the ribbons in a bow under her chin. 'I'm going to see Harry's father. He's a lecherous old man, but I've no reason to suppose he's dishonest. He will hear me out – I will make him listen to me.'

The clerk behind the desk in the office of Gostellow and Son shook his head. 'No one sees Mr Gostellow senior without an appointment, miss.'

Rosina was not in a mood for niceties. 'He will see me, like it or not.' She made for the door that bore the legend *Harold Gostellow* inscribed in gold leaf. The clerk tried to stop her, but she pushed past him. 'Out of my way. I will see him.' She opened the door and went inside with the minion following her, protesting loudly.

Harold Gostellow rose from his seat behind a huge mahogany desk, his eyebrows almost disappearing into his hairline. 'Bolton, what is the meaning of this?'

'I'm sorry, sir. The young person insisted on seeing you. Shall I call for a warehouseman to remove her?'

Rosina shook off his restraining hand. 'Go away, mister. I want words with your employer.'

Harold subsided onto his seat with a throaty chuckle. 'You've been told, Bolton. Do as the young woman asks.'

'But, sir . . .'

'Go.'

'Yes, sir.' Bolton bowed out, closing the door behind him.

Harold leaned forward, steepling his fingers. 'What have you got to say for yourself, miss? I'll give you two minutes of my time and no longer.'

Rosina faced him squarely. At one time she would have been quaking in her shoes, but facing disaster had made her angry and she was unafraid. 'I'll come straight to the point, Mr Gostellow. No doubt Harry has told you his side of the story, and I have nothing to say about the way in which he treated me. But he promised me two weeks' grace before he called in the loan, and he has broken that promise.'

'You've got a nerve, young lady. My wife has been in a state of nervous collapse, and my son has been humiliated by a common girl from the wharves.'

'He tried to seduce me, Mr Gostellow.'

'And you were going to marry him for his money, Miss May. Your father is a worn-out old man who'll never set sail again. You will never be able to repay the money I loaned him for the repairs to a vessel which is only fit for the scrap yard. The property in Black Eagle Wharf is legally mine and I want you out of there by midday, or the bailiffs will evict you by force. Is that understood?'

She drew herself up to her full height. 'Oh, yes. I understand perfectly. You planned this all along. You knew that my pa was ailing and that is why you put him to work in the warehouse with the hay. You are a wicked, wicked man. And I pity Harry having you for a father.' She turned on her heel and stormed out of the office, brushing past Bolton and slamming out of the front entrance.

Outside, the hot July sunshine seemed to suck the air from her lungs. The city stench was particularly noxious today and flies buzzed angrily over the horse dung that carpeted the street. An old woman was huddled in the doorway opposite, dressed in green-tinged black and shivering even though the temperature was soaring. She raised her hand feebly, pointing to an empty tin cup at her feet; her meaning was clear, but Rosina had no money to give her. 'I'm sorry,' she murmured. 'I have little more than you, Mother.' She walked on, biting her lip to prevent herself from crying. That poor woman would once have been young and possibly pretty; she must have had a family who loved her, and a home, even if it was a humble cellar room. What dire misfortune had brought her to this, Rosina wondered. And was it possible that the same fate might befall herself and those whom she loved? She quickened her pace. No, it would not happen, not while there was a fighting chance of survival.

Instead of going straight home, she turned in

the direction of Angel Court. She had not asked Walter if he still lodged in that dreadful place, but she must see him and ask his advice. He had handled her pa's business dealings for years, and he must have some idea of the law. She strode on, praying silently that Walter would be there; if he was out she would sit on the doorstep all day if necessary to await his return. Oh, Will, she thought as she pushed past a group of ragged, wild-eyed street urchins who looked as though they would tear the clothes off her back, given half a chance. Where are you when I need you so desperately, Will Brown? You came to my rescue once; could you not come again?

She crossed the street to avoid a feral dog that was slavering at the mouth. She had heard terrible tales of the disease passed on by a bite from a mad dog. A man lurched out of an alleyway, propositioning her, but she tossed her head and walked on. Perhaps she could under-stand a little now why women sold their bodies to such men. Poverty and starvation did things to decent people, and although she was not yet in such a state, she could see it staring her in the face. A hand reached out of the inky shadows and clutched at the hem of her skirt. Panic seized her and she broke into a run, her breath coming in ragged sobs as she drew nearer to Angel Court. She did not see him coming and she screamed as a man caught her in his arms, pinning her to his chest. She fought and kicked, losing her tenuous grip on self-control in sheer terror.

'It's me, Rosie. It's Walter.'

She went limp, collapsing against him. 'Walter?'

'Yes, it's me. I'm here. Don't be afraid.' He stroked her hair, holding her close to him until she composed herself enough to speak.

'The bailiffs. They came to take possession of the house.' She drew away from him, unable to look him in the face. 'Harry went back on his word.'

He slipped his arm around her shoulders. 'I was just coming to see you, as it happens.'

She was greatly reassured by his presence. Even the most villainous-looking street people drew aside to allow them to pass unmolested now that she was with Walter. As they walked she told him everything that had happened that morning. He allowed her to speak without interrupting, and when she had finished he squeezed her hand. 'Poor Rosie. I would not have had you suffer all that for the world.'

She managed a watery smile. 'I'm tougher than you think. I stood up to old Gostellow. I can't and won't let them take my home.'

They had reached Black Eagle Wharf and a heat haze shimmered on the cobblestones. The river lapped at the wooden supports of the jetties, bubbling and boiling like hot tea. The dock workers were stripped to the waist, their naked torsos glistening with sweat, and their caps pulled down over their eyes to shield them from the glare of the sun. Rosina opened the door and was about to usher Walter inside when she heard Harry's irate voice calling her name. She turned her head and saw him striding towards them, red in the face and scowling.

'What's the matter, Harry,' she demanded. 'Have you come in person to throw us out on the street?'

He stopped, mopping his brow with a large silk handkerchief. 'That is the bailiffs' job. This doesn't concern you, Rosina. I've been looking for you, Brown.' He clapped his hand on Walter's shoulder. 'I might have guessed that I'd find you clinging to Miss May's apron strings.'

'What's this all about, Gostellow?'

'Don't play the innocent with me. I'm on to your thieving tricks.' Harry held out his hand. 'Give it to me now or do I have to call a constable?'

'I haven't the slightest idea what you're talking about.' Walter faced up to him, his jaw hardening into a stubborn line. 'You'd better be careful what you say.'

'Harry, please.' Rosina stepped between them, holding up her hands. 'This has gone far enough. What are you accusing Walter of this time?'

'Not content with stealing from your father, he's taken my mother's engagement ring. The one that you threw at me.'

'That's a lie,' Walter said angrily.

Harry uttered a snort of derisive laughter. 'That's good coming from you – the champion of all liars.'

'You're mistaken,' Rosina said, shaking her head. 'You're wrong, Harry. It was your friend Roland who picked up the ring.'

'Don't be silly. Why would Rivers steal my mother's diamond ring? He's so rich he could buy an entire diamond mine if he so wished.' Harry pushed her roughly out of the way. 'Brown was the only other possible suspect present when you threw the ring at me. He is the only one who could have taken it. Give it to me, you villain.'

Walter squared up to him. 'I haven't got your diamond ring, and if I had stolen it, do you think that I would be stupid enough to carry it about on my person?'

Rosina stamped her foot. 'Stop behaving like playground bully, Harry. If you want the ring back, I suggest you go and see Sukey. You owe her an apology anyway.'

He frowned. 'Are you telling me that Miss Barnum stole the ring?'

'No, of course not. I think you'll find that there's been a slight misunderstanding. If you want to know more you'll have to ask her.'

'I don't believe a word of it. You're just trying to protect him.' Harry jerked his head in Walter's direction. 'Is he your lover, Rosie? Is that why you acted the outraged virgin the other night? A girl of your sort doesn't usually value her virtue so highly—' Harry fell to the ground as Walter hit him with a well-aimed punch to the jaw.

Rosina caught him by his coat tails in an attempt to drag him away. 'Stop it, Walter. Fighting won't solve anything.'

'But it will give me great satisfaction,' he said, taking off his spectacles and thrusting them into her hand. 'Hold these for me.'

A small crowd had gathered round them, and Harry scrambled to his feet, rubbing his jaw. He beckoned to Fred, the sailmaker's apprentice. 'You, boy! Fetch a constable.'

Fred hesitated, but a clout round the head from Mr Cotton, the wharfinger, sent him lolloping over the cobbles towards the dock police station.

'This man is a thief.' Harry had to shout to make himself heard above the cheers and whistles from the men, who were eager to see a fight. 'A common thief, who has stolen from his employer, Captain May, and I shouldn't wonder if he's responsible for the thefts from Captain Barnum's vessels too.'

'Old Walter – river pirate? Hogwash, mate!'

'Who said that?' Harry demanded, glaring round at the grinning faces. 'My name carries a lot of weight around here. Mr Cotton, I want you to take that man's name. I'll see that he is dismissed.'

'Harry.' Rosina stepped in between them for a second time. 'This is ridiculous. Walter couldn't be the – river pirate. He's . . .' She stopped dead, turning very slowly to stare at Walter. Standing there bareheaded in the harsh sunlight, with his hands balled into fists and his eyes blazing with fury, he was no longer the well-mannered, serious-minded clerk from her father's counting house. She glanced down at the spectacles clutched in her hand, and then back at Walter as if seeing him for the first time. Despite the heat and the noise, she was oblivious to the crowd surrounding them: it was as if the world had stopped spinning and they were suddenly alone. She walked slowly towards him. 'Will?' she whispered. 'Will, it is you, isn't it? It was you all the time.'

The hot angry look faded from his hazel eyes as they met hers, and his lips curved into a half-smile. But before he could speak, the sound of running feet and a sharp blast on a police whistle caused all heads to turn towards the approaching policeman.

'Arrest this man, constable.' Harry pointed at Walter. 'Arrest this man. He is a thief and I suspect that he is the river pirate whom you seek.'

An angry murmur rippled through the on-lookers. Rosina stifled a cry of anguish as the constable unclipped a pair of handcuffs from his belt. 'That's a lie,' she cried. 'Walter hasn't done anything wrong.'

'I demand that you arrest this felon,' Harry repeated. 'He stole a valuable diamond ring belonging to my mother, and I daresay a search of his lodgings will produce the necessary evidence.'

Rosina clutched Walter's arm. 'I won't let them take you. I know you're innocent.'

He pushed her gently away from him. 'Go home, Rosie. Leave this to me.'

Harry caught her by the hand. 'So, you don't feel anything for this fellow? It's written all over your face. You tried to cheat me, you little whore.'

'Ahem.' The constable cleared his throat, glancing anxiously over his shoulder at the angry crowd. 'I think this matter will be best handled down at the station, sir.'

Rosina snatched her hand away. Resisting the temptation to slap Harry's face, she drew herself up to her full height. 'I was fond of you. I even thought that I was in love with you at one time, but now I see you for what you are, Harry Gostellow.'

'Don't upset yourself, Rosie.' Walter turned to the constable, holding out his hands. 'I'll come quietly, Constable Dobson. You can search my room, but you won't find anything.'

Dobson ran his finger round the inside of his

stiff uniform collar. 'I'm just doing me duty, Walter. No need for the cuffs. I trust you not to make a bolt for it.'

'I insist that you handcuff him, Constable.' Harry eyed Walter with contempt. 'He's a water rat thinly disguised as a counting-house clerk. You could hang for piracy, Walter Brown.'

'Come along, sir.' Constable Dobson took Walter by the arm.

'Good luck, Walter,' Fred shouted as the constable led him away.

The call was taken up by the crowd and they began stamping their booted feet on the cobblestones in time to the chanting.

Harry turned on them angrily, but Rosina caught him by the arm. 'Please, Harry. Stop this now. You know that Walter is innocent.'

He looked down at her with a hostile expression in his eyes. 'I know nothing of the sort. He's as guilty as sin and so are you. I was besotted with you, but now I see you for what you are – a scheming, manipulative little fortune-hunter.'

He shook free of her restraining hand and was about to follow Constable Dobson and Walter, but Rosina barred his way. 'Harry, I can prove that Walter didn't steal your mother's ring, but you must give me time.'

'Get out of my way, Rosie. I don't want to hear your lies.'

'If you ever loved me, just hear me out.'

'Well?'

His tone was uncompromising, but she was desperate. 'Give me time to prove that Walter is innocent and to raise the money to repay the loan. Call off the bailiffs. You promised me two weeks' grace. Grant me that and I'll be in your debt forever.'

'And do you really think that you can do all that in two weeks?'

'I can but try.'

'You are a fool, Rosina May.'

She saw a chink in his armour; a hint of his old self. 'Please, Harry.'

He nodded abruptly. 'Two weeks. But it won't save your lover from going to jail.' He strode off towards the police station. The crowd had melted away and Rosina was left standing alone on the wharf. She knew immediately what she must do and she headed towards the Barnums' house.

Gertie opened the door. Her plain features contorted into a scowl and she would have slammed the door in Rosina's face had she not put her foot over the doorsill. 'Let me in. I must see Miss Sukey.'

Gertie put all her puny weight against the door. 'She don't want to see you.'

Using all her strength, Rosina gave the door a hefty push, knocking Gertie off balance. She stepped inside. 'Tell her that it's a matter of life and death. I must see her.'

Before Gertie could protest further, Sukey emerged from the parlour. Her face brightened when she saw Rosina and she ran to her with outstretched hands. 'My dear, I'm so pleased to see you.'

'Mrs Barnum said she wasn't to be allowed in,' Gertie muttered.

'Never mind that,' Sukey said, slipping her hand through Rosina's arm. 'Go away, Gertie. And if you dare to tell Mama that Rosie is here, I'll pull your hair until your eyes pop out.'

Clutching her hands to the lank locks of hair that had escaped the confines of her mobcap, Gertie sped down the hall and disappeared through the baize door. Sukey led Rosina into the parlour, closing the door firmly behind her. 'And I shall too,' she said, chuckling. 'That girl deserves a good hair-pulling to keep her in her place. Anyway, never mind her. I've got some splendid news to tell you, Rosie.' She did a little twirl, waving her left hand beneath Rosina's nose. 'I'm engaged to Roland Rivers. Isn't that just too exciting?'

Rosina bit her lip. She was momentarily at a loss for words. Sukey looked so happy that it seemed too cruel to tell her the truth.

'What's the matter? Cat got your tongue?' Sukey threw herself down on the sofa. 'Come and sit beside me, Rosie, and I'll tell you all about it.'

Rosina sat down, making play of arranging her skirts while she tried to think of a way to broach the painful subject.

'Aren't you pleased for me?' Sukey asked, pouting. 'He's terribly rich and really good-looking. To tell you the truth, I didn't much like him at first. But he must have liked me, or he wouldn't have come to the Crystal Palace bringing a diamond ring with him and all prepared to propose.'

'Sukey, there's something you don't know.'

'What is it, dear? If it's about that evening I'm not sure I want to know. Tell the truth, I don't remember a thing about it after the fireworks. Don't tell me that I did something terribly naughty with Roland.' Sukey stifled a giggle, covering her mouth with her hand.

'Don't you recall anything?'

'Absolutely nothing. I don't remember anything until I woke up on that horrid horse-hair couch with the most dreadful headache imaginable. I can tell you, Rosie, I was so relieved when the engagement ring fell into my teacup. My reputation would have been quite ruined if it had got out that I spent the night in a hotel with an unmarried man.'

'I was there, Sukey. Pa, Bertha, Caddie and Walter were there too.'

'I know that now, but anything could have happened to me while I was under the influence of all that champagne.' Sukey leaned towards Rosina, cupping her hand round her mouth and whispering, 'I might not be a virgin now, for all I know. So it's a good thing that Roland is a gentleman, as well as being rich as Croesus and handsome into the bargain.'

Rosina took Sukey's hands in hers. 'Nothing untoward happened that night. We looked after you and Roland shared a room with Harry. You were as safe as if you'd been sleeping in a convent.'

Sukey's mouth drooped at the corners. 'But he had bought me a ring. I know we only met briefly at Cremorne Gardens, but it must have been love at first sight. I've read about men falling hopelessly in love like that in penny novelettes. It is so romantic – he must have intended to propose to me all along.'

'I'm so sorry, my dear. It was all a terrible misunderstanding. Didn't you recognise the ring?'

'It's a diamond solitaire. Just the sort I always wanted.'

'It is Harry's mother's ring, Sukey. The one he gave me when we became engaged.'

'No. That's impossible. I don't believe you.'

'I'm afraid it's true. Look! I'm not wearing his ring. ' Rosina held out her left hand. 'There was a terrible row – you slept through it all. But I broke off my engagement to Harry and I threw the ring at him. Roland must have picked it up and put it in his pocket. Apparently he forgot it was there, and when he came to see you the ring fell out of his handkerchief into your teacup.'

Sukey's eyes filled with tears and her lips trembled. 'He told you this?'

Rosina nodded.

'Why didn't he come to me first? He should have told me himself.'

'He didn't want to hurt you. And he was afraid that your father might sue him for breach of promise.'

Sukey leapt to her feet. 'I don't believe you. I want to hear it from his lips.'

'He's gone abroad on business. I really am so sorry, Sukey.'

With tears pouring down her face, Sukey wrenched the ring from her finger and threw it at Rosina. 'You should have told me sooner. You ought not to have let me go on dreaming of a rich husband. I've told everyone I could think of and now I'll be a laughing stock.'

'What can I say? It was all a terrible misunderstanding.' Rosina picked up the ring, trying not to look relieved. She was desperately sorry for her friend, but now she had the ring in her possession she would be able to give it back to Harry and he would drop the charges against Walter.

'You'd better go,' Sukey said, mopping her

eyes with a lace-trimmed handkerchief. 'I thought you were my friend, but you could have saved me from this humiliating situation. One word from you and I would have known that it was all a mistake, but you chose to keep quiet and allow me to make a complete fool of myself. I hate you, Rosina. I never want to see you again.'

'But, Sukey . . .'

'Go away. Leave me alone.' Sukey collapsed onto the sofa in a flood of tears.

Reluctantly, Rosina left the parlour and let herself out of the house. She hesitated on the doorstep, gazing down at the diamond ring lying in the palm of her hand. Who would have thought that such a small object could cause so much distress? She was deeply troubled by Sukey's plight, and yet part of her was rejoicing that she held the evidence in her hand which would prove Walter's innocence. Walter! Her heart seemed to miss a beat. For that split second on the wharf she had been convinced that Walter and Will were the same person. Had she been dreaming? Was it simply wishful thinking or an overactive imagination? She had never seen Will in daylight. She had never seen him unmasked. But the Walter who had stood up to Harry on the wharf had seemed like a completely different person to the young man who had toiled quietly in her father's counting house. She closed her fingers around the cold, hard diamond.

'And where do you think you are going with my daughter's engagement ring?'

Rosina spun round to face Captain Barnum. She had been so deep in thought that she had not heard the door open behind her. Towering over her, Ham Barnum seized her by the wrist and forced her fingers open. He took the ring from her hand. 'That belongs to Susan.'

'No, Captain Barnum. It does not. I've explained the mistake to Sukey. I'm terribly sorry, but it's all true.'

'I don't care whether it's true or not. The fact is that Mr Roland Rivers gave my daughter an engagement ring. I intend to sue him for every penny he's got. I'll not have my daughter's good name ruined by a libertine.'

'You mean as you ruined my mother's good name?' Rosina glared up at him, unafraid and furious. 'Now you know how my grandpa must have felt when you seduced my poor mother.'

Barnum flinched as though she had slapped his face. 'Shut your mouth, girl. You don't know what you're saying.'

'You know it's true, but that is all in the past now: what matters is that Walter has been accused of stealing the ring and he is innocent. Please give it back to me, Captain Barnum. If you don't then Walter will go to prison for a crime that he did not commit.'

'Bah! That young man deserves all he gets. I've

suspected him of stealing from my boats all along, although I couldn't prove it. He thinks he has some grudge against me, of which I know nothing. Let him rot in jail for all I care. And you, young lady, keep away from my daughter. If you ever come near my house again I'll have you thrown out like the common little slut that you are.'

Rosina threw herself down on her knees in the dust. 'Please, Captain Barnum. I'm begging you . . .'

Barnum went into the house and slammed the door.

Walter's last chance was gone. She rose slowly to her feet, too shocked even to cry. The only person who could save him now had travelled abroad and might stay there indefinitely if Captain Barnum carried out his threat to sue him for breach of promise. She must see Walter. She must find out what had happened to him. Rosina ran, ignoring the concerned comments from the men on the docks as she raced over the cobblestones heading for the dock police station. She arrived breathless and dishevelled with her hair tumbling loose around her shoulders and perspiration streaming down her face. She barged in through the doors, not caring what the men inside would think of her. She marched up to the counter where the desk sergeant was writing something in a book.

'Where is he?' she demanded. 'Mr Walter

Brown was brought in here a little while ago. I want to see him.'

Without looking up, the sergeant continued to write. 'Take a seat, miss.'

'No, I won't take a seat. I want to see Walter. I know he's here.'

'Take a seat, miss, or leave the premises. I'll see to you in a minute.'

Rosina paced the floor, wringing her hands. She could not rest until she discovered Walter's fate. After what seemed like hours, but the large white-faced clock on the wall indicated that it was only a few minutes, the sergeant put down his pen and stared at her. 'Now what was it that you wanted, miss?'

She gripped the edge of the counter, her knuckles showing white beneath the taut skin. 'My friend, Mr Walter Brown, has been wrongly arrested. Please may I see him?'

'You may.'

Her heart leapt in her chest. 'May I see him now?'

'You can see him in court tomorrow morning, miss. He'll be up before the magistrate on a number of charges.'

'But that's impossible. You've got it all wrong.'

The sergeant glanced over his shoulder as an inner door opened and Harry strolled into the room. 'Do you know this young person, Mr Gostellow?'

'What are you doing here, Rosie?' Harry demanded, frowning. 'You shouldn't have come.'

'You're absolutely right, sir. May I suggest that you escort the young lady from the building before she gets herself into trouble?' The sergeant glowered at Rosina.

She forced her lips into a smile. 'Please, sergeant. May I just see Mr Brown for one minute? That's all I ask. One little minute.'

Harry took her by the arm. 'Come away, Rosina. You're making a scene.'

'I'm sorry, miss. Best do as Mr Gostellow says. You can't do no good here.'

Before Rosina could protest any further, Harry had steered her out of the police station. 'You little fool; you'll only get yourself into trouble. Go home, Rosie. There's nothing you can do to save your lover. Walter Brown will go to jail for a very long time. If they can find enough evidence against him he will probably be hanged for piracy, and, if not, I can assure you that after a few years in prison he will wish that they had stretched his neck on the gallows.'

# Chapter Seventeen

The magistrate ordered that Walter be held in custody at Newgate pending trial in the Crown Court, and without bail. Rosina caught only a brief glimpse of him as he was led into the dock and then taken away to the cells after the charges were read and he had put in a plea of not guilty. She left the courtroom in a daze. What chance did Walter stand when Harry could afford the best brief in London? It was all so terribly unfair, and she quite simply did not know which way to turn. As she walked homewards from East Arbour Street in Stepney, she racked her brains trying to think of someone to whom she could turn for advice. It was raining, and after the heat of the previous few days the moisture evaporated in hissing steam as it touched the pavements. She had not thought to bring an umbrella, and by the time she reached Ratcliff Highway she was soaked to the skin. It was less than three months since her birthday when she had collected her new bonnet from the milliner's shop. So much had happened in that short time: she had been a carefree girl then, with the world at her feet; now she and her family were facing ruin and the man she loved – for she was certain that Walter and Will were the same person – was facing imprisonment or even death if the case of piracy could be proved against him.

'Rosie? Come inside, girl. You'll catch your death of cold.'

Old Jamjar's familiar voice brought her to a halt. The shrill chatter of the exotic birds inside the shop echoed in her ears; it sounded as though they were mocking her sad state. 'Mr Jamjar?'

He hooked his arm round her shoulders, guiding her into the dark recesses of his shop. Fronds of potted palm brushed her forehead and the fuggy atmosphere of the interior made her gasp for breath. The pervading odour was a choking combination of damp earth and bird droppings, but old Jamjar seemed impervious to the smell. He helped her to a chair. 'You look done in, girl. What were you doing all alone and wandering about in the rain?' His wrinkled face was close to hers and his beady black eyes were filled with concern.

'I've just been to the police court and seen a friend sent down to await trial. He didn't do it, Mr Jamjar. Walter is an innocent man.'

'And you care a great deal for this friend of yours, if I'm not mistaken?'

Rosina nodded. 'I – I do.'

'And what does the good captain say about all this?'

'My papa is a sick man. He had to go to the country to recover from an illness.'

'Then you need someone to give you good advice, my dear.' He shambled off into the darkness and returned seconds later with a slip of paper in his hand. 'Go and see this man. Tell him that old Jamjar sent you. If Septimus Sumption can't help you, no one can.'

She peered at the spidery scrawl; in the dim light it was difficult to make out the address. 'Thank you, Mr Jamjar.' She tried to get up, but he pressed her back onto the seat.

'You're going nowhere until you've had a restorative cup of mint tea. If you go down with a chill, you'll be no use to anyone.' He disappeared once again into the back of the shop.

All around her the birds squawked and uttered shrill cries as they fluttered about in their cages. She was shivering violently now, even though it was hotter in the shop than it was outside. Her teeth chattered against the china mug as she attempted to sip the drink which he handed to her. The clear brown liquid smelt of mint and something much stronger; she coughed as the raw spirit caught the back of her throat.

Jamjar took a swig of his drink and chuckled. 'That's good navy rum, Rosie, my girl. That'll keep the fever at bay.'

She left the shop with a warm glow in her stomach and a muzzy feeling in her head. The mint tea laced with rum had certainly warmed her chilled flesh and had given her the courage to seek out Mr Sumption at his address in Naked Boy Yard, which turned out to be as insalubrious as its name might imply. Picking her way through piles of rotting vegetable matter and excrement, Rosina bunched up her skirts to prevent them from trailing in the filth. A huge rat ran over her feet as she entered the tenement building and the stench of unwashed bodies, urine and stale tobacco smoke made her retch. She covered her nose with her hand and made her way down a narrow passage, checking the numbers scratched on the peeling paintwork of the closed doors. At the very end she found Sumption's room, and she knocked on the cracked panelling. When she received no answer, she gave the door a push and it opened. She went inside.

She had expected that a man of the law would have some sort of office, even in a rundown establishment such as this, but the only furniture in the room was a truckle bed in one corner, a table piled high with books, and a chair by the empty hearth in which a man lay slumped and apparently asleep. Loosely clasped in his hand was an empty glass, which seemed in danger of falling to the floor at any moment.

Rosina cleared her throat. 'Ahem. Mr Sumption?'

He stirred, opened one eye and then appeared to go back to sleep. She went over to him and tapped him on the shoulder. 'Mr Sumption, I need to speak to you, sir.'

He opened both his eyes this time, staring at her blearily and in an unfocused manner. 'Who the devil are you?'

A miasma of stale alcohol hung around him, and it was making her feel sick. 'Mr Jamjar sent me. He said you might be able to help a friend of mine who is in trouble.'

'Oh, trouble. I'm well acquainted with trouble. You might say that trouble is my middle name, Miss . . . er, what is your name?'

'Rosina May. Will you help me, sir? But first I must tell you that I have no money at present, although I swear on my honour that I will pay your fee as soon as I am able.'

Septimus sat upright, wincing with pain and clasping his hand to his forehead. 'At least you're honest about it. Pass me that bottle.' He nodded in the direction of a bottle, which was just beyond his reach.

Rosina gave it to him. 'Haven't you drunk enough already?'

He took a long draught of the spirit and pulled back his lips in a satisfied sigh. 'Never enough, my dear. Never enough to blot out the tragedy of my talent wasted and my life – a travesty. What did you say you wanted?'

She was not certain how much he was capable of understanding, but she knew that she had no option other than to confide in him. She looked round for a chair, and, finding there was none, she sat down on a pile of leather-bound law books and began her story. He seemed to be taking it in, although he fortified himself at regular intervals with sips from the bottle. When she had finished he was silent for a while, as if mulling it over in his mind.

'Have you any money at all, Miss May? I seem to have drunk the last drop.'

'No, I haven't. And if I had I would not give it to you at this moment. You can't possibly think straight if you're drunk.'

He rubbed his stubbly chin, grinning ruefully. 'I am at my most brilliant best when I'm three sheets to the wind.'

She rose to her feet. 'I can see that I'm wasting your time.'

'No. Stay, please. I'll take the case, even though I'll probably regret it later. Your devotion to your man is most touching. If only all women were as faithful as you, Miss May. I, alas, was not so fortunate as your Walter.'

'Then you will help me?'

He nodded his head. 'It seems to me that your only chance is to persuade the one person who knows the truth to return to London to testify on Walter's behalf.'

'But Roland Rivers has gone to Holland on business and to evade a breach of promise suit brought by the Barnums.'

'Then you must go to Holland and put your case to him.'

She stared at him in horror. 'I can't do that. I haven't any money and I couldn't go all that way on my own.'

'Then your man will go to prison for a very long time, or even worse.'

'You should go to Holland, not I.'

He uttered a snort of derisive laughter. 'Look at me, Miss May. Do you think that a man like Rivers would take any notice of a fellow like me? I think that you are the only person who might persuade him to return to London to bear witness.'

'But I wouldn't know where to begin looking for him.'

Septimus eased himself out of his chair and stood up, swaying slightly. He lurched over to the table and riffled through a pile of books, tossing the discarded ones on the floor. 'Aha, this is the one.' He flipped through the pages. 'It is a directory of London companies and their foreign holdings. Here you are. Rivers and Son, Import and Export Company, trading with – et cetera, et cetera. And their address in Rotterdam is . . .' He tore the page out of the book and handed it to her. 'Go there and doubtless they will know where to find Mr Roland Rivers. The rest is up to you.'

She took the paper, staring at the print until it danced about in front of her eyes like tadpoles. 'I've never been further than Gravesend.'

'My dear girl. This then is your chance to travel. And while you are gone, I will use my contacts within the police to discover if there is any evidence that Walter was involved in piracy. From what you told me, I doubt that they could prove anything, but you never know.' He brushed an unruly lock of mouse-brown hair back from his forehead. 'Now, I really need a drink.' He staggered to the door and opened it. 'Let yourself out, Miss May. I'll see you on your return from Rotterdam.'

'Rotterdam?' Caddie's eyes opened wide. 'You can't go there.'

Rosina continued to pull garments out of the clothes press in her room, tossing them onto her bed in a brightly coloured heap. 'I have no choice. Roland Rivers is the only person who knows the truth about the ring, and he alone can clear Walter's name.'

'But, Rosie, we ain't got no money. How are you going to get there?'

'I don't know how I'm going to get there, not

yet anyway. But things are desperate, Caddie. I'm going to the pawnbroker's shop to see what I can get for my clothes and anything else we have that is of the slightest value.'

'Your lovely clothes,' Caddie said, eyeing the growing pile sadly. 'You was always turned out like you was fresh out of a bandbox. I can't bear to think of you going about like a drudge.'

Rosina tossed a pillowcase to her. 'You don't understand. We'll lose the house as well if I don't do something quickly. Now don't argue, there's a good girl, Caddie. Put everything in the pillowcase while I go down to the parlour and see what I can find there.' She went to the chest of drawers and emptied her jewellery box. The only items of any value were the silver bracelet that Sukey had given her for her last birthday and Walter's gold breastpin. She fingered the locket at her throat, but it contained her most precious possession – the medallion – her only tangible link with Will. She would rather die than part with it. With a heartfelt sigh, she handed the bracelet and breastpin to Caddie, followed by her musical box and Dorcas, her beautiful doll with the wax face and glossy silk hair.

An hour later, Caddie returned from the pawnbroker's shop in the High Street with a purse that felt reassuringly heavy. It was not a fortune but there was enough for Rosina to leave

Caddie with money for food and other necessities, and what was left would go towards Rosina's fare to Rotterdam. After a tearful parting with Caddie and the children, Rosina set off in the direction of Albion Wharf. If anyone could help her then Captain Morgan was her man. He had been her father's apprentice many years ago and was now master of the *River Pearl*, trading to Rotterdam with general cargo and returning with spices for Travers's grinding mill. After a brief respite between showers, the sky had darkened again and there were rumblings of thunder in the distance. Undeterred, she quickened her pace, passing through the white haze of flour dust on Crown Mill Wharf and sidestepping the barrels of beer that were being unloaded from a lighter. She kept her fingers crossed, scanning the water for a sign of Captain Morgan's barge as she came to Albion Wharf: she could have cried with relief when she saw that it was tied up alongside. It seemed as though she was just in time, as the last of the cargo was being lowered into the hold.

She could see him standing on deck. Captain Morgan was an unmistakeable figure, with his flame-red mop of hair barely concealed by his peaked cap, and his thick red beard standing out proud against the dark blue of his pea jacket. She cupped her hands round her lips. 'Captain Morgan. Ahoy there!'

He turned his head, saw her and grinned. 'Rosie! Well now, this is a surprise. Come aboard, lass.'

She hitched up her skirt and climbed nimbly down the wooden ladder to the deck.

'I heard about your father,' Captain Morgan said, tugging at his beard and frowning. 'Bad business, my dear. How is he going on?'

'He's quite poorly, sir. He had to leave London for the country. Doctor's orders.'

'I'm sorry to hear that. But what can I do for you, missy? I don't suppose you come a-visiting me on the *River Pearl* just to pass the time of day.'

'I need your help, Captain. Please hear me out before you say no to what I have to ask you.'

He listened attentively, tweaking and pulling at his beard until it stuck out in small spikes. When she had finished he shook his head. 'I don't know, Rosie. I'm not sure what your dad would make of this. A sailing barge is no place for a young woman such as you.'

'I promise that I won't get in the way. I was practically raised on a barge, Captain. I can make myself useful.'

'Can you cook, lass?'

'Well, er – no.'

'Can you trim a sail or steer a straight course?'

'No, but I could learn. My pa never let me do anything except watch him and Artie, but I'm sure I could pick it up as I went along.'

He threw back his head and laughed, calling to his mate who was busy stowing the last of the crates and closing the hatches. 'D'you hear that, Barney? Miss Rosie thinks she can become a sailor in one easy lesson.'

Barney uttered a hoot of laughter and continued with what he was doing.

'Don't pay him no mind,' Captain Morgan said in a low voice. 'He's a bit simple is Barney, but he's a good deck hand and can handle a barge like one of the best.'

'Please, Captain. I know I'm asking a lot, but will you take me to Rotterdam? I can pay my way.' She took the purse from her reticule and held it out to him. 'Take it all, but please say yes.'

He stared at her for a moment and then he pushed her hand away. 'Keep your money, lass. You look as though you need every penny of it. It's against me better judgement, but if it's as important as you say it is, then I'll take you.'

Rosina could hardly believe her ears. She had been prepared to go down on her knees if necessary. She flung her arms around his neck and hugged him. 'Oh, thank you, sir. Thank you so much.'

His face was as red as his beard and he made a huffing sound as he disentangled her arms from round his neck. 'Now, now. There's no need to thank me. I owe your dad a lot; I just hope he won't be too angry with me when he finds out what I've done.'

'He won't. He'll be ever so grateful, as am I.'

'There's just one thing though. We have to sail on the tide and that is now. There's no time for you to go home and pack up all your folderols and furbelows, and all the things that you young ladies hold so dear.'

Having just pawned everything except the clothes she stood up in, Rosina could brush that objection aside without a qualm, but she must let Caddie know what was happening. 'That is quite all right, but I have to send a message home to say that I am bound for Holland on the *River Pearl*.'

'Barney. Come here, lad.' Captain Morgan's voice boomed out across the wharf, and was eerily followed by a crack of thunder.

Rosina felt as though God had just spoken, and judging by the terrified look on Barney's face as he came lolloping across the deck towards them, he must have felt the same.

'Find a boy to take a message to Black Eagle Wharf.' Captain Morgan put his hand in his pocket and took out a penny. 'Give him this and Miss Rosina will tell you what to say.'

Barney stared at the penny in the palm of his hand and scratched his head. 'Take a message to Black Eagle Wharf? I can remember that, I think.'

Rosina patted him on the shoulder. 'He must

go to Captain May's house. Anyone on the wharf will know which one it is. He is to tell Caddie that Miss Rosina has got a berth on the *River Pearl* bound for Rotterdam.'

He repeated the message slowly, enunciating each syllable, and when Rosina congratulated him on his good memory, he blushed and giggled. He leapt for the ladder and clambered up it repeating the words over and over again. He disappeared onto the wharf and came back a couple of minutes later grinning widely. 'Done it, master.'

'Cast off, Barney.' Captain Morgan went to the stern and took hold of the tiller. 'I hope you're a good sailor, lass. There's little or no privacy on board, or comfort for a seasick passenger come to that.'

Rosina sat down on a hatch cover. 'I'll be perfectly all right, Captain. Don't worry about me. I've never been seasick in my life.'

This bold statement held true while they were sailing downriver, but once they were away from the mouth of the Thames and sailing across open sea, Rosina began to feel decidedly queasy. There was only one small cabin on deck, with two narrow bunks for the master and the mate. Captain Morgan had decided at the outset that he and Barney would sleep on deck, and Rosina could have the cabin to herself. She protested at first, thinking it unfair, but during the cold night on the North Sea she was glad to snuggle down between the rough blankets with a pillow at her head. Next morning when she awakened, the storm had followed them and the barge was bobbing about on what seemed to her to be enormous waves. She found that someone had thoughtfully provided her with a bucket, and she kept to her bunk all day while she suffered the miseries of seasickness.

By the time they reached Rotterdam she had found her sea legs, as Captain Morgan put it, and was beginning to enjoy the voyage now that the sun had come out and the sea was calm. When they docked in the busy port she realised that she was now on her own and would have to find the offices of Rivers and Son. Without a word of Dutch, or any other foreign language, she felt very much alone and vulnerable. Her clothes were travel-stained and crumpled and she had not had a proper wash since they left London. She glanced ruefully down at her grey cotton skirt and the soiled cuffs of her once-white blouse. She had had to put her hair up without the aid of a mirror, and she could feel strands tickling the back of her neck and sticking to her forehead in the heat. But she must put all the vanities aside and concentrate on the business in hand. Walter's fate was far more important than her appearance and she simply had to find Roland.

To her intense relief, Captain Morgan sent Barney with her, declaring that no young lady in his care was going to wander around on her own in a foreign port. Barney may not have been the sharpest knife in the box, but no one challenged her when she was with the big fellow who had a lantern jaw and fists like York hams. They were not to know that his simian appearance hid the softest and sweetest nature, as Rosina had found out during their days at sea. The warehouses and offices were all clearly named and they walked side by side, dodging the horse-drawn traffic and pedestrians alike until they found, more by accident than anything else, the offices of Rivers and Son.

Rosina left Barney waiting for her outside, and patting her hair in place, she went into the office. She asked for Mr Roland Rivers, and for a horrible moment she thought that the clerk behind the desk had not understood, but after a moment's hesitation he smiled and spoke to her in English. 'Mr Rivers is not here, miss.'

'But I must see him. I've come all the way from London to find him. I simply must see him.'

'Not here, miss.'

'But he will come here soon?'

The clerk shrugged his shoulders.

'I will wait for him,' Rosina said firmly. Having come all this way, and after suffering the rigours of the journey on a vessel unequipped for carrying passengers, she could have wept with frustration. But she was not going to give in now. The memory of Walter being escorted to the cells was uppermost in her mind. She popped her head outside the door and told Barney to return to the ship. She would find her own way back, as soon as she had spoken to Mr Rivers.

She waited all morning. The clerk gave her a cup of water, and he offered her a piece of red-skinned cheese and a slice of dark rye bread, which was part of his own midday meal. She smiled and thanked him as she accepted the water, but she could not take his lunch as it seemed little enough to keep a man going all day.

She sat back against the wooden settle and watched the hands of the clock as they moved slowly – too slowly for her liking. The minutes dragged into hours and by late afternoon she was beginning to think that Roland would never put in an appearance, when the door opened and he strolled in as if he had not a care in the world. He walked past her, and then he stopped short, turning his head to stare at her. 'Miss May?'

She leapt to her feet, smoothing her crumpled skirts and wishing that she did not look such a terrible mess. Roland was so smartly dressed that it only made her feel worse. 'Mr Rivers, I . . .' She swayed on her feet, overtaken by a wave of dizziness. She had not eaten anything since the previous night, and she felt herself falling, only to be scooped off her feet and laid down on the settle. Something cold and wet was trickling down her face. She opened her eyes to find Roland staring anxiously at her while he bathed her forehead with a handkerchief dipped in a cup of water.

'Miss May. It really is you. What on earth are you doing here?' He helped her to a sitting position. 'No, don't waste your energy on explanations until you feel better.'

Searching desperately for the right words, she clutched his arm. 'Mr Rivers, I need your help. I must speak to you in private.' His features were going in and out of focus: she felt sick and dizzy, and she rested her forehead against his shoulder. 'I'm sorry. I don't feel so well.'

'When did you last eat? Never mind; don't bother answering, my dear. Save your strength.' Roland stood up, issuing a command to the desk clerk in fluent Dutch.

The clerk muttered a reply and hurried out into the street.

'I've sent for a carriage. My father keeps a company house in the town. I don't think there is anything wrong with you that a hot bath and a good meal will not put right.'

'Thank you,' Rosina murmured weakly.

'Is there anyone I should notify as to your whereabouts? You cannot have come here alone.'

'Could you send a message to Captain Morgan of the sailing barge, *River Pearl*? He brought me to Holland, and he will be concerned as to my safety.'

Roland patted her hand. 'Consider it done, and you yourself need not worry. There will be no repeat of my shameful conduct in Cremorne Gardens, and my housekeeper will look after you.'

A wave of exhaustion washed over her and she closed her eyes with a sigh of relief. Her reputation was the last thing on her mind. She had already decided to do whatever Roland required of her in order to secure his promise to return to London. No sacrifice would be too great if it bought Walter's release from jail. She drifted into a dreamlike state and was barely conscious when someone lifted her into a carriage for a rather bumpy ride over cobbled streets. The next thing she knew, Roland was helping her up a flight of stone steps into a tall, narrow house in the middle of a terrace. Despite its unimposing frontage, the interior took Rosina's breath away. An elegant staircase swept upwards from the grand entrance hall and the air was fragranced with lavender.

A tall raw-boned woman wearing a starched white cap and a black bombazine dress came bustling along the hallway to greet them.

'This is our housekeeper, Mrs Hopper,' Roland said in a matter-of-fact voice, as if it were quite normal to bring a dishevelled and exhausted young woman into his abode. He whispered a few words in her ear and the housekeeper nodded in response. Roland turned to Rosina with a smile. 'Mrs Hopper will look after you, my dear. We will talk later, when you are feeling more the thing.'

'Good day, ma'am,' Rosina murmured, eyeing her nervously. She was surprised and relieved when Mrs Hopper answered her with a cockney twang in her voice.

'Come with me, miss. You look like something the cat brought in. We'll run you a nice hot bath and find you some clean duds.'

Half an hour later, after a luxurious wallow in a deep tub filled with hot water, and having had her hair washed by Mrs Hopper with a sweet-smelling liquid soap, Rosina was wrapped in a bath sheet and sitting at a dressing table in a bedroom at the top of the house. Mrs Hopper handed her a hairbrush and comb. 'Here, ducks. You'd best see to your hair while I find you a clean frock. I'm afraid your clothes are only fit for the ragbag.'

Slowly, as if still dreaming, Rosina tugged the comb through her wet, tangled hair. She could see Mrs Hopper reflected in the mirror as she opened a rosewood armoire and was riffling through a rail of garments, taking out one elegant gown after another and then putting them back. 'I'm truly grateful for all your kindness, ma'am. But my old clothes will do. I don't want to put you to any further trouble, and I cannot take your clothes.'

Mrs Hopper gave a throaty gurgle of a laugh. 'Oh, Lord. These ain't mine, ducks. I might have fitted into one of these here gowns more than twenty years ago when I was following the drum, but not now.'

'I don't understand.'

'I was a soldier's wife, dearie. It's a long story, but my old man was an army sergeant during the Crimean War. He was wounded in the fall of Sebastopol and too sick to be brought home, so I nursed him until he was well enough to travel. We got here eventually, intending to get a passage home to England, but he was took with a fever and died. Mr Rivers senior found me begging in the streets, trying to raise the money to give me old man a decent burial, and he took me under his wing. Paid for everything and set me up in this house.'

Rosina stared at her in a mixture of fascination and horror. 'You mean that he – er – you were his . . .'

'That's right, love. No need to look so shocked. I had nowhere to go and no one waiting for me at home. Besides which, I likes it here and I've had a good life. He could have tired of me and thrown me out on the streets, but he's a kind man, is Mr Roland's father. I mind the house and I keep me mouth shut.' She selected two gowns and held them up for Rosina to see. 'Either of these would suit you a treat. Which is it to be? The grey tussore or the violet-blue silk?'

'If they are not yours, then whose are they? And I'm not that sort of girl, Mrs Hopper. Mr Rivers knows that I'm not. I came here to beg a favour for a friend.'

'And you're ready and willing to pay the price, if I'm not mistaken? Oh, don't look like that, dearie. I'm a woman of the world, and nothing shocks old Mavis Hopper. Take my advice and wear the blue – it will make your eyes look bluer than Devon violets.'

Rosina gazed longingly at the blue silk gown with its shockingly low décolletage and tiny puff sleeves trimmed with Brussels lace. The skirt was cunningly draped across the front, and caught up with a huge bow at the back so that the narrow hem spilled out in a full train. She had seen ladies wearing such elegant garments at Cremorne Gardens and the Crystal Palace, but had never in her wildest dreams imagined that she would have the opportunity to wear such apparel.

'Slip it on, and I'll put your hair up for you. When you're ready I'll show you down to the drawing room where Mr Roland will be waiting. Then you two can enjoy a nice cosy chat over an early supper.'

Roland stood up as Mrs Hopper ushered Rosina into the drawing room, which was elegantly furnished in the style of the English Regency period. Rosina had thought that the Gostellows' gloomy mansion was grand, but now she was seeing how the really wealthy lived, and she could not but be impressed. Roland came towards her, and if she had doubted that the gown suited her, the expression on his face would have put all such thoughts to flight. He took her hands in his with a look of genuine admiration in his eyes. 'Miss May, you look absolutely beautiful.' He kissed first one hand and then the other. 'Quite stunning, in fact.'

'Thank you, Mr Rivers.' She felt herself blushing furiously, and she was even more conscious of the amount of bosom revealed by the décolletage. She could imagine what Bertha would say if she could see her now, and it was not flattering. But Roland did not seem to see anything amiss. 'That gown could have been made for you, my dear.'

'And who is the proud owner, sir?' She had to ask, although she had already decided that it must belong to one of his mistresses. Perhaps he had several of them tucked away in Rotterdam. Maybe that was the real reason for his visit?

'Do take a seat, Miss May,' he replied, smiling.

'But that sounds so formal – may I call you Rosie?'

She nodded her assent as she subsided onto the couch in a billowing cloud of violet-blue silk.

'And you must call me Roland. It seems we are thrown together like old friends, so there is no point in standing on ceremony.' He went to a side table and picked up a decanter. 'May I offer you a sherry, Rosie?'

'Yes, thank you.' She accepted it gladly; she would need all the courage she could muster if she were to get through this evening. Sipping, she eyed him over the rim of the glass. 'You didn't answer my question. Whose gown am I wearing? I hope she won't mind my borrowing it.'

He poured a large brandy for himself and took a drink before answering. His eyes twinkled with amusement. 'So, you think that the boudoir and all the expensive gowns belong to one of my mistresses. Am I right?'

She gulped a mouthful of sherry, nodding her head. He was laughing at her and she felt the blood rushing to her cheeks. 'Maybe.'

'They belong to my elder sister, Vanessa. But I doubt if she will ever wear any of them again, since she has married a baronet, lives in Hertfordshire and is expecting a happy event any day now.'

'Oh!' She turned her head away, unable to look him in the eye.

'But never mind that, my dear.' Roland came to sit beside her on the sofa. 'You must be in very grave trouble if you travelled all the way to Holland on the off chance of finding me.' He put his glass down on a sofa table and took her hand in his. 'What can I do for you, my dear Rosie?'

# Chapter Eighteen

Haltingly at first, but slowly gaining confidence, Rosina related all the events that had occurred since Roland had left London with her father, whom he said reassuringly, had arrived safely in Burnham-on-Crouch and had been in good spirits when they parted.

'So, you travelled to Rotterdam on a sailing barge, and all for the sake of young Walter?' Roland said with a thoughtful frown. 'I'm touched by your courage and your devotion. You must love him very much.'

'What I feel for him doesn't matter. There has been a grave miscarriage of justice and you are the only one who can set it right.'

'But my dear, if I return to London I will find myself on the wrong end of a law suit or else obliged to marry a young lady for whom I have no tender feelings. Much as I would love to oblige you, I'm afraid that I cannot.'

'I tried to tell Sukey that it was all a mistake, but she wouldn't believe me. It has to come from your lips. I'm sure she would understand.'

'With his daughter's reputation in jeopardy,

I'm afraid that her father would not be so forgiving. You are forgetting that I was partly responsible for keeping his daughter out all night.'

'Sukey is a lovely girl, and we were the best of friends until this wretched business. I'm sure you could do a lot worse.'

Roland threw back his head and laughed. 'I'm certain that I could, but that is not the point, Rosie. I barely know the young lady, and I am not inclined to marry someone just to save them from a moment of embarrassment.'

She was desperate now, and she grasped his hands in hers. 'If you won't come back to England with me, will you at least write a letter to Harry? Tell him that it was you who picked up the ring and not Walter: I'm sure he would relent if you were to explain the circumstances of your engagement to Sukey.'

'My dear, I barely understand how it happened myself, and Harry would simply think that I was attempting to escape a breach of promise suit.'

'Please, Roland. I'm begging you to think again. I – I'll do anything that you want of me, if you will save Walter from imprisonment.'

He regarded her with a quizzical smile. 'Anything?'

Before she could answer, the door opened and Mrs Hopper announced that supper had been laid out for them in the dining room.

Roland raised himself from the sofa and offered Rosina his arm. 'I'm sure you must be famished. We'll discuss this matter again later.'

Despite her emotional turmoil, she managed to enjoy the well-cooked and plentiful food that Mrs Hopper had set on the table in the wainscoted dining room. Rosina had eaten almost nothing since the bout of seasickness that had laid her low for most of the voyage to Holland. She ate sparingly, but by the time they reached the dessert of fresh fruit and cheese she was feeling stronger and more optimistic. Roland had been a perfect host and had entertained her throughout the meal with amusing anecdotes. There had been no hint of seduction in his manner, but when they had finished eating she began to feel uneasy. She had convinced herself that she would do anything to secure Walter's release from prison, but now she was facing reality and she was extremely apprehensive. She was in a foreign country, in the house of a man who had once tried to seduce her. She had accepted his hospitality and there was no one to protect her from her own reckless folly. Rosina found herself wishing that she was back on the *River Pearl* with kindly Captain Morgan and Barney.

Roland held out her chair and she rose slowly to her feet. She could feel his breath warm against the nape of her neck. She turned to face him. 'Thank you for taking me in. I'm truly grateful.'

His eyes strayed from her face to the décolletage of her gown, but only for a few seconds, and then he met her worried gaze with a hint of a smile. 'It was my pleasure.'

'I really should be getting back to the ship. I must return to England on the *River Pearl* with or without you.'

'She will not leave until the morning, my dear. I've sent word to the captain to tell him that you are a guest in my home for the night. I'll make certain that you are at the docks in good time before the ship sails.'

She lowered her gaze, afraid of what she might see in his eyes. 'And will you be coming with me, Roland?'

Very gently, he lifted her chin with the tip of his forefinger and kissed her on the lips. 'We'll see.'

He had spoken in the manner that he might have used to placate a fractious child, and she knew that she had to act now, or he would never agree to help Walter. She raised her eyes to his face. 'Roland, I'm begging you to reconsider. Harry has accused him falsely because I hurt his pride by breaking off our engagement. Will you really stand by and see an innocent man sentenced for a crime that he did not commit?'

He traced the outline of her cheek with his finger, following the curve of her throat and caressing her bare shoulder. She braced herself for what was to come, closing her eyes and praying that Walter would understand and forgive her.

'Goodnight, my dear. Sweet dreams.'

She opened her eyes, staring at him in surprise. 'But I – I thought . . .'

'Normally there is nothing that would tear me away from such delightful company, but I am afraid a prior engagement calls. Anyway, you must be exhausted after all your trials.' He moved swiftly to the door and opened it. 'Mrs Hopper will look after you, and I will see you first thing in the morning.'

As the door closed behind him Rosina's knees gave way beneath her and she sank down on the nearest chair. Had she really offered herself to a man who was little more than a stranger? She had come to persuade Roland to return to England with her, and however charmingly he couched the words, he had refused to help. She looked up as the door opened, half afraid that he had changed his mind and decided to take advantage of her, but it was Mrs Hopper who entered the room. 'Well now, dearie,' she said, chuckling. 'This is a turn-up for the books. He don't usually play the gent on the first night.'

'It wasn't like that,' Rosina said, rising to her feet with as much dignity as she could muster. 'Mr Rivers is just an acquaintance, and my business with him was on behalf of a friend.'

'Don't get all hoity-toity with me, miss. You was brought up decent, I could tell that when I first set eyes on you. You must have been desperate to come chasing after Mr Roland.'

'It really isn't any of your business, Mrs Hopper.'

'La-di-dah, I'm sure. Look, love. I'm a woman of the world and I know when a girl wants something so bad that she'll risk everything to get it.'

'It's not what you think.'

'Ain't it? Well, whatever you want from Mr Roland he's no different to his dad. Play your cards right, girl, and he'll give you whatever you want.'

Ignoring the insulting inference that she was an adventuress, Rosina eyed her curiously. 'And was this what you wanted, Mrs Hopper? Were you happy to be the kept woman and never the wife?'

'You're young, ducks. And judging by your innocent face, you don't know nothing about the harsh realities of the world. Being a common law wife and following the drum weren't exactly the life of a lady. I count meself lucky to have a fine house to live in, good food and a kind master.'

She emitted a deep belly laugh. 'And don't look so shocked, missy. I ain't too old for a tumble if the mood takes him, though it ain't so often these days.'

'I – I'm very tired. I'd like to go to bed now.'

'You know where the room is. Top of the third flight of stairs. Don't expect me to keep running up and down after you.'

'Don't worry, I won't trouble you again.' Rosina picked up a candlestick. 'I can find my own way perfectly well.'

Mrs Hopper followed her to the foot of the grand staircase. 'I'd lock your door if I was you, ducks. He might forget he's a gent when he comes home a bit squiffy.'

Ignoring the last remark, Rosina made her way up to the bedroom that had belonged to Roland's sister. Despite Mrs Hopper's apparent unwillingness to wait on her, she found that fresh towels had been placed on the washstand, and the water in the jug was still warm. A fine cambric nightgown was draped on the counterpane and the bed sheets had been turned down. She undressed, washed and slipped the nightgown over her head. She climbed into the bed, revelling in the feel of fine percale bed linen and a feather mattress that was soft as a cloud. She closed her eyes and drifted off into a deep sleep.

She was awakened by the sound of tapping on her window. For a moment when she first opened her eyes she could not remember where she was, but the memories of the previous evening came flooding back and she sat bolt upright. The tapping sound continued and she leapt out of bed with her heart racing. She ran to the window to draw back the curtains and two startled pigeons fluttered skyward, cooing their disapproval on being so rudely disturbed. Their action drew a chuckle from Rosina, but she stopped abruptly as she heard the distant chiming of a clock from a church tower. She counted the chimes – one, two, three, four – when it reached seven she uttered a cry of dismay. The *River Pearl* was due to sail at half past seven. She was not sure how far it was to the docks, but now her only thought was to get to the boat and return home. She threw off the nightgown and struggled into her undergarments, tugging at the laces on her stays with trembling fingers. Mrs Hopper had taken her clothes and she rifled through the armoire looking for something more suitable to wear than the elegant evening gown. It seemed that Roland's sister had lived the life of a very grand young lady and the garments were much too fine to wear on board a sailing barge. But this was not the time to be too particular and she selected a morning gown of grey shantung which boasted the least amount of frills, pin-tucks or embroidery. She was still struggling with the tiny, fabric-covered buttons as she ran down the stairs to the entrance hall.

'Mrs Hopper,' Rosina called out as she saw the housekeeper about to enter the dining room. 'I have to get to the docks immediately. Will you please send someone to find me a cab?'

Advancing so slowly that Rosina wanted to scream, Mrs Hopper shook her head. 'You won't find one round here at this time of day.'

'Then would Mr Rivers allow me to use his private carriage? He promised me that he would see me to the docks so that I can go home to London.'

'That's men for you, dearie. Even the best of them ain't reliable. God knows what time he come in last night. I expect he's still sleeping off the booze and we won't see hide nor hair of him until midday at least.'

Rosina was close to tears, but she was too angry to allow herself to cry. She stamped her foot. 'I will walk then. I won't stay here a minute longer.'

Mrs Hopper marched past her to open the front door. 'Go on, then. You ain't a prisoner here so far as I know.' She pointed towards the far end of the street. 'Go that way and you'll come to the river. Just follow it until you get to the docks, but you'd best make haste if you want to catch the tide.'

With a feeling of panic rising in her throat, Rosina hitched up the long skirts of the gown and ran down the steps to the pavement below. The sun beat down on her head as she raced along the street, ignoring the curious stares of passers-by. She was vaguely aware of their unfamiliar costumes and the wooden clogs that they wore on their feet, but she was too intent on her purpose to take much interest in the sights and sounds of Rotterdam. Although it was still early in the morning, the sky was a peerless blue and the heat was already intense. As she neared the docks she could see a forest of masts, some with sails set, sliding majestically out of the harbour. She stopped for a moment, holding her side as a painful stitch almost crippled her. Then she spotted the unmistakeable reddish-brown sails of a Thames sailing barge. She broke into a jogging trot, but she knew that she was too late. She reached the edge of the dock in time to see the stern of the *River Pearl* as it set out to sea.

She cupped her hands round her mouth. 'Ahoy, there – *River Pearl.*' But the vessel was too far away for them to hear her. She could just make out Barney's large frame as he went about his work on deck and she could see Captain Morgan at the tiller. Rosina looked round in desperation. For a wild moment she imagined that she could steal a boat and row out after them, but commonsense prevailed and she knew that such a reckless act would be fruitless. She ran the length of the dockside, searching for a vessel registered in London, but there was none. She was exciting an unwanted amount of attention from the sailors of all nationalities who had just come ashore, or who were re-joining their ships. The men working on the docks shouted to her, grinning broadly, and although she did not understand the language she could guess at what they were suggesting and her cheeks flamed with embarrassment and humiliation.

She held her head high as she walked past them, trying to ignore their shouts and whistles. She needed time to consider her options and she was heading for the only place she knew, which was the office of Rivers and Son, when a bold young man accosted her, taking her by the arm and speaking to her in a rapid foreign tongue. His meaning was obvious and when she shook her head, attempting to push him away, he merely laughed and tightened his grip. He was dragging her into a narrow passageway between two warehouses and she fought him with all her might, kicking out and screaming, but he was incredibly strong and her rage seemed to amuse rather than anger him. He hefted her over his shoulder and her world was suddenly upside down. Then, without warning, he crumpled to the ground, releasing her so suddenly that she sprawled on her face in the dust. She scrambled to her feet, but was prevented from escaping by another pair of arms wrapping themselves around her. Rosina screamed and bit the man's hand.

'Ouch! There's gratitude!'

'Roland?' She twisted round in his arms and could have sobbed with relief to see a familiar face, even if she had been running away from him just a short while ago. She glanced down at the prostrate figure of the sailor and she shuddered. 'Have you killed him?'

'No, but he'll have a bit of a headache when he comes to. This is no place for you, Rosie. We'd best get you home.'

'You promised that you would see me on board the *River Pearl*. You broke your word.'

'I overslept. It's not the end of the world.' He took her by the hand and led her through the warehouses to the road where his carriage was waiting. 'There are other ships bound for London. I will see that you get home.'

She snatched her hand free. 'You just don't understand, do you? If I don't get back to London soon I won't have a home. Harry has given us two weeks' notice to quit the house in Black Eagle Wharf.'

'I thought that freeing Walter was your main aim.'

'And it is, but I have to fight to keep my home as well. You wouldn't understand that, being such a rich toff.'

Roland handed her into the carriage and

climbed in after her. He did not attempt to sit beside her, but took a seat opposite, watching her closely. 'So what will you do when you return to London? It seems to me that there is very little to be done in the circumstances.'

She settled back against the padded leather squabs, rubbing her bruised wrists. 'If I can't persuade Harry to call off the bailiffs, at least we've got the *Ellie May*, and the repairs should be almost complete by now. My papa is the best barge captain on the Thames, and with Walter's help we can rebuild the trade. With a bit of luck we can repay the Gostellows and get our home back.'

'Is it as simple as that?'

'The way I look at it, yes.' Rosina leaned towards him. 'But I need your help, Roland. All you have to do is come back to London with me and help me clear Walter's name. Will you do that one thing for me, please?'

'Something tells me that I should put you on the next ship bound for London and be rid of you,' Roland said with a sigh. 'I was dragged from my bed this morning by Mrs Hopper, a lady whom it is not wise to cross, and I came hotfoot to rescue you from your own folly.' He flexed his fingers, grimacing with pain. 'And I damned well near broke my hands punching that fellow who was trying to abduct you, so don't ask me for any favours until I've had a cup of coffee and a glass of seltzer.'

Rosina opened her mouth to argue, but he held up a warning finger and she subsided into silence.

Mrs Hopper let them into the house with a supercilious sniff, but she had the good grace not to make any comments about Rosina's dishevelled state or the fact that the borrowed gown was torn and probably ruined.

'We'll take breakfast in the morning parlour,' Roland said, taking off his hat and kid gloves. 'But I suggest that Miss May changes out of that hideous frock. I never admired it on Vanessa and I certainly don't like it on you, Rosie.'

Bereft of speech, Rosina followed Mrs Hopper up the stairs to the room she had thought never to see again, where she suffered a lecture on how to behave in a foreign country while Mrs Hopper selected a yellow silk morning gown lavishly trimmed with black fringing, which she laid out on the bed. By this time the bath was run, and Rosina was just about to climb into the sweetly scented water when Mrs Hopper stuck her head round the door. 'Take my advice, young lady, and stop acting like a niminy-piminy schoolgirl. Use your wits and trade on your good looks to get what you wants.'

Rosina leapt into the tub and ducked as far under the water as she could without actually drowning. When she came up, gasping for air, she found that Mrs Hopper was still there.

'Leave me alone, you old witch. I told you before; I'm not that sort of girl.'

'High morals won't save your man in London, or your pa's boat.'

'You've been listening at keyholes.'

'How else am I to know what's going on in this here house? Anyway, you mind what I've just said. I've watched Mr Roland grow up from a little nipper in short breeches to the gent he is today. He's me blue-eyed boy and I likes to see him happy. So if you know what's good for you, you'll do whatever he wants and be grateful that it was him what saved you.' She shut the door with an emphatic bang, leaving Rosina in the rapidly cooling water. She climbed out and wrapped herself in the fluffy white bath sheet, glancing down at her forearms where bruises were already forming. If Roland had not come to her rescue she would undoubtedly have been raped in that narrow alley, maybe even murdered. She owed him much, and she would be even more in his debt if he could be persuaded to return to London with her and make things right with Harry. She dried herself, dressed in the gown that Mrs Hopper had chosen, and fashioned her hair into a chignon at the nape of her neck.

What happened now was entirely up to her. She went downstairs at a sober pace and found Roland waiting for her in the morning parlour.

He rose from his seat at the table, holding out a chair for her.

'Yes,' she said as she took her place.

He resumed his seat, eyeing her with brows raised. 'Yes to what in particular?'

'Yes, I will be your lady love just once, if you will promise to take me back to London and make things right with Harry.'

His lips twitched. 'Just once?'

She unfolded the white linen table napkin and laid it across her lap. 'I have nothing else to offer. I just hope that Walter will forgive me.'

He poured coffee from a silver pot into a bone china coffee cup and handed it to her. 'It's not the most flattering offer I've ever had.'

'Now you're laughing at me.'

He reached across the table to pat her hand. 'No, my dear girl. To tell the truth, I admire your spirit and your tenacity, but I've never taken a woman against her will. I've never needed to, and I don't intend to start now.'

She sipped the hot coffee, avoiding his gaze. So it had all been for nothing. She had risked so much and it had all been in vain. Her throat ached with unshed tears and she barely noticed that the hot liquid was burning her mouth.

'Don't look so tragic, Rosie.' Roland lifted the silver lid of a muffin dish and sniffed appreciatively. 'English muffins. Good old Hopper – she manages the kitchen like an army sergeant. Do try one.'

She placed her cup on its saucer with an emphatic clatter. 'I'm not hungry. My whole life is in ruins and all you can think of is food. I don't want a blooming muffin.' She pushed the plate away and rose to her feet. 'I'm sorry, Roland. I do appreciate everything you've done for me, but I must find a way to get home. I can't stay here a minute longer.'

He bit into a buttered muffin. 'This is so good.'

'You are impossible.' She pushed her chair back and was about to leave the table when Roland caught her by the hand.

'I'm just teasing you, my dear. Sit down and have some breakfast. We've got a long journey ahead of us.'

'What? You mean . . .'

'There is a ship leaving at noon, bound for Harwich. I will take you to your father, and I will explain everything to him. I'm sure that Harry will respect what Captain May has to tell him, and hopefully that will be an end to the matter.'

It was not exactly what she wanted, but Rosina saw a glimmer of hope in Roland's plan. She flung her arms around his neck and kissed him. 'Thank you. Oh, thank you, Roland.'

He extricated himself from her grasp with a rueful smile. 'Sit down and eat your breakfast, Rosie. I can only resist just so much temptation.'

The steamship docked in Harwich early next morning. After a brief visit to his office, Roland ordered his carriage to be brought to the inn where he had left Rosina, and they travelled on together. As they approached Burnham-on-Crouch, Rosina leaned out of the open window, breathing in the fresh smell of the countryside and the tang of the salt marshes. The corn was ripe in the fields and the harvest had already begun. Men, women and children were working in the midsummer heat, reaping and stooking the sheaves of corn in preparation for threshing and winnowing the chaff from the grain. In some fields this had already been done and golden haystacks stood proud like small windowless houses. The sun burned like molten copper in a bleached sky, and the air was sultry with the hint of thunderstorms to come later in the day. Rosina could not help but be fascinated with this strange, bucolic way of life, which was so different to living in a dirty, noisy and overcrowded city. For the first time in weeks, she felt optimistic about the future. Roland would speak to Pa, and between them they would put things right with Harry. Walter would be a free man, and they would spend the rest of their lives together.

The thatched cottage belonging to Bertha's cousin was a little way out of the village, lazing in the heat of midday on the bank of the River

Crouch. As the carriage drew up outside, Rosina was in a fever of excitement at the prospect of being reunited with Papa and Bertha. She could barely wait until the coachman had opened the door and pulled down the steps, holding out his hand to help her alight. Roland followed her, giving the driver instructions to walk the horses.

She reached the garden gate first, fumbling with the latch in her haste. Bees were busily collecting pollen from stately hollyhocks, and brightly coloured butterflies fluttered amongst the dog roses clambering over the porch. But even as she surveyed the peaceful scene, it struck Rosina that the cottage seemed oddly silent and lifeless. The windows were shut and the curtains were drawn together. She was suddenly apprehensive as she walked up the narrow path to the front door. She glanced over her shoulder at Roland, who was following close behind. He gave her an encouraging smile. 'Go on then, Rosie. Knock on the door. You've been agog with anticipation ever since we left Rotterdam.'

She rapped on the iron door knocker and the sound echoed throughout the house. 'Perhaps Papa and Bertha have already returned to London?' She shivered, in spite of the heat, and some sixth sense told her that something was wrong.

'I can hear footsteps,' Roland murmured. 'Someone's coming.'

Rosina held her breath. Her heart was thudding wildly against her ribs and she had to curb the impulse to beat her fists on the door and demand to be allowed inside.

The door opened just a crack.

'Hello,' Rosina said, giving it a gentle push. 'It's Rosie May. I've come to visit my papa and Bertha.'

The door opened fully and a small, thin woman of uncertain age peered short-sightedly at them both. 'How did you know? It only happened last night.'

Fear pulsed through Rosina's veins and she could barely speak. 'Wh-what . . .'

Roland slipped his arm around her shoulders. 'Pardon me, ma'am. But we've come a long way to see the captain. May we come inside?'

'Who is it, Jemima?' Bertha's voice came from somewhere inside the cottage.

Jemima did not move from the doorway; she turned her head, speaking over her shoulder. 'It's Miss Rosina and a gentleman.'

The sound of scurrying feet preceded Bertha as she pushed past her cousin to fling her arms around Rosina. 'My little pet. You've come. How did you find out?' Bertha collapsed against her shoulder, sobbing as if her heart would break.

Rosina was suddenly more afraid than she had ever been in her whole life. 'What's wrong, Bebe? Has Papa been taken ill again? Speak to me.'

Bertha drew away a little, her face ravaged with grief. 'Oh, my poor poppet. Your dear father passed away last night. There weren't nothing we could do to save him.'

# Chapter Nineteen

The weather broke just as the coffin was lowered into the ground. Roland's coachman, Jenkins, appeared as if from nowhere and produced a large black umbrella, which he dutifully held over Rosina and Bertha. Cousin Jemima wrapped her shawl around her shoulders, shivering and winking away the black dye from her bonnet as it trickled down her face. Roland stood with his head bowed, holding his top hat in his hands. A flash of lightning momentarily illuminated the sombre scene, followed by a rumble of thunder. The vicar hastily intoned the words of the interment, casting nervous glances up at the sky as if anticipating Armageddon. Bertha sobbed noisily throughout, but Rosina held her head upright, too grief-stricken even to cry. She could hardly believe that it was her dearest papa whose body was locked inside the oak coffin. The dead man who had lain in Jemima's parlour had resembled a wax effigy at Madame Tussauds' exhibition; he had looked a little bit like her pa, but the father whom she had loved and respected all her life was gone, leaving just an empty shell.

The rain beat a rhythmic tattoo on the umbrella, and that, together with the vicar's droning voice, was having a hypnotic effect on Rosina. She swayed slightly and was comforted by the touch of Roland's hand on her arm. She looked up and managed to return his smile. He had proved himself to be a true friend during the past few traumatic days. He had organised the funeral and paid all the expenses, waving aside her promises to repay him when she was able. Soon after their arrival, and having done what he could to comfort and reassure them, Roland had removed himself to the inn, where he had been staying ever since, but he had visited the cottage every day. Even Bertha had been impressed by his gentlemanly conduct, although she had been hostile at first, especially when she had learned that Rosina had stayed in his house in Rotterdam. But Roland had charmed Bertha with his winning ways, and had eventually managed to convince her that nothing untoward had occurred.

'Come, Rosie,' Roland said, offering her his arm. 'It's all over, my dear.'

Rosina looked at him dully. She glanced down at the coffin, which was now sprinkled with earth, and she raised her eyes to meet the vicar's solemn gaze. It was all over. Papa had gone to heaven, if one believed in such a place. He was with his beloved Ellie, and the worries of the world were far behind him. Not so for herself. She had a sobbing Bertha to comfort and somehow she had to get them both back to London to face an uncertain future. She laid her hand on Roland's arm. 'Thank you, Roland. Thank you for everything.'

'It was nothing, my dear.' He turned to the waiting coachman. 'Escort Miss Spinks and her cousin to the carriage, Jenkins. Then you can bring the umbrella back for Miss May and me.' He led her to the shelter of the porch, where he shook the vicar's hand and murmured appropriate words of thanks.

Rosina managed to voice her appreciation, and the vicar disappeared into the cool depths of the church just as another flash of lightning rent the dark sky. She huddled in the shelter of Roland's protective arm, wincing as a huge thunderclap followed almost immediately. 'You will come back to the cottage, won't you, Roland? I think Jemima has laid on some refreshments for us; although I don't feel in the least like attending a wake, even a small one.'

'No, I've stayed too long as it is, Rosie. I still have business in Harwich, and then I must return to Rotterdam.'

She stared up at him, barely comprehending his words. 'But I thought – I mean, I assumed that you would return to London with us, especially now, with poor Pa dead and gone.'

'My dear, I told you that I cannot risk it, and nothing has changed.'

'Are you so afraid of Sukey Barnum and her father? Surely a man of your means could buy them off if he so wished?'

'There's something that I haven't told you. A complication far greater than my fear of a mere scandal.'

Another jagged flash of lightning turned the air blue around them. The ensuing crack of thunder almost deafened her, but Rosina was concentrating on Roland. She tugged at his arm. 'I need your help desperately. What is it that you haven't told me?'

'I am already engaged to be married. It's a marriage of convenience and I barely know the young lady. She is impoverished but well connected, and I am wealthy. No doubt it is a match made in heaven.'

She stared up at him aghast. 'Roland, how could you agree to such a union?'

'My father holds the purse strings. He chose the earl's daughter to be my bride, and if I go against his wishes I will find myself cut off without a penny. Ironic, isn't it? I am a man approaching thirty, and still under the parental thumb. When I marry Lady Mary, who is an only child with no surviving male relatives, our eldest son will inherit an earldom, and my fortune will pay for the upkeep of a dreary castle in

Northumberland. So you see, Rosie, you are not the only one with problems.'

'I do see that, but at least you are not facing eviction and destitution. Your heart will not break, because you do not love this lady. I am about to lose everything that is dear to me, and my papa is dead. I have no one else to turn to but you.'

He gripped her hands, looking deeply into her eyes. 'I do love a lady, but she does not love me.'

His meaning was all too clear, and his words came as a shock. 'You can't mean me, Roland.'

His features twisted with genuine pain. 'Can't I? Why do you think that I didn't take advantage of you while you were under my roof? Did you imagine that it was due to some chivalrous feeling on my part? If you did, then you were wrong. I didn't have a business meeting to attend: I did what most men do when they are faced with an impossible situation – I went out and got drunk.'

'I – I don't know what to say.'

'There is nothing that you can say, my love.' He glanced over her shoulder. 'Jenkins is returning with the umbrella. I will see you safely back to the cottage and then I must leave.'

'Oh, Roland. I am so sorry that I put you in this situation. You are a good man.'

He threw back his head and laughed. 'Damned with faint praise!' The momentary glimmer of amusement died from his eyes and he gripped her by the shoulders. 'If things get really bad in London, you have only to say the word and I will come for you. I cannot marry you, Rosie. But I could set you up in my house in Rotterdam. You would be my wife in everything but name, and I swear that you would never want for anything ever again.'

She was saved from answering by a discreet cough from Jenkins as he held out the umbrella.

Roland linked her hand through his arm. 'Jenkins will take me back to the inn, where I've arranged for a hired carriage to take me back to Harwich. He'll drive you to Colchester and put you on the train to London. You should be there before dark.'

Her reply was drowned by a clap of thunder, but she knew that it was useless to argue with him once his mind was made up. They hurried through the pouring rain to the waiting carriage and rode back to the cottage in silence, except for the occasional sniff from Bertha. Jenkins held the horses while Roland escorted them to the door.

Jemima went inside, but Bertha hesitated on the threshold. She eyed Roland with something like respect. 'I thought you was a typical snooty toff, but I was wrong. You're a good man, Mr Rivers, and I'm grateful to you for looking after me precious girl.'

Roland leaned over and kissed her wrinkled

cheek. 'I'm sure I don't deserve such an accolade, but I appreciate it coming from a woman like you, Bertha.'

Rosina could have sworn that Bertha blushed. She giggled like an embarrassed schoolgirl and scuttled into the cottage.

'This has to be goodbye, my love. Unless you have a change of heart later on.' Roland took her in his arms and kissed her hungrily and so thoroughly that it took her breath away. As he released her slowly, and with regret in his eyes, she reached up and kissed him on the cheek.

'Thank you for everything, Roland. I hope that you find happiness with the earl's daughter. She is a very lucky lady.'

Inclining his head, he said nothing as he turned on his heel and strode away down the path to the waiting carriage. I shall never see him again, Rosina thought sadly. She did not, and could never, love him, but her heart was wrenched with pain on losing such a good friend. She stood in the doorway, doubly bereft: first her father and now Roland. She waved until the carriage was out of sight, and then she turned slowly and went indoors.

It was the first time that Rosina had ever travelled by train, and Jenkins had settled them in a first-class, ladies-only compartment, which she and Bertha had to themselves all the way to

Liverpool Street. Rosina would have enjoyed the experience had she not been worried about what might be awaiting them when they reached home. The two weeks was up and she could only hope that Harry would not have been so heartless as to throw Caddie and her children out on the street. Her journey to Rotterdam had proved fruitless, and she had no more proof now of Walter's innocence than she had at the outset.

Bertha was huddled in the corner of the compartment, barely speaking, but Rosina knew that it was not bad temper that kept her dear Bebe silent; it was the nagging fear of what they would find on returning home. Bertha had begged her to stay on in Burnham, saying that cousin Jemima, being the widow of a fisherman, would be glad to have them as lodgers for as long as they wished to stay. Rosina had explained, as gently as possible, that without money, or any way in which she could earn a living in the country, it was out of the question. She had put forward the suggestion that Bebe might like to remain in Burnham, but that option had been treated with scorn. Now they were hurtling towards the city at an alarming speed, and the iron wheels clattered over the points with a rhythmic clickety-clack which eventually seemed to hypnotise Bertha into a deep sleep. Rosina leaned back against the seat, watching the fields and hedgerows flash past the windows.

As they came to the outskirts of London, the urban sprawl grew denser and the trees were more grey than green, heavy with dust, and drooping over the tracks as if too tired to hold up their branches. Factories and warehouses replaced the neat terraces, and daylight was fading as the train pulled into Liverpool Street station. Bertha awakened with a start, and Rosina jumped up to drag her carpet bag from the luggage rack. Jenkins had given her a purse, which he said was money for the cab fare to Black Eagle Wharf. She would have saved the money and walked, but Bertha's face was pale and drawn with exhaustion, and this was not the time for false economy. Rosina helped her out of the station to the cab rank.

It was dusk by the time they reached the house on Black Eagle Wharf. The umbrella cranes were silent and the tiers of moored boats bobbed gently on the water. Rosina's heart sank as she saw that the house was in darkness. She took the key from her reticule and found that it would not fit in the lock. She felt panic rising in her throat. Surely Harry would not have had the locks changed so quickly? She beat on the door with her fists, swallowing a sob.

'He done it then?' Bertha said dully. 'We're too late.'

'He wouldn't have been so cruel. Harry loved me once; I can't believe that he would throw us out on the street.'

Bertha sat down heavily on her carpet bag. 'What do you call this then? Looks to me like he's done just that. What'll we do, poppet? Where will we go?'

Rosina paced up and down, wringing her hands. 'Where is Caddie? We must find her, Bebe. She is all alone with three babies to care for.'

'I can't go another step, ducks. I'm done for and will have to sleep here on the pavement if we can't get into the house.'

'I'll break in if necessary,' Rosina said, eyeing the shuttered window of the office, and realising even as she spoke the words that it was impossible.

Bertha leaned back against the wall, closing her eyes. 'Ta, but I'd rather spend the night out here than in a prison cell.'

'I can see a light in Sam Smilie's window. You wait here, Bebe. I'm going to knock on their door and see if they know what's happened to Caddie.' Without waiting for an answer, Rosina's feet skimmed the cobblestones as she ran to the Smilies' shop. She hammered on the door until she heard footsteps approaching across the bare boards. The door opened and Sam stuck his head out. His eyes widened in surprise. 'Rosie, is that you?'

'It's me, Sam.' Rosina was still wearing the

elegant gown that had belonged to Roland's sister, but it was travel-stained and crumpled and she knew that she must present an odd sight. 'It's a long story, but I've just got home and I'm locked out of my own house.'

'Come inside, Rosie.' Sam opened the door wider.

'I can't. I've left Bertha waiting outside the house. We've travelled a long way today, and ...' her voice broke on a sob, 'and we buried my pa this morning. He's dead, Sam. And I wasn't with him when he was taken ill.' She could no longer hold back the tears and she covered her face with her hands. Great shuddering sobs racked her body and she struggled to regain her self-control.

'There, there, ducks. I am so sorry.' Sam patted her on the shoulder. 'Gladys, come here. I needs you in the shop.'

'I'm s-sorry,' Rosina said, wiping her eyes on her sleeve. 'I'm tired, and I don't know where to find Caddie and the babies, or even where we'll sleep tonight.'

Gladys came hurrying towards them. She came to a halt as she saw Rosina. 'Gawd above, you look like a ghost, child. Come inside and let me make you a cup of tea.'

Rosina shook her head. 'I can't. Bertha is sitting on the pavement outside our house. We're locked out.'

Gladys pushed her husband out of the way and she put her arm around Rosina's shoulders. 'There, there, love. One thing at a time. Sam, go and fetch Miss Spinks. We can't have a woman of her age sitting out on the pavement at this time of night. She'll catch her death of cold. Get on with you, man. Don't stand there staring at me like a codfish.'

'All right, I'm going, woman. Don't nag.' Sam backed out of the door.

Gladys led Rosina into their snug parlour, where a kettle simmered on a trivet over the fire. 'Sit down, love, and I'll make you a nice hot cup of tea.'

Rosina sank down onto the horsehair sofa, gradually regaining control of her emotions. 'Th-thank you, Gladys. You're very kind.'

'Not at all. I knows how bad you've been treated by that young man of yours. Harry Gostellow weren't near good enough for you. I always said that.' Gladys busied herself making tea and fetching cups from a pine dresser.

'I must find Caddie,' Rosina said anxiously. 'Do you know where she went?'

'The last I saw of her she was terrified of going into the workhouse. Said she'd rather drown herself and the little ones than go into that dreadful place.'

'Oh, no! Surely, you don't think she would . . . No, I can't believe that Caddie would take the lives of her babies.' Rosina leapt to her feet. 'I must go out and look for them, Gladys. I can't rest until I find them.'

'I don't know about that, ducks. You shouldn't go wandering round in the dark. If she's done the deed then it's already too late. She'll be found in the drag, that's for sure.'

'Then I pray to God that I find her in time.' Rosina hurried out through the shop, passing Bertha and Sam in the doorway.

'And where do you think you're going?' Bertha demanded.

'I'm going to find Caddie before she does something stupid. And don't try to stop me.'

Sam gave Bertha a gentle push in the direction of the parlour. 'Go in, Miss Spinks. My Gladys will take care of you.' He turned to Rosina. 'Don't go no further than Union Stairs on your own. I'll get a search party together and we'll head towards St Katharine's docks.'

'Wait.' Gladys bustled into the shop carrying a dark cloak over her arm. She wrapped it around Rosina's shoulders. 'You'd best cover up them fancy duds, or you'll be giving blokes the wrong impression.'

Rosina knew that only a lady or a high-class whore could afford such an expensive gown, and no lady would be roaming the docks and wharves on her own in daylight, let alone in the dark. She gladly accepted the loan of the coarse woollen cloak, even though it made her feel hot and sticky. She had one thought in mind as she made her way along the wharves, keeping as much in the shadows as she could, and slipping unnoticed past groups of drunken sailors – she must find Caddie and the children. Rosina reached Union Stairs, peering down the slimy steps to the inky water lapping and sucking at the stanchions. There was nowhere there for them to hide. She wrapped the cloak even more tightly around her body and she hurried on, ignoring Sam's advice not to go any further. She crossed the London dock basin, passing Wapping Old Stairs, and then the New Stairs. She looked into dark doorways, beneath cranes and behind stacks of barrels on the wharves. By the time she reached Execution dock she had only come across drunks, tramps and crawlers sprawled anywhere they could find a space to sleep for the night. The sounds of the river filled her ears: oars creaking as they sliced through the water, splashing and sending out ripples as the watermen plied their trade carrying passengers to and from the moored vessels, or went about the grim business of the drag. She prayed silently that they would not pull Caddie and her babies from the murky waters.

Rosina was becoming desperate as she approached the mouth of the Thames tunnel. Rumour had it that, before the railway track was laid, people had lived in the tunnel alcoves, earning a scant living by peddling their wares to pedestrians. If there were still such places, then it was possible that some of the destitute and desperate might seek shelter there at night. It was her last hope. The mouth of the tunnel was illuminated by gaslights, but that made its gaping maw even more terrifying. The last train had gone but it was filled with strange echoes. She had to pluck up all her courage to enter the black hole, and the sound of her footsteps reverberated off the dripping walls. Water trickled from the curved roof down the slimy brick walls to form deep puddles on the ground. She almost tripped over the prostate body of a man, insensible from drinking cheap alcohol: the smell was unmistakeable. She stepped over him, retching at the stench of urine and human excrement as she went deeper into the tunnel. Dotted alongside the track she could see pinpricks of light where the occupants had lit small fires. No one bothered her as she trudged past their sordid dwelling places.

She heard a baby crying and quickened her pace. A young woman, barely more than a child herself, was huddled in an alcove, suckling her baby. She looked up as Rosina passed her by, her eyes blank and staring, as if all hope had deserted her. Touched beyond measure, Rosina put her hand in her pocket and took out a penny.

She pressed it into the girl's hand. 'It's not much, but it will buy you some food.'

The girl nodded and looked furtively around her as she hid the coin beneath her ragged skirts.

'Have you seen a young woman with three young children, one of them just a babe like your own?' Rosina asked in a whisper.

The girl shrugged her thin shoulders and turned her head away. There was nothing Rosina could do except walk on, guided by the flickering light of another fire. Just as she was about to give up and retrace her steps, she saw a small, ghostly figure dart out of an alcove. She was certain that it was Ronnie. Something about the shape of his head, or the way he walked, made her sure that it was him. She called out softly. 'Ronnie. It's me, Rosie.'

The little boy stopped, staring at her with his thumb plugged into his mouth. Now she was absolutely certain that she had found them, and she broke into a run. Ronnie scuttled away from her like a frightened animal, but she had seen where he went and she followed him. Caddie was sitting on the ground with her back to the damp wall. In her arms she cradled baby Arthur, and Alfie lay sleeping with his head resting on her lap.

'Caddie. Thank God I've found you.' Rosina threw herself down on her knees beside her. Ronnie hurled himself at Caddie, wrapping his arms around her neck.

'Rosie? Is that really you? It's so dark that I can hardly see.'

'Yes, it's me. Don't be scared.'

Ronnie let out a howl that awakened Alfie, who began to sob hysterically.

'Don't be frightened, Ronnie,' Rosina said, bending down to stroke his head. 'It's Rosie. I've come to take you away from this dreadful place.'

Caddie drew her knees up, clutching her children to her breast. 'We ain't going to the workhouse, Rosie. It's all that's left to us now that our home is gone, but I'd rather die. You shan't take us.'

'My dear, no one is going to the workhouse. I don't know how I'm going to do it, but I promise you that I will look after you and your babies. Now, get up and come with me. This is truly a dreadful place.'

Somehow she managed to get the small family out of the tunnel. Caddie gulped a lungful of air, which although dank with the stench of the river was somewhat fresher than that in the depths of the tunnel. 'Where shall us go? The bailiff come the day afore yesterday and they took everything from the house. Then the locksmith come and changed the locks. I had no choice but to come here.'

Rosina lifted Alfie onto her shoulders and she took Ronnie by the hand. 'Well, we're together now and that's all that matters. I'm taking you back to Sam Smilie's shop. I'm sure they'll let us stay there until morning, and then we'll set about finding somewhere to live. After all, we haven't lost everything. The *Ellie May* is at Etheredge's Wharf and I will go there first thing to see if the repairs are completed.'

Caddie nodded tiredly, cuddling her baby a little closer as they set off for Black Eagle Wharf.

Gladys threw her hands up in horror when she saw the state of the children. 'Gawd above! They look like chimney sweeps.' She tickled Ronnie's tummy, eliciting a reluctant gurgle of laughter from him. 'I never saw such a dirty boy in all me born days.'

Caddie collapsed onto the sofa and Rosina took Arthur from her arms. He stirred, opened his blue eyes and then closed them, slipping back into a deep sleep.

Bertha picked up Alfie and set him on her knee while she peeled off his filthy shirt. 'Could we have a kettle full of hot water, Glad? These little 'uns is like to catch something horrible from all this filth.'

Gladys turned to her husband who was standing in the doorway with a bemused expression on his face. 'Make yourself useful, Sam. Go and fetch a bucket of water from the pump.'

He scratched his bald head. 'I will, ducks. But I'm thinking we ain't got room to put these good people up in any comfort.'

'Please don't worry about that,' Rosina said anxiously. 'If we could just stay here for tonight, I don't mind sleeping in a chair and Bertha can have the sofa.'

'I'll fetch some blankets,' Gladys said, wrapping Ronnie in her apron. 'Go and fetch that water, Sam. I'm sure we can make do for now.'

Sam went off mumbling something unintelligible.

'I can't thank you enough, Gladys,' Rosina said, rocking Arthur gently in her arms.

'There's no need for thanks, love.' Gladys took a glass jar of barley sugar from the mantelshelf and broke off small pieces, giving one each to Ronnie and Alfie. 'Your pa was good to us when my Sam got sick with the fever and couldn't work. Neighbours help each other, that's what he used to say when he slipped me a few shillings to buy bread for the nippers. Now I got a chance to help his daughter and it would be a hard-hearted woman who could turn little chaps like these out on the street.' She moved to the table and began cutting slices from a loaf of bread. 'We've only got bread and dripping. I'm afraid it ain't what you're used to, Rosie.'

'You'd be surprised what we've got accustomed to in the past few months,' Bertha said ominously. 'Bread and dripping would go down a treat, and I could murder another cup of tea.'

*

447

Next morning, after an uncomfortable night when she had slept very little, Rosina raised herself from the chair by the range and stretched her cramped limbs. During her wakeful hours she had been racking her brain as to what to do next. She was desperate for news of Walter, and she fully intended to visit him in prison, but first she would have another attempt at persuading Sukey to return the diamond ring to Harry. Her whole future depended on that wretched ring. Sukey had agreed to part with it once, and if Captain Barnum had not intervened, Walter might now be a free man. She stepped carefully over the sleeping bodies of Caddie and her children as they lay curled up on the floor, covered by a threadbare blanket. Bertha was lying on the sofa with her mouth open and her bosom rising and falling rhythmically as she slept. Her legs hung over the edge, and Rosina noticed that her toes protruded through holes in her stockings. Her discarded boots were down at heel and the soles were worn through. Somehow these small observations brought home their impoverished state even more forcibly than the fact that they were now homeless. Bertha had always been so particular about appearances, and it hurt Rosina to see her in such straitened circumstances.

She crept out of the kitchen and made her way through the scullery to the tiny back yard. The pump water was cool and refreshing and she washed her face and hands, smoothing her hair back into a knot at the nape of her neck. Above her the sky was pearl-grey and the clouds were tinged pink by the rising sun. Today she must gather the threads of her old life and look to the future. It was a terrifying thought that she had five people who were dependent upon her for everything. She must think clearly and act appropriately. Shaking the water from her eyes, she put her hand in her pocket and took out the purse that Jenkins had given her. She leaned against the brick wall and counted out the coins. Once again she was struck by Roland's generosity. There was enough here to keep them going for a week or two, if she managed the money with care. First of all she would go out to the bakery in Wapping Street and purchase fresh bread for breakfast, enough for the large Smilie family as well as her own. For they were her family – Bertha, Caddie and the little boys. They might not be her flesh and blood, but she would never, never let them down. She would find a place for them to live and she would seek work. There must be something that she could do, even though she had been raised like a lady and had never had to do anything more arduous than mend a sock or a torn frill on one of her gowns.

Rosina found that Sam was already up and about, opening the shop to catch the early morning trade of sailors, dockers, sackmakers, ropemakers and riggers who wanted to fill their pouches with baccy before the start of their working day. He turned his head and smiled as she came through the door. 'You're up early, ducks.'

'I'm going to the bakery to fetch bread for breakfast, Sam.'

'Lord above us, you don't have to do that. Keep your pennies, Rosie. It seems to me, no disrespect meant, that you'll need to count every last farthing.'

'You're right, but I can't take your hospitality without giving something in return.' She flashed him a smile as the slipped out through the open door. The cool of the night still lingered, and had alleviated some of the worst of the city stench: the cobblestones gleamed with dew. All around her, it seemed as though the sleeping wharves were yawning back into life. Men were hurrying, heads down, towards their workplaces and the cranes were groaning into action as barges and lighters moored alongside, waiting to unload their cargoes. She hurried towards the High Street where she purchased bread that was fresh from the oven and still hot. She had worked out her money very carefully, and she went next to the grocer's where she bought a half-pound of butter and a pot of raspberry and plum jam as a treat for the children. She carried them back to the wharf with a spring in her step.

As soon as she had breakfasted, she would go to the Barnums' house in the hope of seeing Sukey; then she would take the omnibus to the Old Bailey, where she would visit Walter in Newgate prison. Her heart soared at the thought of seeing him again – Walter, who was really Will. He might not have admitted it, but her heart told her that they were one and the same. She could not wait to see his face again, and to tell him that she was working for his release with the aid of Septimus, if he had managed to remain sober long enough to carry out his investigations. Then she would make her way to Etheredge's Wharf to inspect the *Ellie May*.

Rosina stopped for a moment on Watson's Wharf, staring at the red-brown sails of a sailing barge. Her future was inextricably bound with the river. It was not going to be easy, but she would not be beaten. She raised her chin, looking towards the fiery red sunrise in the east. That was where prosperity lay – downriver. She would find a new home, and she would get the *Ellie May* back in business. She would succeed – or die in the attempt.

# Chapter Twenty

'Go away, miss. I ain't to let you in. Master's orders.' Gertie's freckled features contorted with malice when she saw Rosina; she would have slammed the door in her face if she had not put her foot over the sill.

'Please, Gertie. Just tell Miss Susan that I would like a few words with her. It's very, very important.'

Leaning her weight against the door, Gertie hissed like an angry cat. 'Go away.'

'No. I'll stay here all day if necessary. I want to see Miss Susan.'

'Who is it, Gertie?' Sukey emerged from the parlour.

Rosina pushed past Gertie, almost knocking her off her feet. 'It's me, Rosie.'

'I don't want to see you. You're not welcome here.' Sukey retreated into the room.

Ignoring Gertie's protests, Rosina followed Sukey into the parlour, closing the door behind her. 'We used to be such good friends. Won't you spare me just a few minutes?'

Sukey paced the floor, twisting the diamond

ring on her left hand. 'My father has forbidden me to see you ever again. I can't go against his wishes.'

Rosina stood quite still, hardly daring to breathe. 'But you know that I would never do anything to hurt you, don't you?'

'You set your cap at Harry, even though you knew how I felt about him, and then you tried to convince me that Roland had not really proposed marriage.'

'It wasn't like that, Sukey. Roland never meant to propose to you. I told you the last time I saw you that it was all a terrible mistake. He is already engaged to another. A titled lady.'

Sukey stopped pacing. She turned to Rosina with a glint of suspicion in her blue eyes. 'How do you know that? You told me he had gone abroad. Was that a lie?'

Rosina could not meet her gaze and she looked away. 'He did go abroad.'

'You went away too. Were you together? Have you got Roland in your thrall as well as Harry?'

'No. I mean, for goodness' sake, Sukey. Walter is in Newgate because Harry accused him of stealing that hateful ring and worse. When you wouldn't help me who else was I to turn to? Who else knew the truth about the ring other than Roland?'

'Did he or did he not go abroad?'

Rosina knew that she was on dangerous

ground: one false step would send her into a morass of lies. If Sukey found out that she had followed Roland to Rotterdam and that he had accompanied her back to England, she would jump to the wrong conclusions. There was a time for telling the truth and a time when it was inappropriate. Meeting Sukey's hostile gaze, Rosina knew that this was such a moment. She shook her head. 'He took my father to Burnham-on-Crouch in Essex, to stay with Bertha and her cousin while he was convalescing. I saw him in Burnham when he returned from his business trip to Holland. I begged him to come to London and make things right with you, but he was afraid.'

'Afraid!' Sukey spat the word as if it had a bad taste. 'Afraid of me? Don't be ridiculous.'

'Well, maybe not afraid of you, exactly. He feared a breach of promise action.'

'And he told you all this, but he could not tell me to my face?'

'Yes. No. I don't know. Just give me the wretched ring so that I can return it to Harry. Then he will drop the case against Walter.'

'Walter? What do I care if your father's clerk is imprisoned? I expect he deserves it anyway. My pa says he is a river pirate and he should be punished.'

'I – I love him, Sukey. I love Walter, and my papa is dead.'

Sukey sat down suddenly and her lips trembled. 'Your father died? I didn't know.'

'He died in Burnham and I wasn't there.' Rosina wrung her hands, unable to prevent the tears from coursing down her cheeks. 'I was on my way back from Rotterdam and I wasn't there at the end.' She stopped, realising what she had just said.

The horrified expression on Sukey's face hardened into cold anger. 'Rotterdam! So that is where Roland went, and you pretended not to know. You lied to me again. How can I ever believe anything you say?'

'No, it was a mistake. I meant . . .'

'Stop it. Stop lying to me, Rosie. I've heard enough and I want you to leave my house this instant. Go way. I never want to see you again.'

'But Sukey . . .'

'Go now, or I'll have you thrown out. You've ruined my life and my chances of ever finding a rich husband. I hate you.'

It was useless to argue: Rosina could see that, and she ran from the house. She had made such a mess of things. Her heart ached but she would not cry. She might have lost her best friend, but she needed more than ever to see Walter. He must not be allowed to think that she had deserted him in his hour of need. She wiped her eyes on her sleeve and set off for the prison. It was midday by the time she reached the dark and brooding exterior of Newgate. The gatehouse loomed above her and she could sense the feeling of desolation that must exist behind the stone walls.

'That's impossible,' the gatekeeper informed her when she asked to see Walter Brown.

'But surely you must allow the prisoners to have visitors?'

'The prison is open to the public on Wednesdays and Thursdays between midday and three o'clock. You can come in then, but not before.'

'Is there no way that you will allow me just five minutes with the prisoner?'

'Are you his wife?'

'No, sir.'

'Or his sister?'

Rosina took a deep breath. 'Yes, I am his sister.'

The gatekeeper angled his head, holding out his right hand and rubbing his fingers together in a gesture that indicated he wanted payment.

'H-how much?' Rosina asked nervously.

'Did I ask you for money? We ain't allowed to take bribes.'

'I'm sorry, I thought . . .'

'Now if you was to give me a gift, that would be another matter. A guinea would help oil the wheels, so to speak.'

'A guinea? But that's daylight robbery.'

'And that is what your "brother" is in for, so I

believe. It don't seem a lot of money to see a relative what's going to spend a good many years in clink, now does it?'

Rosina fingered her reticule. She could not afford to give the man a guinea. She battled with her desire to see Walter and the need to keep her family fed for the foreseeable future.

'Don't waste my time, girlie. You may be the fella's light o' love, but you don't get in free, so clear off, afore I has you arrested for loitering.'

Once again, she realised what a sight she must present. She had seen enough prostitutes in the Ratcliff Highway to know what they looked like, and that was obviously what the gatekeeper imagined was her profession. She turned and walked away with her head held high and her heart aching. She glanced up at the forbidding edifice, wondering where Walter was confined. She had thought it might help to know where he was, but the reality of Newgate was far more terrible than the place she had imagined. She trudged, head down, away from the prison, not particularly caring where she was going and without any idea as to what to do next. She walked slowly along Newgate Street towards Cheapside. It was a hot day, even for the beginning of September; she was tired and hungry and her spirits were so low that she could barely think. Then it came to her that there was one other person to whom she might turn: a man of the law. Septimus Sumption had advised her to seek out Roland and he had promised to follow up Walter's case. She would go and see him now in the hope that he would have discovered some evidence of Walter's innocence that would stand up in court.

She caught the green Bow omnibus to Whitechapel where she alighted on the corner of Church Lane and she set off walking to Naked Boy Yard. It was late in the afternoon by the time she reached Septimus's miserable rooms, and the stench of stale alcohol assailed her nostrils before he had even opened the door. He stared blearily at her, running his hand through his tousled hair.

'I think you've got the wrong door, young lady.'

Rosina was too tired and anxious to bother with the niceties. She pushed past him. 'I came to see you, Mr Sumption.' She stepped over a pile of discarded clothing on the floor and made her way to the only clear spot, which was a bare patch of tattered drugget in front of the empty grate.

'You'll have to excuse me, but I don't recall ever meeting you before.' Septimus staggered over to his chair and sat down heavily. He reached for a bottle and poured a hefty measure of brandy into a glass.

Rosina stood her ground, waiting until he had gulped a mouthful of the spirit. 'My name is

Rosina May. I came to you some time ago on behalf of my friend, Walter Brown. You advised me to travel to Rotterdam to see Mr Roland Rivers. You were supposed to be investigating the case.'

He held up his hand. 'Not so fast. My head is spinning.' He took another drink, squinting at her with one eye closed. 'I do seem to recall your face. Very pretty.'

'I need your help, sir.'

He threw back his head and laughed. 'My help. That's a good one. Look at me, my dear. I can't even help myself.'

She was in no mood to argue. Rosina moved towards him and took the glass from his hand. She snatched up the brandy bottle before he could reach for it. 'Now, will you listen to me?'

'A woman of spirit. I like that. But you'd better start at the beginning. My memory ain't what it used to be. Just give me back the bottle . . .'

'Not yet, Mr Sumption.' Rosina sat on the pile of law books and began at the beginning, taking him slowly through the events leading up to the present. He listened, apparently attentively, although his eyes did stray rather too often to the brandy bottle clutched in her hand, but he made no attempt to wrest it from her. When she had finished he was silent for a few moments, his forehead creased in thoughtful lines.

'Well,' he said, after a while, 'you are in a pickle, my dear.'

'Never mind me, Mr Sumption. I want you to help Walter.'

'My God, I wish I had a woman like you to care for me. I might not be in the sorry state in which you find me if I had someone to love me.'

Rosina set the glass and bottle down on the floor and she slid off the pile of books to kneel before him. Taking his hands in hers, she looked him in the eyes. 'And I'm sure you will, if only you would stop killing yourself with drink. But that is another matter. I don't need help for myself. I can look after my family and I still have the sailing barge. It is mine now and I intend to make it profitable.'

He smiled. 'I don't doubt it, Miss May. But what do you want from a poor wreck like me?'

'I want you to act for Walter. I cannot pay you at the moment, but I will in time I promise you that. I don't know any other lawyers, and old – I mean, Mr Jamjar of the exotic bird shop spoke highly of your abilities. If you could get Walter acquitted I'm sure it would do much to build your practice up again. Will you help me, Mr Sumption? Please? I'm begging you on my knees to act for Walter when his case comes up before the judge.'

'I'm not sure that I can help you. It's a long time since I accepted a brief such as this.'

'You are my last chance. I know you can do it.' Rosina glanced round at the books and papers littered all about the room, spilling off shelves and piled precariously on every available surface. 'You've got all this book learning. You're a clever man. Please say you'll at least look into Walter's case.'

'I ain't a grasping, greedy sort of fellow, but I have to live. I can't take on a case for nothing, much as I would like to oblige you.'

Rosina's hand flew to the gold chain around her neck. She could feel the locket lodged between her breasts, warm from contact with her body. She had pawned everything else that she owned, but she had clung to this link with Will as a drowning woman might cling to a spar. She undid the clasp and dangled the locket in front of Septimus's eyes. 'Take this as my pledge. I will redeem it when I have funds. It is worth something to you, but to me it is priceless. And, if you see Walter, just show him the contents and he will know that you act on my instructions.'

He took it in his hand, closing his fingers over the locket. 'I need a drink.'

'No you don't. That stuff addles your brain. Please, I'm begging you to help us.'

'Well, it would be a challenge.' Septimus leaned forward and raised Rosina to her feet. 'I'm a worthless sort of fellow, who hides his failures at the bottom of a brandy bottle, but you are a brave and beautiful young woman, and, for you, I will make an effort to stay sober just long enough to make enquiries about your friend. More I cannot promise.'

Rosina left the building in Naked Boy Yard with mixed feelings. She did not doubt his sincerity, but whether Septimus could stay off the drink for long enough to carry out his promise to help was another matter.

It was late afternoon and she had eaten nothing since a slice of bread at breakfast time. Her limbs felt heavy and exhaustion was creeping up on her, stealing her will to continue any further that day. It was a long walk to Limehouse where the *Ellie May* was berthed at Etheredge's repair yard, and an even longer trek back from there to Black Eagle Wharf. She was forced to acknowledge that it was too late either to visit the yard or to find alternative lodgings, and she would have to trespass on the Smilies' hospitality for another night. Her feet were sore and her legs aching as she trudged onwards through the back doubles and narrow alleyways towards the river. For the first time since his death, she was glad that her papa was not here to witness the sorry state in which she found herself. He would be horrified if he could see her now in her dishevelled condition, wandering the mean streets alone, unprotected and open to the insults and indecent proposals from men looking for a cheap thrill in a dark doorway.

Rosina was close to collapse by the time she reached Sam's shop. She had thought to offer them payment for another night spent in their parlour, but as soon as she entered the shop she could tell from Sam's expression that something was wrong.

'What is it, Sam?' she asked anxiously. 'What's happened?'

'It's the scarlet fever, or so my missis thinks.'

Her knees trembled and Rosina clutched at the shop counter for support. 'Who's sick?'

'Me eldest boy, Jim. And Gladys thinks that the youngest two might be coming down with it. We had to send Caddie and her nippers away out of danger and Miss Spinks went with them. I'm sorry, ducks. But you'd best not come in.'

'Where did they go, Sam?' She was desperately sorry for the Smilies, but could hardly believe the continued ill fortune that might leave them without shelter and with nightfall not many hours away.

'Caddie said to tell you that she's taken them back to the tunnel, and you'd know where to find them. I'm sorry, I truly am.' Sam reached beneath the counter and produced a bundle wrapped in butter muslin. 'Gladys packed up a bit of food to keep you going. She's out of her mind with worry, but she's a good woman and she wouldn't see no one go hungry.'

'Thank her for me, Sam. I hope the boys get well soon, and I can't thank you enough for all your kindness.' Fighting exhaustion and a feeling of desperation, Rosina hurried from the shop clutching the bundle; she headed off once again in the direction of the Thames tunnel.

She found them all huddled together in a dark alcove not far from the entrance.

'Where've you been all day?' Bertha demanded crossly. 'You should have stayed to see that we was all right and not gone gallivanting off on some fool's errand.'

Rosina squatted down on the damp floor, ignoring Bertha's outburst, and she unwrapped the parcel of food. 'I'll explain later. You'll feel better when you've had something to eat.'

'Better!' Bertha puffed out her chest, glancing nervously into the dank depths of the tunnel. 'I can't stay in this terrible place a moment longer. I can't believe as how it's come to this – us living like sewer rats or toshers. What would the captain say if he could see us now?'

Caddie laid her hand on Bertha's arm. 'Don't upset yourself so. It can't be helped.'

Bertha shook free from her grasp. 'That's easy for you to say. You're used to living like this but I ain't. My rheumatics is playing me up already in this disgusting hole.'

Ronnie and Alfie fell on the food, cramming bread into their mouths and staring wide-eyed at

Bertha. Caddie hitched the baby over her shoulder, casting an anxious look at Rosina. 'What shall us do? Bertha's right. We can't stay here forever, and my babies might already have caught the sickness.'

Rosina nibbled a piece of dry bread, leaving the heel of cheese for Bertha and Caddie to eat. Their plight was desperate. She toyed with the idea of spending some of the money in her purse on a night's lodgings, but abandoned the thought immediately. They were safe down here, if not comfortable. She managed a weak smile. 'We will have to make the best of it for tonight, but I promise you we will find somewhere much more suitable tomorrow. We will start out at first light and go to Etheredge's Wharf. We still have the barge, and I have found a man of the law who will help free Walter. Once we are back in business, everything will be all right again.' She had spoken with more confidence than she was feeling, but her words seemed to have a soothing effect on Bertha and Caddie. There was nothing more she could do now, other than try to sleep on the hard ground in the eerie, echoing tunnel, listening to the constant drip, drip, drip of the water running down the brick walls.

Next morning, Rosina struggled to maintain a cheerful exterior as the small party made their way to Etheredge's boatyard. The children were fretful and Caddie was almost beside herself, watching them for symptoms of the dreaded scarlet fever. Bertha grumbled all the way, complaining of everything from sore feet to sunstroke. It came, therefore, as a welcome surprise when they finally reached Etheredge's to find that the repairs to the barge were completed. At least one of Rosina's fears was allayed: she had thought that the Gostellows might have gone back on their word, but it seemed that the work had been paid for in advance, and the account had been settled. The *Ellie May* was now hers and the barge was ready to resume trading.

'There's only one thing, miss,' the foreman said, frowning. 'We got plenty of work on hand and we needs the space. You're going to have to move the vessel away from the wharf as soon as possible, and today for preference. We've already kept her here longer than we would normally. We heard that your dad had passed away, and we're all very sorry. He was a good man, but business is business. You do understand, don't you?'

Rosina managed to nod her head and to flash him a bright smile. 'Of course. Leave it to me.'

'Well?' Bertha said impatiently. 'What did he say?'

'He said we've got to move the boat today.' Rosina stared at the swirling waters of

Limehouse Hole, a deep part of Limehouse Reach where ships could turn with ease. She might be used to sailing on a Thames barge, but she had no clear idea how to steer the boat or trim the sails. She cast a desperate glance at Caddie. 'I can't sail her. I don't know how.'

Caddie squared her shoulders. 'I never done it on me own, but I've sailed with Artie afore he got the job with Captain May. We worked a lighter taking coal from the barges to the wharves. I reckon we could manage between us to shift her to another wharf.'

The foreman, apparently overhearing this conversation, cleared his throat with a polite cough. 'Er, excuse me, young ladies. Did I hear you right? Are you thinking of sailing the barge out into the reach on your own?'

Rosina eyed him warily. 'And what if we were?'

'Well, don't take me wrong, miss. But you ain't a freeman of the Watermen's Company by any chance, are you?'

'No, indeed I am not.'

'Nor, if you'll pardon my saying so, are you a qualified skipper.'

'No, but my friend here is accustomed to working on a lighter in the Pool of London. I think we two can manage to shift the *Ellie May*.'

'Look, miss. Again, don't take no offence, but it's a bit tricky on this here stretch of the river. If you'll let me, I'll lend you one of my men. He'll make sure that you gets safely to a wharf downstream.'

'Thank you, sir,' Rosina said, stifling a sigh of relief. 'That would be most kind.'

He tipped his cap. 'It's the least I can do for Captain May's daughter.' He turned abruptly and walked away, shouting instructions to one of his men to help the young ladies make sail and move the vessel to another wharf.

'And what's to become of me and the nippers while you two are playing at being sailors?' Bertha demanded crossly. 'Are we to sit on the muddy foreshore and wait for the tide to come in and collect us like bits of flotsam?'

Rosina exchanged worried glances with Caddie. 'We can't very well take the little ones on the boat.'

Caddie nodded in agreement. 'No, indeed. It would be ever so dangerous.'

'Well, I ain't no nursemaid. Not to a baby and little tykes like them two.'

Rosina pulled her purse from her reticule and took out a shiny silver florin. 'Take them to the Bunch of Grapes pub over there.' She pointed to the building. 'Maybe the landlord will let you sit in the parlour with them until we can get back. You could enquire about a cheap lodging house or some rooms that we might be able to rent.'

Bertha took the coin and stuffed it into her

pocket. 'Well, I suppose that would be all right. Maybe the landlord's wife might let me have a bit of milk for the nippers.'

'Hungry,' murmured Alfie, rubbing his tummy.

'Me too,' Ronnie said, nodding his head. 'Want a drink.'

Caddie passed the baby to Bertha. 'We'll be back as soon as we can, Bertha. You threaten the boys with a good spanking if they play up. I won't stand for badly behaved children.'

'Huh!' Bertha said with feeling. 'They wouldn't dare. Bertha Spinks don't stand for no tantrums. Come on, you two. One word out of place and you'll get a thick ear.'

Rosina watched her as she stomped off towards the pub with the two little boys skipping along behind her. She turned with a start as someone plucked at her sleeve.

'Master has sent me to take you out into the reach.' A tall, gangly young man dragged off his cloth cap and grinned at her shyly. 'Pip, miss. Me name is Pip.'

She eyed him curiously. His weather-beaten face was plain to the point of being ugly, with a nose which had obviously, at some time in the past, met with a fist or a blunt instrument that had broken the bone, and now it had a slightly comical crooked appearance. His lopsided smile was impossible to resist. 'Thank you, Pip. We would be most grateful for your help.'

He nodded. 'Tide's right. We should cast off now, afore it turns.

Rosina hesitated: she was suddenly afraid, although of what she was not quite certain. She had never feared the river; it had always seemed like an old friend, but then her papa had been the master of the *Ellie May*. Caddie on the other hand seemed to have no such forebodings. She was about to descend the ladder from the wharf to the barge when Pip leapt onto the deck to assist her. He swung her down as easily as if she had been a featherweight, and then he held his hands out to Rosina. Taking a deep breath, she allowed him to help her down onto the barge. He looked from Rosina to Caddie. 'Excuse me for being so bold, but do either of you two ladies know how to steer a boat?'

Caddie moved swiftly to the tiller. 'I do, if you'll tell me which way to head.'

Pip touched his cap in a salute. 'Aye, aye, cap'n.' He gave a throaty chuckle, as if delighted by his own wit. Caddie wiped her hands on her skirt and took the tiller. Rosina saw that she was nervous, but there was nothing that she could do, nothing except stand back and watch while Caddie steered the boat and Pip set the topsail to catch the light airs. 'We can't go too far away,' she said, thinking of Bertha and the children waiting for them in the pub.

'It's all right, miss. We can moor close to Duke

Stairs, and it ain't far to walk back to Etheredge's.' Pip turned to Caddie with an appreciative smile. 'You done well, miss. As if you was born to it, like.'

'Me husband taught me how to steer a boat. He said I was a natural.'

Pip's smile faded. 'You're married then, miss?'

'Widowed.'

'Oh!' Pip's face split into a huge grin.

When the *Ellie May* was safely away from the wharf Rosina stifled a sigh of relief. 'That was well done, both of you.'

'Nothing to it, miss.' Pip took the tiller from Caddie. 'I'll take her from here, miss – er, missis. It ain't far to Duke Stairs and I know a place where we can moor her safely for the time being.'

Caddie moved to where Rosina had perched on a coil of rope. 'He seems to know what he's doing, all right.'

Rosina nodded her head, keeping an eye on Pip as he skilfully manoeuvred the vessel around tiers of lighters and dumb barges, heading for a small wharf. He might not be very bright, but he certainly knew what he was doing when it came to sailing a barge. An idea struck her and she rose to her feet, making her way across the deck to his side. 'Mr Pip, do you think it possible that you might be able to work for me? I need to start working the river but neither Caddie nor I are qualified to sail a barge. We desperately need to resume trading, or we will starve. It's as simple as that.'

'That's simple all right, miss.' Pip's brow furrowed into lines and he was silent for a while as he manoeuvred the vessel skilfully alongside the wharf. He passed the tiller to Caddie. 'Hold her steady, missis, while I make her fast.' On shore he might move clumsily, but on board the barge he was as nimble as a performing monkey: he shinned up the ladder with the mooring rope in his hand, made fast and landed back on deck with a flying leap.

'Thank you, Mr Pip,' Rosina said, smiling. 'Where did you learn to handle a boat like that?'

'They trained us at the foundling hospital, miss. But they reckoned as how I weren't bright enough to pass no tests, so they sent me to the repair yard. I always wanted to work on the river, not just on the shore, but I'm a bit touched in the head, like.'

'I don't think that's true,' Rosina said gravely. 'From what I've seen, you are more than competent, but I can't afford to pay you very much, Mr Pip. Not for a while anyway. I believe my papa paid Artie a percentage of the profit on the cargo. And you would only have myself and Caddie to crew for you. I cannot afford to hire a master.'

Pip slapped his sides and seemed to find this hilarious, laughing until he was breathless.

'That's a good 'un, miss. Me, simple Pip Phillips, a waterman! Well, I never did.'

Caddie drew Rosina aside, lowering her voice. 'Do you really mean for us to sail the barge with only Pip to help us?'

'We have no choice. We must find a cargo or we will have no money for food or lodging. And I need funds to pay the lawyer who has taken Walter's case.'

'But first of all we needs a roof over our heads. We got to find a room for the night, Rosie. I got to think of me nippers.'

Rosina patted Caddie on the shoulder. 'I know, and we will. I've kept a little money back for just that purpose. Maybe Pip could help.' She turned to him and found that he had been listening intently with his head on one side. 'Mr Pip, do you know where we might find cheap lodgings in this area?'

'You can call me Pip, miss. And Limehouse Hole ain't exactly the place for two young ladies such as yourselves.'

'Maybe not, but we must find somewhere before nightfall. And it needs to be close by the wharf so that I can keep an eye on my boat.'

Pip's mouth worked silently, as though he was translating his slow thoughts into words. Caddie and Rosina exchanged anxious glances, and when he did not reply, Rosina laid her hand on his arm. 'Don't worry, Pip. We'll ask at the pub. I'm sure they'll be able to help us.'

'There!' Pip said with a triumphant chuckle. 'I've worked it out in me head. You can have me little home on the water's edge and I'll sleep like a king in the cabin on the barge. That way, we'll all be happy.'

Caddie eyed him, angling her head. 'That seems a very generous offer, Pip. Are you sure about this?'

He shuffled his feet, blushing. 'I'd like to help, miss. It ain't exactly a palace, but it'll give you a roof over your heads.'

'You're very kind, Pip. I'm sure it will do nicely.' Rosina set her foot on the bottom rung of the ladder. 'And I'll need to speak to the foreman of the boatyard to make sure he doesn't mind letting you go. I don't want you getting into any trouble.'

# Chapter Twenty-one

The foreman raised no objections to their taking Pip away from his work on the barges. In fact, he almost seemed to be relieved to be ridding himself of the fellow. Before collecting Bertha and the children, Rosina and Caddie followed Pip to his house. It was reached by a boardwalk and turned out to be little more than a wooden shack on stilts, balancing precariously over the muddy foreshore. It was just one of many such dwellings set in front of dilapidated cottages, warehouses, sail lofts and ship's chandlers, forming a crazy wooden village that looked as though it might disintegrate into matchwood in a strong gust of wind.

'This is my little palace,' Pip said proudly as he lifted the latch. 'Take a look inside and you'll be agreeably surprised, mark my words.'

Rosina stepped over the threshold and stood quite still while her eyes became accustomed to the dim light. The shack was constructed entirely of driftwood planks, roughly nailed together to make one small room. Splinters of daylight filtered between the badly fitting panels and a ragged piece of cloth flapped against a tiny unglazed window next to the entrance. An iron pot-bellied stove stood against one wall, with a rusty chimney snaking up through a hole in the roof. The only furniture was a truckle bed, an upturned tea chest, which served as a table, and a wooden three-legged milking stool.

'All saved from the river,' Pip added, puffing out his chest. 'The river has been mother and father to me since I run away from the foundling hospital. I've fended for meself ever since.'

'You poor boy,' Caddie said, her eyes brimming with tears. 'I fear going into an institution. I can't think of nothing worse.'

'No need to fear nothing with Pip on your side, missis. I've always wanted a family. I'd be more than proud to help you and your nippers. I'm a hard worker, anyone will tell you that.'

'Pip, we really can't turn you out of your home,' Rosina said, casting an agonised glance at Caddie. This really was a hovel, and it was none too clean at that. 'Perhaps we should look for lodgings nearby and let you keep your house for yourself.'

'No, miss. I won't hear of it. I will live on the barge until such time as you have enough money laid aside to rent a proper place, as befits ladies of quality such as yourselves. There's everything you could want here – water from the river, driftwood, and lumps of coal washed ashore from the colliers when they unloads onto lighters. Why, you'll only need to spend a couple of pence in the pie and eel shop and you can live like the queen.' He backed out through the door onto the wooden stoop. 'I'll let you ladies have a look round on your own.'

'It's awful,' Rosina whispered. 'We can't bring Bebe and the children to a place like this.'

Caddie picked up the lid on the stove, sending a shower of rust onto the floorboards. 'At least we'll be warm and reasonably dry. It ain't so bad, Rosie. I've been in worse places, and the rent will be cheap. I don't think we've got much choice.'

Rosina wrapped her arms around herself and shivered. 'My papa would turn in his grave if he could see me come to this.'

'Your pa is dead and gone, the same as my Artie. They can't help us now. All we've got is each other. And if you want to help Walter, maybe you ought to give this place a bit of thought.'

'It's filthy,' Rosina said, running her finger across the top of a wooden shelf on which Pip kept his tin mug and plate.

'Dirt will wash away. If three strong women can't keep a place this size spick and span, then my name ain't Caddie Trigg.'

'I don't know what Bertha will say.'

Caddie giggled. 'I can't wait to see her face.'

*

Bertha stood in the middle of the floor with her arms akimbo. Rosina held her breath, waiting for a tirade of complaints. Sounds of merriment were coming from below, where Pip was playing hide and seek amongst the slime-encrusted wooden supports with Ronnie and Alfie. Through the open door, Rosina could see Caddie leaning over the railing, chuckling as she watched their antics. At least someone seemed happy to be here, she thought, as she waited anxiously for Bertha to speak.

'It ain't a palace,' Bertha said at last. 'But it's a sight better than sleeping in the tunnel, and I daresay, with a bit of cleaning up, it might do for the time being.'

'Y-you don't object?' Rosina could hardly believe her ears.

Bertha sat down gingerly on the milking stool, balancing her weight carefully. 'Of course I ain't happy about it. I objects to being turned out of me home after all these years, and it ain't fair that we've had to suffer like this, but we got to be practical. If you can sail the boat with the help of the simpleton, then so be it. I'll make the best of things and I'll look after the nippers while you and Caddie go off and earn us some money.'

'We'll get back on our feet, you'll see, Bebe. And one day we'll have a proper house again, and nice clothes and plenty to eat, just like the old days.'

'That's the spirit, girl. Your pa would be proud of you.' Bertha wiped her eyes on her skirt. 'So proud.'

Rosina flung her arms around Bertha's neck and hugged her, but she had reckoned without the three-legged milking stool, and it tipped over beneath their combined weight, tossing them onto the floor in a tangle of arms and legs. Rosina scrambled to her feet laughing, and she found that she could not stop.

Much later, after Pip had provided them with a pie and mash supper from the shop in Narrow Street, and the children were curled up together, asleep on the truckle bed, Bertha sat on the stool by the stove, in which a wood fire crackled and burned. Pip had returned to the barge, and Rosina was outside on the stoop with Caddie, watching the dusk creeping along the river and enveloping everything in a cloak of darkness.

'We'll need to find a cargo,' Rosina said thoughtfully. 'I wish Walter was here to tell me how to go about it.'

'Well, he ain't. It's just you and me, and we've got to sort it out ourselves.'

'Rubbish!' Rosina said, clapping her hands.

'I beg your pardon?' Caddie stared at her as if she had gone mad.

'I saw a barge being loaded with rubbish on Duke's Shore Wharf. We don't need to buy a cargo of the city's rubbish, Caddie. They must be taking it somewhere downriver and dumping it. All we've got to do is to find out where and who pays for the refuse to be taken away. After all, Mr Gostellow made his fortune with his scavenger cart taking rubbish to the dust mound – I don't see why we can't do the same.'

'But it's dirty work, Rosie.'

'Yes, I know. But because of that it's likely to pay us well.' Rosina glanced down at her stained and torn gown. 'I don't think I'll ever feel clean and pretty again, so what difference can a bit more dirt make?'

Next morning, Rosina went down to the wharf to find Pip. On her way, she watched a barge being loaded with rubbish, covering her mouth and nose with her hand as the noxious cloud of stinking dust filled the air. The men who loaded the barge and those on board, had scarves tied around their lower faces, and hats pulled down over their eyes. Their bare torsos were slicked with sweat and coated with grime: they worked in silence, moving rhythmically like an army of sinister automatons. Rosina suppressed a shudder, and she hurried on her way. When she reached the barge, she found that Pip had set himself to work scrubbing the deck. He leapt to attention when she called him, and, dropping the holystone, he climbed up the ladder to meet her. When she told him of her plan to carry refuse as a cargo, he listened intently, nodding his head.

'So,' she said, when he did not venture a comment, 'do you know how I would go about getting such a cargo? Who should I see?'

He thought for a moment. 'I should say that you need to see – the man in charge.'

Curbing her impatience, Rosina managed a tight little smile. 'Thank you, Pip. That's very helpful. But do you know who he might be?'

'The fat man with the gold watch and chain – he's the gaffer. Can I come to see you later, and maybe play with the little 'uns? I sat up half the night carving a wooden boat for them to play with.'

'Yes, of course. Come round when you've finished your work.' She was obviously not going to get any more useful information from him. Rosina walked back past the wharf where the barge was now fully loaded. As the dust settled she saw that Pip had not been far wrong – the man who seemed to be in charge of the whole operation was dressed more like a city businessman than a dustman, and a gold chain hung across his ample belly, no doubt attached to an expensive watch tucked safely away in his waistcoat pocket. She was once more acutely conscious of her own bedraggled state. She could not do business with anyone while she looked, as Bertha would say, like something the cat had dragged in.

Back at the hut, Bertha and Caddie took the once lovely gown down to the water's edge and scrubbed at it with a piece of carbolic soap. Surprisingly, even though the water was not exactly crystal clear, the material came up almost as good as new. Between them, Caddie and Bertha wrung it out and left it hanging over the wooden railing on the stoop to dry. Luckily it was a warm and sunny September day with a gentle breeze, and by mid-afternoon the dress was dry enough for Bertha to take inside to mend. From the pocket of her skirt she produced a housewife, one of the few items that she had managed to keep about her person, in which she kept needles, cotton and a small pair of scissors. By the time she had finished stitching and darning, the gown was almost as good as new, although it would not bear too close a scrutiny.

When she was dressed, Rosina perched on the stool while Caddie put up her hair. 'There,' she said, standing back and admiring her handiwork. 'You look a treat, Rosie.'

'You should have kept your bonnet,' Bertha said, sniffing and shaking her head. 'No lady goes out without a bonnet and gloves. It ain't proper.'

'Well, I had to pawn it along with all my other clothes. The fat man with the gold watch will just have to take me as I am.'

'Wait a minute, I've got an idea.' Caddie held her hand out to Bertha. 'Can I have your scissors, please?'

Bertha handed them over grudgingly. 'What are you going to do?'

'You'll see. Stand up, Rosie.'

Rosina did as she asked. 'I don't see . . .'

'Wait a moment and you will.' Caddie snipped a rosette of lace-trimmed silk from the bustle at the back of Rosina's gown. 'Turn round and look at me.'

Chuckling at Caddie's unusual bossiness, Rosina turned to face her. 'What next?'

Taking a hairpin from her own hair, Caddie fastened the rosette at a cunning angle over Rosina's left ear. 'There. It ain't exactly a bonnet, but it's a headdress of sorts and it suits you down to the ground. What do you think, Bertha?'

'It'll do, I suppose, but a nice straw bonnet would do better.'

Rosina arrived at the wharf just as the last barge was setting sail. The fat man with the gold watch was just about to climb into a carriage and she had to run the last few yards. 'Wait, sir. Please wait. May I have a word with you?'

He hesitated, frowning. 'What do you want with me, young woman?'

'My name is Rosina May and I am the owner of the sailing barge *Ellie May*. I wish to speak to you on a business matter, sir.'

He pushed his bowler hat to the back of his head, eyeing her with a spark of interest. 'A woman owning a barge? Come, come, young lady, is this some kind of joke? I'm a busy man. I don't like time-wasters.'

'No, indeed. And I am not a time-waster. I can ship your rubbish for you at a very reasonable rate.' She caught him by the sleeve as he started to walk away. 'I'll do it cheaper than the best offer you've had.'

He turned slowly, giving her a piercing look. 'What do you know about barge business, Miss May?'

'My father was Captain Edward May, a shipmaster for thirty years. I've lived on Black Eagle Wharf for most of my life, and, although I don't pretend to be an experienced skipper or businesswoman, I am prepared to learn. And because of my inexperience, I will give a rate that no one else could match, Mr – er – I'm sorry, I did not catch your name.'

'George Gilks. And I have enough barge captains working for me. I have no need, nor do I wish, to deal with a young woman who ought to be at home waiting patiently for a suitable husband to come and claim her.'

He climbed into the carriage, but before he could shut the door, Rosina had leapt in beside him. 'You would not speak to me in such a way if I were a man.'

'No, I would not. Take my advice, Miss May. Go home and concentrate on being a pretty young woman. Leave business matters to men. Now, will you be good enough to alight from my carriage; I have business elsewhere in the city.'

'Give me one cargo. That's all I ask. If I cannot deliver the rubbish to its due destination in good time, and at a cheaper rate than any other barge captain, then I will admit defeat.'

His lips twitched and she saw a glimmer of amusement in his grey eyes. 'You are a persistent young woman, I'll give you that.'

'I mean business, Mr Gilks. I am in deadly earnest; I am not playing games. All I ask is one chance. What have you got to lose?'

Gilks leaned back against the leather squabs, eyeing her shrewdly. 'Have your vessel at the wharf at eleven o'clock this evening and you shall have a load of rubbish to take to Queenborough on the Medway. If you can accomplish that trip successfully and be back here in the same time as it takes the other barges, then I might consider giving you a contract. But I have to tell you, young lady, that I think it highly unlikely that you will even get as far as Queenborough, let alone make the return journey in the required time.'

Rosina shook his hand. 'You will be pleasantly surprised, Mr Gilks. Good day, sir.' She climbed down from the carriage and marched off with her head held high. She knew that she was smiling, and received some odd glances from passers-by, but she somehow managed to resist the temptation to crow with delight. She had not really believed that hard-faced Mr Gilks would give in so easily, but desperation had made her bold, and now they had a chance to prove themselves. She made her way back to the hut with a spring in her step. She looked up into the hazy blue sky, wondering if her papa was looking down at her. She wanted so badly to tell him what she had achieved; he would be proud of her, she was certain of that.

Night came all too soon. Rosina's euphoria had diminished into a welter of nervous tension as she waited until it was time to go down to the wharf with Pip and Caddie. She had hung her precious gown on a nail in the wall, and borrowed Caddie's only change of clothing: a much-darned bombazine skirt and a cotton blouse. She took down the scraps of cloth from the window and tore them into squares to serve as masks against the flying dust. With her hair scraped back into a bun and her sleeves rolled up in anticipation of hard manual labour, Rosina knew that she was as ready as she ever would be.

Under Pip's surprisingly expert guidance, they moved the *Ellie May* and made fast alongside the wharf in time to load the rubbish. Rosina and Caddie tied the cloths over their mouths and noses, standing back to allow the dockers to do their work. Dust flew up and enveloped them in thick, suffocating clouds; the stench was appalling. Rosina coughed and retched and her eyes streamed, irritated by the small particles of grit. The sky was like an inverted bowl of pitch above their heads and the flickering light of the gas flares illuminated a scene which was frighteningly akin to her childhood imaginings of hell.

It was sheer relief when the shovelling and tipping of the rubbish ceased and the hold was full. Pip had instructed them with surprising clarity as to what Rosina and Caddie must do in the way of setting the different sails, while he took the tiller and steered them through the busy river traffic of Limehouse Hole into Limehouse Reach. To Rosina's inexperienced eyes, the dark water was alive with bobbing lights, darting before her eyes like hundreds of tiny fireflies. Pip, however, seemed to know his way instinctively and he steered them skilfully through the maze of shipping. There were moments of panic when she and Caddie set the wrong sail, or when a steamboat chugged past them, taking their wind, but Pip took it all in his stride and gradually they gained confidence in his seamanship. It was exhausting work and they were unused to being up all night. As the first grey-green streaks of dawn appeared in the east Rosina was so tired that she could barely keep her eyes open. The palms of her hands were blistered, and some had burst, creating painful weeping sores. Her back ached and she was numbed with cold. She looked at Caddie who did not seem to have fared much better, but Pip was at the tiller, smoking a pipe of baccy as if he had done this all his life. He met her eyes and grinned. 'This is fun, ain't it, miss? I've never had so much pleasure in all me born days.'

'If you say so, Pip.'

His smile faded to a look of concern. 'You should get some rest, and Caddie too. I can handle the old girl as far as the Medway, no trouble.'

'If you're sure.' Rosina could think of nothing she wanted more in life other than to lie down on the narrow bunk in the cabin and rest her weary limbs. She moved slowly and stiffly to Caddie, who was sitting on the deck with her arms wrapped round her knees. 'Come, dear. Pip says we should get some rest. He'll call us when we're needed.'

Caddie struggled to her feet. 'I could sleep on a bed of nails like one of them Indian gents at the fair.' She stumbled towards the cabin and disappeared inside.

Rosina hesitated for a moment. She sniffed the air and it smelt good. There was only a faint whiff of the rubbish below the hatch covers. The stench from the tanneries, iron works and glue factories had been nauseating, but the industrial part of the East End was now far behind them. She might be imagining things, but she thought she could smell clover, damp soil and just a hint of the salt tang of the sea. She made her way to the cabin and she lay down on her father's old bunk. Was it her imagination, or did the faint scent of him linger in the feather pillow? She closed her eyes, and her father's face seemed to be smiling at her. As she drifted off into a sleep of sheer exhaustion, she thought she heard his voice. 'Well done, poppet. I am so proud of you, my little Rosie.'

Someone was calling her name. It wasn't her papa and it wasn't Caddie. Rosina opened her eyes and saw Pip bending over her with a mug of tea in his hand. 'Morning, miss. I've made a brew.'

She sat up to take the tea from him. 'Thank you, Pip. But how . . .'

'Found a little spirit stove and some tea in a tin. Can't work without a cup of split pea inside you. No sugar though, and no milk. Maybe we could get some afore we makes the return trip.'

Caddie was already sitting up sipping from a cracked china mug. 'We've stopped moving. Are we there?'

'Not yet, missis. I've lashed the tiller so we keeps course for a bit. The only thing is, Miss Rosie, I never learned how to read, and your dada's charts don't mean nothing to me.'

Rosina swallowed a mouthful of hot tea. 'You mean, you don't know where we are?'

'Not exactly, miss. But I'd say we ain't a mile away from the mouth of the Medway. The river's wider here and the currents is stronger.'

'Best get back to the tiller, Pip.' Rosina put her tea down on the floor and scrambled to her feet. 'My pa showed me how to read a chart, but it was a long time ago. I hope I can remember what to look for.'

'My Artie said he always followed his nose,' Caddie said, seemingly unworried. 'Said he could smell land, and he knew by the different scents along the way exactly where they was.'

Pip tapped his crooked nose. 'Mine only goes round corners, missis.' He roared with laughter at his own joke, and shambled out of the cabin.

Rosina took a chart from the drawer and spread it out on the top of the chest. 'I should have studied this last night. We can't afford to go wrong now, Caddie. Everything depends on this trip. Absolutely everything.'

Somehow, more by luck than good judgement, they reached their destination and while the foul-smelling cargo was being unloaded they were able to snatch a few hours' rest. Rosina gave Pip some money and he went ashore to buy provisions, since all they had had to eat since leaving Limehouse Hole was stale bread scraped with a little jam.

As she watched the last of the cargo being shovelled into buckets and hoisted ashore, Rosina turned to Caddy with a sigh of relief. 'We've done it, and in good time. We'll set sail as soon as we've had something to eat.'

'But, Rosie, Pip must be tired out. He needs some sleep.'

Rosina hardened her heart. 'He said he could do it, and our whole future depends on getting back to London in good time. Mr Gilks won't have any sympathy for aching backs or groaning muscles. I'm prepared to stay up all night and help him, and so must you.'

Caddie stared at her wide-eyed. 'I never knew you could be so hard.'

'I'm not normally, but I'm learning fast. If you want to be able to feed and clothe your children, and give them a decent home, then you'll go along with what I say. Otherwise, it will be the workhouse for us all.'

It was dark by the time they arrived back at Duke's Wharf. Pip steered the barge alongside, taking the space vacated by a fully loaded vessel. The foreman watched them from the wharf. Tired and aching in every joint, with her bones feeling so brittle that they might snap at any moment, Rosina climbed up the ladder to meet him.

'So, you've done it then, miss.' The foreman looked her up and down, as though assessing her worth. 'Didn't think you'd make it though.'

'Well, mister, we did. And I require payment.'

'You'll get your money like the rest of them, from the counting house, office hours only. And you've only done half what Mr Gilks said you was to do.'

Rosina stared at him in horror. 'No, I agreed one load at half the going rate.'

'And you've taken only half a load. You'll need to do a quick turn about.'

'Is anything wrong, Rosie?' Caddie had come up the ladder behind her and was standing at her elbow.

'There's been a bit of a misunderstanding. This man says we have to do another trip straight away.'

Caddie's lips trembled. 'But I needs to make sure me boys is all right.'

The foreman curled his lip. 'I told the gaffer that he was making a mistake. Women has no place on the river. In my opinion you should be at home where you belongs.'

'No one asked for your opinion, my man. What you say is not how I understood my agreement with Mr Gilks.'

'Take it or leave it, miss. But don't expect to get paid for the trip unless you keep your end of the bargain.' The foreman turned away, shouting instructions to the men working under him. 'And move that barge if you don't want another cargo.'

'Give me a moment, please.' Rosina took Caddie aside. 'I don't like it, but I'm afraid we must do as the man says.'

'I got to go home first and see me boys. I can't leave them another night, or they'll think their ma has deserted them.'

'Go home then, and I'll see what Pip has to say. If we take another load of rubbish it will take some time for them to fill the hold. I'll come and fetch you, if needs be.'

Rosina forced herself to climb back down the steep ladder to the deck, where Pip was as busy as any housewife tidying up after a party. She put it to him that they were required to do another trip immediately. 'You've been on watch the whole time, Pip. I don't feel I can ask you to do it again without a good rest.'

'I ain't much of a one for sleeping, miss. I've enjoyed meself more in the last twenty-four hours than I have in years, and all I need is a couple of hours' snooze in the cabin while they loads the rubbish, and I'll be ready for anything.'

'Are you absolutely certain?'

'Absolutely, miss. When I was working on shore I felt like one of them slaves they tells you about in the Bible. When I'm sailing on the river, I feels like a bird, flying free with no one to tell me what to do. And,' he added, tapping the side of his crooked nose, 'I can find the way this time. I may not have much learning, but there's nothing wrong with me memory when it comes to sights and sounds. I could smell me way downriver, I tells you, even through this here poor bent beak of mine.'

With her limbs feeling like lead, Rosina hauled herself up the ladder. She went to find the foreman. 'Mr – er – foreman.'

He turned his head. 'Butcher, miss. That's me name, not me profession.'

'Tell your men to load the *Ellie May* then, Mr Butcher. We'll take the cargo, and I will sort matters out direct with Mr Gilks on our return.'

'Mr Gilks,' Rosina said, ignoring his invitation to take a seat in the chair facing his desk. She preferred to stand, keeping her head at a higher level than his and looking down on him. 'Our agreement was for one trip, not two.'

He folded his hands over his corpulent stomach, smiling in a patronising manner. 'My dear young lady, you took only a half-load, therefore it takes two trips to fulfil the agreement, unless my arithmetic is incorrect.'

'No, sir. You arithmetic is right, but your logic is wrong. You're forgetting that I am a barge captain's daughter, and although I may not be an expert when it comes to crewing a vessel, I grew up listening to bargemen's talk. You are trying to diddle me simply because I'm a woman. A man wouldn't stand for it, sir. And neither will I.'

Gilks took a small cigar from a box on the tooled red-leather top of his desk and lit it, eyeing her with a glimmer of a smile. 'Well, now. That's boldly spoken for a young woman such as yourself. But our deal still stands at half the going rate for the full load.'

'Two full loads, Mr Gilks. And I only offered the low rate on the first load. You owe me for one and a half loads.'

Gripping the cigar between his teeth in a rictus grin, he picked up a pen and dipped it in the silver inkwell. He scribbled something on a sheet of paper and held it out to her. 'You win, Miss May. Take this to the counting house and you'll receive payment.'

She took the paper from his hand, read the contents and folded it neatly. 'And will you keep the rest of the bargain? You said if I could prove myself that you would use my barge to transport your cargoes.'

'I did, didn't I?' He puffed away on his cigar, keeping her in suspense. Then he rose to his feet and held out his hand. 'Never let it be said that George Gilks don't keep his word.'

Rosina went straight to the counting house to collect their hard-earned money. It was not until she was outside the building, with a golden sovereign and four half-crowns in her hand, that she was overcome by sheer exhaustion. Somehow, they had all managed to keep going with only the minimum of sleep on the second voyage to the Medway. How Pip survived with so little rest she did not know, but they had done it, and now they were assured of regular cargoes of London's stinking rubbish. She stowed the coins in her skirt pocket. She was shockingly dirty, covered from head to foot in dust and grit. Her hair felt like tow and she wondered if she would ever feel clean again. She longed for a bath in a zinc tub with jugs of hot water to pour over her head, just as she had been used to at home. One day, she thought, as she forced her aching feet to move one in front of the other, she would have a house with a proper bathroom with an indoor lavatory, just like the one in Roland's house in Rotterdam. As she trudged towards Narrow Street, she wondered how many tons of rubbish she would have to shift before she could afford to rent a property that was half as good as her old home on Black Eagle Wharf. She was so deep in thought that she barely noticed a horseman approaching at a fast trot. It was not until he drew his steed to a halt beside her that she recognised the rider.

He leaned from the saddle, staring at her. 'Rosie? Rosina May? Is it really you beneath that mantle of dirt?'

# Chapter Twenty-two

'Harry?' Rosina peered up at him. She was so tired that it was difficult to focus her eyes, but she would have recognised that voice anywhere.

'By God, it is you.' Harry threw back his head and roared with laughter. 'You look like a blackamoor. Damn me, I never thought I'd live to see the day when pampered little Miss Fastidious looked like a chimneysweep's boy.'

'Go away, you brute. How dare you laugh at me? And whose fault is it that I am forced to earn my living in any way I can?'

'It is yours, my dear. You brought this on yourself by breaking off our engagement.'

'No, Harry. It is your fault for taking my home away from me, and for making false accusations against Walter. He is languishing in Newgate awaiting trial for a crime that he did not commit, and all because of you.'

'He is as guilty as sin, Rosie. Maybe he did not steal my mother's diamond ring, but I am certain that he was the pirate who chose to thieve from Barnum. I don't know what scores that fellow had to settle, but robbers become greedy, and it was only a matter of time before he turned his attention to our vessels.'

Shrugging her shoulders, Rosina started walking. She was too exhausted to stay and fight; she could see that it was useless anyway. Harry had his set ideas and nothing would make him change his mind.

'Rosie, wait.' Harry dismounted and followed her, leading his horse. 'I never meant you to sink so low.'

'You didn't care what happened to me. But I haven't sunk low, as you put it. I have my own business now, Harry.' She stopped, turning her head to look him in the eyes. 'There is money to be made from other people's rubbish, as you very well know. I may appear to be down at this moment, but I can assure you that I am on my way up.' She walked on.

He fell in step beside her. 'Gilks told me that he had entrusted a cargo to a slip of a girl. I had a feeling that it was you and I had to find out if it was true.'

'And your curiosity is satisfied. Now leave me alone.'

'George is a good friend of my father's. They were once partners, owning the same dust mound, but Gilks bought my father out when he decided to go into the provender business.'

'I really don't care, Harry.'

'I could put in a good word with Gilks. You could profit from my help.'

Rosina came to a halt, glaring at him. 'What? Are you feeling guilty? Look at me, Harry. I know how I must appear to you, but I am fine. Really I am. I don't need your help.'

He frowned. 'There must be something I can do to make your life easier. I am not a bad fellow, Rosie.'

'If you really and truly want to help me, Harry, go and make your peace with Sukey. Tell her the truth about the diamond ring, and have the charges dropped against Walter. I ask nothing for myself if you will do me that small service.'

'Do you care so much for the scribbling Pharisee?'

'I care about injustice. Now go on your way and leave me alone.'

'If I promise to make things right with Sukey, may I at least see you safely home?'

She did not want him to see the hovel in which they were forced to live, but she was too exhausted to argue. 'Please yourself, Harry. You always do.'

He followed her in silence. It was only a matter of minutes before they reached the wharf. Rosina stopped before they reached the boardwalk. 'You cannot bring your animal down here. I am safe now. You should go.'

Harry shook his head, tethering the horse to a lamp post. 'I said I will see you home, and I will.'

Shrugging her shoulders, Rosina trod the wooden walkway, stopping outside the shack. 'I am home.'

Harry pulled off his hat, holding it in his hands and staring incredulously at the rickety building. 'Good God! You can't live here. It's a hovel.'

Ronnie and Alfie burst out of the door, stopping when they saw Harry and clinging to Rosina's skirts. She laid her hands on their narrow shoulders. 'I'm home, boys. Go and tell Bertha that I'm here.' She shooed them back indoors, turning to Harry with a defiant toss of her head. 'This is my home now. It's humble, but it's clean and it's paid for by our hard work, me and Caddie. I see nothing to be ashamed of, so you can go away with a clear conscience. Just put things right with Sukey and then things will be even between us. Goodbye, Harry.' She turned from him and went into the shack.

George Gilks proved to be an exacting employer and the *Ellie May* was in port just long enough to be loaded and then unloaded at her destination. They worked turn and turn about, arriving back at Duke's Shore Wharf at all hours of the day and night according to the tides, and sailing again as soon as the next cargo of rubbish filled the hold. The only exception was Sunday, and on their first day off Rosina and Caddie slept on their straw-filled palliasses, oblivious to the incessant chattering of Ronnie and Alfie, or the occasional bouts of crying from Arthur. When she awakened, feeling surprisingly refreshed, Rosina dressed and took her cup of tea out onto the stoop where she could count her money uninterrupted by small boys. They were paid for each load and she divided the coins into four shares: one each for the three of them and one which she intended to save towards paying off the Gostellows' loan. Although the ship belonged to her, she could not in all conscience keep the major share, at least not yet. She was learning ship handling with every trip they made, but Pip was virtually the master of the *Ellie May* and without him she knew that they would be unable to work the vessel. She put the money back in her purse, staring ruefully at her calloused hands. The blisters had long since burst, and had eventually healed. Once these hands had been soft and white as the petals of a daisy – the hands of a lady – but now they were tanned by the sun and work-worn. She sighed and put the purse back in her reticule. At least they had food on the table now, and it was a proper table – they had chopped the old tea chest up for firewood. She had spotted the table on the pavement outside a second-hand furniture shop, and had purchased it with some of the money from her first voyage to the Medway. Bertha had gone to the same emporium and bargained hard for three wooden stools, so that now they could sit at the table like civilised human beings, instead of squatting on the floor like cannibals. Rosina smiled to herself; that was Bertha's description, not hers. If they could keep up this pace of work, it would not be long before they could afford to rent a couple of rooms in a proper house. The mere thought of a bathtub filled with hot water was like dreaming of heaven. Sometimes she wondered if she would ever be clean again. The luxurious bathroom in Roland's house seemed a million miles away. As to wearing clean linen and pretty clothes, Rosina sighed. She would have it all, one day. But Walter was still her main concern and she made up her mind to pay another visit to Septimus, to see if he had any news of the court case.

The *Ellie May* was due to sail on the morning tide, and Rosina came to the uncomfortable decision that Caddie and Pip would have to sail without her. For once there was something more important to her than earning money, and this was the day she had set aside for her visit to Naked Boy Yard.

She found Septimus sprawled in his chair, and for a horrible moment she thought that he was dead. His face was pale and unshaven and his mouth hung open, his chin resting on his chest.

His clothes were dirty and he smelled almost as bad as the hold of the *Ellie May*. She approached him nervously and felt for a pulse in his neck, jumping backwards in alarm as he emitted an explosive snort that shook his whole body. He opened his eyes. 'Two ladies, come to visit me?'

With her fright turning to anger, Rosina shook him by the shoulders. 'Wake up, you drunken beast. It's me, Rosina May.'

'Who is the other girl, then?'

She went to the washstand, where she found a jug filled with cold water. It looked as though it had been there for some time: there was a skim of slime on the surface and tiny things swimming around like squiggling punctuation marks. She tipped the contents over his head. Spluttering and coughing, he shook the water from his eyes. 'I'm drowning.'

'You're drunk.'

He peered at her through narrowed eyes. 'It is Miss May, isn't it?'

'At least you can just see one of me now. I need to talk to you urgently about Walter Brown. Do you remember him? He's in Newgate awaiting trial.'

He pressed his fingers into his temples. 'The name is familiar. May I have a moment to compose my thoughts?'

'No,' Rosina said firmly. He had closed his eyes and she was afraid that he was going to sink back into a drunken stupor. She hooked her hand through his arm, in an abortive effort to raise him to his feet. 'Get up, man. I'm taking you to a coffee house. Maybe I can get some sense out of you if you sober up a bit.'

Somehow, although she never knew quite how she managed it, Rosina got him out of the lodging house and along the street to an insalubrious-looking café, where she plied him with black coffee. It took some of her hard-earned pennies, but she considered it an investment. Having eaten two slices of toast and drunk several cups of coffee, he seemed relatively sober.

'Now, Septimus,' she said, leaning her elbows on the table and fixing him with a hard stare, 'can you remember going to see Walter in Newgate?'

He leaned back in his chair, taking a black cheroot from his breast pocket and lighting it. After a couple of puffs, he nodded his head. 'Ah, that's better. Yes, of course I remember seeing Mr Brown. He was a little suspicious at first, that is until I showed him the gold locket, and then he became more forthcoming.'

'And? What then? Is he well? How did he look to you?'

Septimus drew on the cheroot and blew a stream of smoke into the air above her head. 'He looked like a man who has spent several weeks in hell. But I will be defending him at his trial in two weeks' time.'

'Two weeks? His trial is in two weeks?'

'Yes, didn't I mention it before? Fortunately for Mr Brown the case against him is for the theft of the diamond ring. It would appear that Captain Barnum has not so far produced enough evidence to warrant a charge of piracy.'

Rosina leapt to her feet. 'Septimus, you are impossible. How could you not tell me something so important? Have you gathered any evidence that will clear him? Have you spoken to Sukey – I mean, Susan Barnum? Or been in touch with Mr Roland Rivers?'

'No, but I will. All in good time, dear lady.'

She threw up her hands in disgust. 'I trusted you, and you pickled yourself in brandy. How could you?'

'Very easily.

'Well, no more. You are not to touch a drop until Walter is free. Do you understand me?'

'I do, but I can't promise anything. You see, brandy is my friend. It comforts me when I am sad and lonely.'

'You won't have time to be sad and lonely. I will make sure of that.' Rosina picked up his hat and thrust it into his hands. 'Come with me. We'll make a start on the case together. I will keep you company today, not Mistress Brandy.'

'Where are we going?' Septimus demanded as she dragged him by the hand out of the café and through the narrow streets until they came to a cab stand. 'Eastcheap, cabby,' she said, climbing into the waiting hansom cab. 'Come along, Septimus. We're going to Roland's place of business.'

He clambered in and sat down beside her. 'My head aches, Miss May. This is not a good idea.'

'Never mind your head. We'll stop at the chemist's shop later and get you some seltzer, but first I want to find out if Roland is still in Rotterdam. If he is then we will send him a telegraph, asking him to come home for the trial. He need not fear a breach of promise suit now. At least, I hope that I have sorted the matter with Sukey, even if she did find it hard to take.'

'Breach of promise? You are making my head spin.'

She smiled. 'Never mind; that doesn't concern you. We must gather all the witnesses we can to speak up for Walter. I will help you, Septimus. All you have to do is to keep off the drink.'

As they entered the imposing portals of Rivers and Son, Importers and Exporters, Rosina realised that they must present a strange picture. She was dressed in her yellow gown and wearing a second-hand straw bonnet that she had purchased in a dolly shop near Etheredge's Wharf. She had also bought a pair of black lace mittens, to disguise her calloused hands; the moth holes were not too noticeable, unless someone took a close look at them. She had taken Septimus to a barber's shop and he was clean shaven now, with his hair brushed tidily back from his high forehead. She could do little about his clothes, but she had to admit that he carried himself like a gentleman and spoke like one too: in fact, when he was sober she could see that Septimus Sumption might actually be a good lawyer. On making enquiries of a slightly supercilious clerk, she discovered that Roland was still abroad and not expected back in the near future. She had to be content with that, and they made their way next to the telegraph office in Lower Thames Street where she sent an urgent message to Roland, begging him to come home and stand witness.

'Well, now,' Septimus said, holding the door open for her. 'You have done most of my work for me. I'll bid you good day.'

'Oh, no you don't.' Rosina caught him by the hand. 'I'm sorry, but I don't trust you to keep to your word once you are back in your horrible room. I have an idea where you could stay, if my friends will be so kind as to put you up until the trial.'

'No, really, I must protest.'

'If you want to get paid for your services, and to further your career, then I suggest you do as I say.'

Reluctantly, he allowed her to take him to Black Eagle Wharf. It was a long walk, but the weather was cool and dry, and Rosina did not want to waste any more of her money on a cab.

She left him outside Sam's shop, while she went in to enquire about the children's health and to discuss the possibility of the Smilies taking a paying guest for the two weeks leading up to the trial. Sam said that the danger was past, and the boys were recovering nicely. He told her that he would do anything to help young Walter, who was a decent fellow, but he had to ask Gladys first. At his call, she came hurrying from the parlour to greet Rosina as if she were a long-lost daughter, demanding to be told everything that had happened to them all since they had left Black Eagle Wharf. When Rosina finally brought Septimus into the shop, she could see that he was going out of his way to be charming, and that this was having the desired effect on Gladys, whose motherly instincts were instantly aroused. She hustled him off into the kitchen to make him a pot of tea, and Rosina was left with Sam. 'He must be kept sober,' she whispered. 'Don't allow him near a brandy bottle, or Walter's case will be lost. Give him as many cigars as he wants, and I will find a way to repay you, even if I have to haul rubbish for the rest of my life.'

Sam patted her on the shoulder. 'Don't worry, Rosie. We could do with the extra money, and we'll look after the young fellow. I can see that my Glad has taken a real shine to him. Wouldn't surprise me if she didn't get him spruced up like a real gent afore the week is out.'

Rosina kissed his leathery cheek, thanked him once again and hurried out of the shop. She had not gone more than a couple of yards when she saw Harry strolling along the wharf with, of all people, Sukey leaning on his arm. Rosina dodged into a doorway, not wanting to be seen. She would have loved to rush up to Sukey and give her a hug, but she was unsure of her reception. It was enough for now to see that she was on good terms with Harry. He had promised to tell her the truth about the ring, and she could only hope that he had kept his word. As she merged into the shadows, Rosina watched them walk past her, laughing and chatting like old friends. Well, she thought, Sukey had always had a fancy for Harry: she had yearned for a rich husband, and maybe they were meant for each other. She set off for home with a lighter step and a glimmer of hope in her heart.

The *Ellie May* was late returning, and she had missed the tide. Rosina had spent two long hours pacing the stoop and scanning the river for the red-brown sails. When she saw them at last, she knew that they would have to wait until the next high tide to bring them up to the wharf to unload. She blamed herself for not accompanying them on their trip. She had been well aware that Caddie was not strong enough to cope unaided with the heavy work. It had taken the two of them to hoist and lower the mainsail, and although they had both become reasonably proficient with the tiller, there were times when only Pip had the skill required to guide them through the busy waterway or to steer the vessel alongside. They had lost a day's pay, but it would be worth it if she could secure Walter's release from prison.

Every day after that, Rosina went out on the *Ellie May*, working twice as hard as she had before, if that were possible. She had put the wheels in motion and now she knew that she had to trust Septimus to be professional, and the Smilies to keep him sober enough to do his work. She could only hope that Roland had received her message and that he would return to London in time for the trial.

On the day that Walter was due in court, Rosina put on her lamentably shabby gown and bonnet and, having told Caddie and Pip to treat it as a well-earned holiday, she took a hansom cab to the Old Bailey. She found a seat in the public gallery and sat down to wait with her heart beating a tattoo against her ribs and her palms sweating. If she had hoped that Walter's case would be heard first, she was doomed to disappointment. One after another the accused shuffled into the dock to hear the charges brought against them. The lawyers for the defence battled it out with the prosecution and the judge and jury listened with varying degrees of patience. After a recess for luncheon, Rosina's nerves were stretched as taut as violin strings. She was becoming more and more nervous as the afternoon wore on, and could have wept with relief when Walter's case was finally called. She leaned over the balcony to get a better look and her heart was wrenched at the sight of him. He was pale and even thinner than before, but he held his head up high as he promised to tell the whole truth and nothing but the truth.

The charge was read out, accusing him of stealing the diamond ring belonging to the Gostellow family, to which he put in a plea of not guilty. Rosina held her breath as Septimus stepped forward; she prayed silently that he was sober enough to conduct the case. He looked impressive in his wig and gown, and, thanks to Gladys, remarkably clean. His speech was not slurred and he put the facts clearly and succinctly to the jury, calling on his first witness, Mr Harry Gostellow.

Rosina's knuckles whitened as she watched Harry take the witness stand. She saw him glance upwards and it was only then that she realised that Sukey was seated in the gallery, next to her father. Rosina listened intently as Septimus outlined the facts in the case, going carefully through the events which had led up to the moment when she had thrown the ring at

Harry, although he did not mention her by name. She would have been more than willing to appear as a witness, but Septimus had obviously decided that this was unnecessary. She glanced at Sukey in an attempt to read her expression, but she kept her eyes downcast, giving nothing away. Rosina dragged her attention back to Septimus, who had produced the ring and had given it to the clerk of the court to pass on to Harry for examination.

'Is this the ring in question, Mr Gostellow?' Septimus asked in a loud, clear voice, which echoed round the courtroom.

Harry looked at it closely and then handed it back to the clerk. 'It is.'

'Can you be quite certain of that, sir?'

'It is engraved with my mother's initials. There can be no mistaking that this is the ring belonging to my family.'

'Which was retrieved by Mr Roland Rivers, who intended to hold it in safe keeping for you?'

'I object, your honour.' The prosecuting lawyer rose to his feet. 'My learned friend is leading the witness.'

'Objection sustained.' The judge glared at Septimus.

He did not seem abashed. 'I have no further questions, my lord. But I would like to call my next witness.'

The judge turned to the prosecuting lawyer. 'Do you wish to question this witness?'

'No, my lord.'

'Then you may call the next witness.'

'Call Mr Roland Rivers.' The cry was repeated throughout the courtroom.

Rosina covered her mouth with her hand to prevent herself from crying out. She had not received a reply to the letter she had sent to Roland, and had virtually given up hope of his return to London for the trial. She could hardly believe her eyes when he entered the room and strolled towards the witness stand. She sat on the edge of her seat as he was sworn in. He answered calmly and clearly when questioned by the lawyer for the prosecution, and he admitted that the lady in question, whose name he did not want to bring before the public, had been mistaken in assuming that he had proposed marriage and that the ring did, in fact, belong to the Gostellow family.

At this point, Ham Barnum rose to his feet with a mighty roar, pointing a shaking finger at Roland. 'You, sir, are a cad and a bounder. You toyed with my innocent daughter's affections and have ruined her reputation.'

The judge brought his gavel down hard. 'Be silent, sir. Or I will have you removed from the public gallery.'

'This is a travesty of justice. Even if the accused

is not guilty of stealing the ring, I am certain he is the river pirate who stole from my vessel.'

'I will not warn you again, sir. Either be silent, or I will have you taken to the cells and charged with contempt of court.'

Ham subsided onto his seat, muttering beneath his breath. Sukey buried her face in her hands and her shoulders shook. If she could have reached her easily, Rosina would have rushed over to comfort her, but the gallery was packed and she could not move from her seat. She realised that the judge was speaking and she turned her attention to the bench.

'In view of the testimony of the last witness, I can only advise the jury that, with regard to the alleged theft of the diamond ring, there is no case to answer and therefore the only possible verdict must be not guilty.'

A subdued murmur rippled round the gallery and Rosina had to suppress the desire to shout with delight. She willed Walter to look up and see her, but he stood motionless in the dock. The jury were out for the briefest possible time. When the judge asked for their verdict, the foreman stood up and cleared his throat. 'Not guilty.'

It was all over and Rosina made her way as quickly as she could from the gallery to the public area outside the courtroom. When Roland emerged from the court she ran to him and threw her arms around his neck. 'Thank you, Roland. I didn't think you would return to England for the trial. Thank you, so much.'

He held her longer than was strictly necessary and the look of admiration in his eyes warmed her to the core. 'How could I refuse to help a lady in distress?'

'You are such a tease, but I do love you for coming to Walter's aid.'

'How I wish that were true, my dear,' Roland said with a rueful smile. 'He is free now and you have done your part. My offer still stands.'

She was torn between indignation and amusement. 'Don't you ever give up, Roland?'

'We would be so good together, you and I, Rosie.' He tightened his arms around her and bent his head to kiss her on the lips.

She tried to push him away but he held her even more tightly. 'Consider the life you could have in Rotterdam, my dear. And then compare it with the life you will have with him. I can give you everything except my name, but I will protect you and keep you for the rest of my days, if you will let me.'

A shout from behind them made Rosina twist round in Roland's arm. Walter was striding towards them and his face was contorted with rage. 'Let her go, Rivers.'

'Walter, please.' She broke away from Roland, holding her arms out to Walter. 'It's not what you think.'

He pushed her aside and grabbed Roland by the lapels of his jacket. 'You couldn't wait to get your hands on her, could you? I know your sort, Rivers.'

'Walter, stop this. You don't understand.' Rosina made an ineffectual move to take him by the hand, but even as he shook her off she could feel him trembling with fury as he faced up to Roland.

'This is between him and me, Rosie.'

Roland dusted down his jacket with a fastidious flick of his hands. 'She is worthy of a better fellow than you, Brown.'

'At least my intentions are honourable,' Walter snarled. 'Can you say the same?'

'Walter.' Rosina thrust herself in between them. 'Roland came all the way from Holland to speak up for you. He could have stayed in Rotterdam, but he did not.'

'Come back with me, Rosie,' Roland said, taking her by the shoulders and gazing deeply into her eyes. 'I meant what I said. You've seen how I live, and you know that I am a man of my word.'

'What are you saying?' Walter dragged her from Roland's grasp. 'How do you know him so well, Rosie? What has been going on while I've been incarcerated in Newgate?'

Septimus pushed his way through the interested crowd of onlookers. 'Walter, this isn't the time or place to continue this conversation.'

Rosina laid her hand on Walter's arm. 'Please, Walter. Let me explain.'

'Explain what? What did you do to secure his promise to act as witness? I would rather die in prison than have you give yourself to a fellow like Rivers.'

Roland took a menacing step towards Walter. 'Take that back, Brown. This woman risked her life and her reputation to free you, and all you can do is accuse her of some imagined misdemeanour. Leave him, Rosie. Come away with me now.'

Walter fisted his hand but Septimus restrained him before he could land a punch. 'This is no good. Do you want to end up back in court, Walter?'

'Septimus is right,' Rosina said urgently. 'Please, let's leave here now. You are a free man, Walter. We can sort this out later.'

'He's not worth it, Rosie.' Roland held his hand out to her. 'Won't you reconsider your decision, my dear? I'm travelling back to Rotterdam tonight. We could return together.'

Rosina opened her mouth to refuse, but Walter turned to her with a tortured expression in his eyes. 'What happened between you two, Rosie? Did he take advantage of you? If he did, I'll kill him.'

'No, Walter. I swear that nothing untoward occurred.'

'She followed me all the way to Rotterdam to beg me to stand witness,' Roland said, curling his lip. 'She risked everything in order to save your neck. You ought to be down on your knees thanking her; not standing there haranguing her like a sanctimonious preacher.'

'Roland, don't,' Rosina cried desperately. 'You're only making things worse.' She turned to Walter with an attempt at a smile. 'It's true; I followed him to Holland to beg him to return with me, even though he was afraid of a breach of promise suit against him. When I left his house in Rotterdam . . .'

'You stayed with him in his house?' Walter's face paled and he grasped her by the wrist. 'Tell me the truth, Rosie. What did you have to do to persuade a libertine like Rivers to speak out for me?'

She winced as his fingers dug into the flesh of her forearm. 'How dare you accuse me of wrongdoing? All I wanted was justice for you.'

'There he is, Constable.' Barnum pushed his way through the crowd, followed by a police officer. 'That is the man who stole from my vessel on two separate occasions. I want you to arrest Walter Brown on a charge of piracy.'

# Chapter Twenty-three

Roland stood on the edge of the walkway, staring at the wooden shack with a look of disbelief and horror on his face. 'Rosie, tell me you don't live here – in this appalling slum.'

'I do live here, Roland. I wanted you to see this because you simply won't take no for an answer.'

His face creased with concern. 'But, my dear, this only proves how much you need my protection. Walter is back in jail, where he undoubtedly belongs, and if the case against him is proved, he will stay in prison for a very long time. Are you telling me that you will continue with this filthy trade, wasting your youth and beauty on a man who does not deserve you?'

Rosina followed his gaze, taking in the rotting wooden stilts on which the hut perched like a crippled stork: the haphazard way in which the planks of driftwood were nailed together, and the crazily angled tin chimney jutting out of the roof, dripping rust and belching smoke. She could hear the children's voices and laughter coming from inside and Bertha's deeper tones admonishing one of them for some minor infringement of her strict rules. Caddie had just come out onto the stoop to take the dry washing off a makeshift clothes line; she smiled when she saw Rosina and then her expression changed. 'Rosie? What's happened?' She glanced nervously at Roland. 'Where is Walter?'

Pip was shambling towards them from the direction of Duke's Shore Wharf, with his oddly disjointed gait giving him the appearance of a clumsily manipulated puppet. On hearing the anxious note in Caddie's voice, he quickened his pace into a jogging run. 'What's up?'

Rosina held up her hand. 'I'll tell you everything in just a minute.' She turned to Roland with an apologetic smile. 'This is why I won't accept your offer, Roland. My heart is here in Limehouse Hole. We may be living in a shack, but we are all together, and I will wait for Walter no matter how long it takes. I love him and he loves me.'

'He behaved like a madman today.'

'He was jealous of you.' She laid her hand on his arm. 'You are not only a man of wealth and standing, but you are a good man, or you would not have come all this way to speak up for Walter. I thank you for that from the bottom of my heart, but I cannot go with you. My life is here.'

'If that is your last word, then I fear I must accept it.' Roland took off his top hat and tucked it under his arm. He leaned over and kissed her on the forehead. 'I'll always have a special place in my heart for you, Rosie. If things were different I would have been proud to have you as my wife, but if you ever change your mind, you know where to find me.'

She stood on tiptoe to kiss him on the cheek. 'I'll remember that, Roland. I hope you find happiness with your titled lady.'

His eyes darkened and the smile left his lips. For once in his life, he seemed bereft of words. He clicked his heels together and turned abruptly, striding back along the boardwalk towards the road where a hansom cab was waiting for him.

Caddie came hurrying towards Rosina. 'Was that Mr Rivers? Isn't he handsome, Rosie? And what an expensive rig-out he had on. We'd have to work for a year to earn enough to buy the jacket, let alone the trousers.'

'Trousers?' Pip came to a halt beside them and he clutched his sides, gasping for breath. 'That ain't no fit subject for a lady's lips, Caddie.'

'You silly boy,' Caddie said, laughing. 'Fetch us a kettle full of water from the river and we'll have a brew of tea while Rosie tells us everything. Is it good news then, dear? Though I'm afeared it might be on the bad side, seeing as how Walter ain't with you.'

Rosina linked her hand through Caddie's arm.

'I'll tell you everything when we're all together. It's complicated.'

Through sheer necessity, they were back on the barge next day, taking yet another load of rubbish downriver. When they had begun trading, the other watermen had laughed at the oddly assorted trio, and some had been openly hostile at the sight of two women working on the river. But gradually, with each trip, Rosina felt that they were beginning to earn respect. She hated the stench of the rubbish in the hold, the flies and the dust that irritated her eyes and filled her nostrils and mouth, but she kept her sights set on the money they would earn at the end of each voyage. In the hut, the rusty tin on the shelf was growing heavier each day with the money she saved out of her share of the payments from Gilks.

A week after the trial she found Septimus waiting for her on the wharf when they returned from the Medway. Leaving Pip and Caddie to make fast, she clambered up the ladder to meet him. 'Septimus, what news of Walter?'

He took off his hat, shaking his head. 'It's not good, I'm afraid.'

She was uncomfortably aware of the curious glances from the dockers and a hard stare from Gilks, who had just come out of the office. 'Let's walk, and you can tell me everything.'

He offered her his arm. 'Look – no shakes. I've been remarkably abstemious since I took on Walter's case. If I'm not careful I might become a reformed character.'

In spite of everything, Rosina could not suppress a gurgle of laughter. 'I can't see you joining the Temperance Society somehow.'

'Perhaps not, but I've given up my lodgings in Naked Boy Yard and moved in as a permanent paying guest with the Smilies. Gladys takes pleasure in mothering me, and to tell the truth, I rather enjoy it.'

'I'm glad, for your sake, Septimus, but what about Walter? Do you think the charges will stick?'

'Barnum says he has a witness. I've done my best to discover who it is, but so far I have found nothing definite.' Septimus stopped as they reached the roadside and he put his hand in his coat pocket. 'Walter is desperately ashamed of his outburst after the trial. He begs you to forgive him, and he hopes that you can understand why he allowed his feelings to overcome his better judgement.'

'I used to tease him about his iron self-control and lack of emotion,' Rosina said with a heartfelt sigh. 'I confess that it was a shock to see him lose his temper in such a way.'

'He sent you this.' Septimus took her hand and dropped the gold locket and chain into her palm.

'He wanted you to know that Will is very much alive, and that he loves you more than life itself.'

Rosina stared mutely at the locket, unable to speak for fear that she would burst into tears. Walter's anger and his harsh accusations had cut her to the quick.

'I don't understand the message,' Septimus said softly. 'But it seems that you do.'

'I do.'

'There's something more I have to tell you, Rosie.'

She could tell by the sound of his voice that it was not good news, and she raised her head to look him in the eyes. 'What is it? Tell me the worst.'

He cleared his throat and a dull flush brought colour to his normally pale cheeks. 'I told you that Barnum had a witness to the first act of piracy. He wouldn't divulge the name of that person, but he said whoever it was had implicated you in the robbery.'

'No! That's not possible.'

'Think hard, Rosie. It is possible that the fellow could be mistaken, or did you happen to be in the vicinity when the crime took place?'

'I – I was looking out of the window, and I thought I saw a movement on Captain Barnum's boat. I didn't care about him, but my papa's barge was moored alongside the *Curlew*. I went to raise Mr Cotton, the wharfinger, but I slipped and fell . . .' She stopped, unable to go on. The vivid memories of that night had come back in a blinding flash. She could hear Will's voice whispering in her ear. 'My beautiful rose' – that was what he had called her. If only she had known then that Will and Walter were one and the same.

'Go on,' Septimus said gently. 'What happened then?'

'I didn't know it was Walter, but I recognised the pirate's voice. I – I had met him before at Cremorne Gardens. He was masked and I did not see his face but we danced on the crystal platform and he held me in his arms. It was like magic.'

'And you fell in love with him.'

Rosina looked away, unable to meet his gaze. 'I know it sounds silly, but perhaps in my heart I knew all along that the pirate and Walter were the same person.'

'And Walter did steal from Captain Barnum's vessel?'

She could not answer, would not answer. She could not utter the words that would incriminate the man she loved and possibly send him to the gallows. 'What will we do?'

'I don't know yet, but I will go and visit Walter in Newgate. He must have had good reason to target Captain Barnum, and only Walter knows the truth.'

'And what if he won't tell you?'

'He will do anything to protect you and your good name. Walter won't stand by and see you dragged into court as a material witness.' Septimus raised her hand to his lips and kissed it. 'Trust me, Rosie. I will get Walter acquitted if it's the last thing I do.'

She watched him stride away towards the road, but she could not share his optimism. There was some deep, dark secret that Walter was hiding, even from her. She had no idea what it could be, but it must have something to do with Captain Barnum, or why would Walter steal from him and him alone? Barnum was obviously the key to the mystery; she must face him and demand to know the truth.

The *Curlew* was not in port. Rosina had run all the way from Duke's Shore Wharf to Black Eagle Wharf, and by the time she reached her destination she was hot, breathless and desperate to find Captain Barnum. On questioning one of the dockers who was unloading barrels from a lighter, she discovered that the *Curlew* had sailed earlier that morning. She knew the route that Barnum would take to collect his cargo from the farmers of Essex. She had done this trip with her father many times in the past, and although her memory of the route was hazy, she was becoming quite adept at reading a chart. She made her way back to Duke's Shore Wharf. Caddie and Pip would be disappointed – they had been eagerly anticipating a day's rest – but she knew that they would rally round in her hour of need.

With the leeboard raised, the *Ellie May* slid onto the mudflats in the narrow creek. Beneath the vast expanse of sky, the saltings were haunted by the ghostly cries of curlews and the liquid song of skylarks. The acres of mud and brackish water were punctuated by tussocks of marram grass stretching as far as the eye could see, and a group of buildings perched like beached whales on higher ground. At high tide the boat would float gently back into the mainstream, giving Rosina a few short hours in which to find Captain Barnum, although she was fairly certain that he would be ensconced in the alehouse while Barker saw to the loading of the barge just a little further up the creek.

Leaving Caddie and Pip on board, she lowered herself onto the sticky mud. She had taken off her boots and they hung by their laces around her neck. She could remember doing the same thing when she had accompanied her pa all those years ago. She felt as though his spirit was with her as she leapt from tussock to tussock, occasionally having to wade through the glutinous morass until she reached firmer ground. The alehouse was constructed of weatherboard and the roof thatched with reeds; beyond it were a couple of fishermen's cottages and a hay barn. As she went inside her nostrils were assailed by the strong smell of hops and malt mixed with tobacco smoke from the clay pipes clenched between the teeth of two old men seated on a bench. They glared at her as if she had no right to invade their masculine domain, but she ignored them. The landlord did not seem much more welcoming as he eyed her suspiciously from behind the bar where barrels of beer squatted on wooden trestles. He folded his arms across his chest. 'I think you made a mistake, missy. This ain't no place for the likes of you.'

Rosina stood her ground. 'I'm looking for Captain Ham Barnum.'

'And what might you want with the captain?'

'It's all right, Cooper. I know this young woman.'

She turned with a start. Barnum was sitting at a small table behind the door with a pint tankard in front of him. He beckoned to her and she moved swiftly to take a seat opposite him.

'You shouldn't be here, Miss May. You won't do any good by pleading your cause with me. I'll see that young devil hanged and you must take your chances with the law for abetting him.'

His eyes were cold as shards of ice, and Rosina's fingers trembled as they sought the comforting touch of the locket which Septimus had restored to her keeping. Just the feel of the warm gold seemed to bring her closer to Walter.

'You had your differences with my pa, but I still think you are a fair man, Captain Barnum. Walter is not a criminal. I'm begging you to drop the case against him.'

'He did me a great wrong. Why should he go unpunished?'

It was true. Walter had broken the law: that was an undeniable fact, but he must have had good reason, of that she was certain. As she sought desperately to think of an answer which would convince him, she tugged at the locket and it flew open. The medallion landed on the table and rolled towards Barnum. He picked it up, holding it between his thumb and forefinger. 'This is a strange object for a young lady to hide in a locket. It must be a love token.'

When she did not answer, he slipped it into the palm of his hand and examined it more closely. His smile faded and the medallion fell from his nerveless fingers. 'Where did you get this?'

Rosina caught it and held it in her hand. 'What does it matter who gave it to me?'

'It matters to me.' Barnum grasped her by the wrist. 'I won't ask you again, girl. Where did you get that medallion?'

'Let go of me, Captain Barnum. I will tell you nothing until you are calmer, sir.'

He released her, drawing his hand away and rubbing it across his temples. 'What is inscribed on it? Read it to me.'

She peered at the heart-shaped piece of gold, holding it in a shaft of pale sunlight as it filtered through the salt-spattered window glass. 'It is initials – WB.' Her heart missed a beat. Now he would know for certain that Walter had given it to her.

'Winifred,' Barnum said slowly. 'I gave that token to my wife on our wedding day.'

His deep distress was obvious and Rosina shook her head. 'No, sir. You must be mistaken. I believe the initials stand for Winifred Brown, not Barnum.'

Barnum leapt to his feet. 'My God. It can't be. Why didn't I see it before?'

'I don't understand.' Rosina rose slowly, pushing the chair back from the table.

'I should have known him. By God I should. He even looks like her.'

She was frightened now. His eyes were glazed and starting from his head – he looked like a madman. Even the old men had stopped smoking their pipes, and the landlord had come out from behind the bar. 'What's the matter, Captain?'

'You little fool,' Barnum hissed, seizing Rosina by the arm. 'You have no idea, have you? Your friend Walter Brown is none other than my son, William Barnum.' Without waiting for her response, he slammed out of the alehouse.

She was too stunned and shocked to move, and her first reaction was of denial. Captain Barnum must be mistaken. Walter could not possibly be his son – and yet . . . She hurried after him, catching him by the sleeve as he paced up and down, mumbling beneath his breath and shaking his head. 'Captain, please be calm. Could it be that you are mistaken?'

Barnum came to a halt, staring at her with a bleak expression in his eyes. 'I did not recognise my own flesh and blood.'

In her mind's eye she saw Walter, the unobtrusive counting-house clerk, and the pieces of the puzzle seemed to move a little closer together. 'Perhaps he did not want you to recognise him, sir?'

Barnum frowned. 'I had not seen him since he was a child.'

'I heard a little of the story.'

'From your father, I suppose? Well, it would not have been to my credit, and on looking back I am not proud of the way in which I treated Winifred and the boy – but that is ancient history. It is over and done with.'

'Not, it would seem, from Will's point of view.'

Barnum did not appear to hear her; he raised his head and squinted into the setting sun. The saltings were slowly dissolving into the dusk. He sniffed the air like a fox scenting its quarry. 'The tide is on the turn. You must get back to your vessel or you will be stranded here in this godforsaken place.'

'It's over there.' She pointed to where she had left the *Ellie May*. 'But I cannot leave until I have your word that you will not pursue the case against Walter. I mean Will.'

He took her by the arm and began walking briskly in the direction of the barge. 'You must get back on board. These marshes are dangerous, especially at night.'

'Just give me your word and I will go alone. I know the way.'

'And you are as stubborn as your mother was, and just as beautiful. I have three daughters of my own, Rosina. I would not have them walk the saltings alone and in fading light.'

'You really loved my mother, I can tell.'

He lifted her over a rapidly widening channel of salt water, setting her down on firmer ground. 'I was bewitched, besotted and completely beguiled by her. I abandoned poor Winnie and my boy, and I would have gone ahead with the marriage ceremony, even though it was bigamous, if my father-in-law had not found me out. Your father married the only woman I have ever truly loved. I never forgave him for that, God help me.'

His voice broke with emotion and Rosina could almost feel sorry for him, but she was not going to let him off so easily. 'And yet you must have married the present Mrs Barnum fairly soon afterwards. Sukey is only a year or so younger than me.'

'I was a sad and lonely man. Winnie had died of smallpox and her widowed sister took Will in and was raising him as her own. I sent her money, but I could not bring myself to see the boy. I can't say that I blame him for hating me. He has good cause.'

They had reached the *Ellie May*, and she was beginning to float on the incoming tide. Pip and Caddie were leaning over the bows calling out to Rosina to hurry. Barnum lifted her up and tossed her onto the deck. She scrambled to her feet and leaned over the side. 'Captain Barnum, will you at least give me your word that you will visit him in jail, and that you will try to understand why he did what he did?'

Barnum stepped back into the gathering gloom. 'You have my word.'

'The tide is coming in,' Pip said urgently. 'Best hurry, Captain, or you won't get back to your vessel.'

Barnum turned away and his shadowy shape dissolved into the darkness. Caddie threw her arms around Rosina. 'We was so worried. Don't never give us a fright like that again.'

Halfway between tears and laughter, Rosina dashed her hand across her eyes. 'Let's head for home. I've done what I came to do; now it's up to Captain Barnum's conscience. I pray to God that he has one.'

*

Next day, Rosina was back on board the *Ellie May* watching the city's rubbish being tipped into the hold. She could not afford to break her contract with Gilks by taking another day off, and she had to be content with going about what had become a routine task. It was hard to put her worries aside, but the gruelling work left her little time to fret. She was desperate to know whether Captain Barnum had carried out his promise to see Walter, but it was almost a week before she had time to sit down and write a note to Septimus, asking him to come and see her on Sunday, their only day of rest. It was almost midnight on Saturday when they arrived back at Duke's Shore Wharf. As she sank down on the straw-filled palliasse in the shack, Rosina could only hope that Septimus has received her note and that he would have some good news for her.

She was struggling through knee-deep water and her feet were sinking into deep mud. She was shouting Captain Barnum's name, begging him to stop, but he was striding on ahead of her, his booted feet skimming across the marsh as though he were flying. She could not keep up with him – she was sinking – the water was closing over her head – someone was shaking her by the shoulder and calling her name. Rosina opened her eyes and looked up into Bertha's face.

'Wake up, ducks. There's someone to see you.'

Rosina struggled against the mists of sleep. Even as she drew herself up into a sitting position, she was still trembling with fright.

'You was having a nightmare, ducks. Shouting out and calling for Captain Barnum, the old devil.'

Rosina stretched and yawned. 'Thank goodness it was just a dream. But who wants to see me?'

Bertha moved to the table and poured tea into a cup. 'Drink this first. It's that there lawyer fellow and I made him wait outside on the stoop. Maybe he's got good news for you.'

Rosina sipped the stewed tea. It was lukewarm, sweet and bitter at the same time, but it brought her back to her senses. As she clambered to her feet, she realised that it was unusually quiet in the hut. 'Where are Caddie and the nippers?'

'Gone out with Pip. He come round early and took them off somewhere. He was all mysterious and excited about something.' Bertha grinned, tapping the side of her nose. 'He's been sweet on Caddie ever since he first set eyes on her. I wouldn't be surprised if he didn't pop the question today.'

Rosina almost choked on her tea. 'Caddie and Pip?'

'Why not, ducks? He might not be the full

shilling, but he's got a heart of gold and a strong back. The little ones love him, and Caddie could do worse.'

'I – I never imagined . . .'

'No, well, you've been a bit preoccupied, my duck. But you mark my words, there'll be a wedding soon and I'll say Amen to that. Caddie's a good girl and she deserves a bit of happiness.'

A pang of what felt like jealousy seared through Rosina's heart. She could not and did not begrudge Caddie the love of a good man, but somehow the knowledge sharpened the pain of her separation from Walter, and the dreadful misunderstanding that had come between them.

Bertha patted her on the shoulder. 'Cheer up, chicken. Maybe young Septimus has some good news for you.'

'Yes, I certainly hope so.' Rosina rose to her feet, smoothing down her crumpled skirts. She had been so exhausted last night that she had gone to bed fully clothed and she was suddenly conscious that she must look a terrible sight. She raked a comb through her tangled hair, and hurried out onto the stoop where Septimus was waiting for her.

He greeted her with a smile. 'Good morning, Rosie.'

'What news, Septimus? Have you seen Walter? Is he all right?'

'I'll tell you everything in good time.' He gave nothing away by his expression. 'But first, there is something I want to show you.'

'What? Where is it? Don't keep me in suspense.'

He offered her his arm. 'As we men of the law say, you will hear something to your advantage. Come with me. There is a cab waiting for us.'

Her hand flew to her hair. 'I haven't even had time to change or put my hair up.'

'No matter. You look lovely as you are.'

'You are a flatterer, Septimus. But I must tell Bertha where I'm going.'

'No need, ducks. I'm coming with you.' Bertha emerged from the door tying the ribbons of her bonnet beneath her chin. 'I ain't going to miss this for worlds.'

'Of course, Miss Spinks,' Septimus said, acknowledging her presence with a nod of his head. 'This concerns you as well.'

The hackney carriage dropped them off at the entrance to a narrow alley close to Black Eagle Wharf.

'Why have we come here?' Rosina demanded. 'What's going on, Septimus?'

He tucked her hand into the crook of his arm. 'You'll see.'

Rosina turned her head to cast a questioning glance at Bertha. 'Bebe?'

Bertha shrugged her shoulders. 'I'm as much in the dark as you, ducks.'

'Come along then, Miss Spinks,' Septimus said, proffering his other arm. 'I think you'll both be pleasantly surprised.'

He led them down the narrow alleyway leading to Black Eagle Wharf. As they approached her old home, Rosina was surprised to see Caddie, Pip and the children waiting on the pavement outside. What was even more astounding was the sight of Harry standing there with Sukey on his arm. Rosina looked up at Septimus. 'I don't understand. Is this some kind of joke?'

He grinned, squeezing her hand. 'Wait and see.'

'This is a rum do,' Bertha said, panting with the exertion of keeping up with them. 'What are that lot doing here?'

As they drew nearer, Sukey broke away from Harry and she rushed up to Rosina to give her a hug. 'My dear, I'm so happy for you.'

'Will somebody tell me what's going on?' Rosina looked from one smiling face to the other.

It was Harry who came forward to take her by the hand. 'Rosie, you have this man to thank, although I'm not certain he has done me much of a favour.' He jerked his head in Septimus's direction. 'He has worked tirelessly on your behalf and to my detriment.'

'Don't tease her, Harry.' Sukey waved her left hand in front of Rosina's eyes and a sapphire ring glinted in the sunlight. 'We're engaged to be married. It was so sudden.' She slanted a smile at Harry beneath her lashes. 'Harry swept me off my feet.'

'Congratulations, Harry,' Rosina said with a genuine smile of pleasure. 'I wish you well, Sukey. I couldn't be happier for you.'

'That ain't all,' Caddie said, jumping up and down with barely concealed excitement. 'Go on, Septimus; give her the you-know-what.'

Ronnie and Alfie seemed to catch her enthusiasm and they gambolled about laughing and shrieking. Septimus put his hand in his pocket and drew out a key.

'I don't understand,' Rosina said dazedly as he gave it to her, closing her fingers around the cold metal.

'It's all yours, Rosie,' Septimus said, kissing her on the cheek.

'Open the door, Rosie,' Sukey cried, clapping her hands. 'You've got your old home back from the Gostellows.'

Bertha uttered a stifled scream and Pip leapt forward to support her as she seemed close to fainting. 'There, there now. Hold on, missis.'

'Don't be so familiar, young man,' Bertha said sternly, pushing him away. 'I'm quite all right, ta very much. I was just took by surprise.'

'I looked into the matter of the pledge,' Septimus said solemnly. 'It seems that the house is worth far more than the cost of the repairs to the *Ellie May*, and so I took the matter up with Mr Gostellow.'

Sukey pulled a face. 'Don't be so pompous, Septimus. The fact of the matter is, Rosie, that Harry and his pa talked it over. They decided that you had been unfairly treated and that the property rightly belongs to you.'

'Although,' Septimus added hastily, 'the monies for the repair of the barge will have to be repaid to the Gostellows with interest. But now you are back in business that should not be a problem.'

Rosina turned to Harry. 'Is this true?'

'It's true, Rosie. I acted out of pique when you threw my ring back at me. I was wrong to treat you so badly, and I want to make amends.'

'Why? Why now?' Rosina stared at him, totally bemused by the sudden turn of events.

'I am not such a bad fellow, Rosie.' Harry grinned ruefully. 'And now that you are not in the hay trade, and therefore not a competitor, I can afford to be generous.'

'Yes, dear,' Sukey said, eyeing Rosina's dishevelled appearance and wrinkling her nose. 'There might be money in rubbish but it is not the most fragrant of trades, and it does nothing for the complexion. I don't wish to be mean, but you look a perfect fright, if I may say so.'

A gurgle of laughter rose from Rosina's belly to

her throat. 'I know you are right, but at this moment, I don't care. I'm overwhelmed and I don't know what to say.'

Bertha held out her hand. 'Don't waste time talking, Rosie. Give me the key and let me get back into me old home.' She turned to Harry, glowering. 'If there's so much as a scrape on the paintwork, I'll hold you responsible, young man.'

Rosina pressed the key into her hand. 'You go in first, Bebe. I know how much you've missed the place.'

Bertha needed no second bidding and she unlocked the door. She stepped over the threshold making tut-tutting noises. 'It needs a good airing. I can smell mice. We'll have to get a cat, Rosie.' She disappeared into the gloom, followed by Ronnie and Alfie.

'If I'd known as how you lived in a palace, I would not have been so forward as to offer you my little hut,' Pip said, standing back and dragging his cap off his head as if he were about to enter the sanctified portals of a church.

'Your home was the saving of us all, Pip,' Caddie said, shifting the sleeping baby to a more comfortable position in her arms. 'To tell the truth, my dear, I shall be quite sorry to leave it.'

'You and the nippers can stay as long as you like. I'd be honoured to have you living there like me own family.'

Caddie shot him a look beneath her lashes, blushing rosily. 'Why, Pip. That almost sounds like a proposal of marriage.'

He swallowed convulsively. 'What would a lovely lady like you want with a simple fellow like me?'

'Oh, for goodness' sake!' Septimus gave him a none-too-gentle shove towards Caddie. 'Can't you see that she's giving you the hint to propose to her, man? Kiss her, you fool.'

Rosina held her breath and then exuded a sigh of delight as Pip took Caddie in a clumsy embrace and gave her a smacking kiss on the lips. He released her just as suddenly and threw himself down on his knees. 'I got to say it quick, while I'm feeling brave. Will you, Caddie? Will you do me the honour of becoming Mrs Pip Phillips?'

'I might,' Caddie said, smiling. Then, seeing Pip's downcast expression, she leaned down and kissed him on the lips. 'Of course I'll marry you, you silly boy.'

Rosina clapped her hands and Septimus slapped Pip on the shoulder, offering his congratulations.

'Well, now,' Harry said briskly. 'That's enough of that. Susan, I think we are done here for today. I'm sure that Rosie would like to go inside and inspect her old home. There is nothing changed. We had no use for it, after all.'

'Pa has settled a very respectable dowry on me, Rosie,' Sukey said, smiling happily. 'He has become so much kinder recently, and he has told us all about William. I and my sisters are delighted to find that we have a half-brother, and it is so romantic to think that all the time it was Walter, or rather Will, who was the river pirate. It's like something out of a novel.'

Harry tipped his hat. 'Goodbye for now, Rosie. I hope we may be friends.'

'How can we not, after this generous gesture? Thank you, Harry.' Rosina held out her hand and he raised it to his lips.

'I will call on you tomorrow morning,' Sukey said, giving Rosina a hug. 'I am so sorry that I did not believe you before.'

'I will be at work then, but we won't lose touch again, Sukey. I promise you that.' Rosina watched them walk away, arm in arm. So Sukey had got her way in the end. She would marry her rich man after all. Rosina sighed. If only her own story had such a happy ending.

'Are you coming inside, Rosie?'

Caddie's voice broke into her thoughts and Rosina turned to her with an attempt at a smile. 'In a minute. You take your fiancé in and show him the house.'

Pip's face flushed scarlet and he seemed to grow in stature. 'That's right. I'm your fiancé, Caddie, me old duck.' Ignoring her half-hearted protests, he scooped Caddie and the baby up in his arms and carried them over the threshold.

Rosina was left outside with Septimus. 'I can hardly believe it,' she said, shaking her head. 'I don't know how to thank you.'

'If you hadn't taken me in hand I would have ended up in the gutter, Rosie. Now I feel I have a future and it is all due to you.'

'No, I won't have that. You made the effort to give up the drink and it can't have been easy.' Rosina laid her hand on his sleeve. 'Everyone seems so settled and content. I wish that it was the same for me, Septimus. I just wish I could convince Walter, I mean Will, that what I did was for him alone, and that nothing untoward happened between Roland and me.'

Septimus took her by the shoulders and turned her so that she was facing in the direction of the Barnums' house. 'This was my main reason for bringing you here today, Rosie.'

She stared at the approaching figure in disbelief. 'Walter – Will?' She froze for a moment, unable to move a muscle.

Clearing his throat, Septimus patted her on the shoulder. 'I leave you in good hands, my dear.'

'Septimus . . .' Rosina held her hand out to him. She had so much to thank him for but he was striding away and he did not look back.

'Rosie, my own Rose.' Will broke into a run, and, snatching off his peaked cap, he tossed it up in the air. He caught her in his arms and held her in such a close embrace that she was not sure whether it was his heart or her own that she could feel thudding against her breast. He ran his hands through her hair, looking deeply into her eyes, and murmuring her name over and over again as if it were the sweetest music in the world.

Breathless and barely able to speak, Rosina slid her arms around his neck. 'Will, my Will. I can't believe you're really here.'

'I am here, Rosie. I'm a free man, thanks to you, and I have come to beg your pardon for doubting you for a single instant.' He claimed her mouth in a kiss that blotted out the pain and anguish of the past, and promised more – so much more.

She knew now that she had truly come home. Here in Will's arms was the only place on earth that she wanted to be. She drew a deep breath as he released her lips with soft, tender kisses, as though he could hardly bear to let her go. 'Your father – did he . . .?'

'He came to me in Newgate, my love. I truly believe he is a changed man, as I am changed myself. When I came here from Kent, all I wanted was revenge for my poor dead mother. It seemed to me that your father and I had just cause to hate Ham Barnum. I thought my heart was turned to stone inside my chest, but then I fell in love with you. My plan to ruin my father seemed to matter little in the end; all I wanted was to win your love.'

'And you did, Will. I love you so very much.'

'I know that you risked your reputation to save me. When I thought I had lost you to Rivers, I was mad with jealousy. I was out of my mind and I didn't know what I was saying or doing. Then again you risked your life by venturing into the marshes to find my father. He told me everything. You are my own dear, brave girl and I am not worthy of you, Rosie.'

'Don't say that, my darling. Nothing matters to me except that you are free. By some miracle, I have my home back, and I have my business. We can build a new life together.'

He traced the outline of her cheek with the tip of his finger, smiling ruefully. 'I will not have my wife working as a dustman.'

'Your wife?' She angled her head, teasing him with a smile. 'You have not proposed to me, and I have not accepted.'

'Will you, Rosie? Will you marry me and make me the happiest man in the world?'

'I will, Will.' She dissolved into tears, laughing and crying at the same time.

'Don't cry, my love.'

'I – I'm just so happy. I can't believe this is happening to me.'

Will dried her eyes with his pocket handkerchief, and he kissed the tip of her nose.

'We will have a wonderful life together.'

She smiled mistily. 'I am sure of that, but we still have to live. Even if you don't like what I do . . .'

He laid his finger on her lips, and, turning her towards the river, he pointed at the water. 'What do you see, Rosie?'

She was mystified. 'I see cranes, wherries, barges . . .'

'And the barge at the end of the tier is mine. I inherited it from my late uncle when I was little more than a boy. I grew up working the river; it's in my blood as well as yours, my love. When I was released from Newgate, I and my father went down to the Medway to fetch the old girl. With the *Sandboy* and the *Ellie May*, we have the beginnings of our own fleet.' He spun her round to face him. 'You will have no need to roughen your hands with hard work any more, Rosie.'

'And you will be a respectable businessman from now on?'

'I promise.'

'I think I will miss my river pirate.' She leaned her head against his shoulder.

Will wrapped his arms tightly around her. 'He will always be by your side, my beautiful rose.'

To find out more about Dilly Court and other fantastic Arrow authors why not read *The Inside Story* – our newsletter featuring all of our saga authors.

To join our mailing list to receive the newsletter and other information* write with your name and address to:

The Inside Story
The Marketing Department
Arrow Books
20 Vauxhall Bridge Road
London
SW1V 2SA

*Your details will be held on a database so we can send you the newsletter(s) and information on other Arrow authors that you have indicated you wish to receive. Your details will not be passed to any third party. If you would like to receive information on other Random House authors please do let us know. If at any stage you wish to be deleted from our *The Inside Story* mailing list please let us know.

# A Mother's Courage

### Dilly Court

**She would do anything to keep them safe . . .**

When Eloise Cribb receives the news that her husband's ship has been lost at sea she wonders how she is ever going to manage. With two young children, the rent overdue and left with almost nothing to live on, she has no alternative but to turn to his estranged family for help.

She sets off on the long and arduous journey to Yorkshire, but is met with hostility and soon realises she has little choice but to return to London. Virtually destitute and desperate, Eloise is faced with her worst nightmare: she must either go to the workhouse, or abandon her children at the Foundling Hospital. But she is determined to keep them under her protective wing at all costs . . .

arrow books

# *The Cockney Sparrow*

### Dilly Court

**She sang with the voice of a nightingale . . .**

Gifted with a beautiful soprano voice, young Clemency Skinner is forced to work as a pickpocket in order to support her crippled brother, Jack. Their feckless mother, Edith, has fallen into the clutches of an unscrupulous pimp, whose evil presence threatens their daily existence.

Befriended by Ned Hawkes and his kindly mother, Nell, Clemency struggles to escape from life in the slums of Stew Lane. She finds work with a troupe of buskers and is spotted by the manager of the Strand Theatre. Clemency looks set for operatic stardom, but a chance meeting with the mysterious Jared Stone brings danger and intrigue and threatens to change her life forevermore . . .

arrow books

# *The Best of Sisters*

## Dilly Court

### Would fate ever bring him back to her?

Twelve-year-old Eliza Bragg has known little in life but the cold, comfortless banks of the Thames. Living above her uncle's chandlery she has grown accustomed to a life of penury and servitude, her only comfort the love and protection of her older brother, Bart.

But one day Bart accidentally kills a man and is forced to flee to New Zealand. Alone, barefoot, beaten down and at the mercy of her cruel uncle, Eliza realises that her very survival is at stake . . .

arrow books

# *Tilly True*

## Dilly Court

**'I ain't always going to be poor, I made me mind up to that.'**

Dismissed from her position as housemaid under a cloud of misunderstanding, Tilly True is forced to return home. But Tilly is determined to make something of her life and, rather than admit the truth to her poverty-stricken family, she sets out once more in search of employment.

Her journey takes her to the London law courts, a grim parsonage in one of the most notorious parts of the East End and a house of ill-repute. But when she falls for the dangerous charms of Barnaby Palgrave, Tilly soon finds that her troubles have only just begun . . .

arrow books